GOD OF THE GOLDEN FLEECE

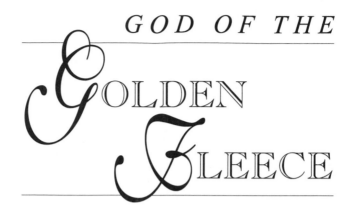

TOR BOOKS BY FRED SABERHAGEN

The Berserker® Series
The Berserker Wars . *Berserker Base* (with Poul Anderson, Ed Bryant, Stephen Donaldson, Larry Niven, Connie Willis, and Roger Zelazny) . *Berserker: Blue Death* . *The Berserker Throne* . *Berserker's Planet* . *Berserker Kill* . *Berserker Fury*

The Dracula Series
The Dracula Tapes . *The Holmes-Dracula Files* . *Dominion* . *A Matter of Taste* . *A Question of Time* . *Séance for a Vampire* . *A Sharpness on the Neck*

The Swords Series
The First Book of Swords
The Second Book of Swords
The Third Book of Swords
The First Book of Lost Swords: Woundhealer's Story
The Second Book of Lost Swords: Sightblinder's Story
The Third Book of Lost Swords: Stonecutter's Story
The Fourth Book of Lost Swords: Farslayer's Story
The Fifth Book of Lost Swords: Coinspinner's Story
The Sixth Book of Lost Swords: Mindsword's Story
The Seventh Book of Lost Swords: Wayfinder's Story
The Last Book of Swords: Shieldbreaker's Story
An Armory of Swords (editor)

The Books of the Gods
The Face of Apollo . *Ariadne's Web* . *The Arms of Hercules* . *God of the Golden Fleece*

Other Books
A Century of Progress . *Coils* (with Roger Zelazny) . *Dancing Bears* . *Earth Descended* . *The Mask of the Sun* . *Merlin's Bones* . *The Veils of Azlaroc* . *The Water of Thought* . *Gene Rodenberry's Earth: Final Conflict—The Arrival*

GOD OF THE

GOLDEN FLEECE

THE · FOURTH · BOOK · OF · THE · GODS

FRED SABERHAGEN

TOR®

° A TOM DOHERTY ASSOCIATES BOOK °
NEW YORK

GOD OF THE GOLDEN FLEECE

Copyright © 2001 by Fred Saberhagen

This book is printed on acid-free paper.

A Tor Book
Published by Tom Doherty Associates, LLC
175 Fifth Avenue
New York, NY 10010

www.tor.com

Tor® is a registered trademark of Tom Doherty Associates, LLC.

Library of Congress Cataloging-in-Publication Data

Saberhagen, Fred.
      God of the Golden Fleece / Fred Saberhagen.—1st. ed.
          p. cm.—(Book of the gods ; 4th)
      "A Tom Doherty Associates book."
      ISBN 0-312-87037-X
      1. Jason (Greek mythology)—Fiction. 2. Medea (Greek mythology)
      —Fiction. 3. Argonauts (Greek mythology)—Fiction. I. Title.

PS3569.A215 G6 2001
813'.54—dc21

                                                                    2001023239

First Edition: August 2001

Printed in the United States of America

0 9 8 7 6 5 4 3 2 1

GOD OF THE

GOLDEN FLEECE

○ *ONE* ○

Proteus

The winning end of a bitter and deadly struggle brought him up thrashing and splashing in salt water, stumbling waist-deep through the warm sea, emerging under a clear sky from which the light of sunset was fading fast. Leftover rage and fear poured fierce energy through his veins, but the memory of the disaster that he had just survived was fading faster than the sunset. Something had hit him in the head, and only fragments of what had just happened were still clear in his mind.

He had a vivid memory of a head as big as a farm wagon, two arms the size of massive trees, mounted on shoulders to match. One of the sea-going type of Giants, almost human above the waist in shape if not in size; but from the hips down, no real legs, only a pair of huge, twisting fish-tails, ending in something like whale-flukes instead of feet. The thing would never be able to walk properly, but it sure as all the hells could swim.

He had been on a ship, and the Giant had come swimming after it like a whale, bent on destruction. The deck and hull crushed in by blows from those tree-trunk arms, the vessel capsized, and everyone aboard had gone into the deep blue sea.

He couldn't remember how he had got away, but here he was. Now if only his head would cease to hurt . . .

When the Giant had reared up out of the sea, throwing everyone into a panic, the ship had been carrying its passengers to . . .

The survivor began to feel a new terror now, subtler than the fear of Giants, but equally unpleasant. It came with the realization that he could no longer remember why he had been aboard the ship, or where it had been taking him.

Or even who he was.

Start again. When the vessel broke up, when the monster sent it to the bottom . . .

No, start yet again. He was going to have to start much earlier than that. But he could not. Because he could not even remember *who he was*.

The man who waded might have broken out in a cold sweat, but it was hard to tell, when every inch of his skin was already soaked by the Great Sea. He could find not a single scrap of memory before his presence on that doomed ship. So, start with the ship, and try to work from that.

He could recall only a few more details, all trivial. Besides one or two clear images of the attacking Giant, there were only some additional colors, shapes, certain ugly noises . . .

The left side of the man's head, where his exploring fingers now discovered an aching lump, still throbbed from the savage impact of something hard. Turning to look backward as he moved, even as his feet kept taking him toward the land, he scanned the empty watery horizon in the direction opposite the sunset. Night was gathering out there, and stars were beginning to appear over the endless sea. Darkness was advancing from the east, but nothing else. There were no monsters in pursuit.

It was horrible that he could not remember where he had been going. Or why he had been on the ship. Or who he was . . .

A helpless groan came welling up, and the wader had to fight down panic. It seemed that virtually a whole lifetime had been swept away.

There was almost nothing left of himself at all, no solid identity anywhere. Who was he? What was he doing here, in what looked like and felt like, and so had to be, the middle of the Great Sea? There ought to be, there had to be, more to him than this, a naked wading body with an aching, almost empty head, laboring under a burden of fear and rage, a terror that wanted to hit back with murderous fury.

Damn the Giant! Could a man's whole self be erased by one medium-hard knock on the head?

Turning his back again on the empty, darkening east, he kept on trudging shoreward in the gentle surf. He was praying now, to every god and goddess he could think of, that his memories, his vanished life, would suddenly come back to him—and it had better happen soon. There were two small fires on the beach some sixty or seventy yards ahead, and a beached ship, with people milling around, and instinct warned him that before he met those folk, whoever they were, he had better have some idea of who he was and what he was doing in the world.

Looking down at himself, he realized that he was wearing nothing that might provide a clue to his identity, carrying nothing—not even a ring on a finger or in an ear. Not even an amulet hung around his muscular neck. The man paused in his wading, suddenly puzzled by his utter and complete nakedness. It was as if he had just left his clothing on a beach somewhere and gone in for a casual swim.

All this time he had been making steady progress toward the shore. Now the gentle waves surged up no higher than the wader's thighs, and every step forward raised him another inch on the sandy bottom's shallow slope. When his thick brown hair and beard had shed their weight of water they would be curly, but right now they were still almost straight, streaming and dribbling little threads of ocean. The unclad body gradually revealed as the water shallowed was no bigger than average, and looked to be in its youthful prime, no more than thirty years of age, strong and slightly rounded toward chubbiness.

Again he looked back into the darkening east, this time over one shoulder, as he kept wading forward. But still there was only watery emptiness to see, shrouded in advancing night.

What kind of reception he might get from the people on the beach ahead he could not guess. But he had nowhere else to go.

What *had* he been doing on that boat or ship, just before he was almost killed? It seemed unbearable that he did not know.

Going somewhere, trying to accomplish something terribly important, yes . . .

A certain great purpose, having some connection with a ship, yes, that was it! Not the vessel whose sinking had almost taken him down with it, but a totally different one. With a flash of disproportionate relief he realized that the ship he had been trying to find was doubtless the very one drawn up on the beach ahead.

Eagerly, now, the man emerging from the sea pressed on. The careened vessel was a new-looking bireme, lean and straight, and big enough to carry forty oars, two banks on each side. The new wood of her hull, except for the spots where it was brightly painted, glowed almost golden in fading sunset light.

One more slender shard of memory fell into place. It was a woman who had imbued him with the sense of purpose, maybe given him his orders—it might have been as simple and direct as that.

It was a blessed relief to feel that things were at least starting to come back. But what exactly the nameless woman had been trying to get him to do remained a mystery. Whoever she was, the man could *almost* see her face in memory, almost hear her exact words—almost, but not quite.

Still he kept wading forward almost automatically, toward the beached ship and the men around her, a sizable group on a long shoreline otherwise deserted.

It looked a pleasant enough place, and the wader somehow assumed it was an island, rather than a mainland shore. Bathed now in fading sunset light were green palm trees, pelicans, and other signs of peaceful nature . . . all reassuring. One last time he looked back over his left shoulder, seeing only the straight line of the horizon, and the gathering of night. The Giant that had almost killed him was evidently miles away by now.

His rage and fear were not gone, far from it, but now they had subsided, enough to be kept out of sight. Now he was close enough to see, in declining sunlight, the name on the ship's prow, above the painted, staring eye. And the word when he could see it—*Argo*—made a connection, established a faint link with all the memories that he had almost lost.

Overhead a gull was screaming, as if in derision, finding rich amusement in the way the world went on, how human beings and others managed their affairs. The *Argo* was long and narrow, the outer row of seats on each side slightly raised. The central deck, barely wide enough for two human bodies to edge past each other, was raised a little higher still, so the two inboard rows of oarsmen would actually sit beneath it, less exposed to sun and rain. In the middle of that raised deck would be a hole to hold a mast, whose foot would nestle snugly in a notch in the bottom planks below. And in fact a suitably long pole had been unstepped and laid aside, and a new-looking linen sail more or less neatly furled. No one was now aboard the ship, which rested tilted sharply sideways on the sand.

Every line of the long ship breathed adventure, and the man approaching could see a great, challenging, staring eye, blue with a white rim, and a thin black outline surrounding that, bigger than his whole head, painted on the near side of the prow, just forward of the name. The other side, of course, would bear another symmetrically positioned eye.

Right now the oars had all been shipped aboard. There was every indication that the rowers were all finished with their labors for the day. Half of them were swimming and plunging naked in the shallow water, mock-fighting with splashes like small boys, uttering rowdy yells, washing away the day's heat and the sweat of rowing. Their bodies were of all human colors, from tropical black to sunburnt blond, except that none of them were old. No gray hair was immediately visible.

The remaining half were up on shore, some clad and some not, mainly clustered around a couple of brisk small fires, from which a smell of roasting meat came wafting out to sea. A meal was in the middle stages of preparation. Someone had been butchering small animals on the beach, and had started the process of tidying up, bundling bones and offal and fat together, into packages that would soon be burned as offerings to certain gods. Meanwhile the humans as always were claiming the good meat as their share, a state of affairs to which no god ever seemed to raise objection.

It was hard to tell if any of the men up on the beach were servants; certainly none of them, at the moment, were wearing the fine robes of aristocrats. There were no women or children anywhere in sight, but plenty of weapons, a good variety of spears and bows and swords; it seemed a very military kind of expedition, or maybe a band of high-class pirates. The man just arriving felt a soothing, baseless certainty that he had come to the right place.

What now? It seemed to him that there was one man in particular he ought to find. The woman responsible for his being here had told him—had practically commanded him—something . . .

And as the newcomer drew ever closer to the gathering, he saw what he had somehow expected, that this was no crew of ordinary sailors. Youth and health and strength were everywhere, along with a kind of inborn arrogance. There was not a single metal slave-collar to be seen, though more than a few magic amulets hung on slender chains around muscled necks. Where scars showed on the hard bodies, they suggested the impact of weapons or claws rather than the lash.

A couple of men had turned now and were watching with interest the newcomer's arrival. But neither of them was the one man he had really come here to find.

Another of those ahead, standing waist-deep in the water at the center of a small circle of attention, had an air of leadership. For one thing he was very tall, and a kind of dominance showed in him, even in this superior company, even unclothed as he was. The newcomer changed the course of his steady, splashing advance to head directly toward this individual.

When the tall man turned his head to look in his direction, the man from the sea stopped a few feet away and said in a clear, determined voice: "Sir, if you are the famous Jason, captain of the *Argo,* I have been sent to join you." The name had popped into his head at the precise instant when he had to have it.

The leader's whole head seemed a dark, luxuriant mass of hair and beard. The closer the newcomer got to him, the stronger his arms and shoulders looked. He said: "My name is Jason." The dark eyes studied the man before him with fatalistic calm. The voice was mild but authoritative. "Where do you come from?"

The nameless stranger had lost his own identity, but he still knew who Jason was. He thought that name would mean something to almost everyone in the world. It was a relief to discover that certain parts of his memory were still intact, things a man would have to know about to function in the world. Jason's fame as a warrior, and particularly as the heroic slayer of the Calydonian boar, had spread swiftly during the last few years. It had been no trouble at all for Jason to recruit forty volunteer adventurers to accompany him on a special quest, even if they had no certainty of what its object was. As soon as the word spread that he was undertaking a great adventure and wanted followers, hundreds of men had come from everywhere, seemingly from every corner of the earth, certainly from as far away as the news had had time to travel. Very few were accepted, of those who applied without a special invitation.

"Out of the sea, Lord Jason."

The leader's voice was still mild. "No need to address me as if I were royalty. I do not—yet—sit on a throne or wear a crown. And I suppose, from the way you look and the manner of your arrival, that you have some tale to tell of shipwreck?" Suddenly Jason's tone became more casual, less interested, as a new thought struck him. "Were you sent to us as a servant? Our original plan was to have several attendants meet us on this island. But I sent word many days ago to cancel that arrangement. What's your name?"

"Proteus." This answer, too, came automatically, for which the man who gave it was deeply thankful; he took the timely access of memory as a hopeful sign that other essential facts might come popping back as soon as they were absolutely needed. Immediately his aching head began to feel better.

Jason was looking directly at him, but still Proteus had the feeling that the leader was giving him only a fraction of his attention. The big man said, as if he did not much care: "I don't remember anyone of that name applying to join my company. Then you *are* one of the servants who were originally to meet us here?"

Up on the beach, one of the young men had picked up a conch shell and was trying to blow it, just for fun. But he had no idea of how to do it properly, and was producing an ungodly noise, making Proteus uncomfortable.

Before he was forced to find an answer for Jason's question, another tall youth came splashing up to the leader and started talking to him about someone called Hercules, who, it seemed, had been a member of the company of Argonauts when they began their voyage a few days ago. Proteus, still distracted by his own secret problems, had some trouble making out just what the difficulty was now. As nearly as he could tell, this fellow Hercules and his nephew, named Enkidu, had been somehow stranded yesterday, left behind either by accident or design, when the *Argo* had put in along the shores of the river Chius, in the land of Mysia.

Other members of the crew of Heroes were now listening in, even as they boyishly traded splashes or just stood around nearby. Some of these made comments indicating they hadn't realized that two of their shipmates had been missing for a day. Evidently, out of this group of some forty young men, many were still largely unknown to one another, though they had been crammed together on a ship for several days.

Meanwhile, Proteus felt a growing certainty that the purpose, the compulsion, that had brought him here required, as a next step, that he find some way to join this noble crew. *She*, the nearly-forgotten but commanding woman, must have ordered him to join the Argonauts. More and more Proteus wanted to know just who that woman was, what had made her think she had a right to order him around. Also he wanted to find out why he felt it necessary to obey—he would be almost afraid to know the answer to that one.

Meanwhile, he was going to do his damnedest to keep secret his weakness, the fact of his ruined memory. Once he admitted that, why would they believe him about anything? And Jason and his crew must not know why he was here. Because it was a matter of life and death, that someone should not find that out . . . come to think of it, it was the nameless woman who had commanded secrecy. With an inward sigh Proteus acknowledged to himself that whatever secret she wanted kept was safe enough for the time being, since he himself could not remember what it was.

And then he was brought back, with a start, to his immediate situation. Jason had just said something that required a response, and was looking at him expectantly.

"I would like to know," repeated the leader, in a tone of patient tolerance, "just what happened to the boat? The one that must have brought you somewhere near this island?"

That question he could answer. "A Giant came up out of the sea, and broke it into bits. I fear that no one else survived."

Naturally enough, this produced immediate consternation among the men who heard him. Some of them went running for their weapons—as if such human toys would help them against that enemy—while others pressed closer to the source of news, urgently demanding more details.

Proteus needed only a couple dozen halting words to give them all the additional information he had available. Sudden, inexplicable disaster, splintered planks and terrified, howling faces, people drowning. Now surrounded by a ring of intent listeners, he explained that the boat had been sunk, he thought about a mile from the island—of that much at least he felt confident—and that unfortunately he seemed to be the only survivor. He'd had a good long swim to get here. It was faintly encouraging that as he spoke of the disaster, a few more of its details—screams for help, and thrashing human arms and legs—took shape in his mind. But nothing that answered any of his own urgent questions.

Several men, speaking at the same time, asked Proteus where he thought the Giant might have gone.

"I have no idea." Probably not to the nearest land; monsters like that one were as much at home in the sea as whales, but with their fish-legs had a hard time getting about on land. He shrugged. Trying to force his memory meant standing in front of a hideous, frightening void, big enough so that it seemed he might fall into it and be lost.

By now all of the men had heard his story, and none were more than moderately surprised. Giant attacks on ships were fairly rare, but certainly not unheard of. Vessels were lost at sea all the time, from a variety of causes, and people went down with them—servants were people, of course, even those who were slaves. But when you came right down to it, they were only servants. Too bad that useful workers had suffered and died tonight, but there were plenty of replacements to be had, and it was no great loss to the world, not to the important people in it. Jason, like his shipmates, frowned on hearing the unpleasant news, but it was not going to change his outlook or his plans. Whatever they might be.

One of the figures standing in the background observed: "Well, that settles one problem for us. There'll be no hangers-on or attendants on this voyage."

"That had already been decided," said another man, a trifle sharply.

"My name's Meleager." This change of subject came from yet

another member of the crew, a big man, almost as large as Jason, who stepped toward Proteus with a hand stuck out in greeting. Plainly the kind who is anxious for you to know his name, and find out who you are, what kind of story you have to tell about yourself.

"Those who know me well call me Mel." His great hand swallowed the hand Proteus put out. "I've been keeping Jason out of trouble since we both were lads."

Mel turned to gesture to another. "And this is Haraldur." A grinning nod from a powerfully built, hairy man who was wearing a horned helmet, though at the moment nothing else.

How long the chain of introductions might have gone on there was no telling, for it was interrupted. Now one of the other men, somewhat older than most of the others, who had been standing by with folded arms and listening, spoke up and reminded Jason that some of the crew seemed to think the problem of whether or not there were going to be servants still had not been finally settled.

"I would remind you, sir, that as matters had stood when we left Iolcus, some of the Heroes enjoyed such a luxury and others did not."

"Yes, Idmon," said Jason patiently. "I understand that."

"Wouldn't have been much luxury for anyone, with half again as many people as we have now crammed aboard the ship," put in another who had been listening.

There arose a weary murmur, suggesting that this debate had been going on for a while and many were tired of it.

Jason looked vexed. "I think you are mistaken. I think all servants and companions have already left us." He looked around, as if his forty—if that was actually the right number—shipmates might be an unruly mob of strangers. "If there are any such still here, it is against my orders."

No one responded to that directly. But a voice from the background said: "If half of the intended servants were sent back days ago, and the other half have just been drowned, it seems to me there's not a whole lot left to discuss."

Someone poked the butt of a spear in Proteus's direction. "No survivors, this man was saying?"

But before Jason or anyone else could insist that Proteus provide more details of the disaster, another man, one of those who had been on shore, came wading briskly up to the leader, who still stood waist-deep in the lapping waves. Urgently this latest supplicant began haranguing Jason about the apparent absence of certain supplies. Someone should have thought to stow caulking materials aboard, and something to use for pitch! Sooner or later all ships leaked and required fixing.

Meanwhile, the news that a whole boatload of servants had been lost was spreading slowly through the ranks of Heroes as they splashed or lounged or worked at getting dinner. Proteus could see them frowning, shaking heads, murmuring. A bad omen, certainly. Probably those who had still been hoping for servants were upset because they would certainly have to do their own cleaning and cooking.

Jason's patience was unruffled. Maybe, thought Proteus, patience was the virtue a leader needed, above all else. Now the leader was trying to explain to his latest questioner about the caulking materials, and other spare parts. The *Argo,* like most ships built for other purposes than carrying freight, suffered from a lack of storage space in general, and not much could be done about it. There were a couple of lockers, fore and aft under the narrow fighting deck that ran down the center of the vessel. Those important spaces had been packed full of necessary stores of one kind or another.

There was talk of the spare sails. Proteus nodded to himself, unsurprised. Some fund of practical experience, though he could recall nothing of how he had obtained it, assured him that on a voyage of any length at least one spare was practically essential, unless you would really rather row. And if you got the finest, most expensive fabric and workmanship—which Jason ought to have done to match the quality of his ship—you could roll and fold the sail tightly enough to stow it away in an amazingly small space.

Jason was going on with his inventory, and now it sounded as if there were as many as two or three spare sails. There were also some caulking materials, but you would have to dig them out.

All this was fine with Proteus. He and whatever other news he might have been able to provide had to wait again. The expedition seemed anything but well organized, and for the moment that was all to the good, because it had spared him any probing, difficult questions.

Somewhere inland beyond the wavering spread of firelight, a male voice suddenly began to moan in pain. Or more likely in passion, as Proteus suddenly realized. None of the men around him were paying any attention to the sound, so he decided to ignore it too. He supposed it was possible that at least one woman had come along on this expedition—but on second thought, it was more likely that there were some in this large crew of Heroes who found the absence of women no detriment to their love lives.

Now one of the figures in the loose gathering around Jason, the slightly older man addressed as Idmon, had turned the conversation back again to the absent Hercules. It sounded to Proteus like this Hercules was a mere youth and a stranger who in a trial of strength had somehow managed to make them all look like weaklings, which in this company would be quite a feat. Inevitably more than a few of the chosen Heroes would have considered him an offensive upstart, and probably out of jealousy or resentment they had somehow arranged for him to be left behind.

Proteus thought that a firm, decisive leader would not tolerate such goings-on among his followers, and he was waiting for Jason to call someone to account for this, try to determine the truth of what had happened.

Large Meleager and horn-helmed Haraldur were shaking their heads, looking vaguely embarrassed. But at the moment Jason seemed anything but firm or decisive. He seemed not the least bit eager to call anyone to account for anything. Watching him curiously, Proteus thought he gave the impression of wishing that all these splashing fools around him would simply go away, taking their worries about their spare parts and their servants with them, and let him get on with his private meditations.

Such an attitude made the newcomer uneasy. This was not the way a captain should behave at the beginning of a serious enterprise. Any voyage on the Great Sea was dangerous, and there was no doubt that Jason was intending a long voyage. Anyone who equipped himself with such a ship, such a crew, and such a plenitude of extra stores, certainly had in mind more than a brief and sunny cruise along the coast. If their leader showed no more enthusiasm for his task than this, Proteus foresaw a hard time ahead for the voyagers at best, and more likely real disaster.

The ongoing discussion soon degenerated into pointless wrangling. Standing by, now and then rubbing his aching head, occasionally looking back at the darkening sea from which he had mysteriously emerged, the new arrival was glad that the argument diverted attention away from him.

He had about decided that it was time for him to casually begin to move up on the beach, and get in line for some dinner, when suddenly there was splashing confusion around him, men crying out in alarm or excitement, everyone looking up. Jason, along with several others, was suddenly ducking and dodging, and Proteus raised his eyes.

A flying shape loomed close overhead, zooming over the waves at no more than treetop height. For a moment, fear of the monstrous in a new form gripped Proteus with paralysis. Screaming gulls darted out of the path of a figure that was much too big to be a bird. The sky was still bright enough to let him see that it was a man flying up there, or at least a figure that looked entirely human, except for the wings of magic sprouting from each ankle.

Joining

For a moment everyone in the water and on the beach was startled by the rushing presence in the air above—then Jason and most of the others relaxed.

Once Jason had recovered from his initial start, the flying figure was no mystery to him. Turning to Proteus, who was still gaping, Jason assured the newcomer that it was no god or monster flying overhead, but only a man named Calais, one of the Argonauts. Calais and his brother, Zetes, had somehow come into possession of two pairs of some god's winged sandals. And now Proteus could see a second flying man in the middle distance, drawing near as if returning from a scouting flight.

"Come into possession?" Proteus marveled. "How?" Given the ruinous state of his own memory, he was not surprised to be unable to recall ever seeing anything of the kind before. But most of the men around him were as awestruck as he, to judge by the way they all gaped at the darting figures in the sky.

The answer to his question came from an Argonaut whose name he had not yet learned. "They're not saying. If some angry deity comes looking for them—well, that will be their problem."

For a moment Proteus stood gazing up at the two flying men, short cloaks streaming behind their backs, coming and going through the last rays of the setting sun, at the height of a good arrow shot above the beach. One flapped his arms in playful imitation of a bird, an action that made no difference in his flight. They waved to their friends below, and called down to them, words lost in the sound of surf.

"Don't tell me they've stolen them from some god, or pair of gods!" muttered one voice. "I've never even seen a god!"

Few people had. Another man put in: "But it looks that way, no? Where else would any human get such gear?"

"Wouldn't be any fun for us if the divine Hermes, say, got angry and came looking for his shoes."

The man standing next to Proteus nudged him with an elbow. "I admit, I've never seen anything of the kind before. Have you?"

"Not that I remember."

"If *I* could fly . . . well." The implication was that the speaker would be enjoying some glorious adventure of an entirely different kind than the one he had signed up for, a better prospect than pulling on a heavy oar for months at a time. Evidently a couple of days at sea, even in the company of world-famous Jason, had been enough to rob that prospect of some of its glamour.

Proteus was beginning to get some sense of the identities of several individuals in the little crowd around him. He suspected he was not particularly good at names, but now he knew Haraldur, Meleager, and Idmon.

A young man addressed as Telamon said to Jason: "Nothing suits you better than to abandon Hercules." A faint groan went up, in several voices; people were tired of that argument. But the reaction did not discourage Telamon: "I've heard it suggested that you planned the whole affair yourself so that his fame in our homeland should not eclipse your own, if we have the good fortune to return." The speaker paused. "Not that I really believe that," he added.

Jason showed no resentment at being challenged in this way. Calmly he denied having had anything to do with the abandonment of Hercules.

"Why should I be jealous?" he asked of everyone, looking around. "If one of my crew, Hercules or anyone else, should gain great glory, that's fine. It will only reflect well on me. All I want is to be peacefully at home, enjoying what is mine by right." After an inward-looking pause he added: "Release from toil is all I ask of the gods."

That struck Proteus as a poor attitude for a Hero setting out to seek adventure. It was as if Jason was tired before he started. But it seemed to have little effect on his forty followers, and Proteus wondered how many were really listening to anything the leader said. But then a few of the men did seem to be made vaguely uneasy by their leader's manner; they exchanged glances among themselves, and no one quite knew how to respond.

Jason seemed to suddenly become aware of this unfavorable reaction, for now he raised his voice decisively, saying he had decided it was time to make clear certain matters that seemed to be generally misunderstood.

Moving quickly, he waded out of the water onto the beach, put on some clothing to indicate the formality of the occasion, and called a meeting.

Proteus, who had slowly followed the others ashore, looked around at the members of the group he was trying to join and said: "I fear I will have to borrow clothing, if I am to have any at all." His hair and beard were still slowly dripping seawater.

"Come along, then." It was the large and hearty Meleager who volunteered to take him in charge.

His new guide led Proteus to the ship, which rested tilted sideways on its rounded hull. Avoiding the large steering oar that projected from the stern, the Argonaut climbed up into the portside outrigger. The bottoms of both outriggers had been solidly planked, to afford sitting and standing space for the outboard banks of rowers, creating what was in effect a triple hull. From there Meleager slid his large body in under the narrow fighting deck, where he pulled open the tight-fitting door of a locker—Proteus supposed there would be a number of other storage spaces distributed around the ship, given the necessity of carrying supplies. The opening revealed a small store of spare equipment, and the newcomer was soon provided with a loincloth and a plain tunic. Any question of his qualifications to join the company had been apparently set aside, at least for the moment.

*   *   *

Presently the Argonauts had all gathered round their leader, who had now put on tunic, loincloth, and sandals, and was standing in the full light of the twin fires.

"All of you must know," Jason began, "or ought to know, that I am the rightful occupant of the throne of the kingdom of Iolcus, where our voyage began a few days ago." He raised his chin as if in defiance, and as he gazed around at the assembled company he looked for the moment every inch a king.

Having achieved utter silence among his followers, Jason went on. "Some years ago my father, as you must know, ruled Iolcus from the high castle above the harbor, where now his brother the usurper sits." The captain paused to look around. "If there are any here with me now who do not already know the story of how my father lost his crown to the treacherous and false usurper Pelias, I will tell it to you."

He took the answering murmur as a signal to proceed, and plunged into the story.

Proteus soon gave up trying to follow the narrative through the technicalities of intrigue; who was descended from whom on which side of the family, and which claim took precedence over which other one. He gathered that Jason's parents were both dead. He couldn't tell if the captain had brothers and sisters or not. Various people were named as being in contention, but they might all be cousins and aunts and uncles. Alliances were made and broken, and hatred flourished everywhere.

Proteus decided that if the legends about Jason were true, he was probably a hell of a Hero when he had a weapon in his hands and an enemy in front of him; but no one was ever going to call him a spellbinding speaker. As for the transfer of power he was trying to explain, events seemed to have followed the path they often did in royal families, a dispute among close relatives. To those not directly concerned the outcome would probably make little difference.

But eventually Jason got around to his main point. Some months ago, when he had challenged the right of his uncle, Pelias, to rule, Pelias had spoken ringingly of oracles and of the will of the gods, and had sworn some high-sounding oath. The details of the arrangement worked out remained vague, but in one way or another the royal uncle had induced or compelled his nephew to set out on this voyage.

Jason sounded like a man fully convinced of the wisdom of his own actions, when he concluded: "The throne of Iolcus must be mine, and it will be, when I have brought back the Golden Fleece."

Brought back the *what?* Proteus wondered silently. Most of the men around him were nodding their approval of their leader's words, and giving the impression that they understood him; but if Proteus had ever heard before of anything called the Golden Fleece, the memory was part of the vast store that had been knocked out of his aching head.

When he tried to recall anything he might ever have known about King Pelias, he had but little better success. The name of Pelias seemed to be associated with a reputation for ruthlessness, but then the same could be said of most successful kings.

Jason's narrative had turned into an exhortation, and every time he paused for breath a polite murmur of agreement went up from his assembled crew, each response a little louder than the last. The second or third time this happened, Proteus joined in, though he had no more idea of whether Jason's cause was really just or not than he did of where the money might have come from to outfit this ship. From the reaction of the other Argonauts, he gathered that Pelias was generally considered mean and untrustworthy, even for a king.

Meanwhile, a couple of volunteers from among the Heroic company had managed to divert enough of their attention from the speech to tend the cookfires, and the smell of roasting meat promised a delicious dinner soon. Proteus's mouth was watering.

He wondered how long it had been since he tasted food—then he thought it might be just as well that he could not remember that.

"The goal of our voyage is the Golden Fleece," repeated Jason, for the third or fourth time, making absolutely sure that no one had missed the point. This time fortunately he went on to provide a kind of definition: the Fleece was said to have come from a god-sent flying ram, the like of which had never been seen by anyone before or since.

"Flying ram?" Proteus asked the world aloud. A couple of his nearest neighbors looked at him, but nobody else paid any attention, which when he thought about it he supposed was his good luck.

Jason, having worked himself into a mood to talk, was recapitulating the story anyway. About a generation ago, this wonderful creature—or maybe it was some kind of a device, worked by odylic magic—had carried a man named Phrixus from the neighborhood of Iolcus halfway across the world to Colchis, where the fugitive had eventually married Chalciope, a daughter of the Colchian King Aeetes, and fathered several children by her.

"Two sons of Phrixus and the Princess Chalciope are with us now," added Jason, and motioned for the pair to somehow indicate themselves. "Phrontis and Argeus."

Two of the younger-looking Argonauts stepped forward into the full firelight, looking round awkwardly, as if they feared they might be called on to make speeches.

But Jason spared the brothers and his audience any such ordeal. He went on with his oration, driving home the essential point by repetition. "Pelias the false king has sworn, by all the gods and in front of witnesses, that if I can bring back the Fleece and give it to him, he will honor my just claim, and resign the throne to me."

Someone in the rear circle of listeners raised a hand. "Captain, this Phrixus is now dead?"

"Our father died several years ago," said Argeus, and went on to explain that he and his brother Phrontis had been mere boys when they left their grandfather's domain. But they could tell their shipmates of the old man's formidable reputation as a tyrant. Shaking his head, the speaker seemed to imply that they could provide plenty of evidence of that in the days ahead.

His brother, Phrontis, now took the floor and had more than a little to say about the journey that lay before them. He recited a list of the various kingdoms where they expected to touch land, on one side or another of the Great Sea. To begin with, there was the island of Lemnos, where women were now said to rule; and after Lemnos they would come to the mysterious domain of Samothraki, where travelers were strongly encouraged to take part in occult rituals. Then Bithnyia, where King Amycus brutally held power—and everyone who had ever heard of Amycus knew what a problem any visitor there was likely to encounter.

Proteus had not heard of Amycus, or could not remember if he had; and apparently he was not going to be enlightened for a while yet.

Young Phrontis, warming to his role of guide, was beginning to be breathless with excitement. After Bithnyia, he said, there were the filthy and odious Harpies that they would have to deal with, and after them the Clashing Rocks . . .

Around Proteus the listening men were nodding, grim-faced in the firelight but still enjoying themselves. Proteus's report of a Giant not far from where they were had not really alarmed this bunch, who were obviously not going to be discouraged by the possibilities of future danger; they had probably been hearing some of the same stories all their lives.

Someone standing back in darkness had a question in a different vein: "This Fleece must be a treasure of considerable value, then? I mean, whether it is really metallic gold or not." Proteus was glad to realize that others in the group were just about as ignorant as he.

Idmon answered: "That is a safe assumption. But the gold itself may be the least part of its value." In the firelight, it was easy to see that there was quite a lot of gray in Idmon's hair.

Proteus wondered suddenly if the crew, or any among them, had been promised shares in any profits of the voyage. That was a common enough arrangement on adventurous expeditions, most of which turned sooner or later into outright piracy. It was a prospect he was going to have to keep in mind, whatever the original impetus might have been that had landed him in this situation.

As for the pledge or promise that Jason seemed so certain of, from old King Pelias, well, it would be a bright sunny day in the Underworld before any king, let alone one with the reputation of Jason's uncle, would give up his throne simply because someone asked him for it.

One of the listening Argonauts now spoke up to raise this point quite openly, though he phrased it in somewhat more diplomatic language. When Jason retorted coldly that he had his uncle's promise, and was going to have the throne, the man who brought it up hastily added an assurance that whether Jason ever became a king or not, he was still eager to go on this expedition for the sheer adventure of it. He did not want anyone to think that he was trying to back out.

There was a chorus of agreement. It seemed that every other member of the crew had come along for the same reasons, and backing out would be the worst thing any of them could think of at this point.

"I plan to honor my side of the agreement scrupulously," Jason informed them all, driving the point home. "And I intend to see that my uncle honors his, one way or another." Another murmur from the men. Somehow the doubts raised about King Pelias and his pledge were set aside again without really being answered.

It was the youth called Telamon who wanted to know: "But tell us, Jason, what course are we are going to steer? I mean, we have heard of the various countries where we may land, but nothing yet of distances and bearings."

That question perked up the interest of the crew, who were already tired of dynastic squabbles and old horror stories. What really mattered was that they had been accepted into this company of famous Heroes, and that Jason himself, *the* Jason, Jason the Boar-Slayer, was leading them to new adventures.

"I will let another man answer that question," Jason said, and with a gesture of invitation stood aside.

A stocky, sturdy fellow, skin dark as ebony, got to his feet. "In case there is still someone on the crew who does not know me, I am Tiphys, your steersman and navigator."

Men looked at him respectfully; evidently he had a reputation. He was a very solid-looking man though not especially large, and Proteus saw that he had removed the compass-pyx from the beached ship, and was carrying it under his arm.

When it was time to shove off again in the morning, he would reinstall it, a job that any experienced navigator could easily accomplish with a few simple, routine rites of magic. Meanwhile, Tiphys acted as if the instrument were his personal property, treating it with the familiar care of a man who handles a treasure that has been passed down in his family for generations.

And he had a ready answer to the question that had already been asked about their course. Tiphys rapidly recited a firmly memorized list of seas and straits and coastlines; Proteus, yearning after his own lost memory, was impressed with the man's knowledge and his ability to recall. Proteus got the impression from listening that the land they were bound for, Colchis, must lie somewhere at the far end of the earth. The contemplated journey was going to last for months, perhaps for many months, even if all went smoothly. And they all knew better than to expect that.

When Tiphys had concluded, Jason asked: "Are there any other questions?"

Someone raised a hand. "Does Colchis lie at the edge of the world?"

"My compass-pyx has shown me that the world is really round. There is no danger of falling off an edge . . . well, argue about that if you like, but I know it goes on far beyond Colchis . . . anyone else?"

When no one else raised a hand, Jason's eye came steadily back to Proteus, who now realized that he had not been forgotten after all.

A silence had begun to grow, and others were also looking at the newcomer. The commander slightly raised his voice. "We must decide if this man Proteus, who comes to us from out of the sea, is Hero or servant. He might have died in a shipwreck with the other menials, but Fate decreed otherwise and he has come bravely through great dangers. If we judge him no more than a servant still, then we must leave him behind. The alternative is to make him one of our number, but before doing that we must see if he is worthy."

Listening to the talk around him, Proteus began to gain some understanding of the controversy over servants. Originally, each qualified and accepted Hero had been allowed to bring aboard one companion . . . friend, relative, servant, catamite, or some combination of those categories.

But Jason, in the aftermath of Hercules's abandonment, had decided that all such hangers-on or attendants had to go. Now that all the chosen Heroes were actually aboard, it was obvious that any such additional number would simply make the ship too crowded; and if not everyone could have an attendant, no one in this company of equals should.

Voices were raised in general agreement. If Proteus was to stay, it would have to be as a full-fledged Argonaut, a member of the company.

People looked at him uncertainly, and he looked back in the same mode. He found it gratifying that his unknown self at least did not feel terrified at the idea of being tested.

"Shall we have a trial of wrestling?" suggested Haraldur the northerner, in the tone of one who expects to get a laugh.

"That didn't work out too well when we tried it with Hercules," someone else recalled. And now there was a ripple of rueful laughter, mingled with resentment.

"Weapons, then." The man in the horned helmet looked at Proteus. "With what tools of death do you feel most at ease?"

"I choose the spear," he heard himself saying. Again, as when he was asked his name, he had no need to give the matter any thought.

Having said that, of course he had to borrow a spear, and several were immediately produced. He frowned at the selection, thinking there was something wrong about each of these weapons's heads, their points, though obviously all were well-made. But he could not have said exactly what the difficulty was, and at last he made a choice. The design of a dolphin had been worked into the spearhead with some skill, and it was good sharp bronze—which of course could never be as hard and enduring as the best steel, but some men still preferred it.

Now, if he could remember that with no trouble at all, along with so much else about the way the world worked, how in the Underworld could there be nothing left of himself except a name? But so it was, and he would have to deal with it.

Balancing the stout shaft in his right hand, Proteus looked about him, meeting expectant glances. "What must I do?"

"Fight three of us to the death. No, no, I'm joking!" And Haraldur bent over double, slapping his knobby knees in high amusement.

After grim news and edgy talk, everyone was ready to enjoy a joke. When the laughter subsided, it turned out that what the company were really proposing was that he should make a throw of a certain distance—someone paced off what was evidently considered a fair distance—and score a solid hit on a log of driftwood, on which some of the Heroes had already been practicing, leaving it chipped and scarred.

Someone jested that they could use as their target the very oaken keel of *Argo*. "She's not going to notice one little pin-prick there." Jason shot the man a look that said he was not amused.

Concentrating intently now upon his trial, Proteus nodded, stepped up to the mark, and with a casual motion of his left arm indicated that people should stand back. Then, without giving himself time to worry about it, he did precisely what he had been challenged to do. He did somewhat better, in fact—the spearhead went in deep, very close to the center of the indicated target. The long shaft stuck there quivering, as if it still had energy to spare.

He heard a muttering behind him: "Stronger than he looks."

The owner of the spear came to reclaim his weapon, and had to work at it to wrench it from the wood. Men thumped Proteus on the back, offering congratulations, bombarding him with their names, half of which he failed to remember the first time he heard them. He was invited to join the others in their dinner.

Jason, after being distracted several times by questions, finally said to Proteus: "Welcome aboard."

"Thank you, sir," the newcomer responded, gnawing fragments of roast meat from a bone. The meat was tasty, but suddenly he realized that what he was really hungry for was fish. Well, no doubt he would see plenty of that in days to come.

"And do you think yourself qualified in every way to join us in our quest?"

"I don't know the answer to that, sir. I've passed your test, I can handle a spear. I'm not sure just what other qualifications you expect."

The mass of dark hair nodded judiciously. "A reasonable reply. Come to think of it, I believe Hercules had something of the same modest attitude."

When it came time to retire for the night, Proteus saw the

steersman Tiphys carefully bring his compass-pyx with him to the place where he lay down to sleep.

The sight of the device stirred something deep in the new-comer's ravaged memory. Proteus asked permission to look at the fine instrument, hoping that something about it would jog his memory into further revelations. Tiphys rather grudgingly agreed.

Use of the compass-pyx was well-nigh universal. Navigation across the open sea, out of sight of land, was difficult enough even with the help of such devices, and would have been all but impossible without it. Probably Tiphys, like most other navigators of reputation, relied upon some special private magical addition to the instrument, an accessory he would try as best he could to keep secret.

The compass-pyx that Proteus was now privileged to look at basically resembled the similar instruments he could hazily remember seeing.

The pointer, or cusp of the device, balanced on a needle-sharp pivot, consisted of a narrow crescent of horn and ivory. A sliver of each of the disparate materials, identically curved and not quite as long as a man's hand, were bound together in a particular way. Some experts swore that silk was the only proper material to use for the binding, but Proteus saw now that Tiphys, like many other expert pilots, preferred the web-stuff of certain mutant spiders.

Once a pilot or steersman had attuned his mind to the device, it indicated with great accuracy the bearing that the ship should take to bring him to his goal. Few people placed any reliance on the compass-pyx on land; its effectiveness on the Great Sea was credited to Poseidon's having long ago given the device his blessing.

There were of course refinements in the construction and operation of the compass-pyx. Some extremely simple versions were good only for indicating true north; others, if the cap/cover was shifted to the first end, pointed to the nearest dry land.

Many swore that the compass-pyx worked best, indeed that it was only reliable at all, if hooked up with a strip of pure copper that ran deep into the central timbers of the ship. Whether Tiphys was going to reattach his instrument in that way Proteus could not tell.

The watches for the coming night had been assigned hours ago, long before Proteus had come wading out of the sea to join their company, and Jason had insisted on taking a turn himself, which was evidently his usual procedure with any kind of duty. So Proteus had no responsibilities as yet; anyway, he thought, his new shipmates were probably not ready to trust him with their lives. Belly satisfied with a good meal, he slept well through the night, stretched out on warm sand. The eternal sound of the surf was in his ears, and his dreams that night were of the sea. In them he was immersed in deep water, but somehow not in the least afraid of drowning.

In the morning, after breakfasting on the remnants of last night's feast, they all lined up along the ship's sides, and at a signal laid hold of her gunwales and pushed her back into the sea again. Proteus immediately scrambled into his newly assigned spot on one of the benches. Meleager was next to him, and he was beginning to recognize the names of others who were nearby.

The oar proved less familiar than the spear had been, but the business of its use was not that complicated, and he soon settled into the proper rhythm.

He felt a nervousness that he did not want to admit, even to himself. But there was no sign of any Giant.

As the new day wore on in rowing, Proteus found himself becoming more and more interested in the tale of the Golden Fleece, wanting to know more about it. He talked with those of the other Heroes who were the least standoffish.

That certainly included Meleager, whose garments, when he was wearing anything at all, looked rich and costly, a picture of size, confident attitude, and youthful vigor.

"Then this Golden Fleece is marvelous indeed," Proteus agreed. "But in what way?"

But Mel had to admit that he was the wrong one to be asking about that.

Every now and then, as the Argonauts talked among themselves, the name of Theseus came up, as it very often did when folks were telling tales of adventure. Everyone had heard the story of the Princess Ariadne of Corycus, her connection with Theseus, and the breathtaking reversals of fortune she had experienced on the Island of Dia.

Speaking of Theseus, almost everyone in the crew seemed to be surprised that that youthful adventurer, sometimes called King of the Pirates, had not shown up and demanded a place. But the time of departure had come and gone, and no one knew where he might be. Many assumed that his name had been on the list of those to whom Jason had sent personal invitations; if Theseus was not a Hero, who could claim that title? True, his remarkable career consisted of little but acts of piracy. But if a consistent concern for others' property was made a qualification, Jason might have a hard time filling his roster.

Jason had only one comment to make when the name of Theseus came up: "From what I hear, he is a thief and murderer, and to call him a king does dishonor to a royal title."

As they rowed, the conversation around Proteus touched on many things: to begin with, women, as might be expected. Then the sea and its wonders, and then something about women. The remote, ongoing conflict between Giants and gods, now supposed to be flaring into open warfare—but such mighty struggles were remote to most of the people of the world, and the conversation soon came back to women.

Proteus listened, mostly, now and then contributing a word or two; but to his surprise, what he had vaguely expected to be the chief subject of speculation, the Fleece itself, was scarcely mentioned.

Though he listened intently, he was still unable to discover just what kind of intrinsic value the Fleece might have, what were its magic powers—everyone assumed it must have some. How big it was, how many standard units of gold it weighed. Gradually it dawned on the listener that few if any of these men who were willing to risk their lives to find the exotic treasure, had any better idea of its nature than he did. They were here because Jason, a magnetic hero who would someday be king of an important country, was going to lead them on a glorious adventure, and so far that was enough for everyone.

Proteus found it oddly restful to spend another night at sea; he thought he could doze, slumped on his rower's bench, almost as comfortably as he would have slept in the safest, driest bed ashore. Most of the other men seemed to be having an easy time of it as well, napping at their oars, while clouds covered the stars. The sea was calm enough tonight, and Jason, who apparently did not completely trust Tiphys and his elaborate compass-pyx, decided to wait for dawn to push ahead.

Around noon on the second day since Proteus had joined the crew, Jason while taking a turn as lookout on the low raised deck—climbing the little mast would have been utterly impractical—caught sight of some green-clad hills. Within a couple of hours the *Argo* was coming ashore, her captain meaning to once more refill the collection of water jugs and jars and waterskins. Whatever part of the world this was, Proteus could not remember ever seeing it before.

When an opportunity offered, and when Tiphys had offered no objection, Proteus took a turn at crouching over the compass-pyx and with the aid of its powers called up a vision of the *Argo*'s destination. It was a mysterious vision indeed, and seemed to have little to do with geography.

Have I done this before? he wondered privately. He thought the answer must be yes. The ease with which he approached the instrument seemed good evidence that he had.

One routine means of operation, he knew, was to whisper aloud the name of the island, continent, or object that you were trying to reach by navigation, while resting your forehead against the ivory box. But in this case nothing of the kind was necessary.

If only he had known the name of his home, he would have tried to get a look at it. A vague attempt to think of home produced nothing. On impulse he tried imagining the Fleece instead.

On each trial the device showed Proteus, behind his closed eyelids, a new view of their mysterious objective, very slightly nearer than the time before but from the same angle. A shapeless mass that seemed to be hanging in the branches of a tree. And against that green it appeared to be golden indeed, but more like the shimmer of morning sun on the ocean, than any material object.

Lemnos

$\mathcal{T}$he next day seemed endlessly long to Proteus. Not that he was particularly wearied by the rowing, but the hours of labor were relieved only by intermittent talk with his new ship-mates. The talk brought him no new knowledge on the subject in which he was most keenly interested—himself. And it taught him very little about the voyage to which he was now committed.

Throughout the long day he was engaged almost continuously in a silent struggle to regain his memory. But all the effort brought to the surface were scattered shards and images, almost nothing any earlier than the Giant's destruction of the ship. At one point the sight and sound of splintered planks came through clearly, then a more detailed look than he had had before at horrified human faces, none of which he recognized. And there was the sound of a man screaming, an ugly noise that ended in drowning bubbles . . . feeling his stomach growing queasy, Proteus gave up for the time being the effort of trying to force his memory.

But of course giving up wasn't as easy as all that. He could not escape his need to know the truth, whatever it might be. And so in a little while he tried again to find some remnant, some walk-ing ghost of his old self. And got no farther than before.

All day the crew had been laboring almost continuously with the oars, which left them generally exhausted. It would have been only sensible if Proteus had found himself worn out too, but at the end of the day his muscles were not aching, and he still had energy. Nor were there any blisters on his palms and fingers, which, as he now thoughtfully noted, had been heavily callused all along. Whatever his true identity turned out to be, it would seem he was no aristocrat.

Maybe a common sailor, then, with an exceptionally well-conditioned body? Or possibly a professional athlete of some kind? Athletes often had to seek other kinds of employment. For all Proteus could tell, he might well have been one of the boatload of servants who had been scheduled to attend the Argonauts, before Jason and the others woke up to the fact that their narrow ship lacked room for so many non-Heroic bodies.

Athlete maybe, servant, maybe. But the more he thought about it, the more likely it seemed that he had been a sailor, one of the crew bringing a load of servants to their destination. In any case his earlier self, who he was beginning to think of as Old Proteus, had been nominally free; his neck was not encircled by any metal collar indicating slavery.

Servant, sailor, or whatever, the evidence said he'd certainly been accustomed to hard, physical work, and not unfamiliar with oars and spears. Now if only he could recall his orders from the mysterious woman—but they lay still tantalizingly out of reach.

It seemed ridiculous to feel uneasy about not getting tired, but the anomaly nagged him. Now stronger than before, the feeling grew in him that the Giant who had destroyed that ship and drowned those men would come and hunt him down if he knew that Proteus had survived. He, Proteus, had been personally stalked by some mighty power that was out to kill him. And if that power knew that he was still alive, it would come after him again.

The next day was also spent in rowing, and, for Proteus, in basically useless mental effort. And so it went on the day after that. On several occasions the *Argo* sailed entirely out of sight of land for hours at a time. Jason and his crew obviously were ready to trust their lives to Tiphys and his compass-pyx, and to the construction of their sturdy ship, and its outfitting with the finest silk and linen sails. From the superb quality of the gear, it seemed obvious that Jason had wealthy backers in his attempt to win a crown. Backers who were not only wealthy, but not much afraid of angering King Pelias. One alternative of course would be that Jason had been blessed with a family fortune, and had sunk that into this endeavor; but the captain made an occasional remark about his growing up in poverty, which seemed to dispose of that idea. Proteus asked a couple of his shipmates what they knew of the expedition's financing, but it seemed they had never thought about such mundane matters. A quest with Jason was sure to be a glorious adventure, and that was enough for them. The new recruit did not pursue the matter further; he had no wish to be suspected of being someone's spy or secret agent.

In the course of these same days Proteus began to notice how strangely often first one flying fish and then another, skimming the waves on a parallel course with the *Argo*, and at no great distance, just kept up with the ship. Maybe the actions of the fish were purely accidental, but now Proteus developed an eerie feeling that some unknown power, for some unknown reason, was keeping the vessel under surveillance. He kept this suspicion to himself.

Now and then during his long hours at the oar he raised his eyes, searching the clouds or the sunny blue, cursed by a vague fear that the *Argo* herself would suffer some direct attack, now that he had come aboard her. But so far there was no hint of anything of the kind.

Three days after leaving the beach where Proteus had joined them, Jason and Tiphys the steersman got together for a long, low-voiced talk. Afterward Jason stood up and raised his voice to inform the crew that their next port of call was going to be the island of Lemnos.

And at the same time, Proteus noticed Idmon opening a locker and taking out a waterproof sealskin pouch. From this in turn he carefully removed a book of modest size. The volume's pages were of parchment, and it was bound in what looked like sharkskin, which Proteus supposed would have some waterproofing effect.

When Proteus asked about the book, Idmon let him know that it was the ship's log, and entries were to be made in it daily, setting down events almost as they happened, so that when the voyage was over a detailed history of it would have been written.

Sitting cross-legged on one corner of the deck, the record-keeper dipped a stubby pen, made from a large feather, into one end of an inkhorn, and started putting words on parchment. When he paused for thought after a couple of lines, Proteus was still curious. "What language is that?"

The scribe looked at him in mild surprise. "An old one. Can you read it?"

It would not have surprised Proteus to learn that half the Heroes had trouble reading even the language they had been speaking all their lives. In this company, scholarship beyond that would be extraordinary. He said carefully: "I think I may have seen it somewhere before."

The scribe seemed about to put another question to him, when both were distracted by a debate that had begun on nearby benches, and had now grown vociferous. For several years now, word had been passed around the world (and in this matter the memory of Proteus seemed to be functioning normally) to the effect that Lemnos was inhabited solely by women. The most popular version of the story said that some years ago the Lemnian ladies, resentful of their husbands' having taken to importing mistresses on a large scale, had risen up in rebellion and slaughtered them to the last man.

Opinions on the truth of this story differed widely among the Argonauts, and a lively discussion went around the benches. Proteus listened, but knew nothing to contribute.

Nobody noticed his reluctance to speak, for plenty of others were eager to do so. Several of the Argonauts claimed to have actually visited Lemnos during the past few years, and these unanimously reported that the tales of mass murder were only rumors. All that had really happened on that island was that a kind of matriarchal government had been put in place.

Others, contradicting the men who claimed to be eyewitnesses, continued to swear that the stories of murder must be correct. When some of the men appealed to Jason, he had nothing directly to say on the question—again his mind seemed elsewhere, as it so often did.

But the dark rumor seemed refuted when, after a few days of moderately rough weather, and about a month after leaving Iolcus, the ship put somewhat warily into the small harbor of the city of Myrina, the only real port on Lemnos.

It was easy to see that the island was of substantial size though not as big as some—Tiphys said a little less than two hundred square miles. Here and there faint columns of smoke went up to enormous heights, over land much of which looked quite empty of human habitation; one of the older Argonauts said the smoke came from volcanic activity, that the ground here was always smoldering somewhere. Gentle hills in the western and southern parts of the island built up gradually to a single mountain, called Skopia, Tiphys said. The sharp-toothed crest stood about fifteen hundred feet above the level of the sea.

Once in the harbor, the visitors were relieved to see some of the wilder stories proven false. There were a fair number of men about—though it was true there seemed fewer males and more women than you would ordinarily expect to see on docks and quays. The waterfront was not particularly busy, but by no means deserted. Proteus observed one fellow standing at the end of a dock, who seemed to be posing with tensed muscles while he watched the *Argo* glide by, as if he wanted to impress the newcomers with his physique. If that was indeed his purpose, the effect was spoiled by his thin arms and pot belly.

Shortly after they had tied up, it was a woman who came to meet them as port official, with book and pen in hand, and escorted by a small armed guard who were also women. Briskly the official asked the newcomers their business. Jason met her courteously, and Proteus watching from a little distance thought they were having a reasonable conversation. In the end the visitors were granted full freedom to come ashore.

As the Argonauts gradually relaxed their vigilance, stepped off their ship, and began to see more of the town, it became obvious that for some reason the male population of Lemnos seemed content to leave both the business of government and the government of business to the women. It wasn't that the men were totally idle; but they seemed to be contenting themselves with an intricate system of activity involving both gambling and philosophical debates.

When Proteus, keeping a borrowed spear casually within reach, talked to a couple of the local men about the apparent lack of excitement on their island, the locals, turning calmly arrogant, informed him that they were expecting to depart within the hour. They said they were going to take part in a great adventure, whose nature they were not at liberty to discuss.

When the visitor looked around the harbor and asked which of the few visible ships they planned to take, they were unable to contain their great secret any longer. Each man swore soberly that they were waiting for Theseus to sail in and welcome them aboard his pirate ship for a cruise of pillaging and looting.

Their visitor thought the pair looked poorly equipped for any such adventure. When Proteus tried politely to convey that he still had doubts, he expected for a moment that the two were going to attack him, for they glared wildly and knotted their fists. But then they turned their backs on him and wandered off down the dock, arm in arm.

Another Argonaut, watching their slightly unsteady progress, snorted. "They're on drugs."

"That would explain much," put in a third.

The port official, a gray-haired woman with a look of harried pride, was looking after the pair also, with disdain. She explained that the fathers and sons and husbands of the island, or a great majority of them, were now spending most of their time and energy on taking some drug, or some combination of substances, that was supposed to make them clever, powerful, and handsome.

Then she added: "And what you are thinking about them is quite right. The drug does not work—not in the way they think it does. The only notable real effect, as you will observe when you meet more of them about the island, is to make them see themselves as Heroes."

"And to make the rest of us see them as idiots," Proteus muttered. Somehow it made him feel a little better to see men who were worse off than he; there was no keeping their weakness secret from the world.

In passing he noted also that there were few small children to be seen around the island. Perhaps over the last few years the men of Lemnos had lost interest in other things besides work.

The idea of leaving all the practical affairs of life to women was one that a number of Argonauts found shocking. It led to a discussion of the half-legendary Amazons, another topic on which the men had strong opinions and very little knowledge.

None of Proteus's shipmates claimed to have ever actually visited Amazon country, though several said they were determined to get there before they died—rumor had it that impressive warriors were welcome there, and were royally entertained until they had impregnated large numbers of women.

Whatever the truth about the Amazons, Lemnos was real, and hard enough to understand. Those who said they had visited this port before observed that the situation seemed to have deteriorated since their last visit—by that they meant there were now even fewer men to be seen in public.

Leaving aside the organization of society, Lemnos did not seem to be a wealthy land. Every rooftop seemed to carry some kind of cistern, ready to catch rainfall; streams of fresh water were small and scarce. Sparse crops grew on hillsides visible from near the middle of town, and the workers in those tilted fields appeared to be almost entirely women.

But, soon after the port official had reported to the modest palace, messengers came from the queen, with word that the Argonauts were invited into their town and houses as friends.

And Jason was invited, alone, to visit the queen in her palace.

The Argonauts spent the interval when he was gone staying close together, trading stories and whetting blades, vaguely suspicious of some kind of treachery.

After about three hours, Jason returned to his men, looking quietly excited, more so than Proteus had ever seen him. When his crew had gathered around him, Jason reported that he had had a long conversation alone with the queen, and she had actually offered him the kingship of Lemnos.

A number of the Argonauts began to laugh at that, but Jason remained solemn. No, he was not joking. Then he raised a hand, quelling the beginnings of an excited celebration, and told his men that he had turned the offer down. At that a sudden silence fell.

Proteus felt inwardly relieved at the announcement, though he could not have said why Jason's political and dynastic plans should matter to him one way or the other. But then Proteus made the odd discovery that, for some reason that was still shadowy in his own mind, it was important to him that the Argosy go on.

Jason gave the impression that his decision had cost him a struggle, but once reached, it was firm.

Speaking into a continuing, wondering silence among his men, he said: "You will be asking yourselves why I have rejected a crown."

No one had any comment to make. Answering the question that had not been asked, their captain went on to offer several reasons for his refusal, chief among them the vow he had made and had to keep. "Not that I could have accepted in any case. I have made a solemn vow to return to Iolcus with the Golden Fleece, and that's what I will do."

There was also the fact that the current king of Lemnos would have had to be deposed. But rumor had it that that individual seldom took any interest in affairs of state, or in his queen for that matter, being totally absorbed in his life of drugs and games. His existence did not appear to be much of an obstacle.

Meanwhile, Proteus was thinking that Jason's true reason for turning down a throne might well be quite different: Lemnos was small and mean, almost a joke as an independent kingdom, and it would only retain its independence until some real monarch thought it worth his while to snap it up.

Not much else of interest to Proteus happened during the adventurers' short stay on the island. There was a little excitement—vicarious for most of the crew—when three or four of the Argonauts sampled some of the drugs to which the men of the island were so ruinously addicted.

Proteus and a few others were standing at dockside, uneasy about getting far from their ship in this strange place, when the unmistakable sounds of a fight breaking out reverberated through the thin wooden walls of the tavern.

Haraldur brightened at the noise. "Sounds like fun. Let's go!" A couple of others shared his enthusiasm.

Proteus by contrast experienced only a vague sinking feeling at the prospect of a fight; but he went along, walking rather than running after his shipmates. His lack of eagerness did not matter, because the brawl, such as it was, was very nearly over by the time the first of his shipmates reached the tavern doorway, where Proteus looked in just in time to see Meleager felled by a thick glass bottle bouncing off the back of his head. The bottle did not break, and the thin Lemnian who had wielded it looked surprised at his own success.

Mel's shipmates lumbered forward, generally towering over the natives, exacting vengeance. Weapons hardly seemed required, in this tavern, in this town. And anyway, a spear was always awkward at close quarters. Proteus stood leaning on his, and watched.

The worst of the skirmish, from the Argonauts' point of view, was that Meleager had to be carried back to the ship, where several minutes passed before he fully came around.

Jason on hearing the story of the fight was plainly angry, the first time Proteus had seen him in that state. "Was it not possible to stay out of trouble for a few hours?"

A chastened Hero stammered out that drugs had been at the bottom of the dispute. The captain on hearing this blasphemed several gods and sent out a search party. A couple of Argonauts who had sampled the local pharmaceuticals had to be hauled back aboard by main force. Jason on hearing this went to look them over. Realizing their condition, he sternly warned them that any man who jumped ship from this voyage would open himself to lifelong embarrassment; then he ordered them tied up until the effects of the drug had passed.

One man had to be restrained from jumping into the harbor, saying he meant to swim to Colchis, pick up the Fleece, and be back to Lemnos in time for dinner.

The captain's indignation was quietly mounting. "If any of you have carried any of those drugs on board, I hope you'll pitch them overboard."

Haraldur, smiling slightly, had a comment: "It might be fun to watch a sunfish that thinks it's a shark."

Some men laughed, but Jason was not amused.

Fortunately there were no immediate repercussions from the brawl. In an effort to discover how much local resentment, if any, the fight had created, Proteus and several other Argonauts strolled to a different quayside tavern where they entered as casual customers. This like the other grog shop was one of the few places where local men were still working, tending bar.

Whining music came from a corner, where female musicians of gnarled and charmless age sawed at their stringed instruments. The wine was not bad, and now he had consumed enough to make him feel well-satisfied with the world for the time being.

Looking round at his shipmates, Proteus decided that after all, getting truly smashed would be more trouble than it was worth— now that he had begun drinking, he had the feeling that serious competition in this field was not and had never been a regular part of his life.

The bartender who had been hovering nearby suddenly cleared his throat. "So, Jason is going all the way to Colchis."

Proteus raised an eyebrow. "That's the plan. Certainly no secret about it."

The man leaned toward him over the stained wood. "Take me with you." He looked a bit old to be starting out as an adventurer.

"You serious?"

"I am. Anything to get away from Lemnos." The tone was one of quiet desperation.

"Don't want to be ruled by women?"

The bartender shook his head, and looked at the musicians. "It's not the women who are driving me crazy. It's the men."

Proteus was shaking his head. "Sorry, but we're allowed no attendants aboard. It's been decided." Then he looked up at a familiar voice, and was surprised to see Mel back on his feet again so soon. Well, some skulls were thicker than others.

Another Argonaut joined in, making some drunken proposal to have the new applicant prove his worth by throwing spears. "Or maybe bottles? How 'bout that?" That was horrifying; glass bottles were rare enough to be considered of some value.

By now Proteus had had enough to drink so this even seemed a good idea to him. "Why not? It worked for me." But in the end the discussion came to nothing.

＊　　＊　　＊

When the native men felt themselves insulted, which Proteus got the impression happened dangerously often, they were not shy of challenging some of the Heroes to fight. The resulting contests— if that was really the right word for them—tended to be very one-sided. Fortunately for the diplomatic atmosphere, no one was actually killed, and the native men bore no resentment. As long as they remained alive, they seemed able to convince themselves that their side had won, or at least that they had gone down gloriously, succumbing only in the face of overwhelming odds.

Meanwhile, some of the younger women had begun eyeing the visitors with frank interest. Three Heroes besides Jason received offers of marriage, none of which were accepted. Local prostitutes had seen their business fall off sharply, their bodies less attractive than the images produced by drugs in the minds of their former customers.

They stayed in all three days on Lemnos.

"Three days." An oarsman grunted at his task. "Only three days? I thought it was longer."

Another shook his head. "Three days was plenty long enough. An unpleasant spot, for all that it was full of horny women."

Mysteries

$\mathcal{M}$eleager's head was still sore from the knock sustained in the Lemnian tavern. But soreness was the least of his problems. He had not had much to drink, and had stayed away from the drugs, but his behavior had certainly turned odd.

Jason, as Mel's oldest friend aboard, was seriously concerned. "Let me take a look at him."

Proteus moved closer, watching over the shoulder of the would-be physician. External damage was slight. Mel's eyes were open most of the time, and he was capable of moving about, and sometimes responding to simple questions. He announced that he was ready to take his turn at rowing, but when he got to the bench he only sat there with the long oar idle in his hands.

When encouraged, and reminded of what he was supposed to be doing, he would pull steadily for a stroke or two, and then again forget where he was and what he was about. He just sat there looking round at his shipmates as if he wondered who they were. Proteus, on observing this behavior felt an inner chill, and rubbed his own head thoughtfully. The swelling had gone down and the spot no longer hurt, but a vast domain of vital memory remained totally out of his reach. Still, that crack might have left him much worse off than he was.

Another man, who claimed to have had some training as a physician, pronounced judgment on the case of Meleager. "I have seen this kind of thing before. He may come out of it, or he may not. Time will tell."

Everyone who thought he knew something about medicine took a turn asking Meleager questions, and peering into his eyes and ears and nostrils; none of these orifices were bleeding, which the self-appointed experts said was a hopeful sign. At last a consensus was reached that he should be watched, and allowed to rest as much as possible. His fate rested in the hands of the gods.

A few days later, the Argonauts were beaching their long ship at Samothraki. This was a rocky island, presenting barren cliffs to the sea around almost its whole circumference, but Proteus thought it beautiful in its own unwelcoming way. And it was certainly much different from their last port of call. Here there were springs and streams, obviously a good share of rainfall, and a single mountain four times as high as the single peak that Lemnos had. Samothraki was about ten miles long by seven wide, smoothly shaped with a regular coastline which offered few natural harbors. A shipmate with a mind for practical details told Proteus that exports included fruit and vegetables, especially onions.

More interesting to most of the crew than onions were the mystery rituals for which Samothraki was also well known. It was to discuss these, and the invitation issued to all the Argonauts, that Jason called a gathering of the entire crew beside the ship.

"There is a cave over there"—pointing to a spot on the cliffside that bulked up only a few yards from the harbor's mouth— "where certain rites, usually forbidden to visitors and strangers, are to be conducted; and we have been invited to take part."

Many were interested but everyone was wary. "We have? How did that happen? Who knew we were coming here?"

Jason would say only that the invitation had reached him through intermediaries. And Idmon casually let it be known that he himself had been an initiate for some time.

"What sort of rites are they?" someone asked. "What would be expected of us?"

"There are mysteries of which we must not sing," said Idmon, in a tone that suggested he was quoting someone or something. "I will say only this: that when you have passed through, you will sail on with greater confidence across the formidable sea."

Around Proteus several of the other men were making gestures and mumbling words that they doubtless thought had some magical efficacy. It came as no great surprise to him to discover that there were several would-be mystics and/or would-be sorcerers among the crew. But it turned out that no more than half a dozen men in all were eager to be introduced into the secret rites of the Cabiri.

That was a new name to Proteus. "Who or what in all the hells are the Cabiri?" he demanded of some of his shipmates. He didn't think they were divinities, for he had the feeling that among the vast store of largely useless rubbish his memory had somehow managed to retain, he could have found the names and folk histories of most of the gods—probably no human being knew them all. He could only hope that "Cabiri" wasn't familiar as mother's milk to everyone in the world with an intact memory. But it was still a new one to him, and there was nothing he could do about that.

The men to whom he put the question looked aghast at him, and one of them chided Proteus for a lack of reverence. But he got the impression that a majority of his shipmates probably did not know much about the Cabiri either. It was only that no entity of more than human power ought to be so casually treated.

For the rest of the day, and through the early hours of the night, when his shipmates whispered to one another about the Cabiri and their mysterious rituals, Proteus could only nod and smile, as if he really had some idea of what the others were talking about.

When the subject came up, Proteus felt a deep, instinctive reaction that he would be wise to avoid taking part in any secret rites himself. This feeling was only strengthened when he got his first close look at a dim hollow in the rock, fifteen feet or so above the high-tide level of the sea, and approachable only by a narrow ledge along the face of a low cliff. His first impression was of a shallow cave, no more than a grotto, but he supposed the appearance was deceptive. As he watched, a hummingbird came darting out. This, the Argonauts were told, was the entrance to the place where the mysteries were to be revealed—or rather, where glimpses of certain secrets were to be granted to a select few.

It all sounded somehow repellent and even unconvincing to Proteus. He asked: "What will these Cabiri look like when they appear?"

"Appear?" The informant, who obviously wanted to seem knowledgeable, shook his head. "They're not going to do that. They never do."

It turned out that the men who were to be initiated had been warned not to expect to actually see any of the Cabiri in the course of the rituals.

As the afternoon drew on toward dusk, Jason, dressed in a fancier tunic than usual, came looking for Proteus, and found him mending a small fishing net. "There you are. Do I understand that you mean to take no part in the ceremony?"

Proteus looked up from his work; the fact that his fingers knew how to tie a variety of useful knots seemed to bolster his theory that he had been a sailor. "That's right, Captain."

The big man shrugged. "I don't expect to gain much benefit of it myself, or to enjoy it either, but my position requires that I join in—those who made the offer may be offended if I decline. Half a dozen of our shipmates have decided to accompany me into the cave. I want to assign you, among others, a post to guard."

"The ship, you mean?"

Jason shook his head. "I have others assigned to stand regular watches, and most of the crew will be aboard anyway. You and one other—Telemon, I think—will be posted just outside the cave. Just in case there is anyone who means to do us harm, while some of us are busy and distracted in the ceremony. And while I think of it, it would be a good idea if you who are standing guard brought a few extra weapons to your posts. We will be allowed to carry no arms into the cave—but it would be good to have some available at no great distance."

Proteus stood up, trying to wipe the slime of fishy cordage from his hands. "Any reason to suspect any kind of treachery, Jason?"

The captain shook his head again. "No more than a feeling. Would you rather not be chosen as a guard?"

"No, I feel honored. I'll do my best."

Shortly before midnight, Jason and those of his shipmates who had chosen to take part in the ceremony entered the cave bearing torches, accompanied by several masked and robed figures who had come to escort them.

As soon as the chosen ones had passed inside, Proteus and Telamon, his fellow sentry, took up their positions, one on each side of the cave's mouth, below torches burning in sconces fixed to the rock. They had each, as inconspicuously as possible, brought along a few extra weapons, as the captain had requested. Proteus saw that swords and short spears, along with a couple of battle-hatchets, were stashed just inside the cave. No one could see the cache from outside, but men inside, expecting to find weapons there, could easily put their hands on them.

By the captain's orders, all of the remaining Argonauts were staying close to the ship. Tonight, Proteus thought that those orders would certainly be obeyed. Samothraki did not seem a promising theater for ordinary revelry.

Proteus knew, in the general way that he knew most things, that there was a simple art to standing sentry, as to most other military tasks. From somewhere in his demolished past the rules appeared when they were needed. Don't stand in one place, like a statue. Move often, but not predictably—if an enemy is watching, never allow him to be sure of where you will be a few heartbeats from now. Walk your post, whatever it is, with an irregular timing. Turn left this time, turn right the next time round. Of course there was very little room for any of these tactics on their small ledge.

Time passed quietly at first, and it began to seem the only danger might be utter boredom. Proteus and his fellow sentry exchanged a few words. Whatever the people in the cave might be up to, they weren't making much noise. Only a few strange sounds came drifting out from time to time, and the more Proteus tried to listen to them, the stranger they sounded. Some of them might have come from human throats, a kind of quiet chanting, and others from the squeaking strings of untuned musical instruments.

Apart from that, the night was peaceful, and exotic smoky smells came drifting from somewhere well inland. The moon lay sparkling on the sea.

Now Telamon whispered restlessly: "Why are these things always held in caves?"

Proteus shifted his grip on his borrowed spear, whose owner so far did not seem worried about getting it back. Fortunately spare weapons were in good supply on this voyage. " 'These things'? You've been to other parties like this one?"

His shipmate looked around uneasily. "One or two that were close to it. And I've heard stories about strange things happening here on Samothraki."

"I hope you told Jason. What are the strange things?"

The other man only looked wise, as if reluctant to speak.

Proteus asked him: "How long is it all going to take, do you suppose?" The question ended in a cough, for suddenly a cloud of strange smoke had come swirling out of the cave to embrace them in its crude pawlike eddies. If it smelled that strong out here, those inside would have to be careful not to choke themselves.

For Proteus, some odd flavor in the smoke rattled certain keys on the ring of memory. Suddenly, impulsively, he filled his lungs with one deep breath, trying to fit the key into the lock and turn it.

The dark fumes made his head swim. He wheezed, and for a moment felt light-headed.

He had sniffed exactly the same pungent and intoxicating smoke before, but *when*, and *where* . . . ?

Proteus had the feeling that someone, somewhere, was urgently trying to tell him something.

A disembodied voice was saying to him: "You have managed to get yourself aboard the ship—excellent!"

"Yes, indeed I have," he said aloud.

And Telamon, at the other end of the short walkway, turned to him puzzled: "Are you talking to me?"

"No. No, I . . ."

"Proteus. Proteus!" His name was now sounded in quite a different voice, coming from a different place, some source firmly rooted in cold reality. A man's urgent whisper, repeated two or three times before Proteus focused on it. This voice was absolutely real, not coming out of any vision in his head, but from a place in the real world only a couple of feet behind him, on a rocky ledge outside a cave on the isle of Samothraki.

Telamon must have heard it too, for his young and almost beardless face had gone taut. "What was that? Did you hear—?"

"Good to see you on the job," said the whisper behind Proteus.

Something was also moving, silently, behind his fellow sentry; and in another instant Proteus was treated to the sight of his cheerful young companion being murdered before his eyes, his throat cut from behind with ruthless efficiency.

A single file of armed men, three or four of them at least, all utterly unfamiliar to Proteus, each of them as menacing as Death himself, had approached the sentries' position along an almost unnoticeable natural catwalk that ran just below the ledge of rock. These intruders all had dark paint of some kind smeared over their faces, and on every bit of exposed skin, trying to make themselves invisible in darkness.

The first two of them had climbed up, nimble and silent as a pair of cats, to the level where Proteus was standing, the nearest of them no more than a good spear-thrust distant from him. Meanwhile another, the whisperer, had somehow climbed into position directly behind him.

There passed a long and breathless moment, in which the intruders could easily have cut down Proteus in his half-befuddled state. But they only stood there gawking at him. This time it was the man first in line who spoke to him in a whisper, with fierce urgency.

"Proteus! You stoned, or what? Call Jason out of that hole." A jerk of the head toward the cave mouth. "We bring him greetings, from an admirer." And the fellow grinned, and shook his own spear in his brawny hand, leaving no doubt as to what kind of greeting he wished to give.

"I see," said Proteus. He leaned over the open side of the ledge, and for a timeless moment stared down at young Telamon, whose body had been pitched onto the rocks below, where it lay unmoving in what looked like a terribly uncomfortable position, trickling blood, that flowed dark in the moonlight, into the lapping waves.

Feeling his head clearer now, Proteus turned back. "Greetings to you," he added quietly, and with a flick of his wrist changed his grip on his own spearshaft. A moment later he had thrust the keen point hard and deep into the painted killer's throat.

Filling his lungs at the same instant, Proteus raised a cry. "Argonauts, to me! Assassins! Murder!"

From here it was impossible to see any portion of the *Argo*, but the ship lay at anchor only a few yards away. It was as if her entire crew had been sitting waiting for a signal, so quick was the reaction. Instantly Proteus was answered by friendly war-cries, and he could hear a tramp of feet and rush of bodies.

The men who had come here to kill Jason were offended, outraged, surprised beyond astonishment. "Proteus! Have y'gone mad?" barked out the second one in line.

And now a sudden rush of bodies stirred the atmosphere, drafting a wave of fresh air across the entrance to the cave. More of the anonymous attackers had been waiting in reserve, and here they came.

From the other direction rushed the Argonauts, meeting the painted enemy, head on. Forced to abandon all hope of stealth, the attackers were yelling like evil spirits now, a good way to throw victims into a panic.

But tonight the men they were attacking were hardly in the victim class. Proteus heard another voice, whether of friend or foe he could not tell, shouting out his name.

Two of the enemy were hacking at him, but neither was quite fast or strong enough to do him any harm. The spear in his hands felt as if it belonged there, though it was no perfect weapon, and in his hands it held like a defensive wall. Now he used the short blade like a sword, cutting with the iron edge against a bronze sword thrust at him, then thrusting back one-handed, to get a longer extension of his arm against a dodging foe. And as he fought, he let out rhythmic yells, a rallying cry for help.

The fight went on, in the timeless-seeming way of all fights. Some Argonauts advanced in single file, along the one narrow ledge readily available for passage. Others were managing to go round, scrambling and splashing along the rocky shingle below the ledge and cave, but that way took longer.

Still, thank all the gods, the crew of the *Argo* had the advantage of numbers. With no shortage of nerve and energy, brawny bodies moved with the spring of youth and the skill of veterans, pouring along the ledges and rocks and shingle into the shallow water before the cave. With heavy splashes, bodies of friend and foe were going off the rocks and into the deep water, one, two, three of them.

And at this point, better late than never, Jason and his few comrades in ritual came pouring out of the dark cave mouth with weapons in their hands, stumbling and retching in black smoke. It was easy to suppose that the attackers, suddenly outnumbered, had never expected anything of the kind.

And then abruptly, in the way of most fights, the bloody brawl was over. But in the mind of Proteus the eerie shock of it lingered on.

He stumbled, and someone took his arm and asked if he was wounded, and he shook his head. For a moment the world had turned gray before him, as if he might be about to faint, but then it cleared again.

It was not a reaction to the sudden treacherous attack, the blood and death, that set him reeling. Some part of his weakness came from the poisoned smoke and visions; but the true horror, what really made him gasp and stumble, was the fact that the attackers had known him on sight. Their leader had called him by name, and in the easy tones of comradeship. *Good to see you on the job. Call Jason out for us. So we can kill him.*

"Look out!"

And the fight that had seemed to be finished was not over after all. This time some of the enemy came from above, from the rocks over the cave mouth, as well as from below.

Proteus took a hard grip on his spear again, and used it to good effect. Those of the enemy who were not slain were driven howling in retreat.

He ran through one antagonist, saw and heard the man die with a gurgling cry, and clubbed another with the shaft of his handy weapon.

"Who are these bastards, anyway?" a slightly wounded Argonaut was gasping. "Are they Samothracians?"

"Damned onion farmers!" growled another shipmate.

Jason, once he had cleared his eyes and lungs of the befuddling smoke, used his steel sword with considerable skill and a kind of fatalistic calm.

When things got very hot for Proteus on the narrow ledge, swords coming at him from front and rear at the same time, he went off the ledge in a long dive that carried him past the shore-line rocks and into deep water.

Surfacing, he threw away his spear and reached ashore, grab-bing two of the enemy, each by an ankle. In another moment he had pulled them off the rocks and into the rough waves.

Neither antagonist proved to be a swimmer, at least not in a league with Proteus. He shifted his handgrip on each man, getting them by their necks, and held them under water. As soon as they went limp, he let them go, and swam quickly to see what he could do for his beleaguered comrades.

To his surprise he discovered Jason in deep water too, grap-pling with a brawny foe who sought to stab him. Proteus reached the struggling pair in time to see that Jason stayed afloat while his enemy went under.

Now once again it began to seem that the struggle had been won. First Zetes and then Calais, on winged sandals, came over-head dropping rocks and then flying low to strike with sword and spear, striking terror into the enemy's heart. Whatever reserves they might still have had on hand turned away in screaming flight.

And then at last it was really, finally, truly over.

How many of the damned determined bandits there had been was hard to determine, because naturally some had run away. Esti-mates among the Argonauts ranged from a couple dozen to a hun-dred. Whatever their numbers, they had not been ready to take on forty well-armed men. Not forty who knew what they were doing when they had their favorite tools in hand.

Jason was looking around at everyone, not finding the face he sought. "Where's Mel?"

"He came running with us," a man told him, "when we left the ship. I saw him go into the water."

Roll call was taken hastily. Meleager had disappeared, and they had to assume he had gone into the water in the fight, and drowned. Jason dove in to look, going deep and coming up for air, bringing up only another dead enemy by mistake. There were currents here, and it was easy to suppose a missing body would never be found.

Meanwhile, men argued in the darkness on the shore. More torches were being brought, but one increment of light after another was added without doing any good. "But who in all the hells were they? Druggies who followed us here from Lemnos?"

"No, no. No men from that island would have wit or strength to get themselves this far, let alone fight like that."

"From King Pelias, then," murmured someone else. And no one spoke up to cast doubt on that suggestion.

Jason urged his men to try to find one of the attackers still alive, so they could hear his answers to some questions. But that was not to be. Many of the mysterious ones had run away, but everyone still within reach of the Argonauts was dead.

Proteus felt inwardly relieved; he wanted to hear the answers to those questions too, but not at the price of having one of the villains call him by name, and reproach him in front of his shipmates for being a traitor to the assassin's gang.

Jason, having given up the hopeless diving in search of Meleager, stood dripping over the first of the face-down corpses, thrust his foot under its shoulder, and turned the dead man over. There was a silence. "Anybody recognize him?"

There were blank stares, and shaking heads. Wiping the dark paint from the dead face did no good.

The captain went on to turn over the second in the same way, with no more helpful result. So it went with the remaining enemy dead.

When he had finished that fruitless task, Jason turned and

vowed eternal loyalty to his friend Proteus, whom he credited with saving his life.

He laid a heavy hand on the shoulder of the shorter man. "I owe you my life, and I will not forget it."

"I would have done as much for any shipmate, Captain. Maybe you can do the same for me some day."

Still feeling lingering traces of the smoke, he went instinctively to plunge his head into the sea again. Under water, he groped around halfheartedly in darkness, but of course there was no trace of Mel. He came back to the surface, gulping a deep breath of air. The new attack he had been half-expecting had come, but it had not been directed at him. He supposed that fact ought to make him feel relieved, but it did not.

He was gnawed by the dark certainty that the attackers had only spared him at the start, because they thought that he was one of them.

Jason, and those who had been in the cave with him, had had enough of Samothraki rituals, and there was no thought of resuming any efforts along that line. Tersely the captain ordered his crew to reassemble at the ship. No attempt had been made to harm the *Argo*.

"They were no ordinary pirates," Jason mused. "I expect that what they chiefly wanted was to murder me." He looked at Proteus. "Did you hear them—say anything?"

"Nothing that I could understand, Captain." And that was certainly true enough.

Certain well-dressed Samothrakians, substantial citizens no doubt, came to express their horror, amazement, and regret. It seemed that none of them could recognize any of the dead.

That mattered not to Jason, who had already made up his mind. "I have no doubt that they were sent by my uncle. My arch-enemy. The usurper."

Idmon asked him: "Is it possible that those who invited you to take part in the ritual have some connection with—?"

"With the attack? I do not think so. No." The captain shook his head decisively. "But of course there were others here on the island who knew of the invitation."

But then, Proteus observed to himself, their leader was developing a strong tendency to feel doomed anyway. Now he had better cause for pessimism than before. Yet there was something about him that made his followers want to stand by and protect him, unite their fates with his.

Men kept searching for Meleager, alive or dead, until the hour before dawn. At that time Jason called off the search. Several Argonauts swore that they had seen Mel fall into the deep water, and he had never come out, and that was that. The voyage must go on, and the only reasonable assumption was that Jason's old comrade had died of wounds or drowned.

All the crew were able to agree on at least one thing, as they started to pull out of the harbor: They were eager to see the last of Samothraki.

Some of the men seemed chastened after the brawl, even though they had not been hurt. But others were in high spirits. "Nothing like a good fight, with blood spilled, to weld a crew together"—that was Haraldur's idea. And in an excess of good feeling he pounded one of his shipmates on the shoulder, fortunately choosing the man's unwounded side.

Some of the men began to sing, in raucous voices, an ancient-sounding chanty that Proteus naturally could not remember ever having heard before.

"So far, we have lost men, and blood, at every stop since leaving home," Jason groaned, sounding near despair. "How far can we go on like this?"

Proteus wanted to grab the leader, shake him, remind him to put a better face on things. But no one else seemed disposed to try to rally their commander, and they knew him better than Proteus did.

When it came Proteus's turn to catch some sleep, he curled up on the curving planks at the foot of his rower's bench. He had slept in this position before, but right now, despite having been awake all night, he could not have slept in a feather bed. He was haunted by the friendly words of the first man he had killed, just outside the cave, and the look of confident familiarity in his victim's face.

Good to see you on the job. Call Jason out of that hole. We bring him greetings.

He couldn't tell Jason that the sneaking murderers of Telamon and Meleager had expected him, Proteus, to help them butcher Jason too.

Proteus knew in his bones that he had not come aboard the *Argo* to do her captain any harm. The only purpose he now seemed to have in life was to help this captain and this crew complete their mission. Other men might have a vision of more glorious goals, but not the reborn Proteus. This ship had become his only home on earth, and Jason and the Argonauts his only friends.

With a faint shock he realized that one way or another, the voyage must someday be over. He wondered what he could possibly do then, and could come up with no ideas. But there was no point in worrying about that now. His chances of surviving that long were probably not great.

Seeing the glum look on his captain's face, he took it upon himself to make an effort to cheer Jason up.

Boxing

*P*roteus, scanning the faces of the crew, decided that any of them whose secret goal had been gold and riches must be beginning to be disappointed. Of course those who had really joined the Argosy purely in search of adventure ought to be well satisfied.

"We have only been at this for a month and a half, but one cannot say that the voyage has been lacking in adventure." That was Haraldur's assessment of their situation now.

Idmon was shaking his head. "Adventure is always a story. It means something happening to someone else, hundreds of miles or years away from the people who enjoy it. Our story is too real to us to be adventure; but others will call it that."

"Call it excitement, then," said Proteus, and no one could dispute that. It would have been hard to make a reasonable argument that things had been too dull. In a sense the great gods were smiling on them, because good weather held, and the breeze was favorable, as it had been through most of their days at sea. But there were dead and wounded now, and the bloody proof that powerful enemies were determined that the Argosy should fail.

Jason had no comment to make about adventure. He was still beset with the gloomy feeling that a doom hung over him and his enterprise. He was making another day's entry on the parchment pages of the logbook, inside their rugged sharkskin cover.

The *Argo* pushed on, fast enough to put up a small white wave at her bow, with the great majority of her crew still alive and well.

One more Hero, a man of comparatively little fame, died aboard of wounds suffered at Samothraki. He was buried at sea, along with Telamon, whose mangled body had been conveyed on board. Various volunteers agreed that they would try to notify the dead men's next of kin when they got home.

It turned out that no one knew what their late shipmates' preferences might have been in funeral rites, and a majority thought it did not matter.

It was Idmon who said: "When you go down to the Underworld, you go down, that's all. Doesn't matter what happens to the clay you leave behind."

Others disputed that, though not with any real vehemence. Everyone on board had heard at least one ghost story—except, possibly, Proteus, who could not remember any—about a spirit rendered unhappy by some improper treatment of its no longer habitable corpse. It seemed that at least half the crew believed such things were possible.

When someone asked Proteus where he stood on the question, he replied that he only envied men who could be so sure of anything.

Several among the Argonauts who considered themselves most skilled in medicine took turns at looking out for the wounded, who were relieved of rowing duties for several days, and lay on the deck or sat and called encouragement to the rowers, or made light of each other's wounds. Each made it a matter of pride to resume his labors, at least part time, as soon as possible.

Casualties had made the crew a bit short-handed on the oars, but the weather continued favorably, there was no urgent need for speed, and they pushed on.

Proteus was still haunted by the memory of the assassin who had approached him with such cheerful confidence. The son of a carrion-eater had actually greeted him as a bosom comrade. *Good to see you on the job.*

He kept trying hard to find some alternate explanation, but kept coming back to only one. Old Proteus—that is, himself, back before he'd lost his memory—must have been involved up to his eyebrows in a plot to assassinate Jason. Might the plot have been led by the mysterious woman he could half remember? Maybe. But his memory could produce no indication that she had ever wanted anything of the kind.

So far none of the Argonauts had questioned Proteus regarding those bewildering first moments of the attack—exactly how Telamon had been taken by surprise, and how he, Proteus, had managed to survive. But his shipmates might grow curious, and one might bring the subject up at any time, either innocently or with suspicion. It would be a good idea to get some answers ready against that possibility.

. . . and still he kept coming back, in his mind, to that scene in front of the cave. The leader of the assassins had actually *expected* to find Old Proteus there, planted among the Argonauts so he could betray them. The carrion-eaters hadn't doubted for a moment that he was going to call Jason out to be killed. Surprise had come into their leader's face only at the last moment, when Proteus's spear point was already sunk a handsbreadth in his throat . . .

. . . and still he kept coming back to it, he couldn't leave it alone. Old Proteus must have been a secret agent, working for some deadly enemy of Jason.

The discovery raised several practical questions. To begin with, why—on staggering out of the sea and into his new life, with almost everything about the old forgotten—why had he felt from the very start an urge to *help* Jason and promote the Argosy's success? Why had he not stayed loyal to the assassins, instead of cutting them down without a moment's hesitation?

Proteus looked down at his own hands, tanned and strong and callused. What kind of man did they belong to? That still seemed to be a mystery, but he thought the evidence so far did not leave much room for optimism.

Dark thoughts were interrupted by Tiphys, who had been in

his usual position kneeling before the binnacle, resting his forehead on his compass-pyx. Suddenly the navigator jumped to his feet and announced that he was ready to steer a course for Colchis.

"We are on our way to the land where the Golden Fleece lies ready for our taking," the sturdy man said in his precise voice.

Proteus thought that might be a slightly optimistic way to put it. At best there were still several intermediate stops to be made, and the next of these was Bebrycos.

Someone observed: "We probably ought to have dropped off our wounded before we got to Bebrycos."

This brought on a heated discussion, resulting in a general consensus that King Amycus of Bebrycos, who claimed to be a son of Poseidon, might have a reputation as the world's worst bully, but he could hardly enhance his reputation by stooping to pick on wounded men. "It's not the hurt ones who have anything to worry about. Amycus likes to pick out some big, strong lad, and beat him into a jelly."

"Son of Poseidon?" The speaker blasphemed several gods. "Son of a mad bitch is more like it."

"That may be. But he's a real man."

Haraldur the northman observed: "I'll go along with what the proverb says: There are no good kings, but there are certainly bad ones."

That comment brought a general murmur of agreement; Proteus noticed that Jason did not join in. If he was giving any thought to their next stop, beyond the plan of provisioning there, he did not show it.

Several of the Argonauts had visited Bebrycos in recent years. It was a pleasant enough place, according to their stories, or would have been, except for its monarch. It now had the reputation of being a good place for travelers to avoid, but at this point in the Argosy no one aboard—except possibly Jason himself—had any idea of avoiding an adventure.

Besides, some bad weather was finally blowing up, and the look of the sky combined with the chronic need for fresh water removed any doubts as to what the wisest course would be. Jason ordered the Argonauts to put in at the chief port of Bebrycos.

It was hard to credit the idea that the bully-king really insisted on boxing with every visitor—that would scarcely be practical, however great his appetite for combat. Some of the rowers could still not quite get it straight.

"You mean he challenges every ship? *Every* ship?"

"Well no, he doesn't fight every man aboard. But each crew must choose a champion."

"To go against the king's?"

"To go against the king himself."

"Amycus must be a tough one, doing his own fighting. To what does he challenge them, exactly?"

"Boxing."

"Hah, that's not so much."

"With gloves of hardened leather. They say Amycus has never lost a match, and more of his opponents have been killed than have been only stunned. Broken jaws and noses are routine. Many have had their teeth knocked out, and more than one has lost an eye."

"Huh. And what about him, in all these years of pummeling? Doesn't he get beat up? Has he never lost a bout?"

"Not that I've heard of."

The island of Bebrycos was of moderate size, and its geography was unremarkable. Several merchant ships were currently in the harbor, taking on cargo in a routine fashion. The port was unre-markable, and there seemed no particular shortage of trading vessels. No doubt the king had learned to be selective in his challenges, not wanting to drive away useful shipping. Gradually a small crowd began to assemble at a distance of a few yards, first idlers, then more substantial-looking folk. They had the air of people assembling to watch a sporting event, leaving space for an arena.

"There are a fair number of ships," someone was saying two benches behind Proteus.

And the answer from still farther back: "Oh, I suppose he may let some get by, when he's feeling tired, or just on a whim. But if he knows that Jason is here, with a ship full of young men looking for adventure—"

"It's not likely that we'll be given a free pass. No."

"Well." The speaker looked around at his shipmates, who were a tough and hardy-looking crew indeed. "I'd say it's not likely that we'd want one."

And indeed, they had not long to wait before word came from the king. They had been tied up at a dock for less than half an hour, and had not quite finished taking on fresh water. Boredom must have been rife at the palace; or maybe the news of Jason's Argosy had somehow got here ahead of him.

One of the minor officials of the court, a curly-bearded man who hardly troubled to hide his wicked amusement at what he considered to be their plight of having to sacrifice one of their number, let them know that the king was upset at not having been invited to take part in the Argosy. The suggestion was that long months ago Amycus had gone so far as to hint, through intermediaries, that he wanted to be asked. But Jason had chosen to ignore the suggestion, if in fact it had ever reached him.

Not that Amycus would condescend to join their expedition now, of course, the court official hastened to assure them. Not even if they begged him.

Only silence answered that remark. Moments later, Proteus heard Jason muttering that this monarch would serve as a model to him, of how not to behave when he came into his own kingdom.

"Here they come," someone said, and Proteus turned to look.

Amycus was having himself carried down to the docks in a litter, on the shoulders of eight brawny, gold-collared slaves; the king when he climbed out of the litter and stood beside it on his own two feet looked bigger than any of the bearers. He was a startlingly huge brute, looking every inch the champion boxer, a match for his reputation. Proteus thought that half of his opponents would probably be paralyzed with fright before a blow was struck.

Besides the slaves who bore the king's palanquin on their shoulders, he was accompanied by a numerous mean-looking escort, large well-dressed men the majority of whom were certainly not slaves. This crew settled in along dockside, where the construction went up in great stair-like steps of stone, as if they were looking forward to a show. Settled in, they began to pass around flagons of wine among themselves.

So far, no one had offered anything at all to the visitors.

"The hospitality here is not exactly lavish," one Argonaut commented.

Jason said in a taut voice: "Let's see if we can get some drinking water somewhere. But none of us should stray far from the ship. I suspect we may be leaving in a hurry."

"Best keep our weapons handy," Idmon advised. But no one needed to hear that.

Jason had hardly time to respectfully greet Amycus before the monarch threw down a black mantle with gold clasps he had been wearing, and a thick, crooked staff carved from mountain olive wood. Now the king stood forth in only a loincloth, obviously proud of his appearance and daring anyone to match it.

A few of the visitors might have done so, but none of them moved; this was not going to be a posing contest. Proteus, along with most of his shipmates, stood back with folded arms, watching with keen interest. The king looked to be in his middle thirties, in the prime of health and strength. His nose had been seriously flattened some time ago, testifying to the fact that at least one opponent had landed him a good blow. But the deformity only made him look all the more formidable.

In another moment, King Amycus repeated his challenge, in a loud and arrogant voice that suited his appearance.

"I feel like a little workout with the gloves today. If anyone among this crowd of weaklings thinks he can fight, let him step forward now! It will be better for the rest of you if one is willing to sacrifice himself." His substantial following of attendants and hangers-on made sure to applaud this speech swiftly and loudly.

If the king had hoped to overawe his visitors, or at least throw them into uncertainty and doubt, he had come to the wrong crew. Most of them only looked at him. Only one man responded to his challenge, and that very quickly, suggesting some kind of prearrangement.

The king looked somewhat puzzled at the figure who stepped forward. It was a man called Polydeuces, with whom Proteus had not yet exchanged more than a couple of words. Though Polydeuces was reasonably tall, he was far from the biggest in the company of Argonauts. Actually he was a slender youth, though strong and long-armed.

His eyelashes were long, his young face almost beardless, and gentle in appearance—or would have been gentle, were it not for the slight deformation caused by scar tissue on forehead and cheekbones. His eyes held sparks of youthful enthusiasm.

Though not minded to undergo a boxing trial himself, Proteus felt little personal fear of Amycus—nor indeed of any man, when he stopped to think about it. In the back of his mind there nestled a comfortable certainty that he himself had already survived at least one encounter with some mysterious opponent who must have been even more formidable. But he was somewhat surprised that none of the other Heroes stepped forward and tried to argue that they were better fitted for the contest than this slim youth. He had to conjecture that many of his shipmates knew something about Polydeuces that was not apparent to the latest man to join the crew.

Now one of the king's close associates, a court official of

some kind who seemed to be acting as his second, walked out between the combatants and dropped a pair of rawhide gloves at each man's feet.

Amycus spoke up again, using the same tone of arrogance: "It may be the custom to cast lots for the gloves, but we're not going to do that."

Polydeuces nodded agreeably. He was being calmly polite as he took off his fine cloak (he had told his shipmates it was a present from his girl) and laid it carefully aside. "What does Your Majesty have in mind?"

"A decision that should make you happy—if your guts are not too upset just now to preclude any feeling of that kind. I don't want it said later that I played any tricks, so, therefore, I hereby make you a present of whichever pair of gloves you like."

Polydeuces murmured a quiet thanks. Without seeming to care one way or the other about the decision, he casually bent and picked up the pair that had been tossed in front of him.

Meanwhile the king's second, or steward, had been busy outlining the space on the dock in which the bout was supposed to take place. This was done quickly and efficiently, as if it had often been done before. Then the same official went through a swift recital of rules, in a high-pitched, sing-song voice, which Proteus had trouble understanding. Nobody seemed to be paying the slightest attention to the recital anyway.

When the formalities had been got out of the way, the two contestants lifted their large fists and went straight at each other.

The crowd roared, following the example set by their monarch's close associates, as if their champion had already disposed of his opponent.

Haraldur shrieked out something that sounded like: "Berserker!" Some kind of strange northern battle cry, thought Proteus, shooting him a glance.

Subtle strategy played no part in the king's plan of battle. Steadily he advanced, firing one punch after another, giving Polydeuces no chance to pause. But that seemed fine with the younger man, who had the necessary skill to avoid these bull-charging tactics.

At one point the king, missing badly with a roundhouse swing, overbalanced and slipped to one knee. But Amycus was up again a moment later, red-faced and furious.

The crowd of onlookers was now growing rapidly, and on impulse Proteus scanned the faces nearest him. He was startled to encounter a pair of eyes looking back at him with what seemed to be recognition. They belonged to a youngish woman wrapped in a scarlet robe, a style of dress that in many places indicated the wearer was a prostitute.

"Got yourself a good thing going there, hey Proteus?" The woman, moving close beside him now, nudged him in the ribs. The gathering of people was now so dense that he thought the gesture might have gone unnoticed by anyone else.

The woman's face, not unattractive, was as unfamiliar to him as were all the other faces in the world, excepting only those of Jason and his crew. This one was leering and almost winking at him with an expression that claimed intimacy.

And she knew his name.

Her voice was so low that he felt sure no one else could hear it through the cheering. "Oh, you don't have to let on you know me. Glad to see you've come up in the world. I know you're the kind to remember your old friends." And she raised one hand a little, rubbing thumb and forefinger together in a gesture of universal significance.

At the moment Proteus had not a small coin to his name, and said so, a little roughly.

His rough words and a hard stare changed the woman's attitude completely. What came into her face was not greed or annoyance, but the look of deep and serious fear. She murmured something that sounded apologetic, in a whisper so low that Proteus could not really hear it, and backed away.

The roar of the crowd swelled up at just that moment, and he turned his head long enough to make sure both fighters were still on their feet. When he looked for the woman again he could not find her. Briefly he was tempted to go diving into the crowd in search of her, but this was not the moment to separate himself from his shipmates.

The circling figures in the ring had completed a preliminary period of sparring, feeling each other out, and now some hard blows were being exchanged. Actually Polydeuces, when you looked at the two men closely, seemed to have the slightly longer arms.

The young Argonaut kept circling, almost dancing, with the air of one who had played this game before; he was plainly faster on his feet than was the king, who simply kept plodding forward, going always toward his opponent.

There was now good evidence of something that Proteus had never doubted—the effect of hardened rawhide gloves was not to cushion blows, but only to armor the fists that struck. Soon both men were bleeding from the face, and from their arms, where the hardened rawhide tore loose patches of skin every time an arm caught a punch intended for head or body.

The Argonaut declined to stand toe-to-toe with Amycus, but kept stepping back and counterpunching.

"Stand still and fight, damn you!" Amycus roared, sounding a trifle short of breath.

"In good time, Majesty." Polydeuces spoke clearly; he still seemed to have plenty of wind left. His arms were bruised, covered with swellings and leaking red, but the muscles still had a good spring in them. His eyes were bright, and now he was the one who seemed to be enjoying the contest.

Polydeuces nodded to himself; it was as if he had so far mainly been taking the measure of his opponent, and now thought it time to get down to serious business.

Growing truly winded now, and obviously less confident than he had been at the beginning, the king lunged close to the Argonaut, and assayed a mighty swing that Polydeuces deftly turned aside, with just a touch of rawhide knuckles on the king's thick forearm at the precisely proper moment.

Now Proteus thought that the king, beginning to be winded, must have passed some secret signal to his official, probably in the form of smoothing his hair with one gloved hand. Because for no apparent reason the official immediately tapped a gong, signaling for a break between rounds.

Several Argonauts loudly raised objections about this procedure, but it did them no good. The steward explained coldly and clearly that no, the fight was *not* over. Having a pause every so often was simply the way they did things here.

A shipmate standing beside Proteus asked him: "I wonder what other new rule will be discovered?"

No one ever learned the answer to that question.

Evidently Polydeuces decided not to wait and see. Almost in the instant when fighting was resumed, the Argonaut struck overhand, a kind of punch he had not thrown before, catching Amycus on the right eyebrow and tearing loose a flap of skin that pulled the eyelid down and away with it, so that the right eye of the stunned king stared out, more wide-eyed than it had ever been before, through a gush of blood at his onrushing doom.

In the next moment Polydeuces threw a left hook, getting all his wiry weight behind the rigid curve of arm. It landed squarely just above the king's right ear. Proteus winced at the sound of impact, and thought he could pick out, in certain fine components of that noise, the crunch of breaking bones within the skull.

The sweeping right-hand punch that followed might have fractured a sturdy jawbone, but it missed its target, because the king was already falling, had already landed on his knees, eyes staring into eternity. A moment later, Amycus toppled forward on his face, never feeling what happened to his nose when it hit the dock. His fall had an utter finality to it, like that of a man with an arrow in his heart, or a slung stone embedded in his forehead.

There followed a long, breathless pause, before the winner stepped back, and several supporters of the king rushed to his side to learn if he still breathed.

Meanwhile, Jascn had already stepped in front of his men and was issuing quick commands with silent gestures. The Argonauts closed ranks and kept their weapons ready.

"The king is dead!" The words were first spoken in hushed tones, then taken up by other voices, shouted across the docks and to the rooftops. There was strong emotion in the yells, but Proteus found it hard to tell as yet just what the emotion was.

Moments later, some of Amycus's shocked supporters had drawn swords and were doing their best to kill the Argonauts. Fortunately, the crew were at hair-trigger readiness to defend themselves.

Before anyone had had time to draw a good long breath, a major fight had broken out. The royal bodyguard, well-equipped with spears and hardened clubs, grabbed up their weapons and came charging at Polydeuces. But the fistfighter's shipmates were ready to defend him with their own spears, swords, and axes. In the first moments of armed combat, some of the high officials who had been closest to Amycus went down.

In retrospect the boxing match took on the aspect of a game, compared to what strong men could do to each other with edged weapons. For a long minute, there was bloody slaughter on the dock. None of those who took part were strangers to the art, and none of them turned and ran. Proteus, wishing for a shield, stood a little back from his comrades in their rank, hoping to be able to use the greater length of his weapon to the best advantage.

It was the royal party who broke off the conflict after the first clash. No doubt they were realizing that their king's death meant they were faced with other matters more important than seeking revenge for one whom they had never loved.

Jason backed away muttering: "Is there some curse on our voyage, that we must fight and die wherever we come to shore?"

Fortunately for Jason and his men, it was soon plain that most of the populace were more interested in hurrying home with the day's news, or in settling some old scores among themselves, than in punishing the visitors. And those leaders who had come to watch the fight, and who might have led a charge against the foreigners, were suddenly more occupied with seeing to their own futures now that everything had changed.

As they were accomplishing a slow retreat to the ship, weapons still ready, Proteus barked at Polydeuces: "Did you have to kill him? Wouldn't a simple knockout have done as well?"

The long-armed youth only grinned back, somewhat vacantly, as if the blows his own head had taken had left him a bit stunned.

Jason, for once seeming to exert some active leadership, gripped his own short sword and barked orders.

Once they were all aboard their ship, Jason had them row out a little way into the calm water of the harbor, where they prepared to defend against further attacks.

Jason was murmuring something, and Proteus looked around. "I couldn't hear you, Captain."

"I said, it is not good for any king to die in such a way."

The minutes dragged on and then an hour, and it was as if they had been forgotten. There were no more attacks aimed at the visitors, though they could see and hear that wild fighting had broken out in the streets of the city.

Idmon was talking in low tones, saying that certain factions must have been waiting in hopes of a chance like this. Two merchant ships had cast loose from their moorings, and were dipping oars at a good rate, and hoisting sail as well, but obviously their only intention was to make a prudent withdrawal, not to bother the *Argo*. Proteus could see two places, well inland, where buildings were burning. The columns of smoke gradually disappeared as darkness fell, but the glow of flames only became more lurid.

Zetes and Calais volunteered to fly ashore and reconnoiter, but Jason in his commander's voice told both of them to remain on the ship. The sight of flying men might bring on an attack, or at least draw the islanders' attention to the Argonauts again. "I think we can see all we need to see from here."

Toward morning, the situation quieted, as the various combatants on shore were becoming exhausted; there arose from somewhere inland sounds of cheering that could be interpreted to mean that one new leader had emerged victorious.

"What in the Underworld are they celebrating now?" someone wanted to know.

"Most likely that a new king has been chosen. Or one of the contenders has announced that all the people want him, which comes to the same thing."

"A likely interpretation." Idmon nodded. "Of course there may still be other contenders, as you call them, with different ideas. Whoever comes out on top will almost certainly want to consolidate his position in the palace and the capital before undertaking his next move."

"With any luck we will be gone by then. As soon as we have the tide, and the breeze—that now seems to be coming up. Hoist the anchor stone!"

The Argonauts pulled out of the harbor while the night was at its darkest, and at first light ran up their sail, catching a lucky wind that drove them on, in the direction the steersman had determined they should go.

Tiphys, who like most of his shipmates had come through the

fight unscathed, now seemed a little more at ease than he had been. "Won't be any need to navigate for a couple of days, lads. There'll be plenty of land in sight. But the wind's not with us this time. Now you've had a little exercise, you'll be all loosened up for rowing."

A universal groan went up.

Harpies

$\mathcal{O}$he keeper of the logbook dipped his quill pen into the inkhorn, and recorded on tough parchment the fact that almost two months had passed since the voyagers departed from Iolcus.

Singing at their oars, inventing some ingenious new verses of an old song at the expense of the late, murderous Amycus, the crew of the *Argo* drove their sleek vessel on up the swift and swirling watery channel that the steersman and the Colchian brothers called the Bogazi.

And Idmon on that day copied into the log some of the impromptu verses, not bothering to cipher them into an antique translation.

Even Jason was more cheerful now than when they had left Samothraki. He told his crew that the name "Bogazi" meant "Ox Ford" in some ancient language. What an "ox" might be he did not know, but one of the more scholarly adventurers spoke up to say he thought it meant an animal, some type of mutated cameloid.

"Be ready for a long row and a hard one, lads," their navigator cautioned, leaning on the steering oar. The channel was almost twenty miles long, and varied in width from half a mile to more than two. At the start the scenery on both sides was of well-wooded shores, dotted with villages and what appeared to be the villas of the wealthy. But as they progressed slowly upstream, both banks became wilder, less populated.

Of the entire crew, only the two grandsons of Aeetes had ever traveled this route before, and their passage had been years ago, going in the other direction. Therefore their memories of the way were hazy. Few other members of the crew had ever seen any waterway similar to this one. Proteus, along with the great majority of his shipmates, could only shake his head in wonder. His damaged memory still offered him no clues as to whether he had ever beheld the like. But the steersman soon offered a simple explanation of the strange watercourse: this was in effect a great, salt-water river, a channel connecting two salt-water seas. Farther up the strait, he said, the land on both sides would be completely wild and uninhabited.

And Tiphys went on to explain, to the untraveled and geographically unsophisticated in the crew, that there were times when the Bogazi reversed its flow, certain seasons when it reacted strongly to the pull of the tides, as fresh-water tidal rivers were wont to do.

But now, approaching the peak of summer, the northern sea was receiving a great influx of fresh water from several large rivers, so the flow in the strait was consistently one way—the wrong way, from the Argonauts' point of view.

The vessel's painted prow encountered relatively few waves, but most of the time it was necessary to struggle against an increasingly swift and steadily rising current of cold water. Only when sail and oars could be made to work together was it possible to make satisfactory progress.

Two full days of hard labor at the oars, and the skill of Tiphys as steersman, were needed to win an upstream passage through the twenty miles or so of the strait.

Was it only his imagination, Proteus wondered, or did the *Argo* really make notably better speed when he was rowing, which was most of the time, than on the fairly rare occasions when it was his turn to rest?

Sitting at his oar, a position in which most of his waking hours were spent these days, he closed his eyes. Pull. Pull. Steadily, not too hard. Around him Heroes groaned and gasped, testing the limits of their endurance and the strength of their quivering arms, while what he chiefly felt was boredom. There, two benches away, was Polydeuces growing weary, who had outlasted Amycus.

Again it made Proteus uncomfortable to realize that he could have been pulling harder and faster than he was, without putting himself in any danger of exhaustion. In fact he thought he might even be capable of breaking the pine blade. As a practical matter there was of course nothing to be gained by his exerting an all-out effort; that would only have upset the rhythm of the bank, slewed the ship away from the exact course the steersman was trying to hold, as Tiphys sought to find a slower downstream current or an eddy.

A man would have to be crazy not to prefer strength in his own body over weakness. But the oddity still bothered him, because he could find no explanation for it. He couldn't remember being considered especially powerful, or notably capable with either oar or spear. Of course he could not remember ever being called a weakling, either. When he tried to compare the muscularity of his own body with those visible around him, he had to rate his frame as no better than average for this crew of adventurers.

It would be truly wonderful, Proteus thought, if he could remember being simply ordinary—but that comfort also was denied him. The woman standing on the Bebrycan dock had known him—probably had known nothing good about him, for one glance of annoyance from his eyes had been enough to send her in white-faced retreat.

The gaping void of ignorance about himself, the unavailability of information that had to exist somewhere, was like an infected wound, hurting more the longer he had to live with it. When the horror threatened to become too much for him, as it did now, he fought it in the only way he could, by turning his attention to other matters.

Every now and then, at intervals during the day, the steersman put in to shore. Anchored by stones or tied to trees, *Argo* clung to the bank for a short time, giving the rowers a chance to rest. Those who wanted to switch places at the oars could do so; sometimes it eased the strain to shift from port to starboard, or from an inside bank to one of the shorter oars on an outer bench. As soon as the men had caught their breath they plunged back into the relentless struggle.

There were times when Proteus, rowing, fell into almost a hypnotic state. The briny water in its mad rush to the lower sea seemed like a living thing. From somewhere in the back of his mind came a suggestion that he speak to the flow as if it were a living being: *Why do you fight against us, Water? What god has you under his control, to force us so viciously downstream—and why? Or can this be simply nature?*

Just when it seemed they were about to be swept helplessly back where they had come from, a strangely powerful eddy current, coming into being as it were from nowhere, caught the *Argo* and whisked her lightly upstream, so close to the right bank that the raised mast brushed branches on the shore, and came away plastered with the leaves of an overhanging oak. Tiphys cried out in amazement, at the goal achieved so suddenly, when all his skill and the steady effort of the men for an hour had availed them almost nothing.

Panting, the rowers rested once more at their oars, this time for once losing no ground as they did. Some of the men were wondering aloud what god had been so kind as to help them. Proteus rested with them, and was silent. But in his heart he had begun to be afraid of what he did not know.

The next day they were out of the swift current of the strait, and into a much broader sea; and the day after that, they found the stretch of coastline and the harbor that they wanted, and brought their ship to rest. In fact they were still almost within sight of the coastline of Bithnyia, but it seemed to the weary men that they had rowed a thousand miles since leaving it behind.

During the last night before making port the men unwrapped such bundles of extra clothing as were still unopened, and huddled together for warmth. Though it lay at no great distance from Bebrycos, this was a harder, colder land, on the surface less hospitable than that ruled by the late Amycus. But here the welcome from the people was the very opposite of that. As if glad to see any visitors, they brought out food and flowers to the ship when it was tied up.

The next time Proteus slept, for once dry and snug ashore, his slumbers were uneasy, and he woke in terror from dreams of a murderous Giant.

They had now reached Salmydessus, the land ruled by blind King Phineas, who, as Idmon informed his shipmates, was tormented by Harpies—or at least that was what the stories said. No member of the crew had ever set foot on these shores before. And only a minority had ever seen a Harpy.

Following their experience in Bebrycos, the adventurers were nervous on first landing, but soon began to relax. The strangers of this land gave strangers a hospitable welcome.

The great wonder of this country was the peculiar curse that had afflicted its monarch for more than twenty years. According to a number of reliable reports, King Phineas hardly dared show his face outside the stone walls of his palace, for every time he did, a flight of ghastly Harpies appeared in the nearby sky and attacked him. For some reason that the newcomers had trouble understanding, it seemed impossible to fight them off, and the king's soldiers had even given up trying. The foul, unnatural creatures also devoured any food in sight, eating some of it, and scattering and befouling what they could not swallow or carry off.

Some of the Argonauts did not know what Harpies were, and the monstrous creatures had to be explained to them. Proteus could remember what they were supposed to be, though he doubted that his knowledge was based on any personal experience.

There were whispered rumors among some of the commoners

that it was in fact the blind king's Scythian wife who caused him trouble. The queen's true feelings in the matter remained mysterious to the Argonauts, for she never appeared during the course of their visit, and her absence was never explained. Meanwhile, it was oddly true that none of the king's own soldiers or advisers had been able to help him overcome his strange curse.

Proteus had hardly been an hour in this land before he heard from a native one explanation of its royal curse that he found especially intriguing: that the king of Salmydessus had incurred divine wrath, more than twenty years in the past, by offering help to the refugee Phrixus, he who had come this way mounted on the famous and mysterious Flying Ram.

Both grandsons of King Aeetes were keenly interested in learning the truth of this story. If it proved accurate, they were determined to meet the man who had once helped their father in his time of need.

Argeus seemed the more scholarly of the two Colchian brothers, the more interested in finding things out just for the sake of knowing them. He thought the rumor very interesting, but doubted that it was true. "I don't know why the gods should have been angry at our father."

No one could offer him any enlightenment on that point; but of course gods were never obliged to explain anything they did to humans. Jason announced that one reason he wanted to stop here was a hope of hearing more details about the ancient flight of the Golden Ram, from Iolcus to Colchis.

Phineas proved to be quite the opposite of Amycus, glad to entertain interesting visitors, and quite willing to discuss the matter of Phrixus, especially with folk who brought him interesting stories in return. And he told the Argonauts matter-of-factly that he had seen the Ram, on that day more than twenty years in the past.

"What was it like?" asked Tiphys. "This Flying Ram, I mean?" In answer, the king only spread his hands, and shook his blind head slightly, as if to say that some things were beyond description.

"Yes," said Proteus slowly. "It would be good to glean any further word that we can about the Golden Fleece." Others nodded and murmured their agreement.

"Long years ago, when my eyes were young and keen—" he began his tale to the Argonauts.

Alas, the king's knowledge of the events proved very limited, and second-hand at that. He spoke of how a creature he described as a giant, flying ram had been stolen in Iolcus by a fugitive named Phrixus. Flying away on the strange beast had enabled Phrixus to escape from some unspecified trouble, but when the flight reached Colchis, it had come to a violent end.

Blind Phineas seemed glad to tell what little he could of the story again. Proteus, watching the people of the royal household, got the impression that they had grown so weary of the subject that they closed their ears to anything that the kind old man might have to say about it.

The hearing of King Phineas proved very keen, or at least, through long practice, it was finely attuned to certain peculiar noises. He suddenly broke off his tale of the old days, before any of the Argonauts' young ears had picked up the sound of what was coming.

The old king, showing an unsuspected agility, almost jumped to his feet. He raised one hand before him, its fingers spread and twitching; and the sentence he had begun to utter broke off in a wordless cry.

A moment later, Proteus could hear it, the leathery flap of distant wings, followed presently by the scream of high-pitched voices, taunting in an ancient language that he could only halfway understand.

The king was still standing in front of his chair, his whole body trembling. Now he pointed, quite accurately despite the quaking of his arm. "There! There! I hear them, and you can see! The curse is come upon me yet again!"

Following the direction of the old man's gesture, Proteus caught sight of what at first seemed to be a flight of odd-looking, thick-bodied birds, visible in the clear afternoon light. They were bearing in from the dim, gray north . . . from the direction of a line of ragged cliffs that he supposed might offer a good variety of nesting places.

Around him the Argonauts were murmuring in alarm, and snatching up their weapons, while the king's own guards, who ought to have defended him, were only tugging on his garments, intent on getting him safely indoors, and then seeking shelter for themselves.

"Will you not fight for your own king?" one Argonaut demanded of them.

The soldier looked startled, as if the idea had not occurred to him. "Fight against the Harpies? We dare not. It is the will of the gods that our king is punished so."

Jason was outraged. "The will of the gods? To humiliate an honorable king in such a way? That cannot be!" Jason could not seem to bear the thought that any monarch should be subject to such abuse and humiliation, especially such a worthy monarch as Phineas.

Proteus was shading his eyes to study the approaching threat. The creatures now appearing in the sky were not much like birds at all, beyond the fact of having wings, and some of them with beaks. What he saw now were little more than large, inhuman heads with great pinions attached, and wiry legs ending in bird-like feet with savage claws. Of course the true scale of size was difficult to determine, but surely such shapes lay outside the ordinary forms of nature. Odylic magic had to be involved.

The creatures were closing in on the king's palace with remarkable speed. As soon as their captain sounded the alarm, the brothers Zetes and Calais went sprinting back to the ship to equip themselves with their borrowed sandals, while Jason stood shouting after them to hurry. The refitting took longer than some of their shipmates thought it should have. Earlier, someone had told Proteus that the magical footgear in the brothers' possession was really about the only reason Zetes and Calais had been accepted into the company of Heroes. But eventually Calais and Zetes were back, moving much faster than they had run away, flying now and brandishing swords.

Meanwhile the other Argonauts unanimously refused to be driven indoors, but stood their ground with spear and axe, sword and bow and sling.

When the foul Harpies swooped near the earth, they proved so hideous at close range that men found it was a joy to fight them.

Seemingly stunned by meeting such ferocious resistance on the ground, the enemy emitted astonished cries, were wounded by arrows and slung stones, and were soon in full retreat.

But their detractors had to admit that at the moment Zetes and Calais were acquitting themselves well, fighting back to back in a mid-air skirmish with half a dozen of the winged heads, all of the Harpies streaming long, tangled hair.

Flying near, the attackers opened beaked mouths that shrieked and honked with laughter, then swerved away as the fighting men once more responded fiercely. Some of the heads and faces were more birdlike than human in design, and others strongly resembled bats. It was hard to be sure of size at first, but when they came near, Proteus realized that they were built on a scale somewhat smaller than humanity.

By this time any lingering doubt about the Harpies' vulnerability had been dispelled. They were not ghosts, or visions, but as solid as so many crows or vultures, and with no sweeter voices. They could be hurt by sharp blades, carved up like so many crows if they persisted in attacking.

The first wave of the monsters had drawn back, but the attack was not over. There were dozens of the Harpies now visible, and more were still approaching, as if attracted by the noisy uproar in the sky. The flying bodies too far away to be picked out individually made a small black cloud.

Jason took a hasty glance around and assured himself that so far none of his men had fallen, though the ground was littered with crumpled winged shapes. "Where are they all coming from?" Jason demanded.

Pointing into the distance, one of the natives shouted: "The creatures nest there in the high cliffs, where their caves are out of reach of climbing men."

"If this were my land," Jason vowed, "they would not roost there unmolested."

Among the attacking creatures Proteus saw one or two whose scalps were each thickly overgrown with a crop of hissing, writhing snakes. Another gripped in one set of talons what appeared to be a living snake, thick as a man's arm, and raised it like a weapon, ready to strike with the reptile's fanged and gaping mouth.

Moments later one of the larger creatures, its wings laboring frantically, drew close enough for him to see its bloodshot eyes, while squawking words at him. The language was one that Proteus had never heard before, but the content of menace, the intention to inspire terror, were unmistakable.

Suddenly it displayed a thin, bone-like arm, wielding a kind of twisted javelin. Evidently this version of the damned thing had six limbs in all, counting its wings. Proteus could also see the claws in which its thin legs terminated.

A moment later Proteus discovered, almost too late, that the flying horror, whatever it might be, also used its beak for a weapon. A savage thrust of head and neck just missed the Argonaut, and tore splinters from the shield of wood and leather that he raised in self-defense.

With his back against a stone wall now, there was no way to retreat, and no place to run. Instinctively Proteus thrust back with his spear, feeling the bronze point go into solid flesh. Another Argonaut dealt the thing a hacking blow, decapitating the snake, whose head stayed where it was, while the thick body writhed and fell away.

One of the flying creatures struck in midair by Calais dropped like a stone. Another, wounded, screamed and fell away, laboring to stay airborne with a damaged wing.

It was a battle against nightmare things. Those that entirely lacked legs looked grotesquely helpless when they fell to earth. One of these had been forced down in front of Proteus, and it could only lie there, like a winged egg, the ugly face tilted far to one side.

Proteus finished the beast off with his spear, then squinted upward, trying to shade his eyes from sunlight with one hand, and got a surprisingly clear view of some of the swordplay in the sky.

Even as he watched, another Harpy, stone-struck by a slinger on the ground, fell like a wounded bird, half-gliding, half-plunging toward the small river at the bottom of a nearby ravine.

He soon decided that after all, the beasts were probably not much more intelligent than birds, despite their ability to utter words, and the almost-human look their faces sometimes wore. Running in pursuit of the flailing, falling, flapping form, Proteus got a good look at one of the first Harpies that had been brought down. It lay on the ground surrounded by a growing litter of dead flies.

One of the other Argonauts called his attention to the fact that first one fly, and then another, had fallen buzzing to the earth and quickly died, evidently of poison, after being attracted to the fallen Harpy's wounds, or to small spots of its spattered blood.

*   *   *

Idmon, wiping dark foaming blood from the blade of his short sword, and giving counsel in his usual calm fashion, said it was obvious that they were flying more by power of magic than by strength of wing.

"These could not fly, nor could Giants walk, if they depended upon the powers of nature only." He was inspecting a slight scratch inflicted on his left shoulder by one monster's talons.

The struggle had taken longer than Proteus at first thought it would. But eventually the skies were clean again. Now word spread among the men on the ground that the Harpies, slow-witted monsters for all their physical agility, must have mistaken Zetes and Calais for flying gods, and fled away in terror.

One of the winged brothers landed, wiping his sword in triumph. "Ho ho! It's a glorious business, fighting in the air. I think the dull-brained beasts have taken us for gods, because we fly, and now they fall all over themselves getting out of our way."

Others looked at him in envy. "How about letting me try those sandals of yours sometime?"

"Not likely." The refusal was quick and definite. "Anyway, they're dangerous to wear. My brother and I were a long time practicing before we set out on this voyage."

A good argument was brewing, but Jason aborted it with practical questions. "Any casualties on our side? Apart from a few scratches?"

"Doesn't look like it, Captain."

That there might be none was really too much to hope for. Tiphys, like Idmon, suffered a scratch in this skirmish, from one of the monsters' claws, but brushed it off as only a slight wound.

When they told King Phineas that his enemies had been driven from the field with heavy losses, he seemed afraid, at first, to believe in his good fortune. For half an hour he kept wondering aloud whether his tormentors would return. But Idmon eventually persuaded him to come outdoors again, and told the king: "Now that they're convinced you have divine protection, I doubt very much that they'll be back."

Clashing Rocks

*P*hineas, in gratitude to Jason and his companions for ridding him of the monstrous pests that had tormented him for so many years, decreed a night and day of feasting and celebration. While preparations for this festival were under way, he engaged in conversation with Jason and a few of the other Argonauts. The blind old king had wrapped himself in a shawl, and emerged again from his castle to enjoy the relative warmth of the late afternoon sun, on a high terrace.

For the first time in many years, he told his guests, he felt certain that his fiendish tormentors were not going to hurl themselves at him out of the sky.

The king's hospitality went further than mere food and drink. Now, several dozen comely young women appeared as if from nowhere, the slave collars of some of them so thin as to be almost invisible, or to be mistaken for mere necklaces. These began to attach themselves to Argonauts in a most friendly manner.

Jason, as befitted his rank, was naturally the first to be offered his choice of partners. The captain still seemed to be debating which, or how many, to select when another girl approached Proteus, who was more than ready to enjoy such entertainment.

His smiling companion took him by the hand and led him a short distance apart, where she drew him down onto a natural couch of soft grass, warmed by sunlight and lightly screened by tall flowers. Yes, *this* he could remember doing, and he was certain that Old Proteus had enjoyed the experience many times. But there were no names or faces attached to the act.

A quarter of an hour later, when Proteus returned to the public area, he was somewhat startled to note that Jason was there, seated in a low chair almost at the feet of Phineas, and deep in intense discussion with the blind monarch.

It was hard to believe that the captain had declined the offer of intimate companionship, for he had appeared eager at the prospect. The alternate explanation was that Jason must have finished very quickly with his girl, or girls, and hastened back to sit beside his host. It was not hard to see that the captain's true interest lay here, in the chance to engage a friendly king in discussion of the questions and problems pertaining to royalty.

Proteus had not much curiosity on that subject, but had begun to have a fair amount regarding Jason. He sat down casually on a low wall nearby and listened with some interest to the talk between the king and the adventurer.

At the moment, Jason seemed to be answering some question about his own aspirations to become a king. The adventurer was speaking in hushed tones of the holiness, the blessed state of royalty.

And in return the king, gently shaking his sightless head, told Jason: "There is no need for you to envy any man who wears a crown. Even leaving aside the fact that your fame in the world is greater than my own, you now possess youth and strength, good eyes and freedom. You can enjoy a woman, run a race, watch a sunset, digest a feast—do you not think I would trade all of what you call my high estate, my royal glory, for the kind of wealth that you enjoy?"

Jason was respectful but stubborn. "Thousands of men are young and strong and free, my lord Phineas. But only a very few are granted the distinction and honor of being kings."

The blind man shook his head again. "Am I to suppose that you would change places with me this instant, if some god were willing to perform such a transformation?"

Jason's answer came without a moment's hesitation. "Most gladly, sir."

Proteus, silently watching and listening, shook his head on

hearing this confirmation of his captain's madness. Apprehensively he looked to right and left, and even scanned the skies, wondering if some deity might have overheard. But the blue vault looked empty, and he chided himself for his own foolishness.

The king sighed. "No wise god would ever grant you such a wish. For good or ill, each man must live his own life, must read the knucklebones as they are cast for him by Fate."

Then Proteus must have made some movement, or uttered a sigh that attracted the blind man's attention, for the face of Phineas turned toward him where he sat five or six yards away. The king said: "There sits a man who has a certain smell about him—the smell of the sea." And his thin lips split in a faint smile.

"Or of fish, at least, my lord king," said Jason by way of explanation. "There sits Proteus, my good friend, my shipmate, and trusted adviser, besides being an excellent catcher of fish."

The blind eyes kept wavering in his direction. "What do you think, Fisherman Proteus? Would you rather be king, or god?"

Proteus did not answer immediately, but the king let him have time, seeming to divine that he was not left speechless by the question, but giving it serious thought. At last he responded: "Neither, Lord Phineas. It would be enough for me to know who I really am."

"There speaks the beginning of wisdom," said the old king softly.

Presently the talk took a less philosophical turn. When Jason asked Phineas for advice on the next leg of their long journey, the king took the opportunity to warn his guests about the Clashing Rocks, which were said to represent a considerable danger at this season of the year. Not that he had ever seen them himself. Nor, he thought, had anyone who was currently available at his court. But he had heard terrible reports, of crushed and sunken ships.

"I have questioned Argeus and Phrontis," Jason assured the king, "who are King Aeetes's grandsons. They have heard the stories, like everyone else. But neither of them has any memory of any phenomenon called the Clashing Rocks. They passed this way but once, when they were only children, and probably at a different season."

Among other pieces of advice, the king cautioned his adventurous visitors to accept the gifts of warm clothing he intended to make them before they pressed on. The Argonauts were ready enough to believe what Phineas was telling them about the weather they should expect, as the air, even now in what ought to be the middle of summer, had already grown much cooler than most of them were accustomed to.

"What sort of reception will we be given when we reach the land of Colchis?" Jason wondered aloud.

Phineas asked Jason if he was acquainted with any of the Colchian royal family.

"Only with the king's two grandsons, who are valued members of my crew."

"Then they can tell you much more than I. Aeetes and I have never been friends, but certain things are more or less common knowledge. He has two grown children who still live at home. His son Apsyrtus must be thirty years of age by now—how time flies!—and his younger daughter, Medea, perhaps half as old. But wait, I am forgetting the older daughter, who you will doubtless encounter also. Chalciope, the widowed mother of your two shipmates."

Before the evening of celebration was over, blind King Phineas with the willing aid of members of his court pressed gifts on all the Argonauts. Warm clothes were abundant, as the king had promised. Proteus, allowed to choose from an assortment of fine weapons, got a good spear of his own. He thought it might have come from the same workshop as the borrowed weapon he had been using, for this spear, too, had the image of a dolphin worked into the metal head. He liked the balance, and the straight, keen point; yet still the vague impression persisted, that this weapon was lacking in something that would have made it the perfect spear.

Meanwhile Phineas, shaking his head, and briefly reverting to his look of depression, did not seem to think that family ties were going to mean much to his royal colleague, King Aeetes. He told Jason: "Beyond what I have already told you about the weather, there is little I can say that will be of help. You are obviously determined to go on with this."

For once, on leaving port, the Argo received an encouraging send-off. Proteus thought that Jason looked a little nervous until he had taken roll call again, and assured himself that no one had jumped ship in the welcoming land of kind King Phineas.

Swathed to a greater or lesser extent in garments of itching wool, Jason and his followers somehow maneuvered their long ship on upstream, watching vigilantly for the Clashing Rocks, which had been described to them as "perpetually shrouded in sea-mist."

"I see no magic rocks as yet," Haraldur cried. The northman happened to be taking his turn as lookout. "What I see are giant blocks of ice. Bergy bits, we call them at home."

"What in all the hells does that mean?"

"They are like crumbs from a true iceberg."

"From a true *what*?"

A majority of the Heroes had spent most of their lives in practically tropical climes, and from their complaints it seemed they would have much preferred another brisk swordfight to this kind of thing. "What sort of rock is it that floats with its head out of the water?" said one through chattering teeth.

"Only one kind that I know of—ice."

"*Ice*?" The cry had a sound of outraged disbelief. "Whoever heard of chunks of ice the size of houses?"

But someone chipped off a bit of one of the drifting things, and snatched it aboard—and as it melted in their hands, there was no doubt of what it was.

"Not all the oceans of the world are warm as a steam bath, like the one you mostly sail in." Now that the air had begun to turn frigid, Haraldur seemed to come alive, and was invigorated. He drew deep breaths, pounded his broad chest with energetic fists, and urged his shivering comrades to enjoy themselves.

What actually appeared now, in front of the ship and rushing downstream at it, was a series of ice floes, punctuated now and then by a fragmented berg—all ghostly silver and white, looming out of the white and silver mist. *Argo* absorbed a glancing blow from one of these that was fortunately very small, snapping off like toothpicks two oars whose rowers did not get them out of the way in time, and, as if in afterthought, hurling oarsmen this way and that.

"Man overboard!" One man who had gripped his oar too tightly had been sprung by it into the icy water.

Without pausing to think, Proteus sprang to his feet. In the next instant he had dived over the gunwale, launching his body high and wide off the stern to stay clear of the oars. The briny cold closed over him, but it seemed to him that he had no time to feel the shock.

A few quick strokes brought him to the side of the man who struggled convulsively, and at once Proteus had him in a grip that his frantic thrashing could not break.

Fortunately the current was bearing the ship straight down upon them, and very quickly Proteus had it within reach again. Someone threw a rope, and the victim still had the energy to seize it with ferocious strength—in another moment he had been hauled back on board. Then another rope, for Proteus, and he only had to catch hold to be pulled in and over the low gunwale.

Hands pounded him in triumph, deep voices roared congratulations. Now it was necessary to get the ship in to a bank, stop its rapid drifting, lest it be quickly carried all the way back to the mouth of the Bogazi.

But the next shock of glancing impact of a mass of ice, right against the starboard bow, was enough to stagger the few Heroes who were not on rowers' benches. They had all been served with a warning that they must avoid contact with any larger bergs.

That was advice easy enough to understand, but Phineas warned them it might be hard to put into practice.

In the legends that later generations were to build on *Argo*'s trip, the enormous power of passing time turned floating towers of ice into huge bulks of metal or stone, swung back and forth by currents, quite capable of crushing to splinters any ship that happened to be caught between them when they closed.

The northerner Haraldur said that he understood where the house-sized chunks must be coming from. They were nothing new to him, as they were to all the others.

"They are pieces of what we call a glacier, in my country, where such things are common enough."

More of what he called bergy bits, and even larger chunks that he named growlers, came riding the swift current down through the strait, in a flow made torrential by the late spring thaws.

Each mass of ice came trailing little wisps of cloud behind it, adding an air of magic to what Proteus now realized was a wonder purely natural. Gradually, as the day wore on, the whole scene became enveloped in mist, making it difficult to tell where either shore might be. Or how far away the next berg was, or the one after that, or to steer out of the way of any of them. Tiphys and Idmon had both grown feverish, and the skin around their respective Harpy-scratches looked puffy and inflamed. But so far, both men refused to admit that such small wounds might make them really sick. By now, all the wounded from the earlier fights seemed well on the way to full recovery.

The thoughts of the crew were on the ice, not on their injuries. Even a ship bigger than *Argo* could easily have been bashed to pieces, or crushed between huge chunks.

Visible bits of wreckage, maybe items of clothing, a broken oar, showed that this had happened to at least one vessel, somewhere upstream from where the Argonauts were laboring.

And now when the voyagers emerged again from the strait into an open sea, they saw that the cliffs on the land side were not of earth, or rock, but rather a towering wall like nothing most of them had ever seen before.

"By all the frozen hells!" Jaws dropped, and men forgot to row.

"What in the name of all the gods is that? Don't tell me that it's . . ."

"But it is."

The mass loomed bigger than any castle any of them had ever seen, yet it was no part of the natural rocky earth. It was gray-white, mottled here and there with suggestions of pastel color, smooth, sheer, and enormous. It was well over a thousand feet high, and still calving off huge bergy bits.

"I can't believe it—that's all ice?"

Only Haraldur had anything reassuring to tell his shipmates. He stood shading his eyes with one hand and squinting up. "I tell you, I have seen these things before—though none quite that high," he added under his breath.

And Proteus pointed. "There goes another. Look." Up at the top of the high wall, a slow crumbling, for some unseen reason. A majestic tumble and a huge, slow splash.

The weather was also turning much colder than most of the Heroes were accustomed to. Even bright sun did not bring what they considered real warming.

"If this is summer, what in the Underworld is winter going to be like here?"

"Just pray that we'll be long gone from here by then."

Somewhat cheered by surviving the perils of the ice, but gloomy with shivering and chilblains, and with their ship's sides scraped and dented, some of the joints of planking strained, the Argonauts landed in the home of King Amycus's arch-enemy, Lycus. They had heard something of this monarch before leaving home, and they expected him to be ready to offer a warm welcome to the conquerors of his old foe.

News of his hated rival's death had already reached Lycus by heliograph, and he was impatient to know details.

The latest monarch to offer the Argonauts his hospitality, a jovial rascal by the look and sound of him, made no effort to restrain his delight at the news, and ordered Polydeuces pointed out to him that he might pay the boxer special tribute.

He sat in his high chair, midway between two roaring fires, one at either end of his great hall, and waved enthusiastically for them to enter. "Cracked his head-bones, did you? With your fist? Ha haaa, I like it! No, I love it! Come in, gentlemen, come in! Sit down, let's bother with no ceremony! What can I do for you? Servants forward, ho, fill and refill their cups! You must all be my guests for many days."

And so it turned out that the Argonauts enjoyed a whole barrage of feasts, and entertainment in every way equal to what they had enjoyed at their last stop. But with regard to their mission, Lycus could offer little in the way of practical help, and could do little more for the Argonauts than entertain them with a hunting party. Jason was reluctant to delay his sailing for another day, but realized that it would be rude to decline the offer. Meanwhile the great majority of the men were eager to remain a little longer in a place where many pleasures, not only those of the hunt, were readily available.

Several parties mounted cameloids and rode out into the royal hunting preserve, a few square miles of rugged land, where there were cliffs not unlike those in which the Harpies had been said to nest. Proteus scanned the skies at intervals, but there was no sign of any similar monsters here.

Unhappily, he had not much success in seeing signs of a boar, either.

But Idmon saw one, at extreme close range. The boar's tusk gashed his thigh, and he died, bleeding to death inside his suit of borrowed furs before any effective aid could reach him. By that time his mind was wandering, and none of the treatments attempted by King Lycus's physicians did him any good at all. Those who attended him at the end were certain that his weakness and inattention during the hunt were a result of his fever, caused by the single scratch on his arm inflicted by a Harpy's filthy claw, a small but ultimately fatal wound.

And an even harder blow now fell, in terms of the practical hopes for the success of the voyage. The fever of Tiphys, who had also been scratched by a Harpy's claw, grew worse and soon he too had breathed his last.

The navigator's chief concern in his last illness was how to dispose of his compass-pyx. He asked that it be brought to him, as he lay dying, and lay for an hour or more with the device clutched to his chest, as if trying to make up his mind how best to bequeath it.

In the end he chose Jason as his heir, though Jason was not the most skilled in the use of such an instrument.

Two weeks after their arrival in the domain of King Lycus, a double funeral was held. The company of Argonauts was again a little smaller than it had been. Idmon's counsel would be sorely missed, and in the loss of their navigator they had suffered what several of them feared might be a crippling blow.

Three months had now passed since the Argosy began. Four Argonauts had died on the journey, and the missing Meleager had to be presumed dead.

Medea

ason still intended that the log should be faithfully kept up—he had told his shipmates that he wanted as complete a record as possible of everything that happened on the voyage. Proteus supposed that the captain had some idea that written evidence might be useful to his cause, when he had brought home the Golden Fleece and stood confronting the current occupant of the throne of Iolcus.

"Captain, my thought is that nothing you bring before the king—excuse me, the usurper—is going to help you depose him. Nothing, that is, short of an army strong enough to do the job."

"We will see what we will see." And that was all that Jason had to say.

The business of log-keeping was under discussion now, because with Idmon dead, someone else had to take over the job. Anchaeus, who had assumed the duty of making entries, went on with the task, which was currently a joyless one.

In the process of selecting Idmon's replacement, the question had come up as to how many of the Heroes could read and write—when the captain called for a show of hands, it turned out that a substantial minority were practically illiterate, even in the common tongue that all of them could speak.

Proteus, glancing curiously through the log book, was struck by the fact that though Idmon at various times had used several little-known languages—maybe just to keep in practice with them—he, Proteus, could read all of them without any trouble. The only explanation that occurred to him was that sailors tended to get around the world a lot, and Old Proteus had evidently been no exception.

*   *   *

According to the new navigator's best projections and calculations, they had now covered well over half the distance between Iolcus and Colchis, where, as Argeus and Phrontis repeatedly confirmed, the Golden Fleece hung unsecured in its tree, just waiting for someone daring enough to lift it from the branches and carry it away. The distance had been halved between Jason and the treasure that he so keenly coveted, yet the captain of the *Argo* was moodier than ever, downcast over the two most recent deaths among his company.

This was a cause of gloom that Proteus could understand. The loss of Idmon and Tiphys at the same time was a hard double blow, and it was not surprising that the commander took it as an indication that there would be even greater tragedies to come.

Proteus also thought that he himself would probably have done well as the new navigator, particularly with the superb compass-pyx the successor of Tiphys had inherited. He would have liked to try, and had an instinctive feeling that he would have done well; it seemed to him very likely that he had some experience along that line which he could not remember in detail. But no one else had suggested that he take the job, and there seemed to be several other worthy candidates. And if he had said he wanted to replace Tiphys, naturally everyone would want to know, among other things, exactly what experience he had in using a compass-pyx. He was certain that he had some, but there was nothing specific he could have said.

When the captain kept on fretting about the losses his crew had suffered, Proteus wanted to tell him to quit bellyaching and get on with the job. But even when Jason was behaving stupidly, he retained his knack for making people want to like him and do things for him. Proteus was aware of being somehow subtly manipulated, but that did not dampen his enthusiasm for helping the captain to succeed.

He told Jason: "Captain, none of the bad things that have happened on this voyage were your fault. And everyone who volunteered to join your company knew the quest would be dangerous."

But it seemed he might have saved his breath, for the captain
gave no indication that he heard. Instead Jason only voiced
another complaint or two. "I do not want to think about how many
men I have lost since leaving home. The whole enterprise seems
to be under a cloud."

Proteus kept trying to give good counsel. "Some of your problems are certainly the work of enemies. Any man who wants to be
a king is going to have enemies."

"That is true. Someone arranged that attack back on Samothraki. I wonder if I have other mortal foes besides Pelias?"

Proteus wanted to avoid speculating on that subject. "And
some of them are just bad luck. You could hardly have ordered
Polydeuces not to win his fight, but when he won that set off
another battle."

Proteus found himself taking extra turns at an oar, making
sure that the sail was well cared for, baiting extra hooks and casting lines whenever they stopped, to keep the crew supplied with
fresh fish. King Phineas had seen that they were amply provi-
sioned on leaving his domain, but storage space on the slender
vessel was strictly limited, and more than thirty hard-working men
consumed a large amount of food.

In the privacy of his own thoughts, Proteus often asked himself why the *Argo* and its crew should be so important to him.
Until that sunset when he had come wading almost mindless out
of the sea, he had never (as far as he knew) laid eyes on this ship
or any of the people now aboard. The only answer he could find
(and it was not very satisfactory) was the lack of any other purpose in his reborn life—except, of course, that of discovering who
he was. Attaching himself to Jason and his cause had provided a
kind of answer—at least he now had an identity as a member of a
crew. By now, his own presence on the *Argo*, working hard for the

success of the voyage, seemed to Proteus the most natural thing in the world.

But in connection with his own work, Proteus now faced another puzzle, one he could no longer dismiss as only a figment of his imagination. The ship really did make better progress when he was rowing than when it was his turn to rest, even though he never worked his oar harder or faster than anyone else. As far as Proteus could tell, none of his shipmates had yet become aware of this phenomenon. If any of them ever did, he meant to try to make a joke out of it somehow.

While Proteus uneasily enjoyed a feeling of accomplishment, things were obviously different with Jason. Sitting on a rower's bench—he continued scrupulously to take regular turns at the oars—the big man mumbled gloomy forebodings.

But the other Argonauts, to some extent following an example set by Proteus, persuaded the leader to brace up, and take some satisfaction in the fact that his marvelous goal was drawing nearer, hour by hour.

Proteus, in his ongoing concern for their success, was relieved to take note that no one but Jason was really grumbling. The others had all come for the sake of adventure, and so far no one could complain things were too dull.

Now at last they were drawing near their long-sought objective, or so the new steersman assured them, when he raised his head from the compass-pyx. And from here on it would seem that navigation should not be difficult.

After passing various sights, and avoiding a few more icebergs, the *Argo* came in sight of certain mountains, blue with distance, looming over the watery horizon. Phrontis and Argeus reacted with great excitement. Now, they said, they knew for certain that they were coming home.

Those high blue crags came nearer hour by hour, taking on

the aspect of solid rock. It seemed now that they had come to the end of the open sea, and were entering the broad estuary of a sizable river. Jason gave orders to lower sail and yard and stow them in the mast-cage. Next they unstepped the mast and put it down to lie beside them, on one side of the long deck.

The current in this broad stream was comparatively gentle, nothing like the mighty flow they had had to contend with in the salt-water strait.

Men were calling back and forth across the benches, telling each other that they were in fresh water now. The smell of it was different, as always, and Proteus could feel the difference in the *Argo*'s lessened buoyancy. People were reaching over the side to scoop up handfuls of the stream that was trying to push them back to sea, and taste it. And it seemed to Proteus that whatever beneficial effect his rowing might have on the ship's progress had become decidedly weaker since entering the river. Still, pulling an oar as hard as everyone else did not tax him to anywhere near his full capacity.

Another day went by, and then another. The distant mountains came a little closer, then began to recede again, as the waterway the ship was following turned its course. The river was guiding them steadily inland, into what certainly must be the kingdom of Colchis, though so far they had had no contact, beyond a casual wave or two, with any of its inhabitants. They had to assume that word of their presence was being carried overland, much faster than they could row upstream, to the ears of the king in his capital city.

Now occasionally there were people along both shores, one or two or three at a time, laborers working in the fields, some riding cameloids. Faces kept turning in the Argonauts' direction, taking note of the foreign ship with the two broad staring eyes painted on her prow. Proteus supposed they might easily be taken for pirates, except that few people would believe that pirates could be so bold here near the center of Colchian power.

"We are almost home," Phrontis murmured, and it sounded as if he might be praying.

On the right bank as they proceeded upstream, Proteus saw, a short distance inland, the tops of a grove of tall trees, full green with the exuberance of what was undoubtedly a brief summer in these parts. Proteus supposed he might well be looking at the sacred grove supposed to hide the Fleece. What species of tree they might be he had no idea; if at any time in his life he had been a forester, that knowledge was all gone. But there was no spot of gold to be discerned among that forest of branches, and no sign of any dragon, or indeed of any living animal or bird.

And here Jason for the time being gave up taking his regular turn at rowing; it was as if he were expecting at any moment to be summoned to some great deed. With a sword now belted at his side, he stood or paced hour after hour on the slender foredeck, watching hungrily, having things pointed out to him by one or the other of King Aeetes's grandsons. Argeus and Phrontis were visibly excited at returning to the land of their birth, and kept pointing out remembered landmarks to anyone who would pay attention.

Argeus took one hand off his oar long enough to point into the midst of the grove of tall trees. "Up there. See? There is where they say the Fleece lies spread out on the leafy branches of an oak, while a great snake keeps watch and ward over it."

His benchmate did not seem at all impressed. "Yes, I see. What does the great snake eat all this time, do you suppose? Acorns and pine cones?"

"Maybe there are enough would-be thieves to keep him well-fed."

There was much speculation, some of it ribald.

"Aye, it's there among those trees somewhere," agreed Anchaeus, looking up from his rower's bench. "If all the stories we've been told are true."

"Are all the stories ever true?" demanded an Argonaut who

liked to argue. "But if even half of them are based on some foun-
dation, then the Fleece should be over there; somewhere in that
very grove."

"See any glowing eyes, peeking out between branches? The
treasure's supposed to be guarded by a dragon."

"I thought it was a snake. What happened to the snake? Ran
out of thieves and acorns?"

"Dragon must have ate it," was another irreverent comment.

"Oh, it'll be guarded, certainly. By what, or who . . . I suppose
we will find out when we talk to Grandfather. I'll be glad to be
free of these damned oars for a few days."

One of the Argonauts, at least, was not notably quick-witted.
"They say King Aeetes is brother to Circe the enchantress."

"Aye, so they do."

"Then let's see—if the king here is Circe's brother, or half-
brother, then his daughters are Circe's nieces."

"They certainly are."

"And the king's son, Apsyrtus, who must be about thirty now,
is Circe's nephew."

"Yes. Absolutely. I think you've got it now."

None of this was really news to Proteus, who was listening to it all
with half an ear. Most of it fell into the vast category of imper-
sonal things his memory had managed to retain, through the
destruction of the old Proteus and the violent creation of the
new—if creation was the right word. But it struck him now that
there was probably a genuine relationship between Circe and
King Aeetes—the enchantress was no goddess, by most accounts,
and it would be unprecedented, Proteus thought, for any monarch
to try to gain status by adopting her into the family. It was more or
less expected that anyone asserting rights to a throne would work
hard and imaginatively at manipulating his or her family tree,
until some evidence could be discovered, or invented, for claiming
at least one deity among the ancestors. Some families, by twisting

their genealogies into complete fantasy, tried to establish half a dozen divine connections. Of course, folk tended to credit Circe with powers at least equal to those of many a minor goddess. And Proteus thought that the relative modesty of this claim tended to make it more credible.

Circe, he knew, was probably as famous as any other mortal woman who walked the earth. And besides that, she . . .

His hands stopped what they were doing, and for a moment he held his breath . . . in his chronic struggle to remember something of his own past, he had just brushed against something of great importance . . . but before he could seize it, it was gone again, hard to recover as a smooth rock at the bottom of a stream. Damn! He'd almost had it!

There was *something* else that he really ought to be able to remember about the enchantress, Circe . . . he supposed it was even possible that Old Proteus had met her. Why not? Even if the great ones of the world tried to keep themselves apart from common ordinary humans, they must sometimes encounter such folk, including sailors and fishermen.

And now he himself had met Jason, who was not a god, of course, but so famous that people would probably begin to think of him as one.

Abruptly it struck Proteus as odd that he had never heard Jason making out a claim for gods among *his* ancestors. But no doubt a deity or two would appear from nowhere, as a matter of common knowledge, as soon as Jason had managed to set a golden crown upon his head. Zeus would suddenly become his grandfather, or Hera his great-aunt.

"Not *the* Circe?" asked the slower-witted, marveling Argonaut, his thought lagging a speech or two behind the conversation, which had otherwise moved on.

"I don't know of any other." His bench-mate and sometime tutor looked at him impatiently. "People aren't likely to tag their daughters with that name, are they?"

That debate was drowned out by another one, more practical, between two other men: They were in disagreement about exactly how far upstream they had come, and which way they ought to be going.

"But which side of the river is the city on? Yes, as I thought. This one—that's the side where we want to land."

"Want us to take it right into the harbor, Captain, tie up to the central dock?"

"No, I think not," Jason said. And to Proteus the captain's increasing nervousness was evident.

But Jason's voice was calm enough as he gave directions to the steersman. They would land on the bank opposite to the supposed location of the Fleece—no use giving any of the local people grounds to suspect that the visitors had some particular interest in their famous treasure.

On the approaching shore, as the grandsons now pointed out, the wharves and piers of a real city were coming into view, though still a long way upstream. The number of people on shore actually watching the *Argo*'s arrival at this point in the river was quite small; Proteus was not sure that anyone would observe their landing.

They were within a mile of the real port when Jason chose their landing spot. A squall of rain had come to blur the river and the surrounding landscape, and it seemed entirely possible that they were unobserved when he gave quick orders to the steersman to turn them hard port into a marsh.

By the time the vessel came to a stop it was half-hidden by tall reeds from any curious watchers who might be passing on the water, or along the far shore. Here the *Argo* rested conveniently beside a narrow tongue of firm land, so the crew would be able to stand on something solid when they disembarked.

The men looked at one another when they shipped oars and dropped the anchor-stones, but no one made a comment on this odd choice of landing places. Proteus thought that anyone who saw them pulling in here was very likely to take them for pirates trying to hide.

Before anyone actually set foot on shore, Jason brought out from some hidden pocket a small flask of gold he had been saving, and poured into the river a libation of fine wine, saying as he poured that his offering was made to Earth, to the gods of the land.

Having done that, he sat for a while without speaking, as if reluctant at last to leave the ship, while his crew got up and stretched, and tried their feet ashore. Men got the impression that he did not know what to say; and if it had been anyone but Jason, they might have thought that he was frightened.

At last Anchaeus had to gently prod the captain. "We have come to our goal, Jason, the land of Colchis. Now we must consider how to go about getting what we came here for."

The captain nodded, but remained silent. His face wore an expression now all too familiar to his men, suggesting he did not know what to do next. It seemed marvelously strange to Proteus that Jason had led them this far without having made any firm plan for immediate action when they got here. At least their leader ought to have had one ready in his own mind. There had been no shortage of time to think and talk things over, and two members of the Colchian king's family had been on hand for consultation. But Jason seemed determined to rely mostly on his own stubbornness and intuition. Soon it was plain that nothing would be done until the morning, and Jason gave orders to make a kind of camp ashore. The men got busy, killing a few snakes who did not seem to mind the chill weather.

It was as if the mere thought of Aeetes, the stories of fits of rage, of cruelty beyond the ordinary, inspired dread. Though the Argonauts continued to talk bravely, in general it seemed to Proteus that they were more afraid of the king they were about to meet than they had been of any of the other difficulties they had encountered so far, including the boxing bully.

It had been easier to confront the brawler who only wanted to knock your teeth out. Polydeuces said to Phrontis: "From what I hear of your grandpa, I'd rather get into the ring with Amycus again." And the boxer rubbed his cheekbones, where the scars of that match were still not fully healed.

"So would I," offered Haraldur, overhearing. "He's dead!"

By now it was obvious, at least to Proteus, that the grandsons of Aeetes were going to be of less help than their shipmates had been fondly hoping. The two had only fairly remote memories of their grandfather, from a time when they had been really only children. But they had a great fund of second-hand tales about the king, and could testify to their shipmates of the old man's formidable reputation. As the time for the expected confrontation drew near, the Argonauts were more and more interested in hearing what Phrontis and Argeus had to say, but the brothers seemed to look forward to the meeting less and less.

The night had been so cold under a clear sky that a thin film of ice formed over the tall green grass of the marsh, to be dispersed like a bad dream, or like the feeble ghost of an iceberg, in the light of the morning sun. The men who had slept ashore blessed Phineas for having provided them with blankets.

In a way, the lack of any Colchian reception at all was worse than the hostility some of the Argonauts had more or less expected. No one had approached them or their ship since they had landed, and it was hard to say if any of the local inhabitants even knew they were lodged in this trackless marsh, three-quarters hidden by tall reeds.

And now there was a decision to be made, that could not be put off any longer. It was time for Jason, and whatever Argonauts he might choose to come with him, to actually go to the palace and formally announce first their presence, and then their mission, to the king.

The intruders' first good look at the distant palace, in clear morning light, did nothing to ease their nervousness. The upper sections of several towers were just visible from where they were moored among the reeds.

Jason issued orders in a quiet voice. "I ask those who are not coming with me to stay quietly on board, or very near the ship, with your arms ready, while I go up to Aeetes's palace with the sons of Phrixus and two other men."

Jason also chose Proteus and Anchaeus, as his new chief counselor, to accompany him, so there would be five in the party in all.

"Do we go armed, Jason?" Proteus wanted to know.

"Of course." The answer came without hesitation. "Who knows what we may meet along the way?"

Leaving the ship, the five men soon found a faint, irregular path that led them quickly to dry land beyond the reeds and water. From there, they passed on to higher ground.

Once they were sure that the way in front of them lay all on solid ground, they stamped and scraped the mud off their feet as best they could, and trudged on, still heading upstream though they were out of sight of the river now. The slate-colored tops of the palace's twin towers remained in sight, and what they saw as they drew closer confirmed it was a much more impressive building than any they had encountered since leaving Iolcus.

As the men walked on, the two grandsons of Aeetes entertained their shipmates with further descriptions of some of the people they might expect to encounter at the palace. Naturally Argeus and Phrontis were especially looking forward to a reunion with their mother, the king's older daughter, Chalciope.

"Mother must be about forty years of age by now. And I suppose our Aunt Medea must be fifteen or sixteen," said Argeus, who was scarcely any older than that himself. "I remember her as a mere toddler—now I have heard rumors that she, like our great-aunt Circe, likes to deal in witchcraft."

Proteus grunted something noncommittal in response. It seemed that everyone had heard those stories.

"And I," said Phrontis, "that Aunt Medea has something of a temper."

Once the delegation of Argonauts had got a hundred yards or so inland from the marshes, beyond the osiers and willows bowing over the wet ground, they entered a region where taller trees stood in rows, as if they had been deliberately planted years ago. It was not far from the city, in an area where one would think the need for lumber and firewood would be great; yet in these groves the absence of stumps showed that no trees had been cut down for a long time. The only likely explanation was that they had been set aside for some religious purpose.

The grandsons of the king confirmed the fact. "Look." Argeus was pointing upward.

There were corpses, swathed in wrappings and dangling on ropes from the tall trees' highest branches. Some were mere skeletons, with most of their wrappings fallen free, or undone by scavenger birds; others were comparatively recent, and rotting. Most of the stink of the freshly dead went upward, but now and then a thoroughly unpleasant whiff came drifting down.

Aeetes' grandsons explained to their shipmates that the Colchians would think it sacrilege to burn the bodies of their men. Here only women and children were cremated, a process which in many other lands was considered the only proper ending for dead warriors.

"How strange," mused Jason.

"The world is a strange place," said Proteus. No one was going to argue that point with him today.

Before they had emerged from the trees, they were met by a thick mist which spread gently from inland toward the river. It was so heavy that they almost had to grope their way.

Proteus was reminded of the thick smoke billowing out of the ritual cave on Samothraki, though here the smell was of nothing worse than earth and water. "Is this mist natural to this place?" he asked the brothers. "Or does some god wish us to pass through the city unseen?"

Phrontis and Argeus only shook their heads, as if to say they could remember nothing like this fog.

"Some power wants us to get lost and fall into the bog, more likely," grumbled the Counselor.

The palace was perhaps a mile from where they had left the boat and most of the crew. As they drew nearer, now following a broad road, more people passed the Argonauts in the mist, some closely enough to take apparent alarm, despite Jason's cheerful greetings, at the sight of five armed strangers.

And at last there appeared in front of them a high stone wall that could belong to nothing but the royal palace. Phrontis and Argeus remembered the way to the front gate.

On reaching the very entrance at last they paused. Two of the visitors at least were no strangers to palaces, yet even they found much to marvel at on surveying the king's courtyard with its wide gates, and the rows of towering stone columns, that seemed to have no purpose other than display.

Anchaeus remarked that the royal castle in Iolcus, perched on a crag as it was, was taller than this structure, and probably would be more easily defended. But in all other ways the home of King Aeetes seemed superior.

"Look at that, would you!" Yet another tower was looming out of the mist.

"It's impressive."

The guards who eventually appeared inside the closed gate showed no surprise when Jason told them his name, and told them that he had come, escorted by his trusted friends, to see the king.

After only the briefest delays the visitors were ushered in, by sentries whose demeanor gave no clue as to whether such visitors might or might not have been expected.

There were gravel paths, curving artistically among neatly tended beds of flowers.

Another, lesser gate let them into an inner court, from which several sets of folding doors led out again, evidently to various rooms.

Here the visitors were kept waiting only briefly, before being welcomed by a well-dressed functionary, who without bothering to introduce himself said the king was busy with important business, but had sent word that his visitors should be entertained at dinner.

Given the early hour, it seemed likely that dinner would be hours away, but no one was going to quibble. "Then the king knows who we are?" asked Jason.

The man very slightly inclined his head. "Sir, your ship has been observed for several days by people along the river. Very little that happens here escapes His Majesty's attention."

But still the man made no move to escort them further. Now he was looking at their weapons with evident disapproval, and making small throat-clearing noises.

At last Jason asked him directly if he and his companions had unknowingly committed some offense.

"Sir, the king would be grievously offended if visitors should carry arms into his presence. We will not permit an armed invasion."

Jason turned his gaze on Argeus and Phrontis. Both native Colchians looked uncomfortable, as if realizing they ought to have known better, and to have warned their shipmates in advance.

"We thought we might encounter bandits on the way to the palace," the elder grandson offered lamely. The only response from the official was a look that made most of the delegation feel they owed him an apology.

But Jason, refusing to take offense, unbuckled his sword and tossed it on the ground, no better place of storage having been offered. His shipmates in turn all followed his example, Proteus being the last to give up his spear.

Then their guide at last led the way into the inner palace.

Challenge

At every moment, with every new chamber that they entered, each new turning of a corridor inside the palace, the Argonauts were struck by some new detail, a fresh glimpse of size or elegance. To Proteus it seemed that everything here might very well have been calculated to stun the first-time visitor with an impression of overwhelming wealth and power. Well, this group was doubtless less susceptible than most. Neither Jason nor his Counselor were strangers to royal display. And this palatial exhibition half-awoke strange memories in Proteus, rather than striking him with awe. Why strange? he asked himself. Well for one thing, because the light in King Aeetes's halls, while bright enough, seemed somehow wrong. For any display as magnificent as this the dominant illumination ought to be greenish, or maybe blue . . .

He shook his head in wonder at his own thoughts. Maybe the effects of that knock on the head were even more long-lasting than he had suspected.

But this palace was indeed impressive. It was not only the height of the walls and hugeness of the rooms, but the marvelous tapestries, fountains, and statues to be seen everywhere. Any visitor who came from a truly rustic background would almost certainly be overawed and overwhelmed, but it seemed that none of the visitors fit that description. With the possible exception of Proteus himself, all backgrounds looked about equally familiar to Proteus. He could call up some general idea of what the inside of a palace ought to look like, as well as the inside of a fisherman's hut, and what he saw around him now matched with the former. Maybe, he thought, he had once been a member of some royal bodyguard. But where?

Where else, but at the court of the king—or usurper—who had chosen Old Proteus to be his secret agent?

Jason's face as he looked around inside the palace wore an expression of faint sadness, as if he might be comparing the grandeur here with that of the castle that ought to have been his— and that someday would be his, as he had sworn.

To Aeetes's grandsons, of course, these marble halls were, if perhaps not exactly their childhood home, at least familiar to them from their early lives. Phrontis commented that everything looked smaller than he remembered it; but Proteus watching the two brothers got the impression that their life here had not been par- ticularly happy or comfortable. They did not presume to behave in any way other than like visitors.

The visitors were conducted to a dining hall, where a large table was laid, as if in expectation of their coming, with utensils of gold, silver, and fine crystal. Attendants were already bringing in food and drink, as if a party of visitors had been expected. Jason and his companions were bidden to sit down and enjoy his majesty's hospitality; their guide said in his neutral voice that cer- tain members of the royal family would greet them presently, and eventually they would be joined by the king himself.

Ordinarily it would have seemed somewhat early in the day for banqueting, but rations aboard ship had been lacking in variety for some time, and sometimes in quantity as well. The Argonauts were ready for a change, and fell to with a will. The wine and food were excellent, and seemed all the better after weeks of largely frugal fare.

Almost an hour had passed at the table, and they had practi- cally finished a sumptuous meal, before the members of the king's family began to join them, one by one.

As soon as the entrance of the Princess Chalciope was announced, everyone at the table rose.

Proteus turning to the doorway saw a vaguely worried-looking woman of about forty years of age, wearing fine silks trimmed with fur. For the moment the princess ignored Jason's formal greeting, as she hastened to embrace her two sons. In a loud voice she reminded everyone that she had not seen Argeus and Phrontis since they were mere children. Now they were fully grown, but their mother swore that she would have known them anywhere.

Another figure was now pausing in a different doorway, about to enter the great hall, and inspecting the scene before him with what seemed sardonic interest. Proteus was certain of the young man's identity even before his name was mentioned. He wore gold and rich garments, worthy of a prince. Proteus thought that he did not seem especially formidable—until he recalled one of the king's grandsons earlier telling him: "I remember Uncle Apsyrtus—he seems very pleasant, most of the time." And then the youth had fallen silent, with an unhappy look.

Argeus looked that way now, as he caught sight of the waiting figure, and cleared his throat. "Good day to you, Uncle."

The older man nodded slightly. Obviously, if the decision depended on Uncle Apsyrtus, there was going to be no demonstrative family reunion. Phrontis in turn murmured something in the way of greeting, and bowed slightly.

Then, before any general conversation could begin, the king came in, not bothering to have himself announced. He was an old man of unhealthy but commanding appearance, dressed in silk and furs.

Proteus at his first sight of King Aeetes was struck with a maddening feeling that there was something familiar about the monarch's face—it seemed almost certain to him that this king had played some role in the life of Old Proteus, that he could not remember. But when the eyes of Aeetes rested on him, briefly, they betrayed no sign of recognition.

As soon as the king had taken his seat at the head of the table, his two grandsons stepped forward and bowed to him.

But before any conversation could begin, Chalciope, looking

toward the doorway again, called out: "Come in, Medea dear. Come in and meet your grown-up nephews. And there are other travelers here, who have come all the way from your father's old home to visit us."

The king's youngest legitimate child now entered the banquet hall, a blond and elegantly dressed small figure. Old Aeetes greeted his daughter with a look of approval, and Proteus thought that the way he looked at her, and his murmured greeting, indicated some sincere affection.

Medea was dressed simply, more or less in the style of her older aunt. The girl's long blond hair was done in an intricate knot, and she was attended by a mousy-looking young maid. Suddenly Proteus was disinclined to believe the rumors that would have had this almost childlike person dabbling in witchcraft.

And Proteus noted that Apsyrtus appeared to be studying his sister carefully, as if he were trying to gauge her reaction to the visitors. And Medea seemed somewhat interested in the visitors, as was only natural when people were arriving from halfway around the world. He thought she paid particular attention to the two young men who were actually her nephews, though they surpassed her in age by a few years.

The glance that Medea returned to her older brother suggested that there was no love lost between the siblings. But that took only a moment; and now she gazed with frank curiosity at her two nephews.

So far there had been no sign of any queen or royal consort, and Proteus thought there probably would not be. According to the king's grandsons, Aeetes was now on his second (at least) wife (and queen), Eidyia, a woman of considerable beauty but who was seldom seen abroad. Rumor held that one of his intermediate consorts had not been entirely human, but rather an Oceanid or Nereid, called Idyia, Hecate, or Nearea, in various versions of the story.

*   *   *

There being no more interruptions, the king now methodically and formally greeted all his visitors, in a reserved voice, and heard their names from Argeus. Then in a grandfatherly way, he inquired of his newly-arrived grandsons how they had prospered on their long sojourn away from home.

Argeus began to tell their story, haltingly at first, then speaking more smoothly as the old man gave him an encouraging nod. Vaguely Argeus described how he and his brother had left home, filled with youthful determination somehow to recover certain unspecified possessions that their father had once owned in other lands. But they had to admit that effort hadn't worked out. And at this Phrontis nodded, smiling in rueful agreement.

Of course, Grandfather sir, they had really been on more than one long voyage. Speaking now in alternation, the two young men went on to inform the elder king of how they had come to hear of Jason's quest, bound for their homeland, and had made a great effort to meet the famed adventurer.

Here Aeetes raised one finger to interrupt their narrative. A certain rumor had reached the court, he said, to the effect that Jason had actually rescued them from shipwreck, in the middle of some earlier voyage. The king wondered aloud whether that might be true.

No, majesty, his grandsons explained, interrupting each other in their eagerness. At one point in their adventures they had indeed needed rescue, though not by Jason. It was simply that the ship they had been on at that time had failed. But the *Argo*, the ship that had now brought them back to Colchis, was quite a different matter.

Now they had come to a subject on which any sailor would be ready to enthusiastically hold forth. The young brothers explained eagerly what a superb ship *Argo* was.

Then the elder grandson, showing more enthusiasm than social awareness, started to introduce his shipmates all over again.

"This is our captain, sir. Jason has led us here halfway around the world, by means of a long and difficult voyage, hoping you will make him a generous present of the Golden Fleece."

Two heartbeats after those last words were uttered, it struck Proteus that the banquet hall had suddenly grown very quiet. All eyes were on Aeetes, who, looking gently puzzled, raised a commanding hand. "Stop! Just stop a moment there. There must be some misunderstanding. *What* is it I am to let him have?"

The grandsons looked at each other helplessly. If there had ever been a plan of how to deal with this inevitable moment, that plan had been forgotten. What they remembered of their grandfather made them stutter and stumble as fear began to grow in them, neither of them wishing to speak the words that must now be said.

But at last one of them had to come out with it. "The Golden Fleece, sir. If, of course, you will do so freely and willingly. He has not come here to try to force you into doing anything . . ."

The young man's voice trailed off into a tense silence, for it was obvious to everyone that the king was no longer calm and welcoming, that in fact, though he had scarcely moved and was still silent, he was in a mounting rage.

Now the king, with a surge of energy surprising in an elderly man, jumped to his feet, with the result that everyone else scrambled to stand up also. A vein stood out on Aeetes's forehead as his words poured forth. "You villains!" At the moment he was glaring directly at his grandsons. "Get out of my sight at once. Get out of my country, before you meet a . . . Get out of here. Get out before I feed you a Fleece that you won't like."

Now the monarch was becoming almost incoherent in his rage. "Fleece, is it? I think I know better than that. You have in mind some plot to seize my throne. If you had not eaten at my table first, I would tear your tongues out and chop off your hands, both of them, and send you back with nothing but your feet . . ."

The floors and walls of solid stone seemed to be vibrating with the king's fury. But Jason, standing taller than the king, looked him squarely in the eye. And when the raging monarch had to pause for breath, began a soft and reasonable reply.

Proteus, wondering at his captain, thought: *So, this man can be very brave when ninety-nine out of a hundred would be speechless with fear. How strange, then, that I have seen him shudder and draw back at times when it would seem a Hero would find it easy to be brave.*

Meanwhile, Jason was still speaking. Proteus thought it was probably his fatalistic attitude that allowed him to infuse his voice with an hypnotic calm. "My lord, if you were offended by our show of arms at your front gate, I ask you to overlook that. We acted only in ignorance, no worse. We have not come to your city and palace with any such designs as you suspect.

"Destiny has brought me here, sir. Fate, and the would-be cleverness of a usurper. If you could find it in your heart to be generous, know that I will make your name and your virtue famous through all the halls of my homeland."

The king had now slumped back in his chair, his face a study in sullen deliberation. Meanwhile, everyone else remained standing.

The look on Aeetes's face told them all that his anger had not been dissipated. But now it had assumed a quieter and more thoughtful form. When he spoke again, his tone was calm and reasonable. To Jason he said: "Sir, there is no need for you to make me any more long speeches. If it is really the Golden Fleece you want, and nothing more—why, I will let you have it."

A breathless silence hung in the great hall. Obviously the king was not quite finished.

At last Aeetes went on. "That is, if you still want it when I have told you what you must do to get it." The old man looked up, almost smiling. "You should not confuse me with your ruler back in Iolcus, the man you hate so much, as you describe him; I am willing to be generous to honorable visitors."

Whatever Jason might be feeling, Proteus had to admire his ability to hold his voice level. "What test will you set us, sir?"

Now the smile had come fully back to the king's face. "It will be a test for *you*, sir. You alone."

Jason nodded his acceptance.

Aeetes said: "I propose to try your courage and abilities by setting you a task which, though formidable, is not beyond the strength of *my* two hands." And the king held them up, displaying many rings, and a set of arthritic knuckles. It was plain that his body had once been strong, but was now becoming gnarled with age.

He went on in the same tone: "Are you at all used to agricultural work? No? A pity." Again Aeetes paused for a time, looking from one to another of his audience, savoring the tension as it built. "There is a certain field of land in my domain, one that I want plowed, and sown with a certain, special seed, and harvested—all in the space of a single day."

There was a faint gasp of indrawn breath, almost inaudible, from the other side of the table. Proteus noted with a start that Medea had suddenly taken on a worried look, as if she had just realized what her father was driving at. And the inexpressive face of Apsyrtus had now developed a faint smile.

Meanwhile, the king, still steadily regarding Jason, went on. "Sounds impossible, hey? It's not, I assure you. I have performed the feat myself—do you think that you are up to it?"

"I will do my best, sir, if you will tell me or show me just what to do. What tools am I to use?"

"Aha! A good question. We come now to the most interesting part." The old man shifted in his chair. Obviously he was now truly beginning to enjoy himself. Proteus supposed there was nothing like a fit of rage to get the juices flowing. "What tools you are to use, and what crop you are to sow—and reap. Ha! Ha ha!"

Aeetes waved one gnarled hand, vaguely indicating a direction. "There's a place across the river—yes, over there. That's where you will yoke two very special cattle to your plow—they are Bulls with feet of bronze, and live flames in their very breath.

And after plowing with these cattle, you will sow the field with nothing less than Dragon's Teeth. And—should you survive those early phases of your test—you will then be privileged to deal, to the best of your ability, with the resulting harvest." And the king's smile broadened once again.

The dining hall was very quiet as the king went on. His voice had fallen till now it was very low, but all in the large room could hear him clearly.

"I will tell you how I myself have managed the business in the past. After I have yoked the Bronze Bulls and plowed with them, I sow the furrows with the teeth of a monstrous serpent—never mind how I come to have such kernels—you will see.

"And then you will watch, and we will all watch with you, as those teeth grow up in the form of armed men—yes, that is what I said. But you see, I know how to deal with that crop of warriors, using my spear as they rise up against me on all sides.

"By the end of the day, I had done with my harvesting. Now if you, young man, can do as well as I did, you may carry off the Golden Fleece and take it home with you."

There was a heavy silence in the room. Proteus thought, with a sinking heart, that whatever power of will had kept the young man going seemed to be wilting away.

Jason stood before the king almost as if paralyzed, staring at the floor. *Say something, you fool!* Proteus wanted to shout at his captain. Had they not all been on their feet, he would have kicked him under the table. *Whatever you come up with will be better than just standing there like a lump of dirt, as if you were afraid to open your mouth . . .*

Into the silence the king said: "I am not unreasonable. You may have a certain minimal amount of help—someone to hand you the yoke for the Bulls, for example—but no more assistance than I myself enjoyed when I managed to achieve the feat. And that was very little, as anyone who watched me can attest."

"When is this test to take place, Majesty?" It was Proteus who had nerved himself to ask the question.

The old eyes flicked at him appraisingly. "Tomorrow, at dawn." The king returned his gaze to Jason. "And if you hesitate to yoke the bulls or shirk the deadly harvesting, I will take the matter up myself in a manner calculated to make others shrink from coming here and pestering their betters."

With dignity old Aeetes got to his feet again. Then he turned his back on his stunned visitors and marched out of the dining hall with a springy step, his head held high. Whatever might happen in the morning, he obviously expected to enjoy it.

Moments later the steward, looking no more and no less hostile than when he had ushered in the visitors, showed them out again. Their weapons had been moved from where they left them, thrown in a careless pile outside the outer gate, like so much garbage waiting for disposal.

"Not exactly a warm or joyous welcome," Proteus observed after a moment. No one else had anything at all to say.

But when they had put the outer gate of the palace behind them, Argeus spoke up, saying that during the course of the meeting he had received several friendly glances from his young Aunt Medea. These he interpreted to mean that she would surely be willing to help, in one way or another.

"Yes," said Jason vaguely. "We must try to take advantage of that."

Phrontis quickly put in that he felt certain their mother would want to do everything for them that she possibly could.

And Argeus tearfully apologized for so clumsily blurting out the object of their visit.

Jason only shrugged, and clapped the young man on the shoulder, as if to say that the Fates must have wanted it that way. "It was necessary that we should tell the king sooner or later. I am not sure that any other way of telling him would have made the matter easier."

They all turned at the sound of softly running feet behind them, to behold a maidservant trying to catch up. Between gasps, the girl told them she had been sent by the Princess Chalciope, to invite the sons of the princess to come back through a side door of the palace for a private visit with their mother.

The young maidservant said: "If you are Argeus, and Phrontis, there is one in the palace who wishes to have a private talk with you. The king will not object."

This seemed to offer some hopeful prospects. After exchanging a few words with the captain, the two native Colchians went back with the messenger, while the three remaining Argonauts retreated gloomily to their ship.

After they had walked a few hundred yards in depressed silence, Proteus asked the captain: "What will you do, sir?"

Jason trudged on a few more paces before answering. "One thing is certain, Proteus. I will need help, if my mission is not to end in inglorious failure. Doubtless more help than Aeetes is willing to allow me."

"Of course." But Proteus fell silent, having said that much. At the moment he did not see how any help could be provided.

Possibly the captain had no ideas along that line either, for he made no immediate announcement of any plan. Instead he sighed, and asked: "Did you ever feel a great ambition, Proteus?"

"I don't think so, Jason. At least I can't remember having any."

"Then you are fortunate."

When they got back to the ship, Anchaeus discovered some favorable omens to tell Jason about, in an attempt to cheer him.

Meanwhile, back in the palace, Chalciope had eagerly welcomed her sons on their private visit, and hastily arranged for her sister to join them.

Medea had come with her maid, who stood by listening quietly. The younger princess said she was also eager to save her two nephews from the king's wrath, and had a question for her sister: "Are you implying, sister, that you would welcome my aid in the form of some kind of sorcery?"

Chalciope paled at the suggestion, but would not be discouraged. "I want to save my sons from our father's anger," she said simply.

The younger sister turned to the two young men.

"Tell me something, Argeus, Phrontis."

"Yes, Aunt Medea."

"When you are free again to go anywhere in the world you wish—where will you go?"

The youths looked at each other hopelessly. "That's hard to say," Phrontis replied at last. "There is much of the world that we have never seen as yet."

His brother nodded. "If Grandfather lets us go anywhere." He swallowed. "If he even lets us leave Colchis alive."

"My father is a grim old man," Medea agreed at once, surprising all her hearers. "I do love him, and I think he has some affection for me. But he can be impossible to live with. I really sympathize with anyone who tries to be his wife."

She paused there, and with a visible effort put some inner struggle behind her.

"But let us be practical. You are my nephews, and I mean to arrange matters so you will remain alive, and free to travel."

"Thank you, Aunt," said Phrontis.

"And what of our shipmates?" Argeus asked.

"Why, I will do all I can to save them, too, of course." And Medea smiled reassuringly.

Then she turned to her older sister. "To accomplish that, dear sister, I must talk with the captain of the Argonauts in secret."

Chalciope, with an arm round each of her sons, stared back at her half-sister. "That would be very dangerous!"

"It will be more dangerous, I think, if I do not."

*   *   *

The sons of Chalciope carried word to their captain of the time and place of the proposed meeting. Meanwhile, Medea equipped herself with whatever magic ointment she thought Jason would need to deal with the Bulls.

Of all the maids who served Medea, there was only one the princess truly trusted, the one who had come with her to meet the foreigners, and that young woman was called by her mistress "Mouse" because of her generally quiet and self-effacing ways.

The Mouse was, as usual, privy to all her mistress's secret preparations. The maid on learning of the contemplated project in odylic magic was not surprised. But she did appear concerned.

"Why do you hesitate, girl?" Actually the princess appeared to be a few years younger than her servant. "How long have you been with me now? Two years? You have helped me many times before in matters of this kind. Things that had to be kept secret."

Mouse nodded her dark head. "True, my lady, we have done a few such things together."

"Many times, I say."

The Mouse was obviously not going to argue.

As soon as the Mouse learned that Jason's voyage had originated in Iolcus, she was anxious to hear any news the Argonauts might have brought from there.

The princess was momentarily puzzled. "News? What on earth could it matter to you what news there is?"

The maid made a small dismissive gesture. "I—I once knew some people who lived there, my lady."

"Well, you'll be coming along with me when I go to talk to our visitors, so you can listen, I suppose." Medea's voice was preoccupied, she was intent on her own plans.

"What will you talk to them about, my lady?"

"Why, about the dangerous situation in which they find themselves. And how I can help them out of it."

"Is that all, my lady?"

"What else?"

"I'm sure I don't know, my lady."

"What else could there be? Here, these are the spells that I must work if we are to be successful." And Medea's arm shot out, thrusting toward the Mouse several pieces of parchment covered with close writing and intricately drawn diagrams.

Part of Medea's preparation for this effort was to clothe herself entirely in black.

She discussed her preparations with her maid, who catechized her on whether she had gone down the list correctly.

Carefully the maid unfolded the crumpled parchment. "It says, my lady, that you are to draw off the juice in a Caspian shell, after bathing your entire body in seven perennial streams—"

"Yes, yes. As for the 'Caspian shell,' we agreed last time on what that means; but what exactly what is a 'perennial stream?' Have you any better idea than I do, Mouse?"

"I think, mistress, it means a spring or river that runs all year long. I fear we'll have to amend that part of the preparation. I doubt there are seven perennial streams within a hundred miles of here. Visiting them all in one night will not be possible."

Medea sighed. "Well then, we must do the best we can. We might leave that detail out. Then we have: 'and calling seven times on Brimo, nurse of youth . . . night-wanderer of the Underworld, Queen of the Dead.' And so on and so forth. That should be easy enough."

"Yes, my lady."

The list went on. There were certain dark roots that had been harvested, against some such eventuality as this. The princess began to recite, as if she were quoting from some old play or story: " 'The dark earth shook and rumbled under the Titan root when it was cut' . . . ah, what an adventure that was, Mouse, gathering those roots. Remember how the earth shook, when we tore out the plant? It really did, you know."

"How could anyone forget a thing like that, my lady?"

It was no more than an hour later when Proteus and Jason received through an intermediary a secret message from the princess, telling them that a meeting had been arranged in a Temple of Hecate. The messenger described this to the visitors as a half-ruined building that had been long unused, ever since the worshipers of that dark goddess were driven away.

The temple stood hard by the arboreal cemetery. They could probably find it without being specially guided. The one who had brought the message stood ready to guide them there.

"Do you suppose this is some kind of trick?" Jason pondered.

"Aeetes won't have to bother with trickery if he decides to butcher us. We can't afford not to take chances."

When the young couple met to speak for the first time, they knew that they were not entirely alone. Each was well aware that at least one companion, considered a loyal friend, was looking on from no great distance and overhearing at least part of their talk.

Proteus, who by now had earned his leader's trust several times over, had once more been chosen by Jason to accompany him as a bodyguard.

In asking him to come along, Jason gripped him hard by arm and shoulder. "I have lost Idmon and I have lost Tiphys. Let me not lose you."

"I am here, Jason. I am likely to stay here. I hope this is not another ambush, like the one on Samothraki."

"I do not think it can be. If it is . . ." And the captain gave a fatalistic shrug.

"If it is, we'll get through it somehow." *And if tonight another*

grinning assassin should call me by name, I will make him tell me
who I am. Before I turn him inside out.

Argeus and Anchaeus also went along as additional body-
guards, at least partway.

The temple, a middle-sized old building fallen greatly into disre-
pair, was dark, and an open doorway yawned on one side of the
ground floor. Jason and Proteus as they approached could see a
round room some thirty feet in diameter, illuminated by a single
candle burning, unattended, on a stand in the center of the room.
Entering the building cautiously, the Argonauts looked up stair-
ways and into closets. All seemed innocently empty.

"I will wait in here alone," Jason decided, standing by the
table where the one light burned. "Stand guard for me outside, at
a little distance, if you will."

Proteus took up his position, and for a few minutes the night
was still around him. Then, even as he thought he heard in the distance, approaching along an unseen path, what sounded like the
soft footsteps of two women, he was suddenly distracted by the
appearance of another figure, near at hand. This was no more than
child-sized, and it approached from the direction of the palace in
almost ghostly silence.

Seen at close range, this proved to be a mere lad, looking no
more than nine or ten years old. Despite the chill night air, the
boy's pale skin was totally unclad save for a kind of rich cloak or
mantle that he wore oddly bunched up around his shoulders. In his
left hand this strange attendant was carrying a small bow, no bigger than a child's toy, while in his right fist he clutched two little
arrows.

The boy was walking straight toward Proteus and, just as the
man was about to challenge him, came to a halt in front of him.
Then he tipped him a conspirator's wink, and startled him by
addressing him in a rasping, unchildlike voice, and with a

strangely familiar manner. "Good to see you're on the job, my friend. The great ones are taking no chances."

"They seldom do," Proteus heard himself respond. He had no clue as to where that answer had come from, or just what it meant. Meanwhile he was thinking, in a kind of desperation: *Is this going to be the cave entrance on Samothraki over again? Another attempt on Jason's life?* But he dismissed that idea in a moment— no one who wanted to finish off the captain would dispatch a child armed with toy weapons to do the job.

Still, he could not keep from thinking: *Here we go again.* In his gut there was an ugly, sinking feeling that in recent days had become all too familiar—here was one more encounter with one more utter stranger who seemed more familiar with him than he was with himself.

He was about to demand some explanation from the boy, when along the same path came the princess herself, attended by the same mousy maid who had been with her in the banquet hall. Both women totally ignored the lad with his bow and arrows, as if he were some perfectly familiar attendant, and both smiled briefly at Proteus as they passed him. He caught a whiff of something strange, unpleasant, and thought it must be something that they were carrying—the maid held a little jar. He hoped that it was no one's idea of perfume. For a moment he was reminded of the smoke swirling out of the cave during the ritual of the Cabiri.

Meanwhile the boy had remained standing quietly at a little distance from Proteus, and now he spoke to Proteus again in his rasping voice. "Oh, and the great ones said to tell you: If you encounter an agent of King Pelias, kill him on sight."

Without waiting for an answer the youth walked on, following Medea and her attendant into the temple, leaving an open-mouthed Proteus to stare after him. Once the lad was inside the great room, he behaved as if he were indeed performing some kind of ritual, choosing a roughly circular path that took him clear around the waiting Jason, who totally ignored him. The boy came to a stop when he had reached a spot some fifteen feet behind Medea and her maid. The princess was facing away from him, alertly confronting the man she had come to see.

Proteus, puzzled, advanced a few steps toward the doorway and stood staring into the gently illuminated room. No figure however strange would have been very surprising back on Samothraki, as part of the Cabiri ritual. But what in the Underworld was an attendant like this boy doing *here*? He must have some connection with the magic that Medea was said to practice. Proteus decided he could only wait to see what would happen next.

What happened next came much too quickly for Proteus to do anything about it, and it completely froze the marrow in his bones. One moment the boy was simply standing there, his back against the gently curving temple wall. The next moment he had nocked one of his toy arrows to his little bow. Without a moment's pause he drew the small shaft to its full length and let it fly. Proteus, unable to lift a finger to prevent, stood watching the thin silvery streak go darting fast as thought toward the Princess Medea's unprotected back.

Bulls

roteus stared helplessly through the doorway into the interior of the temple, at a scene so close that he could see it almost perfectly, yet just out of reach. A moment ago, the small lamp near the center had shown him four faces in its circle of light—now there were only three. The boy had disappeared.

Reacting quickly to the bowshot, Proteus was on the point of leaping forward, but even before he moved he could see that there was nothing to be done. The archer had vanished simultaneously with his arrow, at the moment when it reached the body of the princess. And there stood Princess Medea, with her maid complacently beside her, not in the least troubled by young archers or little arrows, still facing Jason across the little table as their conversation got under way. To all appearances the princess was undamaged, and seemed completely unaware of any misfortune.

But an abrupt change *had* taken place. A new look had come into Medea's eyes, and the glow of some sudden emotion had inflamed her cheeks.

Proteus, on the very brink of dashing into the temple, held himself back. He would only make a fool of himself, by reacting to a mere vision, probably the lingering aftereffect of a dose of poison gas.

And during the long, frozen moment of his hesitation, he took note of the little attendant maid, still standing beside her mistress. The two were almost exactly of a height, and of similar slender build, the most notable difference being that the maid's hair was black instead of blond. What drew his attention to the maid right now was the fact that her big dark eyes were fixed on him. The girl looked nervous but was smiling at him slightly, as if she meant to be reassuring. Had she seen what he had just seen, the strange boy and the flying arrow? If not, then some high power had sent him, Proteus, a personal vision. The gods alone knew why they might do that. But if the young maid had seen the same thing . . . Proteus vowed to have a private talk with her, as soon as he could find a chance.

Between the couple who had arranged to meet, it was Jason who spoke first: "Lady, I am alone. Why are you so fearful of me? I am not a lecher, as some men are, and never was, even when I am at home in my own country."

"My lord Jason, you mistake me utterly. I am not afraid of you." And as Medea spoke she took the small glass bottle her maid had been carrying, and handed it over to him. Proteus watching from outside the doorway could see that the contents were some dark and muddy stuff. Just before handing it over, the princess with a firm pull extracted the cork. Again the fuming smell of Samothraki stung the air, stronger this time.

Now, to the observer watching from just outside, it seemed as if she were in some way confidently taking charge of the tall man.

"Pay close attention," she was telling Jason. "Your life may depend on following my plan."

Jason started to interrupt, but then appeared to think better of it, and the princess went on. "When you have met my father and he has given you what he says are teeth from a Dragon's Jaws, anoint your body with what I have just given you, using it like oil."

The captain, listening respectfully, nodded. It was as if he could not find a word to say.

The girl's voice went on, charged with strong emotion. "If you do as I say, you will survive, and pass the test my father has set for you. Then you will be able to carry away the Golden Fleece. Take it home with you, or take it anywhere you like."

As she finished her speech, Medea's hands were clenched before her, and Proteus thought she was trying to keep from throwing herself into Jason's arms. She paused briefly, then in a voice charged with emotion added: "I ask only that if you ever manage to regain your home, you will remember my name, even as I will always remember you."

Her voice broke there. Proteus, staring incredulously in through the doorway at the princess, saw that she was weeping. She seemed like a woman saying farewell to her beloved husband or brother, rather than opening a conversation with a stranger she had seen for the first time only a few hours ago.

Jason too was obviously confused by the princess's display of emotion. But he seemed much in sympathy with it. Soberly he said to Medea: "Never will I forget the offering of help that you are making now. Of help and . . ." He had to pause there. The surge of love in the young face before him was obviously genuine.

At last the captain went on. "If you come to us in Iolcus . . ." He paused again, and took a deep breath, reading to the best of his ability the message in her eyes. Then he went firmly on, with the air of a man leaping over a precipice. "There will be a bridal bed for you, which you and I will share."

. Medea's mouth opened in a soundless gasp. Jason seemed to have trouble getting control of his voice. The night around the abandoned temple was very quiet. At last he went on: "Nothing shall part us in our love till Death at his appointed hour removes us from the light of day."

What is going on here? thought Proteus to himself. *Have these two secretly known each other for years? Or have all three of us gone mad?*

Once the princess heard the Hero's pledge of marriage, her voice regained some measure of its normal tone. "So now, Jason—my friend—I will reveal to you the magic secret of the brazen Bulls.

"The secret has, strictly speaking, very little to do with magic. The truth is that the metallic things are no more dangerous than real oxen."

Jason was staring in fascination at the short girl before him. "Someone," he observed, "has told me they breathe fire." He sounded as if he dearly hoped that she was going to tell him otherwise.

Medea did not deny the point, but brushed it aside. While the glow of new love remained in her eyes, her speech was all practical business. "And so they do, in a way. So does a blacksmith's forge. But as the sparks from the forge are harmless, so are the apparent flames from the Bronze Bulls. Unless a man is foolish enough to hold his hand deliberately in them—I'm not sure what would happen then. So, too, the Bulls may knock down any human clumsy enough to stand right in their way.

"But they will *not* attack you. Because they care nothing about humans, one way or the other, nor do they care what humans may be doing near them, even right in front of them. They have no life in them, but are the lifeless engines of some ancient art."

Jason continued to watch the girl intently, as if he were still trying to guess what had made her do as she was doing.

There was a pause. Then Jason, as if waking suddenly from a kind of trance, asked: "How do you know so much about the Bulls?"

"Trust me, I do know." Medea nodded solemnly. "Perhaps as much as my father, and no one knows them better than he. Once, years ago, he put his knowledge to good use, plowing and sowing with the great bronze creatures, convincing all his subjects that he had the powers of a demigod."

"What are these Bulls?" The man put the question in a tense whisper.

And again Medea surprised her hearers: "I think the Bronze Bulls were once part of the Flying Ram, which twenty years ago brought Phrixus, who was to be the father of Phrontis and Argeus, here from over the sea. You know of the Flying Ram, of course?"

Jason was looking almost dazed. "I have seen its image in a statue."

Medea went on to explain that Phrixus had died before she was old enough to remember much about him. But in later years she had seen with her own eyes that the strange metallic things, by then called Bulls, could still be harnessed to a plow, and made to plow a field. Once when she was still a little girl, she had seen her father perform that feat, though how he had learned to do it was more than Medea could say.

"I might as well confess it to you, though the gods know what you will think of me when you hear it—some time after that, but when I was much younger than I am, I actually played with the Bulls myself! I did some of the very things the king now brags about."

Even the Mouse seemed astonished to hear that, and turned on her mistress a gaze of wonder.

Jason too was staring at the princess incredulously, and Proteus realized that he himself must be gaping in much the same way.

Medea, still focusing all her attention on Jason, went on with her explanations. She told him that it was in the nature of the Bronze Bulls that they would follow docilely enough the guidance of any human who walked between them with a hand on each.

And she had another revelation: though Aeetes had impressed his people by working parts of the trick, he himself had never sown more than one of the Dragon's Teeth at a time. Medea as a child had seen her father do so once.

"And did a warrior indeed grow from that strange seed?" Jason asked, in an almost childlike voice.

"Something grew." The memory made the young girl frown. "But it was more like a ghost than like a warrior."

That was a strange answer, and it took Jason a while to think of his next question. "And did your father duel with this apparition, and cut it down?"

The princess hesitated. "I did not see that part. I think he waited, a day or more, until the thing in the field had grown weak—but don't worry, the stuff I have given you will be a sure protection when you must fight!"

"Of course," said Jason, putting some conviction in his voice. And he looked down at the little bottle of dark stuff in his hand, now firmly recorked.

Proteus made himself look away from Medea, and shook his head to try to clear it. He was becoming more and more impressed by the Princess Medea's performance—he had the feeling of being slowly, delightfully, drawn in under a spell of true high magic. At a more practical level, he was beginning to be convinced that she might know what she was talking about regarding the handling of the Bulls.

But Jason, though he had already promised to marry the young woman in front of him, seemed not totally convinced that everything she told him was the truth. He said doubtfully: "A king may do many things that are prohibited to mere natural man, or woman."

Medea looked right back at him. "Only because he is a king? I do not think so. But a true Hero ought to be able to do more than a mere man."

Jason took thought. He said at last: "I hope you will believe, my lady, that it is not a mere lack of courage that makes me seem to hesitate. Any of my men will tell you that I have slain the Calydonian Boar—no, let me be precise, exactly truthful in my claim—I led a group of other men in killing that great beast, and so I gained whatever Heroic reputation may now be mine. But I am willing to confess to you that all the javelins I hurled at the beast may well have missed it. Still, I stood my ground when the Boar charged, and kept fighting till it was dead."

Proteus on hearing this remembered the late Meleager once telling him that when danger threatened, Jason's tendency was to stand still and endure it fatalistically—or, if it was something he could reach with a weapon in his hand, to hack away at it in the same spirit.

Mel had concluded: "In some situations such tactics are indistinguishable from great courage, and sometimes they bring victory."

You might also say, Mel had added, that Jason's real talent is in finding people who will somehow deal with difficult matters for him, or at least show him how to deal with them.

Proteus realized that he had somehow missed part of the conversation between Jason and the princess. "I believe you," Medea was saying now, her voice a lover's breath. "I believe whatever you say, and I do not care about your reputation. I know you are a Hero."

A soft footstep sounded behind Proteus, and he turned to see Haraldur, who in a whisper asked how the meeting was getting on. Proteus shrugged, and made a strong gesture enjoining silence.

Now Medea had returned to the subject of the Dragon's Teeth, and was apparently telling Jason all she could about them. Where her father the king had got them, she did not know.

Whatever Jason thought about this, he could hardly admit himself terrified to try a feat that this little girl assured him she had safely accomplished.

Of course she had stripped first, and anointed herself with the magic ointment. "That was in the days before I had my Mouse to help me," she explained, and turned her head briefly to the small maid at her side. "I'm sure my magic is much more effective now than it was then."

"I rejoice to hear it," said Jason solemnly.

When it had come time for the captain of the Argosy to bid the princess farewell—and after repeating to her his promise that included a bridal bed—the light in the temple was extinguished. Jason fell into step beside Proteus and Haraldur, and the three of them headed back toward their ship. Most of the walk passed in silence, as each man considered what had just taken place.

*   *   *

After returning to the *Argo*, Jason saw to it that everything was in readiness for a quick departure. He meant to do his utmost in the morning, but after their disastrous interview with the king, it seemed quite likely that desperate flight would soon become their only option. And then he urged his men to try to get some rest.

Assembling his entire crew, he told them all that he had been given hope by the princess, but he did not spell out the details of her pledge or his promise of marriage. He concluded his short speech with a warning that they must not interfere with the trial even if things should appear to be going against him.

There was much restlessness that night aboard the *Argo*, and in the small camp on the adjoining narrow ridge of dry land. All thoughts were on Jason, and the test that their captain must undergo, beginning early in the morning. Many people wanted to offer him advice on magic or on demons, and a few actually did so. Others kept urging him to get some sleep, and in the end he did manage a few hours.

The sentries posted near prow and stern of the moored ship were continually nervous, and there were several false alarms.

Proteus was restless. Unable to sleep, he moved back and forth along the offshore outrigger for a while, stepping over the outflung limbs of sleeping shipmates, working his fishing lines, not quite as effectively as usual. But his thoughts were not on fish.

Wherever he looked, whatever he tried to do, a certain flash of memory kept getting in the way. Not the same old one. The face and words of the assassin on Samothraki had been supplanted by that terrible, heart-stopping moment when the peculiar boy had loosed his silver arrow at Medea's unprotected back. The dart could not possibly have missed her. There was nowhere else it could have gone but in between her silk-clad ribs. And the princess had totally ignored what ought to have been a mortal skewering. She had simply gone on talking to Jason; but from that moment, a great love for the man in front of her had shone as clear as lamplight in her face, and sounded in her voice.

And in the very instant when the small flying arrow disappeared, the figure of the archer had also vanished. There was no reason to think that any of the other people on the scene had ever been aware of the lad's presence.

Was it possible that he, Proteus, had only seen a vision, some aftereffect of the drugged smoke inhaled days ago? But he could not convince himself of that. So the little archer and his bow were more than natural, and more than merely a vision.

That drastically narrowed down the possibilities.

What ancient Boy was it who shot Arrows that did not kill, that wounded in only the strangest and most subtle way, inflicting only the most delightful pain? Proteus knew the inescapable answer—everyone did—but he did not want to think about it.

He had no choice, though. This time he had been recognized by a god, by the Lord Eros himself, known to some as Cupid, who had come on the scene to help Jason by causing the Princess Medea to fall in love with him. And in passing Cupid had recognized an old acquaintance, and stopped to chat with Proteus.

Good to see you're on the job, my friend. The great ones are taking no chances. Then, as if the god and the dingy assassin were working for the same cause, the Boy had made a point of passing on to him the latest command of the great ones—any secret agent of King Pelias should be killed on sight. But apparently, and luckily for Proteus, Eros had failed to understand that Proteus *was* the very secret agent whose death was to be accomplished.

Maybe, Proteus thought helplessly, he had lost more than his memory when the seagoing Giant wrecked and sank that ship. Maybe he was going crazy. Such an assumption would simplify matters enormously. But he had a feeling that the real explanation was going to turn out to be something even worse.

When at last he lay down and tried to rest, his sleep was fitful and troubled by strange dreams.

*   *   *

Most of the Argonauts were stirring before dawn on the morning of the trial, and soon every man was up. Each member of Jason's crew did his best to fortify himself for a hard day, some with rituals of prayer and token sacrifice, others simply with breakfast. The morning's fish catch, taken by Proteus whose luck at the game still held, was large enough to be considered a good omen, a pair of sturgeon or pike big enough to feed a crew of forty, along with a round of fried cakes left over from the night before.

Proteus beheaded and gutted his catch with swift, sure movements of his new steel knife—another gift from King Phineas. Yes, he was a good fisherman, skilled and lucky too, as old Phineas had thought. Careless of whether or not anyone was looking, he hungrily devoured a few bites of the raw, freshwater fish, earning himself some queasy looks from some of his more finicky shipmates.

The *Argo* and her crew had hardly begun their passage across the river, in misty morning light, when they caught sight of the king and his party, in several boats, performing the same crossing several hundred yards upstream. No salutations were exchanged.

Crouching beneath the raised deck to be out of sight of the Colchians while his shipmates rowed, Jason smeared himself all over with the ointment given him by Medea. Then he applied the same treatment to the head of the spear that he was carrying. The bad smell seemed to quickly evaporate once the stuff was put to use, and it became almost invisible as well.

As he did this he talked nervously to Proteus, telling him he had waited until now to use the stuff because he wanted it to be as fresh as possible when he put it to the test.

Plowing

ulling sturdily at their oars, the *Argo*'s crew grounded their ship lightly not far from the royal vessel, on the riverbank near the broad meadow where the trial was to be. Visible a few hundred yards farther inland were the treetops of the towering grove where the Fleece was said to lie spread out on branches.

This time Jason carried a spear with him as he went ashore, because he had been told it would be needed in the trial. He had cautioned his men to bear their weapons with them as usual.

An officer of the king was waiting for him, and handed him a warrior's helmet, fashioned of bronze in an antique style. The helmet was inverted to make a bowl and Proteus, standing near, could see that the bowl was half full of what appeared to be sharp teeth.

The officer's tone was cool and punctiliously correct. "These are the Teeth of the Dragon, sir. The king has told you what you must do with them."

The captain nodded. "He has." Proteus was relieved to see that Jason looked calm and capable, ready to play the part of a captain of Heroes.

The Argonauts had all disembarked, following their leader. Two men had been assigned to keep a close guard on the ship. All the others arrayed themselves a few paces inland, with *Argo* riding at anchor close at their backs, and the field of the trial in front of them. This piece of land was lying fallow, and had the look of having done so for many years. But on close inspection it was possible to see the old, shallow ridges and furrows indicating that it had once been plowed.

Proteus had the feeling that this morning none of his shipmates really envied him the distinction of being chosen as the captain's close attendant. Now Jason passed on to him the helmet, doubly weighty with its cargo.

Proteus had heard no prohibition against touching the helmet's contents, so when Jason had turned away again he picked one of the supposed Dragon's Teeth out of its antique container and looked at it closely; and again he experienced a maddening moment of half-recognition. The object reminded him that there was *something* he ought to remember, in connection with things like this. Some association he ought to be able to make . . .

So strong was the feeling that he came near calling out to everyone that these teeth had nothing to do with dragons. In fact he was almost certain that they were really not teeth at all.

Proteus sifted a handful of the hard little objects through his fingers. They seemed about the right size to be useful in the mouth of a large animal, and almost the right shape, at least for a planteater. But he did not think that they had ever grown in any living jaws. Choosing one at random, he took a moment to study it intently. Mottled gray in color, beveled almost to a chisel edge on one end, and doubly pointed at the other, suggesting the roots of human teeth.

About fifty yards from where the *Argo* had nosed ashore, and the same distance inland, the king's attendants had been busy erecting a royal pavilion, a top and three walls of painted canvas, a sturdy tent that had doubtless seen its share of military campaigns. Aeetes, after keeping everyone waiting for another quarter of an hour, emerged from this shelter to make his official appearance on the scene. Several of his boats had carried across the river a full complement of attendants, and about a hundred heavily armed soldiers, a formidable bodyguard.

Meanwhile Proteus, scanning the field before him, its long grass silver-gray with morning dew, could see nothing of any cattle, either bronze or fleshly, and it crossed his mind to wonder if the whole challenge might be no more than some monstrous jest.

The Prince Apsyrtus was in attendance also, chatting with several military officers. And yes, there were the king's daughters, dressed in different finery than they had worn last night. Evidently Aeetes wanted everyone to witness the ignominious failure that the adventurer was going to meet, one way or another.

The king was gorgeously arrayed this morning, and looked confident, well satisfied with himself and with his plans. Aeetes called an expansive greeting to the assembled Argonauts, and then with fists on hips, planted himself in front of Jason. "And are you ready to meet the Bulls?"

"I am as ready, sir, as I will ever be."

"I take that to mean we should proceed. Sir, the field is ready, and so are your tools. Go to it."

Jason took a step or two into the field, and stood looking round him uncertainly. Still there were no Bulls in sight. The plow stood ready in the field, quite an ordinary-looking implement, fairly new and solidly constructed. A few yards from it lay the yoke, a heavy beam almost as long as a man's height, with curves carved smoothly into one side where it must be made to fit over the necks of the strange team.

Aeetes made a gesture to an aide, and that man did something that Proteus could not quite see.

Some fifty yards away, out near the center of the empty field, there came a stirring of the grass on the near flank of a low mound, over as wide an area as a man might span with his two arms. As the foreigners and most of the natives stared in wonder, a section of sod just that wide ripped open and peeled back, without apparent cause. Meanwhile, a door-sized aperture also yawned in some hard surface just beneath.

Proteus could hear the sound of the sod tearing, like the ripping of some heavy cloth, and then a muffled rattling noise, not quite like anything he had ever heard before.

"The Bulls," murmured one of the Argonauts standing a little

behind Proteus, who had advanced a few steps in his capacity as
authorized squire or attendant.

But of course, Proteus reminded himself, *they are not really
bulls*. Medea in her secret instructions had insisted steadily on
that point several times, but somehow he, and perhaps Jason, had
not really grasped the fact until now. In the mind of Proteus matters became a little clearer than before.

At a glance he was certain that the two dark, bulking shapes
were not even of flesh and blood. They were a couple of—of
objects, things, that were alive only in the sense that a ship might
be said to have life, or the wind. Now the pair of them, moving
bull-like forelegs, had climbed clear of the opening in the mound
and were standing, side by side, where everyone could see them.
From time to time there was a small orange flare, as if the creatures were really breathing flames of fire. None of the Argonauts
actually turned and ran, but Proteus could feel the impulse surge
through the ranks. He was not totally immune to it himself.

At the first puff of visible flame, a little murmur of alarm went
up among the onlookers. But the Argonauts retained their compo-
sure; Jason had told Proteus to once more pass the reassuring
word that the captain had reason to believe he would be able to
deal with whatever might happen today.

Now the two beasts that were not really beasts came moving
forward side by side, leaving behind them the opening in the shallow hillside. Proteus was strongly reminded of something that he
could not quite place, or fully visualize—it lay there in the ruins
of memory, as did so many other things, just eluding his grasp
every time he tried to pick it up.

The more he looked at the two creatures before him, the more
certain he was that no blood flowed in their veins. To begin with,
they were only calf-sized, not built on the scale of full-grown cattle. Their horns were stubby, little more than symbols, possibly
projections designed for some other purpose entirely. (And it

struck him also that the end of each horn had a broken look, suggesting that something had been attached above it. Here and there on the upper surface of each Bull were small, shiny, irregular spots, suggesting the stumps of broken metal branches.

And when these creatures moved, they did not change position casually or randomly, in the manner of normal animals or people. Instead, the Bulls either stood stock still or acted with seeming purpose, as they were doing now, when they moved a little apart from each other and turned their heads in the direction of the thin crowd who gaped at them from the field's edge. Proteus knew he had—somewhere, sometime—seen well-drilled soldiers act in such a way.

Somehow the idea that the two things that the king called Bulls might actually be demons had not occurred to Proteus as a serious possibility. And it had been obvious at a glance that they were not human beings, much less gods.

Coolly and thoughtfully Proteus surveyed them, wondering how he himself might try to do battle against such objects if he were forced to attempt it. They looked very strong, but still he thought there were some grounds for optimism.

Their unblinking eyes as blank as glass. They had no mouths that Proteus could see, and the weight of each rested upon two skillfully jointed, mechanical-looking legs in front, and two wheels in the rear, where a normal animal's hind legs would be. At first glance the creatures, or devices, gave an almost comical suggestion of beasts with their front legs on the ground, sitting in the very carts they were supposed to pull. And Medea had said at the secret meeting that they were components of the mysterious Flying Ram.

And now Jason, looking woodenly calm as he was wont to do in moments of desperation, had turned to him, was making a small gesture, wanting to make sure that when it came time to use the helmet half-full of the small, strange objects that were not teeth, Proteus would be ready to hand it over.

Now he muttered sharp oaths to himself. He had seen *something* of the kind before, but he was damned if he could say where, or when, or what . . . groaning with the futile effort of trying to reestablish some kind of connection with his unknown self, he dropped the pebble-like thing back into the helmet. There was someone who would be very glad to see a thing like this—someone, but who? Not the still-nameless woman whose orders had caused him to be here. But someone connected with her . . . He had now come that far, groping into the past.

The urge to know who he was, to try to establish what his life was supposed to be about, swept over him again. It was maddening, like an itch that could not be scratched or even precisely located. Like an itch, it was worse at some times than at others, but it never entirely went away. How could he accomplish anything else until he had freed himself of this nagging urge? And yes, what he really ought to do was bring this mysterious object, this fake tooth, to . . . to someone who would dearly want to see it . . . *someone*, but *who*—?

Jason was now as ready for his trial as he was ever going to be. In the next moment, before anyone could begin to question his courage, he sprang into action, charging directly toward the silent, waiting bulks of bronze. It was, thought Proteus, as if he were determined not to allow himself time to think.

Despite all orders to stay clear, Proteus took a tight grip on his borrowed spear and stood ready to jump forward and do what he could to rescue Jason if that proved necessary.

Fortunately the leader, once he had committed himself to action, lived up to his reputation as a Hero and stood in no need of help. He seemed to have decided he was going to treat his strange opponents as if they were the domestic animals they could not be.

Shooting out an arm, Jason grabbed the bull on his right side by the tip of its left horn, and gave a tremendous yank that got the creature moving toward him. A moment later, he brought it down on its knees with a sudden kick on one of its bronze feet. Meanwhile, the other Bull made a lurching, sideways movement toward the man, and was brought down in the same way with a single kick.

Now Jason took a solid stance, feet planted wide apart, and though the flame-like flaring of light at once enveloped him, he stood his ground unburned, and, still clutching one animal's horn in either hand, held them both down on their fore-knees where they fell.

Proteus had already handed the helmet on to Polydeuces, who was standing near. There was a long thong attached to the helmet, and by this Jason slung it around his neck. Now he picked up the heavy, massive wooden yoke and started to move it into position.

In tribute to this auspicious beginning, a murmur of relief and hope went up from the Argonauts. Proteus could see Medea, her whole life in her silent gaze as she watched the contest. At her side, the silent little servant called the Mouse again turned the gaze of her great, dark eyes to Proteus, as if for some reason she found him almost as interesting as the Hero in his struggle.

Meanwhile, Apsyrtus had his full attention fixed on Jason and the Bulls, as if the prince found this a more fascinating show than he had ever seen before.

Now Jason had gripped the wooden yoke, and was managing to fit it tightly over first one Bull's neck and then the other. In the next moment he had lifted the sturdy wooden pole between them and fastened it to the yoke by its pointed end. Now he grasped his spear and pricked both bulls on their flanks, in rapid succession. Then he slung the spear on his back again, and seized both handles of the plow in a firm grip.

When the spear-point stabbed against one of the creatures' sides, it made a sound as if Jason were tapping an iron shield. But it got his strange team moving. The iron plowshare began to cut the sod and turn the soil.

Scooping his hand into the helmet and bringing out clusters of pointed little objects, he cast them far from himself with many a backward glance lest a deadly crop of earthborn men should catch him unawares.

The bulls, thrusting their bronze hoofs into the earth, toiled on, and Jason kept pace with them.

Steadily the sun climbed in the sky. Hours passed while it turned through the zenith and began to sink. Hour after hour, Jason walked without pausing, plowing a long, straight furrow, guiding the Bulls through a sharp turn, and plowing back again across the field. Despite the duration of the struggle, few of the onlookers let their attention lapse for any reason. And those who did were soon drawn back irresistibly to watch.

The plowing was a lurching and uneven business, and Proteus suspected an experienced plowman driving a normal team could have finished the job sooner.

A murmur of amazement went up among the watching Argonauts, and every man among them gripped his weapons. Proteus saw to his amazement that the strange crop had indeed begun to grow.

It did not really consist of earthborn men, he could feel sure of that now. What was coming out of the earth and shooting up like corn were rows of objects that looked like miniature, dusty whirlwinds. The rows were as straight as those of planted corn, and they covered all parts of the field that Jason had already plowed.

Under his incredulous stare the things took shape and seemed to prosper, row after row of them emerging steadily from under the soil, growing as tall as men—but what were they?

Proteus had the sensation that the hair on the back of his neck was trying to stand up. For a moment he saw that first eruption from the ground as a tiny spout of clear water, the emergence of a spring. But there was no splash and flow of liquid. And as the odd little spout mounted swiftly to the size of a man, it lost its near resemblance to a fountain, taking on more the aspect of a cloud, or rather of some object spinning so fast that the details of its surface were no more than a gray blur. Now he understood a little better Medea's difficulty in describing her childhood view of a similar planting.

Some Argonauts were later to swear solemnly that in a matter of only a few minutes, the field in the wake of Jason's plow had bristled with stout shields, double-pointed spears, and glittering helmets—Proteus was willing to agree that there were shapes that might have been mistaken for such things.

The sight of the grotesque things suddenly triggered shadowy memories. Acting on impulse, Proteus snatched up a fist-sized rock that had been turned up by the plow, and handed it to Jason, meanwhile telling him in a fierce whisper: "Throw this among them! Hard as you can!"

Jason did not argue, but spun round and let fly with his strong arm, as hard as he could, so that the missile went bouncing far away along an irregular row of the earthborn things. An instant later, Proteus had crouched down behind the plow, pulling Jason down with him.

It was almost as if he had hurled a stone into a hornet's nest. Each impact along the row triggered a violent reaction. Each of the earthborn men, if that was what they were, struck out at his neighbors in some fashion. No actual weapons could be distinguished, not by mere human eyes at least, but the impression of combat was unmistakable. With explosive speed, the struggle spread from row to row, all across the field. First one by one, then in squads and detachments, the creatures fell back into their mother earth, as if a grove of small trees had been flattened by a gale. Jason had to do no more but crouch down with Proteus, while the creatures of the dark soil mowed each other down with amazing rapidity.

In less than a minute, the field was as barren as it had ever been.

When the time came, later, for creating legends, some Argonauts and some of the king's supporters too—none of them with quite as good a view of the field as Proteus enjoyed—were to swear that in the plowed field on that day they had seen armed men slaughtering each other; and there would also be testimony to rivulets of blood, running in the newly-plowed furrows. But Proteus, watching coolly and carefully on the day when it all happened, saw no bodies and no blood, but only a swirling and scattering of grayness, a vague, blurred wreckage that melted back into the earth even faster than it had sprouted out.

Proteus was not the only Argonaut whose eyes and mind saw clearly. One man behind him muttered: "Whatever those things were, they were not fighting men. And this king has built his warrior's reputation on knocking down such scarecrows?"

"Myself, I'd rather face some man with a sword," his fellow muttered.

Whatever the true nature of the peculiar crop, there was no doubt that the harvest was complete. The field was still again, and quiet, and whatever had been summoned up out of the earth had now gone back to it again. And it was time for the audience to leave.

Proteus's last sight of the two Bulls showed them standing motionless, a pair of bronze statues at one side of the broad field.

The king, without acknowledging in any way the upstart's victory, had turned his back on the scene even before the last of the strange creatures had been destroyed. His aides and his family hastened to follow Aeetes as he stalked away. Apsyrtus lingered a moment, surveying the scene thoughtfully, before he went.

Medea and her sister naturally followed their father and brother. Proteus thought that both women were looking deathly pale.

Proteus was just about to board the *Argo* again when the young maid who had been attending Princess Medea came hurrying up to him.

"My mistress wishes to see you."

This time, when she was near and looking directly at him, the maid gave Proteus an impression of wiry energy. He also immediately got the idea that for some reason she was seriously afraid of him, though she was trying to conceal the fact.

"You mean she wants to see Jason," Proteus told her. "Or is it that she wants me too?"

The young woman shook her head. "I mean what I said. Not Jason, not right now. You are the only one called Proteus, aren't you? It's you she wants."

"All right. Yes, I am the only Proteus among the Argonauts. What's your name, girl? Did I hear the princess call you 'Mouse'?"

"You did."

He was intrigued. "Is that your real name?"

"I answer to it quick enough."

"Have you a liking for it?"

"I like my mistress well enough, who gave it to me."

Proteus was on the brink of asking whether she had seen Cupid and his Arrow, but quickly decided he had better let that question wait. Hastily he told Jason what was going on, and said he would rejoin the captain and his crew as soon as possible.

When the messenger had conducted him to where the princess was waiting alone, Medea said: "We can speak freely in front of the Mouse, here. I would trust her with my life."

Looking into Medea's eyes, Proteus could not fail to see that the glow brought to her eyes by Cupid's Arrow still persisted.

Softly and eagerly she said: "Good Proteus, I am so glad you came to talk with me."

"It is my pleasure, princess."

"You are Jason's friend, are you not? His good, reliable friend?"

"I trust I am." And from the corner of his eye he noted that the Mouse was standing back a little, looking as if she seriously disapproved of this line of talk, perhaps of this whole meeting.

But to Medea it was obviously very important. "You are ready to stand by him, to risk your life to protect his?"

"Princess, I will take that risk for any of my shipmates." He could go as far as that and still tell the perfect truth.

But the princess was staring at him in such a way that he realized she had hardly heard his answer; she had already assigned him a role to play, and needed no confirmation. Now her tone was almost envious or jealous. "Have you known the Lord Jason for many years?"

"I'm afraid not, my lady. Only for a few months."

Still she was not really listening. She had her own idea of who he must be, and how he must serve Jason. "He seems to speak to you, to rely on you, more than on any of the others."

"I don't think any of us in the crew are really his old friends, my princess." Meleager would probably have been able to make some such claim, but none of the other Argonauts. Struck by an odd thought, Proteus added: "Somehow I doubt that our captain has any old friends."

That answer caught Medea's full attention, and she reacted with shocked surprise. "Oh, how can you say that? I'm sure you're wrong!"

"I have been many times wrong before, my lady." He did not want to waste this opportunity. "My lady, I have a question for you."

She was surprised again, but not unwilling to accommodate him. "Ask it."

"Now that Jason has done what the king demanded of him, what is going to happen?"

The princess had her answer ready at once.

"My father will be angry, of course—even angrier than he is already. But I think he will take no action immediately. He likes to think things all the way through before he moves, when that is at all possible. He will move cautiously when he moves."

"I understand you, Princess. So, we have a little time in which to get away, before your father takes action, as you put it. As soon as we can get the Fleece into our hands, we must leave directly. I fear that you will have put yourself into great danger by giving us your help."

"You are right about the danger, of course. So you must leave as soon as possible, even if you are unable to get the Fleece."

He was shaking his head. "No, my lady, we will not do that. Jason will insist on having the Fleece, because he still believes that if he brings it home, he can trade it for the throne of Iolcus. And even if Jason were willing to leave without his treasure, I think the crew might desert him if he did, having come this far and gone through all that we have endured."

"They wouldn't do that!"

"Forgive my directness, lady, but they would. They would consider him a false Hero, not worth following. And Jason absolutely needs the Fleece. Or he's convinced he does, which comes to the same thing. He believes it means a throne to him. Whether that is true or not—" Proteus shrugged. "But if he goes home without it, he will certainly have no kingdom. Whatever supporters he might have at home will desert him . . ."

"Not you, Proteus! Tell me you will never fail Prince Jason." And Medea reached out to grip his arm.

It was the first time Proteus had ever heard his leader awarded that title. It seemed to him misplaced, but he was not going to dispute with a princess over her choice of words. Now he admitted: "To serve him seems to be the only goal I have in life, my lady."

That answer pleased the princess very much indeed. "You do swear by all the gods you most hold sacred?"

"If it pleases you, I will."

"Thank you! Thank you, kind friend! I am so glad to hear that! Let it be always so."

And Proteus bowed silently.

Fleece

In the light of a glorious sunset the Argonauts recrossed the river in their ship, and put in very near their old landing place, about a mile downstream from the city and the palace. This time there was no question of trying to conceal their presence, and no one bothered to push *Argo*'s prow so deeply into the marsh.

The keeper of the ship's log, Anchaeus, careless now of whether Colchians might be watching him or not, lighted a lamp on deck, and tried to decide on the right words to set down a short description of the amazing events of the day just past.

He also noted that it was an apparent advantage of the cold weather that there were fewer mosquitoes in the swamp than might otherwise have been expected. But of Jason's triumphant success in his struggle with the Bronze Bulls Anchaeus wrote very little, and that in cautious words; and he set down nothing that he might have known of any secret understanding that might have come to exist between the captain and the princess. Jason had reminded him that it was not impossible that some enemy would soon be reading the log.

The last of the sunset had long faded from the sky, and the time was near midnight, when the Mouse came to where the princess waited in her room alone.

When the servant was slow to begin, Medea prodded her. "Have you seen the king?"

The maid looked over her shoulder before answering, and her voice trembled slightly. "Yes, mistress, and never in the years since I came into your service have I seen my lord the king so angry."

"Who are you to judge my father's angers?" But Medea herself realized that was a foolish question, and she did not pursue it. "What was he doing?"

"Only talking, my lady princess. To the prince, and to the other men who counsel him. But it was the look on his face . . ." Mouse shook her head.

Medea briefly closed her eyes. "I can well imagine. Go on."

The maid went on to describe how the king and Apsyrtus had summoned her for questioning in the royal council chamber. But when she was brought to them, they were not ready to hear her yet. She had been carelessly told to wait in an anteroom; and while waiting there she had been able to look out through a doorway and see the king and the prince, and overhear much of what they were saying to each other, and to the king's other advisers who were in attendance.

Not only had the maid overheard the talk, but she had made some shrewd judgments about the speakers. Aeetes was enraged by Jason's success, but at the same time impressed by the physical power and skill shown by the leader of the Argonauts. He had demonstrated more courage than Aeetes would have given him credit for, it seemed well within the realm of possibility that the foreigner might have had effective magical assistance. All these things made the king wary, but it was really the continued alertness displayed by the Argonauts that had kept him from impulsively taking any action against the visitors.

The maid also told how Apsyrtus had argued with his father that it was hard to see how the foreigner could have done what he had done without some kind of help from within the king's inner circle.

The prince had asked: "How many, Father, know the full secret of the Bulls? How many besides yourself?"

Apsyrtus as the heir had been fully informed of such matters. But Aeetes did not see how there could be anyone else. Certainly

Phrontis and Argeus, who had left the realm as children, must be innocent of any such secret knowledge.

The Mouse hesitated before she added: "My lady, I think your father at first suspected your brother of some treachery."

Medea's red lips formed a round O. "Are you mad? That could never be. My father trusts Apsyrtus as he trusts no one else in the whole world."

"Then perhaps I am mad indeed, my lady. I can only tell you how it seemed to me."

"But what about my elder sister, whose sons are most in danger? And what about me? Did suspicion rest on either of us?"

"I would say, my lady, that neither the king nor Prince Apsyrtus seemed to consider either of you a real possibility."

Medea sighed with relief. Then she said, as if looking into some awful distance: "I think the king has a hard time imagining that any blood relative would really turn against him. Or that any might have reason to do so. That is why he is so angry with his grandsons." Her gaze came back to within the room. "Or that any woman might find it in her to be so bold and active. Truly he would deem it quite unnatural if she were."

Her servant thought about it. "My lady, the king mentioned the Princess Chalciope only once. That was when he said to his advisers that she would certainly be trying somehow to save her two sons from his wrath. I think he meant that your illustrious sister would come to plead with him, and of course she is going to do so."

"And he had nothing at all to say about little Medea?" And she touched her own breast with a forefinger.

"I heard nothing, beneficent lady."

Again the princess allowed herself a sigh. "Father has, I hope, no reason to suspect that I have ever bothered my head about such matters . . . I was only a little girl the last time he put his bronze toys through their paces."

* * *

Even as the maid reported to her mistress, the meeting in the council chamber was still going on, into the early morning hours.

The king and his advisers had to consider soberly that there were almost forty of the foreigners, a not inconsiderable number, all of them well armed, and good fighters if appearances and reputations meant anything in such matters.

Prince Apsyrtus said: "And also they are very much alert, tending to post guards, stay together, and keep their weapons handy. It would not be a simple matter to wipe them out. Hardly the kind of thing that could be accomplished quietly and unobtrusively."

One of the officers of the royal guard suggested: "Your Majesty might invite them all to a banquet, get them to lay aside their arms . . . but I doubt they would fall for any such trick now."

After the first three words, Apsyrtus had begun shaking his head. "*I* certainly wouldn't, in their place. Not after the way you have already spoken to them, Father. An invitation would only put them more on their guard, or send them fleeing—the usefulness of such treachery is overrated."

Aeetes shook his head. "They will be very reluctant to leave Colchis without the Fleece. And that, as we know, is too well guarded for them to simply snatch it up." He grumbled something more. Any way he tried to calculate it, trying to wipe out the Argonauts quickly, with only the relatively small number of troops he had handy in the palace, actually no more than a hundred, would most likely result in a prolonged pitched battle.

"And some inconvenient losses on our side," his son concluded. "Sir, to get the job done swiftly will mean using overwhelming force. I think you will have to summon reinforcements. Four hundred men would not be too many. Even so, we will have casualties. Of course that's not necessarily bad; I think our home guard could use a little real practice."

The king agreed with what Apsyrtus told him. Everyone knew that the king trusted his only son, at least more than he trusted anyone else.

Prudently the king and prince dispatched messengers, beginning the process of gathering the necessary force. To do so properly would require at least two days. It was Apsyrtus who suggested calling for warships; it was not impossible that the Argonauts would suddenly decide to run away, even without the Fleece they said they had come for.

"Should we set a close watch on their ship?" asked an officer.

"No, don't bother." The king smiled faintly. "It will be interesting to see just what they do, if they think they have their freedom. But send fast messengers, and while today's sun is bright, use the heliograph as far as possible. Order all my distant forces to be on the lookout for the *Argo*, and stop her if she should suddenly depart."

Meanwhile, Medea, still alone with her maid in the gray hour before cockcrow (she was much too excited to think of sleep), confided to the Mouse that her plans went far beyond simply aiding the foreigners. Whether her father suspected her yet or not was actually not of the first importance. "He will probably get around to doing so sooner or later."

"So what will you do, my lady?" As she spoke, the Mouse was busy about some trivial household chore.

Medea was standing looking out her bedroom window, which was half covered by a screen of stonework, at the dark void of the sky. "I will take control of my own life, so it no longer belongs to the king to do with as he wills. I mean to get away from here— clean away."

"In the ship of the foreigners?" The Mouse's voice was a frightened squeak.

The princess nodded. "And you are coming with me."

"My lady!"

"Of course you are. Don't be dull, Mouse. And don't be rebellious. If you don't come with me, and I am caught, I will see that you are implicated, and however bad the result may be for me, it will be worse for you."

"But *why?*"

"Why do I want to leave home, when I have such a delightful future before me if I stay?" The princess's tone grew mocking. "If I stay, I will probably soon be a queen somewhere—that is, I'll be the wife of one of two or three old men with whom my father would like to establish some alliance. Of course none of them are really *that* old, I might have thirty or forty years of humoring them into their senility." And her voice changed again, became fierce as she grabbed Mouse by her wrist. "This is the first real chance that I have ever had to get away, and it will probably be the last. I am not going to let it slip by."

Again she asked Mouse: "Are you sure that Father does not really suspect me?"

The maid gave her a helpless look. "I don't know what is in your father's heart, my lady. All I can tell you is what I heard him say. And he only asked me one or two questions, about what I might have heard the foreigners saying. Of course I had little enough to tell him about that. And he had no idea that you had met with the Lord Jason privately."

"That is good," said Medea, and for a moment she seemed lost in dreams.

Mouse cleared her throat. "It seems to me, my lady, that we now face serious practical problems. How will the Lord Jason, how will anyone, be able to get the Fleece, guarded as it is?"

That brought her mistress back to business. "I mean to see to that. And you of course are going to help me."

"I fear the Bronze Bulls were as nothing, my lady, compared to the one who guards the Fleece."

"I know that, Mouse. So Jason will now need a magic ointment that is much different, much stronger than the stuff I gave him to control the Bulls. So powerful that you will not dare to dip your finger in it—unless I show you how." And the lady demonstrated with her own small, white fingers the very action she had warned against.

"Of course, my lady."

"Do you know," the princess now remarked, seemingly diverted for a moment by a pleasant memory, "I think that ointment to protect against the Bronze Bulls really worked?"

"Of course, my lady. It seems obvious that your magic ointment was really very effective."

"Oh, Mouse! How wonderful!"

"Yes, my lady."

"And all my plans aside, I am truly in love with him—gloriously, marvelously in love! It happens in the stories, but I never thought that it would really . . ."

"I understand, my lady."

Medea talked about how suddenly her overwhelming love for Jason had come over her. Her heart was bursting with it, so she had to talk to someone, and she could trust no one but the Mouse—and, to a lesser extent, her sister Chalciope.

She could not begin to understand why, but she loved the strange dark foreign captain so terribly. She feared to do anything that would cause him to doubt her, or think less of her in any way.

Mouse was blinking at her. "So, my lady. So maybe this time you will also be successful in finding some effective protection against the one who guards the Fleece!"

That sobered Medea in an instant, and once more brought her back to business. For a little while she had actually forgotten about that guardian. "We must pray to all the gods that what I do will be effective. It must be!"

If Mouse had understood and reported the council's deliberations accurately, and the princess had no reason to doubt she had, a day or two must pass before the king moved forcefully against the

Argonauts. So at the first hint of daylight, beginning a day of expected peace and tranquility, princess and maid took to their beds to rest. Medea slept much of the time, or tried to sleep, and dreamt of her strong lover who was going to carry her away.

Around midafternoon, Medea took care to appear for an hour or two in the palace, and to act as if nothing very remarkable were on her mind. Then bringing the Mouse with her, Medea withdrew to the privacy to her own room, where the two young women began their most secret preparations.

What had worked against the Bulls was mere milk and honey compared to what was needed now.

"Once Jason has the Fleece in hand, he had better not delay his departure from Colchis by the space of a single heartbeat."

"That is very true, my lady."

"But the trouble is, if he departs from these shores without me, he is never coming back, and I will never see him again."

"That may well be so."

"You know that it is so. And I know that my heart will break, my life will be nothing without him; nothing! Have you ever loved anyone, Mouse?"

"My lady, I—"

But the lady had not really expected any answer, and pressed on without stopping to hear one. "I had thought that I knew what it meant to love, but now I realize that I had no conception of the thing at all. I will die, Mouse, if I am separated from Jason." And it seemed that the princess believed that it was so. "Therefore I must go with him."

The thought ran through Medea's mind that when a girl in one of the romantic stories ran away from home, she almost invariably left behind on her pillow a lock of her hair and a note, usually tear-stained, for her mother to find, saying only that she was going far away. But Medea's mother was long dead, and the king's current consort would not be much interested. If she left a note for anyone it would be Chalciope. Anyway, any such storybook gesture would be foolishness—some spy or snoop would be likely to discover the message before she could get to a safe distance.

Keeping all preparations to a very minimum, Medea went out to meet the Argonauts, taking with her as attendant only the faithful Mouse.

Neither of the young women carried with her anything but the clothes she was wearing—which in the case of the maid amounted to little more than a simple shift, and a woolen cape against the chill of the night air. Meanwhile the princess had on sandals and a couple of additional light garments, with a fine, soft, dark mantle over all.

Getting out of the palace unobserved was a trick that they had worked more than once before; they had learned it did not hurt to have the aid of a muttered spell or two, an invocation of Hecate.

They came to some doors that opened simply for them, in the ordinary way. One was held fast by a large, clumsy lock, that Mouse knew well how to pick, having picked it several times before, in the course of earlier adventures. Others, in apparent obedience to Medea's swiftly chanted incantations, swung open of their own accord. The princess ran in soft sandals down narrow alleys, holding her mantle over her forehead with one hand to hide her face, and with the other lifting up the hem of her skirt.

And the maid ran ahead, darting silently on small unshod feet, less worried about disclosing her own identity.

They passed under the trees where Medea had sometimes come to climb—or more often, to send her young maid climbing—in secret search of corpses, whose parts she needed for the most powerful spells and ointments. From there on they could only guess their way.

Guardian

*P*hrontis happened to be the one standing guard, some yards inland from the ship, when he heard the two young voices softly calling. He called to his brother who was nearby, and the two young Colchians agreed that they were hearing the voices of their young Aunt Medea and her maid.

Jason, summoned at once, also recognized the voice of the princess. He sent Argeus hurrying to alert the other men, and soon all were awake and listening, practically speechless with astonishment.

The men marveled. "The *princess* has come to us? The young one? Are you crazy?"

"That may be," said Jason. "But I, too, know her voice." And he lit a torch at their small cooking fire and led the way toward the visitors.

When presently the two young women were guided in among the wondering men, Mouse gave Proteus a glance that he interpreted as asking for his approval. Not knowing what to make of this, he replied with a slight smile and nod. The maid seemed reassured.

Medea meanwhile went straight to stand in front of Jason, and raised her voice, as if to make sure that all the men could hear her.

"It seems that my father has discovered everything, and I am doomed if I stay here."

The Argonauts were all silent, wondering. And as soon as those words fell from Medea's lips, her maid looked at her for a long moment, in silent astonishment—that soon enough turned into genuine fear. *I think the princess is lying*, thought Proteus, and looked over Medea's shoulder, into the darkness she had come from.

"Were you followed, princess?" he asked abruptly.

She turned her gaze to him. "No, but all is discovered. We must sail away, and quickly, before the king can organize any pursuit."

Proteus immediately took note of that "we"—it suddenly made a kind of sense of her story. Meanwhile the princess was still speaking.

"Before we go, I will put the guardian of the Fleece to sleep," she was telling Jason, "and you yourself can lift the treasure from the tree." She paused, impressively, with the men all staring at her. "But one thing first. Jason, here in the presence of your men I want you to call on all the gods to witness the promises that you have made to me."

It still seemed to Proteus very doubtful that all had really been discovered; if so there would already be a hue and cry. He caught Jason's eye and slightly shook his head. But if the princess could really help them lay hands on the Fleece, then even if she was determined to come with them, accepting her offer might be their only real choice.

When there was really no time for hesitation, Jason could be decisive enough. "Then get aboard the *Argo* quickly," he commanded. "And your maid, too." Of course the servant must not be left behind, able to confirm that her mistress had really run off with the foreigners.

The maid began to move, but Medea reached out to grab her and hold her where she was. With neither woman stirring an inch, but only looking at Jason, he drew a breath and did as the princess had demanded.

"Dear lady, I swear—and may Olympian Zeus and his Consort Hera, goddess of wedlock, be my witnesses—that when we have returned safely to Iolcus I will take you into my home as my own wedded wife." And with that Jason took Medea's right hand in his own.

But marriage would have to wait. Flight came first, and for that very little preparation was required. Some Argonauts bent to their oars, while others began pushing and pulling on reeds and cattails to get the boat out of the marsh.

No one in the countryside around them raised an outcry at the sound, or tried to interfere with their departure. It seemed that no one had observed it. If Aeetes was setting a trap, thought Proteus, it must be an elaborate and subtle one; and the king did not seem the type for schemes like that. With Apsyrtus things might well be different.

But no trap had been set for the Argonauts or their ship in the river. There were only a couple of distant, moving lanterns to show how little traffic of any kind existed at this time of night.

They had left the fire burning at their campsite, but the *Argo* was showing no light at all as the men bent to their oars. Proteus was not trying to measure time, but the passage across the river seemed amazingly swift.

"Can we locate the place in darkness?" Jason fretted as they climbed ashore in darkness. In whispers he detailed several men to guard the ship, and hold her ready for a quick departure.

The young woman who was now clinging to his side gave him sturdy reassurance. "The Fleece itself will be our guide as we come near. It will show itself as bright as a golden cloud at sunrise."

"Are there no guards?"

The princess shook her head, whose long blond hair was now bound up closely under a scarf. "No need to worry about any human guards. No one but the king himself, and Apsyrtus, will go near the place."

"Then what about the famous dragon? Or snake, as the case may be?"

"Let me explain that later. With my magic to defend you, you need not worry about that—but just to be on the safe side, we will move as quickly as we can."

They made their way along a narrow path that wound between tall, dark trees.

Proteus found himself walking beside the Mouse, who boldly took him by the arm and pulled him a little nearer in the darkness.

When he bent down his head she whispered in his ear: "It sounds like the Lord Jason is expecting some kind of serpent guardian, and it really isn't that."

He kept his own voice very low. "What, then?"

"Maybe you should warn Jason, I don't know if he will listen to me, or if the princess is going to tell him the whole truth. The guardian of the Fleece is really a kind of Giant."

Those last two words echoed harshly in the mind of Proteus, awakening blurred nightmares—visions of a splintered and demolished ship, of human death on every side. "A Giant. Are you sure?"

"Oh, very sure. The kind that lives mostly in the water."

Proteus did not argue, but that seemed to him to make no sense. For longer than anyone could remember, Giants and gods had been engaged in a bitter war for supremacy over the whole world. That any one of those immense beings, traditionally antagonistic to all humans, would want to devote long years to guarding a treasure for King Aeetes was hard to believe.

Medea, walking with Jason at the head of the little column, led them along a path so faint that finding it at night, without a guide, would have been hopeless. Now Proteus, straining his vision, thought they might be entering the very grove of tall trees that housed the treasure. And now, still a little before dawn, before any of the foreigners had actually expected it, there was a light ahead, as faint and golden as the early dawn itself, but on a smaller scale. Only moments later they arrived at a small clearing in the trees, at one side of which the Golden Fleece hung waiting for them.

Their whole group, almost forty people, were standing in a kind of clearing in the grove, an open space twenty yards across, formed by the dead trunks of the other trees that must have been knocked down by the Ram in its violent descent from a long flight. The tree that actually held the Fleece was on one edge of this clearing, and at the crest of a low ridge; just beyond, the wooded land fell off sharply into an unseen valley.

Proteus as he stared, trying to make out some details of that dim fire in the darkness, recalled the fragments of the story he had been hearing from various people over the last few months. The tale had been passed down, from Medea's sister, of how the strange object had been flung into high branches by the force of the crash. Now, as the eyes of the Argonauts accommodated themselves to the deep darkness of the grove, they could see how beneath the broken tree trunks, and scattered for some distance all around, lay bits and pieces of strange material, the wreckage of something that once had been the Golden Ram, that had brought Chalciope's husband to this land.

Phrontis and Argeus were exchanging excited whispers; from what Proteus could overhear, he gathered that this was the first visit either brother had ever made to the sacred grove.

The light of the Fleece was not really strong enough to let them view each other's faces. Presently, at Jason's whispered order, one of the men uncovered a dark lantern he had been carrying, and they could all see a little more of their surroundings.

During the twenty years since the Ram's arrival, the grass and bushes had grown back thickly over what must once have been a deep hole in the soft ground . . . it seemed marvelous that the father of Phrontis and Argeus could have survived the impact.

The sons of Phrixus mourned and said hasty prayers over the spot, and Proteus could hear them mumbling promises to certain gods that later they would offer sacrifices.

Beside the hole there was a mound, overgrown with grass, and Argeus now whispered it must be the base of the altar that Phrixus had set up to Zeus. To Proteus, it looked more like a mound of dirt thrown up by some tremendous impact, as if a Giant's club the size and weight of a falling house had here struck at the earth.

Once he started to look around, it was easy to pick out other fragments, miscellaneous and unidentifiable, left over from the crash landing. Similarities in appearance strongly suggested to Proteus that the Fleece and the Bulls had once been part of the same creature, or machine, the remaining parts of which lay smashed and scattered irretrievably.

Jason had now approached the hanging Fleece, and was reaching up with one hand to touch it tentatively. It would not be easy, Proteus thought, to reconstruct the details of that flight and its hard ending. Rooting with the toe of his sandal under some leaves, he uncovered a strange bit of metal, all twisted and black, as if it had been scorched. In the light of the single lantern, and the faint glow of the Fleece itself, he could see how other similar pieces were embedded in the ground, some in the trunks of trees. He bent quickly and picked up a bit of softer stuff, not glowing like the Fleece. It felt something like wool and something like grass, and it rang musically when it was touched. When he tried to squeeze it hard, his fist suddenly felt weak, and he hastily cast the object from him.

But all these things were only momentary distractions; they had come here for the Fleece, and there it was. To get directly beneath it, Proteus had to move around to the other side of the spreading tree that held the treasure up, some six or eight feet above the ground, within reach of a tall man.

In the moment when Proteus got his first full look at the object of their long voyage, the doubts he had begun to have of its divine origin were swept away, and he was struck with wonder. So were all his shipmates, Jason included. Only Medea and her servant, both of whom had seen the sight before, were less impressed. The princess kept glancing back nervously over her shoulder, in the direction where the unseen *Argo* waited, as if expecting her father's palace guard to appear at any moment.

In spite of all else, the Fleece drew Proteus's attention back to itself again. As if someone had frozen a sheet of golden flame, and somewhat dimmed its light . . .

The sight of it conveyed somehow the power of a huge waterfall, though it was not actually in motion. Still the tiny bits of substance that made it up seemed never still. It was quite big enough, as it sagged in heavy folds among the branches, to make a cover for a royal bed. Everyone present could feel the power of what hung there in the tree, or imagined that they could. The edges appear frayed, the strands composing them growing thinner and thinner as they stretched farther from the center, until they indeterminately raveled out into invisibility.

Proteus stared at the branches of the tree that held the Fleece, thinking to himself that they must have been transformed over the years, under the strange weight of such a golden burden. It was somehow disquieting that they seemed no different from any other branches on the trees around.

No two Argonauts were affected in exactly the same way. Some fell on their knees as if in worship, some hung back in fear, refusing to come near the tree. Meanwhile others' faces showed that greed had come alive in them. In the darkness before dawn the faint golden glow of the treasure before them transformed each man's countenance, so that he seemed something other than what he truly was.

The stuff where it was the thickest and most solid had the color of pure, raw, glowing gold, so intense that beside it Medea's hair, escaping from her scarf, had acquired a pale and lifeless look. Men stretched out their hands to touch it as it went by. Proteus impulsively reached with his fingers to brush the thing in passage. The feel of it was warm, with slow pulsations of even greater warmth perceptible.

"Take it, Jason, and let us go," Medea said.

Proteus could see how the muscles hardened in Jason's arms when he lifted down his trophy from the tree, but it was not too heavy for a man to handle. Folding it into a manageable bundle took a little time, and somehow the careful bundling was soon spontaneously undone.

But moments later, when Jason tried to run with his prize in the direction of the ship, he discovered that the Fleece somehow resisted any but the slowest acceleration.

The fabric hung as low as Jason's feet, as he held it in his arms, and the golden glow of it lit up his face. The very ground before him as he walked was dimly transformed to radiant gold. When Proteus touched him on the arm, he started nervously and looked up with a little cry. "What's that?"

"I said, Jason, we had better get into the ship and get moving as quickly as possible."

The leader seemed to emerge from a kind of trance. "Yes. Back to the ship. Shove off, and get everyone aboard as fast as possible. I'm coming as fast as I can, this thing is hard to carry." And he struggled with his burden, trying to form it into a more compact load.

"Shall I help you?"

"No, I'll manage."

For a moment Proteus dared to hope that they might manage to carry the treasure away without hindrance or delay, that the legends of one or another inhuman guardian were no more than legends. But that moment ended when a strange sound turned all their heads. It had come from somewhere behind the grove they had just left.

"You'd better hurry, Captain."

Jason was almost gasping. "I know that, Proteus—but by all the gods, this is the strangest thing. Every time I try to run, it seems to grow in weight and slow me down, as if I were pushing some enormous rock."

But Proteus had turned his head away. "Damn all the gods, what's that?"

There was a stirring, not loud, yet somehow vast, coming from the little valley that lay just beyond the tree that had held the Fleece—a sound like the crackle of trampled underbrush, but grown huge, made up of the crushing and snapping of many branches of large trees—

In a moment Proteus's imagination created an awesome image—despite the Mouse's warning, he wanted it to be a dragon or a snake—but he knew, with the fearful certainty of nightmare, that it was really a Giant coming toward them now, one of the transformed, mutant kind whose legs and lower body had wholly metamorphosed into twin fishtail coils.

Moments later the bad dream had come true. An enormous head, surmounted by a whole thicket of hair, appeared just beyond the crest of the low ridge passing through the grove. The skull was impossibly, miraculously large, the span of an axe-handle's length between the eyes. Proteus had seen people living in huts with smaller domes. The head was very nearly human in its shape, but far too large to ever have fit on any human body. It was easier to imagine a man or woman riding inside it, peering out through one of the face-sized eyes.

Proteus sharply reminded himself to learn from the maid the source of her knowledge—if they both survived the next minute or two, which promised to be perilous.

The fragmented memories Proteus had begun to regain regarding Giants informed him that most of that race were any-thing but comfortable when not in deep water. But there did exist a type, or subspecies, whose lower limbs were practically reptilian—and that was what floundered and rolled before him, almost like a great whale out of water.

It might be floundering now, confined as it was to land, but it was nevertheless advancing with deadly speed, faster than a man could run. Tree trunks bent and broke under the weight of the massive, practically legless, amphibious body as it lurched and flopped and crawled toward the Argonauts, most of whom were petrified. A thousand twigs and little branches broke, making a ferocious crackling like that of a burning forest. Proteus's stomach went queasy when he realized that the Giant had freed one enormous hand from crawling duty and was actually swinging a thirty-foot tree trunk as a club. Birds and animals of every size uttered screaming cries and fled from the Titan's path.

Now that the Argonauts had been discovered, they had no choice—they were going to have to kill this hideous creature, or die trying, before they left this spot. At the moment, the men were falling back on every side, though to their credit most of them did not simply turn and run, but were backing away in good order, readying their spears and slings and arrows.

In a moment memory had transported Proteus back to a near-drowning in deep water, floundering in the middle of the Great Sea amid the wreckage of a demolished ship. The monster that had been trying to kill him then was very much like the one before him now. Both were Giants, and the identification brought with it something close to ultimate terror.

Medea met the challenge as bravely as any Argonaut. Displaying the courage of desperation, she attempted to take charge at once, while her maid could only fall down and hide her face. Proteus felt a surge of admiration. Standing as tall as she could with her arms raised, she did her best to stop the monstrous creature with her magic.

Meanwhile Proteus stood by with his spear ready, from the corner of his eye catching a glimpse of Jason who at the moment appeared to be paralyzed with terror.

As far as Proteus could tell, it was very likely that the girl's chants and her drugs were about equally ineffective. The intruders were going to need some other means of defense if they were going to survive.

And now Medea seemed to be coming to the same conclusion. "Run!" she cried to Jason. "Get to the ship!"

Jason had demonstrated his great strength in managing the Bulls, but something about this new task restrained him to a snail's pace, even when he tried to run.

Proteus raised his spear in the direction of their fallen foe, covering Jason's advance, and did not lower it again.

When the creature advanced, half-lurching, half-rolling forward with surprising speed, he hurled the spear as hard as he could, and with remote surprise saw the weapon bury itself up to the last hand's breadth of its shaft in the great monster's naked, hairy belly.

Jason, needing two hands to manage the Fleece, had dropped his spear, and Proteus now swiftly grabbed it up.

The surprising strength in his arm was matched by unsuspected skill. His second cast hit the Giant squarely in the middle of his chest, as easily as striking a wooden knot upon a log. At the same time, the other Argonauts around him were standing firm, shooting arrows or slinging stones. With a hail of missiles falling on the creature, it was all but impossible for anyone to see, in the poor light, whose stone or point was really doing the important damage.

The enormous monster was roaring like a thunderstorm. It had dropped its bludgeon, and was flailing with two arms themselves like mighty tree trunks.

Running forward, Proteus armed himself with a third spear, snatching up one that had landed short when cast by a shipmate. His next throw struck home in the Giant's left eye. The huge being let out an awful noise, and slapped his great hands protectively up over his face. Seizing yet another spear from the litter of fallen weapons, Proteus rushed forward and thrust it deep into his enemy's side. With a hoarse, terrible cry, the Giant fell. Moments later, writhing and crawling, he made a floundering retreat that carried him over the ridge again and down its far side.

Proteus ran after the thing just far enough to see what was happening to it. Downslope, the twitching arms were breaking off great branches. Sliding and slithering, the huge body dragged itself toward the lake and swamps below, visible as a sheen of water in the faint brightening of the morning sky.

Turning swiftly, Proteus ran back after his comrades, and had soon rejoined them. No one else was much concerned with the final fate of their fallen enemy, and it seemed that no one but Proteus quite understood what a key role he had played. They had won the fight somehow, with a hail of spears, stones, and arrows—a near thing there, for a while, but every man of them was used to winning fights. And now they had the glorious treasure to be marveled at.

Jason was on his feet again, apparently unhurt, stumbling on in the direction of the *Argo*, desperately clutching his treasure in his arms.

The young maid wept in fear as she crept aboard the ship, while the princess was fiercely jubilant. But Mouse was determined to serve her mistress, and even more determined that she herself would not be left behind. In only moments all the oars were working, and the ship was under way, headed downstream toward the open sea.

Their departure was just in time. Now there was plenty of daylight to see in the distance King Aeetes in his chariot, pulled by giant cameloids, at the head of a body of troops, chasing them along the riverbank. The king and his mounted troops gained ground but just missed catching up. There had been heavy rain upstream during the night, and the current was swift. Rowing downstream went much faster than the laborious coming up.

The captain stood looking back from his slight elevation on the deck. "He must have got together five hundred men, somehow. Row!"

Evidently the princess had keen eyes. "Yes, that is my father. And my brother too, I recognize their chariots, and the beasts that pull them. But they cannot catch us now!"

Even when they were almost a quarter of a mile downstream, Proteus thought he could still hear the great king's roaring in his rage. It might almost have been the bellowing of a wounded Giant, but Proteus knew that it was not.

They needed no further warning to know that a Colchian fleet would soon be in close pursuit.

The King of Colchis had been robbed of two great treasures, and what he would do to the robbers if he caught them was not something they wanted to think about.

Trapped

$\mathcal{T}$he scribe Anchaeus made mental notes of what the current logbook entry ought to be; he could hope that he was going to live long enough, and would soon be able to find the time, to actually scratch the words on parchment.

As the mouth of the river broadened and the banks fell away, delivering *Argo* to the sea again, all hands were fully occupied in propelling the ship or keeping lookout. And all rejoiced in glorious success!

One man shouted as he pulled his oar: "A hundred years from now, folks will still be making songs about Jason and his splendid voyage!" And for the moment at least that seemed believable.

"What top-notch pirates we'd have made!" cried out another.

The Argonauts, rowing in good rhythm now, were leaning hard into their work, but they all had enough breath left for a song, and the man who wanted to start a song got a good response on his first try. The Fleece was safely aboard, and so was the princess who had helped them and asked their protection in return.

When the Mouse's eye fell on the book, whose keeper had momentarily left it lying in the open, she whispered innocently that she liked books and would like to read this one. Then without waiting for an answer, she picked it up and looked at it. Most of those who saw her were surprised that she could read.

Meanwhile the princess was too busy staring back over the stern, and murmuring an occasional incantation, to pay any attention to a book.

Proteus at the moment was not listening to the songs, nor did he much care what was being entered in the log or who was reading or writing. Instead he was thinking furiously to himself, wrestling with private doubts as to whether any Giant ought to have been mortally wounded by a simple weapon in the hand of a mere human. True, the arrows, slings, and spears of some thirty strong young men could do a lot of damage. But Proteus had the feeling that most of those missiles had been no more than flea bites to the Giant. No, it was the spears that he, Proteus, had thrown, that brought the monster down. And the spear that he had thrust finished it off, sent it crawling in search of deep water in which to die. Even in the bad light before dawn, he had been able to read their huge enemy's reactions in sufficient detail to feel sure of that.

Others had probably seen the matter differently, as was usually the way in combat. Now some Argonaut was calling, with triumph in his voice: "Which way will you turn us, steersman? Find us another battle, or another monster?"

"And maybe another treasure, too!" chimed in another voice.

Judging from the comments, a good portion of Jason's crew had now had their fill of adventure for the time being, and would have voted to return home along the same course that they had followed outward bound. That route had certainly had its perils, but now it had the great advantage of being to some degree familiar. Meanwhile a minority of others, elated by their triumph, were in a mood for fresh adventures.

But there was no reason to expect Jason to call for a vote. Such decisions were better left in the hands of the steersman/navigator, assuming that he knew his business. The current occupant of the office could be heard muttering his hearty wishes that Tiphys had not died.

There was really no reason to doubt the new man's competence, and no one protested when he informed them they would have to begin their long journey home by a new route. He went on to explain that the decision was being forced on them, by the sheer need to get away from Colchis as fast as they could, and to avoid the forces that would soon be trying to hunt them down.

Once that was settled, Jason gave his men a little talk, toning down the mood of celebration. For the moment they were indeed free, but it would be foolish to think they had seen the last of that king's far-flung forces.

Proteus had to agree. They could all bear witness to the king's anger when Jason succeeded in the trial; and it was all too easy to imagine Aeetes's reaction when he could confirm that the Fleece was gone. Medea had reminded them that even before Jason's triumph, her father had sent word to his distant forces, by means of several fast, light ships, that the *Argo* was to be intercepted should she try to leave—and that order would remain in force until countermanded by the king himself.

Some hours later, when the day was far advanced, the steersman appealed for help to the Colchians aboard; he was having some trouble understanding what his compass-pyx was showing him, and thought their knowledge of the surrounding geography might be of benefit. Princess Medea and her maid, proceeding in the easy fashion of people used to working together, began to draw with charcoal on an empty rower's bench a crude map of the maze of waterways ahead.

"Then it is likely we will be cut off," the navigator muttered, after a few minutes spent studying the sketch.

"We might try to slip through at night," one of Jason's advisers suggested.

The steersman raised his head and squinted at the sea and sky. Now he looked gloomier than ever. "That might work if we knew exactly which points were blocked against us. Also the skies are gray. Also traveling at night, in strange waters and under clouds, is a good recipe for getting lost, compass-pyx or not."

On returning to his post, the steersman spent the next few hours of the long day with his forehead almost continually pressed to his small ivory box, so that his face bore the marks of it when he straightened up. Only now and then he briefly raised his head, to inform Jason of some slight course correction that he thought they had better take.

As the day wore on, the princess spent most of her time standing alone (except for the almost constant presence of the faithful Mouse), holding on to a rail on the raised central deck. The two young women alternately looked back at the shores of their homeland, which were fast disappearing, and then cast their eyes ahead at the watery horizon, beyond which lay whatever new life they were to have.

Right now, Medea, the Mouse, and the man who clutched the steering oar were the only people on the ship not rowing. Medea, looking down at Jason laboring steadily on his bench, talked encouragingly to him as he pulled an oar. If the events of the last two days had exhausted him, he did not show it.

Proteus, pulling an oar steadily on a nearby bench, thought that the chief looked worried, even more than usual. Well, now Jason had good cause to fret, having made a deadly enemy of one of the world's most powerful monarchs. Not that it was easy to see how the captain could have avoided that outcome.

At last they were blessed by a favorable wind, so the sail could be hoisted and the oarsmen rest. Medea, thinking and planning aloud, considered it certain that there would be a determined pursuit, and likely that her brother Apsyrtus would be leading its main body.

"I'm sure that Father will send him, and not come himself. He'll not feel secure enough to leave his kingdom on any prolonged chase. And besides, he is an old man now."

When the wind began to fail again, and the men resumed their rowing, Proteus found himself taking the next shift right beside Jason—one of them sitting inboard and pulling on a long oar, the other outboard on a short one.

Now and then Medea glanced at Proteus and smiled, in the manner of a woman pleased by what a clever servant had done for her. He smiled back at the princess, and thought his own thoughts regarding her. A beautiful woman, but no more so than many others. Also, of course, as unreachable as a star for any common sailor, which made it possible to consider her objectively.

Meanwhile, Jason was speaking jerkily, getting out short sentences between pulls on his oar: "You need not worry, princess. No one's going to overtake us."

Medea looked at him thoughtfully. She said simply: "Perhaps not. But I know it is my brother coming after us." And she turned her head, looking back in the direction from which they had come. "He is more like our father than any man should be. But at the same time he is more cunning, so that I fear him even more."

Jason signaled to the man who had been resting to relieve him at his oar. Then the captain opened the door of a locker beneath the central deck, and set about trying to refit it as a kind of private nest for Medea, where she might be able to rest in a small sheltered space.

He said: "Come lady, I will prepare a place of greater comfort for you."

Her attitude seemed to say that it did not matter, that he should be devoting his time and effort to more important things. "I doubt that any such place can be prepared within a thousand miles of here."

But Jason only smiled at her, and set about doing what he had promised. The finished space was so small that Medea's attendant could not share it with her, but would have to sit just outside.

Proteus smiled at the maid, who was obviously frightened, and finally saw one corner of her mouth turn up in response. He sighed inwardly, foreseeing problems. All of the Heroes understood that the princess was firmly attached to Jason, and most of them would have thought her unattainable anyway, by reason of her royal blood. But here was another young woman, fairly good looking if no great beauty, and certainly of inferior social status. Several dozen young Argonauts would have her almost continually in sight for the duration of the voyage, with no reason to think that she was not fair game. However the girl chose to behave toward them, there were likely to be quarrels, which the crew could ill afford at any time, particularly now.

The presence of two passengers who never rowed really made the ship only a little more crowded, but the change seemed greater than it was.

"Good thing we are not trying to haul twenty or thirty servants," someone commented from a nearby bench.

"Aye, that would have been unmitigated disaster," said the speaker's mate. "Anyway, I think by now that most of them would be dead, or have deserted."

Princess Medea had already emerged from her nest, and was assuring Jason in a low voice that, yes, there were enough openings in her newly created private quarters to allow in sufficient air and light; she might have barely room to turn around inside, but for the moment nothing could be done about that.

Having thanked her rescuer for his trouble, the princess did not seem much interested in the little nest. Nor did she hear Jason when he muttered grimly to himself that the only reason that any spare space at all was now available was that the reserves of dried fish and hardtack, cheese and dried fruit, spare oars, and fishing gear that had formerly filled this space had by this time been put into action or consumed.

The wind no longer favored their passage, so the crew rowed all day, with only brief pauses for rest and natural needs, stretches and changes of position. Then they rowed on well into the night, favored by a clear sky with so many familiar stars that the compass-pyx became for a time unnecessary.

As the next few hours passed, Medea continued to spend most of her time out in the open, staying as close as was practical to the man who had pledged her his love.

Tireless rowing afforded Proteus no escape from his own thoughts.

Again and again, behind the private screen of his closed eye-lids, he could see that damned, deceptively tiny Arrow darting toward the princess's unprotected back. It had to have gone on to pierce her heart. Ever since then she had been crazily in love with Jason. So there was no doubt that the Boy who shot the Arrow had truly been Eros.

Then I have seen a god—that is the first marvel. I—alone of the ordinary mortals who were present—*could see him very clearly.*

Proteus had never seen a god before—or had he? The truth was, of course, that he could not remember. He knew that most people lived their lives and went to their graves without having any personal encounter with divinity. But on the other hand, many in the world's long history *had* met gods face to face, and no doubt some were still doing so.

One of the things that everyone knew about gods was that they could readily pass for ordinary humans, and might, just for their own amusement, choose to go about in the world as such. For every single one of them had been born a mortal human being, only to be transformed at some point in his or her life by somehow acquiring a god-Face.

But Cupid, on that memorable evening when he met Proteus, had not been interested in disguising himself. Instead he had made himself invisible—to everyone but Proteus. Because Cupid had a job to do, and also had something he wanted to say to Proteus. A few words that made less sense to the hearer the more he thought about them.

Like the whore on the dock in Bebrycos, little Eros knew me. Like that sneaky killer on Samothraki, he said he was glad to see me standing where I was. And then Cupid added, almost offhand-

edly, that I should kill a certain nameless man, an agent of King
Pelias, as soon as I laid eyes on him.

Why would the divine Lord Cupid stop and talk with Proteus
the common sailor as if they were old pals? Especially when Old
Proteus was almost certainly the very agent, or one of them, that
the great ones wanted dead.

It sounded like even the great gods must be monumentally
confused. There had to be an explanation, somewhere, but Proteus
was not at all sure he wanted to know what it was.

In the morning of the third day of their flight from Colchis, the
fugitives tied up their ship on an unfamiliar coast, at the mouth of
a river that the navigator said must be called Halys. Only he had
any idea of where they were, and not even he could say which way
they ought to go next.

Zetes and Calais were prevailed upon to fly, and soon took
wing above the morning mist. Within the hour they were back
with word that if the *Argo* held on anything like her present
course, she was about to leave the open sea behind. They had now
reached the fringe of what appeared to be a great continent, its
coastline fragmented into a maze of islands and estuaries. Within
the space of a hundred miles, the mouths of several sizable rivers
emptied confusedly into the sea.

"We should be staying in the open ocean altogether," someone
complained to the current steersman.

He snapped back at the questioner. "Don't talk nonsense!"
And the flying scouts confirmed as much: "That way we're hopelessly blocked, by a score of ships almost as fast as we are. Maybe
faster, if their crews aren't worn with rowing."

"Then how are we ever going to get home?"

"Look here." The steersman unrolled one of his several parchment charts, and thumped a knuckle on a spot. "We must be
here—approximately. Of course we must eventually find our way
back to the open sea. But to escape our pursuers, we must enter

one of the mouths of this great river, then make our way upstream to a big freshwater lake . . . then out of that again by a different river, and so eventually back to the sea."

"Can we do that?"

"Easily enough—if there were no Colchian ships upstream from us. Which I fear is not the case. But we must do the best we can."

Making their way along the coast in a generally westerly direction, they were now passing through an area more heavily populated, and small boats frequently appeared at a distance, their occupants gawking at *Argo*, taking in the staring painted eyes that decorated her prow, and her many oars. No doubt a majority of these observers assumed that the Argonauts were pirates.

"Good thing we're not come here on that type of enterprise," Haraldur observed. "I don't see a lot of easy game." The small boats all seemed possessed of darting speed, as if the arms of their crews were energized by fear.

Above the *Argo*, as the steersman turned her into one of the great river's multiple mouths, and began to feel their way into the watery maze, towered rocky bluffs, crowned with an irregular line of trees.

The air was distinctly warmer now, and most of the cold weather had been left behind in Colchis. Mosquitoes began to be something of a problem.

After another mission, the flying scouts brought back a more detailed description of the pursuit. What they said left little room for optimism.

"Then it is as I feared, my brother leads them." And Medea's fingers almost convulsively knotted the fine scarf she had been wearing around her head when she fled the palace.

When Jason tried to be reassuring, it almost seemed that the princess could not hear him. "Some of my father's ships are very fast. And their captains are all terrified of him. They will not dare fail in their duty."

"Then the worst has happened," Jason groaned. With a sinking feeling, Proteus observed that the leader was slipping into one of his black, fatalistic moods. And it seemed true that the *Argo* had been cut off from escape.

Before long it was certain that the enemy knew where the Argonauts were. They had seen the *Argo* from a distance, and would be coming after her.

They passed channel after channel that the steersman refused to enter, because the compass-pyx gave him no hope that any of them could ever lead to freedom.

And there came a moment when he raised his head, and looked at his shipmates despairingly. "It is no use. There is no open way."

"Even if we go back the way we came?" asked Proteus.

"That would be the worst choice. That way leads only to an all-out battle against great odds."

The intrepid flying Argonauts took to the air again, but the only result was to confirm that the Colchians had the river blocked, both upstream and down, where it flowed amid a myriad of islands. The pursuers had now occupied most of these islands, with one notable exception.

"They have not occupied this island," observed Proteus, pointing to the nearest one.

"There's a big temple on it," the captain pointed out.

Not really very big, thought Proteus. But certainly a temple. Who but worshipers would build so elaborately on this scrap of land, where there were certain to be floods.

"But whose?" Anchaeus asked.

"Artemis, I'd say," said someone else. There was an image of the crescent moon atop its modest tower.

"Who among our crew is devoted to Diana?" Jason asked, evidently hoping to gain advantage from the goddess. It seemed to

Proteus an unlikely source of aid, and that the captain was grasping at straws.

Men who heard his question looked around hopefully, but no hands went up. Adventurers as a rule had little connection with that great goddess, also known as Artemis. She was, among other things, the divine personification of the moon, eternally chaste and honorable, the patroness of childbirth and hunters, of fisherfolk and unmarried girls.

Jason looked out over the heads of his waiting crew, and raised his voice. "Who here can claim a friendship with any god? We stand in need of all the help that we can get."

Only silence answered him. That was the kind of claim that no one was eager to make—not when you came right down to it. The men were all weary, and they were all frightened, though their fear would have to grow a long way yet before it disabled these tough warriors.

Proteus suddenly recalled that Diana was also considered the twin sister of Apollo. And she had some close connection with Hecate, who in turn some said was Circe's mother. But the knowledge seemed of no current use at all.

"We are trapped, Jason. What are we to do?" asked another Argonaut, one who often gave advice, but now had none to give.

Now that the worst had happened, the captain seemed to be recovering his nerve. "If we cannot use the ship, we might as well get out of it and stretch our legs. I suppose we ought to go ashore."

Presently most of the crew had disembarked, stretching their legs and accomplishing what little exploring there was to do. Proteus was only slightly surprised when the Mouse seized the opportunity of being briefly alone with him; her meaningful glances had convinced him that she must have something to communicate in private, and a serious talk between the two of them was overdue.

They were walking for the moment in the shade, as much out of sight and hearing of all their shipmates as they would ever be able to get while on the island. Bushes more or less surrounded the couple, and someone might possibly be hiding in the bushes, but Proteus was certainly ready to take the risk.

After exchanging a few completely banal words with him, the young woman stopped in her tracks and said to him quietly: "Well, here I am."

Proteus stared at her. Somehow it had not sounded like a sexual invitation. The Mouse's hands were clasped in front of her, her shift still decently arranged if more than a little soiled by long days of being worn without a change. And there was nothing of the wanton in her pose.

When he remained silent, the young woman pursued him with a query: "I want you to tell me what our task is to be."

The request sounded simple enough. Except that he had no idea what the girl could be talking about. "Our task?"

She lifted her chin a little. "No need to dodge around with me. You are Proteus, and I was told to expect your coming on Jason's ship."

Another mysterious recognition—but this one was something more. He thought he could feel his jaw drop open. "Who could have told you I was on his ship?"

Restrained impatience showed in the girl's voice. "The same master we both serve in secret sent word to me. You pretend ignorance very well, but don't you see that now you are keeping up the pretense beyond all reason? That you are only making our job harder?"

He blinked at her. "And what is this job?"

She lifted her head with a look of brave defiance. Proteus realized with a slight shock that the Mouse was deeply afraid of him, just like the woman on the dock. No, not quite like that. Here he faced not only fear, but hatred.

But Medea's maid was not going to be conquered by her fear. "You are going to have to tell me. I will say it once more, I have been told to expect your arrival at the court of King Aeetes, as a member of Jason's company. A man of your name, your exact physical description." She paused. "So I would recognize you, even if I had not seen you before, in Iolcus." She paused, and now her loathing was more plain. "Even if I did not know *what* you are."

What am I? Who? He almost spoke the words aloud, but held back in fear of betraying his own ignorance.

Seeing his continued blank stare, the Mouse drew a breath and shook her head and tried again. "I am to obey your orders absolutely—whatever they may be." It had cost her a struggle to say that, but she had managed to put aside her dread, and smother her extreme revulsion.

"Ah." Proteus felt a sudden rush of anger. Not at the Mouse, but at the unfairness, the helplessness of his position. Half the people in the world seemed to know far more about him than he knew about himself.

Groping blindly for solid facts, and struck by what seemed a clever inspiration, he asked the girl: "I suppose this secret master is a god?"

"Don't be a fool." Now the maid was daring to be angry. "You'll have to talk sense to me sooner or later." But the Mouse did not turn and run away. She was not about to disappear, as had the others along the way who had dropped their enigmatic hints and vanished. His own anger was replaced by a tremendous inward excitement. Proteus found it almost difficult to breathe; he had the feeling that at last he stood on the brink of some huge revelation.

"How did this master, the one you say we serve, manage to send word to you?" That was the safest question he could think of at the moment.

The girl shrugged slightly. "Through one of a troupe of traveling players. They visit everywhere, talk with everyone."

"Ah, I see." That much at least was understandable.

The Mouse was silent while they walked on a few more paces. Then, with a sudden light breaking on her face, and in the tone of one who at last has caught a glimpse of sunlight through the clouds, she ventured: "Is it possible that he didn't tell *you* anything about *me*? Didn't even let you know that I'd be here, an agent in place to help you with your plan? By all the gods, that would have been a ghastly blunder on his part. But such things happen."

Craving solid information as he did, Proteus was ready to accept that "he" as certain proof that the secret master was not a woman. Which didn't help him much, because the only giver of orders to Old Proteus that he could remember had certainly been female. "You're right," he said. "He told me nothing about you."

"That explains your caution." His fellow agent—for so she seemed to be—was not going to let it go at that. "Then what *did* he tell you? Certainly he gave you some mission to accomplish when you reached Colchis? And I still think I must have been meant to play some part in it. Else why arrange to plant me here at all?"

The Mouse sighed, peering sideways at him in cautious puzzlement. "But I don't suppose he could have foreseen that Jason would manage to get the Fleece and the princess both on board, and would now be sailing free again."

"That would have been hard to predict," agreed Proteus. He strolled on in silence, furiously trying to think. Then he shook his head. "And I don't suppose we can count our current situation as sailing free."

"All right, all right." The maid's voice was vehement but she kept it quiet. Still afraid of him, yet still daring to be bold. "Don't tell me what the plan is yet. But I stand ready to follow your orders. I have no choice about that, as you well know." She paced for a few steps in silence, then added: "I only hope it doesn't involve anything that would hurt my lady. I've come to have a true regard for her."

"It doesn't involve anything like that," Proteus decided firmly.

"I'm glad of that at least. And glad to hear you admit that after all there is some plan, some thing we must accomplish."

Some of their shipmates were coming in sight, and their talk was broken off.

The temple island was roughly circular, not more than a hundred yards across. A hasty reconnaissance showed that they had the place entirely to themselves, except for a small handful of unarmed temple attendants.

A new arrival on the island needed only a minute or two to get a feel of its size. It was indeed so small that it was possible to stand near the middle of it and look out through trees and brush, to see the surrounding water on all sides.

The *Argo* was too big to hide, and within an hour of the Argonauts' going ashore, their Colchian pursuers had discovered where they were. Two warships took up symmetrical positions on opposite shores of the river, so they could keep every inch of the island's shoreline under observation. But so far Jason and his people were not molested.

One battle-scarred veteran said: "If I were the Colchian commander, I'd be setting fire to the good ship *Argo* right about now."

But another who looked equally experienced was shaking his head. "I wouldn't. Not if I thought I could sail her home as a prize. Ships as good as ours are rare."

Jason asked the princess whether Apsyrtus would be reluctant to attack them on an island dedicated to the goddess, and Medea brightened a little, agreeing that he probably would.

Now the captain and his royal passenger sat down together, borrowing an anteroom of the temple for the purpose, and tried to draw up a more complete map of their position, using charcoal on a plain board.

Proteus, invited by Jason to consult with them, watched the drawing grow. Here and here and here were the various islands, mostly overgrown with wild vegetation. Through all this twisted the courses of several rivers, or the branches of one river, if you preferred to think of them that way. Here, now firmly blocked by the enemy, was the way they had come into the maze. Way over *there*, seemingly out of reach, was the open sea they must eventually travel to get home.

Jason mused: "Your brother must feel very confident that we cannot get away—unless he lets us slip through his fingers. How long we will be safe on this island I do not know."

Medea answered: "Apsyrtus bears me no love—there will be no slipping through. But as there is a temple here, and he is a patient man, we probably will be safe from any violence—until we starve to death—or grow too weak to take up arms. Then he and his men will come and carry me away."

Proteus cleared his throat. "You say, my lady, that there will be no slipping through. But would it not be wise to establish some kind of contact with Apsyrtus? True, he may refuse to negotiate with us on any point at all. But we can't be sure of that until we try."

Medea looked sad, and quietly frightened. "I think there will be no trouble establishing contact. If I know my brother as well as I think I do, he won't simply order an attack. We will probably be getting a message from him, urging us to surrender, as soon as he knows exactly where we are. He is good at war, but he more enjoys diplomacy."

And sure enough within the hour, as if to confirm her prediction, a messenger from Apsyrtus came bravely alone in a small boat to ask for a parley.

Together Jason and Medea and Proteus went to talk to the man, who remained in his little rowboat some ten yards from the shore. He said: "My lady, your brother himself plans to come and speak with you."

Jason cleared his throat. "What escort does the prince plan to bring?"

The emissary shook his head. "No more than half a dozen men, sir, to row his boat. I will be one of them, and if you want us to stay in the boat, we will all—except the prince himself, of course."

What better meeting place than in the proposed sanctuary, one of the smaller chambers inside the temple of Artemis?

"Let us go," said the captain, "and make sure that those who are in charge of the temple have no objection."

When the door of the temple opened, Proteus saw the faces of a few young acolytes looking out, solemnly afraid. The priestess who came to meet the visitors was a quiet, frightened-looking woman who, when Jason courteously questioned her, quickly gave her permission for the meeting, and then withdrew to some inner, private room.

Murder

*T*he Temple of Diana, standing as near the exact center of the island as could be estimated, was an old structure, grown shabby through lack of maintenance. The lower walls were discolored on the outside, evidence of having been at least once inundated when the island flooded.

Proteus thought that even when the structure was new, it could never have pleased the goddess much. It was plainly built of wood, and consisted of only a few rooms on the ground floor plus a kind of attic, with one main entrance and a couple of side doors. Here and there a panel, indoors or out, had been intricately carved in abstract designs, and stained in an attempt to add a touch of elegance. Proteus wondered if the building had originally been dedicated to some other deity altogether, or intended as something other than a temple.

No sooner had Jason agreed to a meeting, than Apsyrtus sent word to say he would be delayed—his sister interpreted this as an attempt to play on their nerves. A full day passed in this manner, with Argonaut sentries posted against surprise at several places around the shore. Meanwhile most of the men took the opportunity to catch up on their sleep, lying with weapons ready to their hands.

There was plenty of confirmation that the Argonauts were indeed effectively surrounded. A worn sandal and some fruit peelings drifting downstream testified to the careless presence of Colchians above. But sudden attack did not seem to be the real danger for the Argonauts, not when all Apsyrtus had to do was wait. It was easy to see that obtaining food for forty people was very rapidly going to become a problem.

Proteus was invited to listen in while Jason and Medea discussed the situation. By now, Jason had come to depend heavily on him for advice, and Medea was beginning to share the captain's view.

And the Mouse was present too—Medea maintained she had no secrets from her maid, and obviously relied on her as an adviser.

It was the Mouse who called their attention to the fact that a small boat was openly approaching, coming across the channel dividing the temple island from the next one over in the maze of waterways.

Taking a few steps to the shore, the princess looked out over the muddy current, shading her eyes with one hand. "Here comes my brother."

Silently a small group gathered to receive the visitor. Medea's brother seemed at ease, sitting in the stern of a small boat, and was dressed much as when Proteus first saw him in his palace. He was smiling faintly, and gave them a small wave as he approached. His curly hair and beard appeared to have been freshly trimmed and oiled, and his personal appearance revealed no traces of a hard voyage.

Even before disembarking, Apsyrtus complimented Jason on his seamanship, and the speed of his ship. "Your men are blessed with strong arms, and I envy you your swift vessel. Would it be impertinent to ask how you came by it?"

Jason was curt. "I have friends, and some of them are wealthy. There are many who see the justice of my cause."

"I see. Admirable. And what does your ship's name mean, by the way—*Argo?*"

"I have heard different answers to that question," said Jason distantly.

"Of course the superiority of your vessel and your crew will avail you very little, will it?—if your opponents are ahead of you as well as behind, and they have you outnumbered by about ten to one."

The captain said nothing. Apsyrtus looked directly at his sister and then away again. Evidently he had nothing in particular to say to her at all.

Jason was in no mood to prolong the verbal fencing. He asked: "On what terms will you allow us to go on?"

"May I not come ashore, where at least there is some shade?" Medea's brother showed his hands, open and well-manicured. "You can see that I'm unarmed."

"Yes, come." Jason gestured, and Proteus and the other Argonauts moved back.

The boat eased close to the riverbank, and Apsyrtus stepped to the muddy bank—the six men, apparently unarmed, who had rowed him remaining impassively in the boat—and when his sister offered him a formal greeting, responded coolly in a few essential words.

Proteus got the impression that the prince was ready to be tolerant of these amateurish adventurers who had foolishly tried to defy the power of Colchis. He was even faintly amused by their behavior.

Now with a word and a gesture he drew Jason aside, casually, deliberately leaving Medea out of their conversation. "I would have a word with this gentleman alone, dear sister." But the prince seemed willing to accept the presence of a bodyguard, and made no objection when Proteus silently walked along. Meanwhile Medea did not protest, or appear surprised. She waited, arms at her sides, chin lifted, a picture of royal poise despite the deterioration in her dress.

When the three men had gone a little way, Jason said: "If you come to parley, you must have some terms to offer us."

"Oh, I do." The Colchian prince had kept his gentle smile. "Nothing very harsh. To begin with, I am perfectly willing for you to keep the Golden Fleece. No, I mean it, really." With an amused attitude Apsyrtus raised a hand in a forestalling gesture. "The offer is genuine and I have no trickery up my sleeve. Believe me, I've no need for that."

Jason was silent, looking at him. Apsyrtus, taking note of the captain's expression, said in his aristocratic rasp: "Let me say again, Jason, that I plot no treachery. Really, keep the Fleece!" His long arm, pale and perfumed but still corded with wiry muscle, made an elegant gesture of pushing something from him. "If you want to know my true feelings on the subject, I consider the damned thing useless, nothing but a chronic cause of trouble. It's been hanging on a tree in that forest for as long as I can remember, and it seems impossible to realize any wealth from it, or derive any practical benefit. And once it's gone, we'll have no need of a fish-tailed Giant always lounging around, practically in our capital. The one that you disposed proved not much of a guardian in any case, and I suppose we should actually thank you for driving him away, however you accomplished it."

Jason, now looking downcast, murmured something.

"I understand your caution about taking me at my word," Apsyrtus went on, "but I've been considering the matter for years, and that is my conclusion. No, the Fleece is yours." Again he made an elegant small pushing motion, this time with both hands. "You honorably fulfilled the terms of your wager with the king."

"I did not consider it a wager."

"Whatever you want to call it, you succeeded, tamed the Bulls. I won't ask how, or who may have provided you with help."

Nor were Jason or Proteus about to volunteer any information on those subjects. The three men walked on.

"And Medea?" Jason asked after a few paces.

The elegant Colchian shook his head. "Oh, well, on that point I'm afraid we have nothing to negotiate. My father will settle for no less than having his daughter back. I assure you, my own head would not be safe if I went home without her.

"In the matter of his two grandsons, the king has announced formally that he wants to bring them to trial to answer for their crimes—he considers it a crime to have guided you to Colchis." Apsyrtus raised a hand, forestalling objection. "But between you and me, he doesn't really care about them. I say that Phrontis and Argeus can go on with you, and good riddance."

"She does not want to go home," Jason said, casting a glance back at the distant figure of Medea. Proteus looked too, and saw that her face was turned in their direction.

But the prince did not reply to that, or even look back at his sister. He seemed to be waiting for Jason to make a more meaningful response.

It took the captain of the Argonauts a while to find the exact words he wanted to use next. "I suppose King Aeetes intends to punish her."

"Well . . . my father *is* an angry man," Apsyrtus agreed, judiciously. "In fact, I don't believe I have ever seen him as angry as he is now. Probably you've heard the story that's recently been going around about that other king? The one who's said to have poked out the eyes of his sluttish daughter with long bronze pins? You mustn't think anything of the kind will happen to Medea. No, I very much doubt that any punishment my father has in mind would go as far as death or mutilation. If he did have some such idea, I'd certainly talk him out of it. My sister"—he nodded in her direction, without looking—"is after all a valuable asset to the crown. Eminently marriageable. Even after an—episode like this. Some new version of events will be developed. It will turn out that she's had a chaperone with her all the while she's been away from home."

"As a matter of fact she has. Her maid, the one called Mouse."

"Ah, there, you see? That will help."

With Proteus moving silently on their heels, the prince and the captain walked on, debating a little more around the fringes of the situation. Such matters as whether Aeetes had any additional complaints, what living conditions had been like for the princess aboard the *Argo*. But Apsyrtus was now taking it as settled that Medea would have to come home with him.

At length a silence fell. Proteus, nervously shifting his grip on his spear, had been waiting for some clever counterargument from Jason. Persuading people to do things for him was what Jason's life was all about. But now Proteus could tell by his leader's face that there was nothing of the kind in prospect. Proteus thought to himself: *I can't believe it. He's simply going to cave in. Unless he is planning some deception. Jason has the wit for that, if he would use it. He gave her all that talk of faithfulness and marriage. But the truth is he really cares for nothing and no one but his own ambition.*

Apsyrtus was evidently reaching the same conclusion. Confident now that he had won, Medea's brother remarked how unseemly it was for a young unmarried girl of royal blood to be living, day after day and night after night among a group of men, whether chaperoned or not.

Now the details of the surrender were being discussed, with some attempt at a face-saving arrangement for Jason. The Temple of Diana was conveniently at hand, and could be put to a good use.

The captain tentatively agreed that Medea and her maid would be put in charge of the temple priestess for a few days; and in that time the temple authorities would hear the case and judge whether she was to be sent back to her father or not.

Again an elegant gesture from Apsyrtus. "I am sure they will come to the right conclusion. Then, you see, there will be no point in our having a battle. You can take home the Fleece, as proof of having honorably succeeded in your mission. And I can go home too." By now the prince had evidently realized that Proteus was present as something more than a mere bodyguard, and was talking to him almost as much as to Jason.

Apsyrtus seemed to have no doubt at all as to how that judgment would come out. Proteus had to bite his tongue to keep from shouting protests and bitter accusations. It was only with a great effort that he kept quiet, and wooden-faced. He would only be placing himself and his shipmates in greater danger if he let an enemy see violent disagreement in the camp of the Argonauts.

* * *

When the meeting was over, Apsyrtus calmly climbed back into his small boat, which had been more or less keeping up with the men as they walked along the shore, and was briskly rowed away, in the direction of one of the large warships across the channel.

After waving a farewell, Proteus and his captain started back to rejoin the other Argonauts near the ship. Jason for once did not ask his opinion, and Proteus did not offer it. Instead, a taut silence grew between them.

But when they returned to camp, Medea was waiting for them and demanded to know what had been decided. Her voice was loud enough for most of the men to hear, and a small crowd of interested Argonauts began to form.

Jason would have been glad to avoid the confrontation, but he saw no possibility of doing so. "I will get to keep the Fleece," he began, and paused.

"I see. What else?"

The captain glanced momentarily at Proteus, but could see no help in that direction. He sighed. "You are to go back to your father."

For the first time since they had met, Medea was glaring angrily at the man to whom she had been fastened by Cupid's Arrow. It took her a while to get out any words at all. "I don't believe it. You must be lying."

Around them, the men had now formed a solid circle of still, listening faces. The maid seemed about to weep.

What had once been Medea's attitude of supplication was gone, had turned into something else entirely. Jason's soul was quailing before that gaze.

"My—my lady, I only wish it were not true." It was the first time that Proteus had heard him stammer.

The princess boiled with rage. She swore with fishwife oaths to set the ship on fire, to break it up and hurl herself into the flames. Clenching her fists, she screamed out her appeal to the sky. "Gods, give me power! Great Loki, give me fire to burn! Among all these spineless Heroes, is there not one with manhood enough to stand by me?"

Jason was obviously frightened, but he forced himself to regain some measure of calm. "Enough, my lady. I am no happier about this business than you are. But we are seeking to stave off a fight, encircled as we are by a vast horde of enemies, and all on your account."

"On my account? On *my* account?" Her beauty had been transformed, by an anger so great that it must push all else aside, so that Proteus marveled. Now she was her father's daughter. Now Proteus, glancing back over his shoulder at the poor little wooden temple, half-hidden among trees, thought he knew what the chaste and terrible Artemis must look like when she was calling some human to account for some offense.

At the moment, the Mouse was doing her best to make herself invisible.

But Jason, who had faced the angry king with patient argument, was not about to be unnerved by a mere princess. He was speaking with relentless calm. ". . . and if we faced them in the field, we should every one of us be slaughtered. Would it not mortify you even more if we were killed and left you to them as a prize?"

Proteus could see that prospect gave the lady pause, despite her rage.

Jason pressed on, looking at her hopefully. "I said that your brother and I came to an agreement, and we did. But what he and I have said to each other is not necessarily the final word in this matter. Any agreement can be repudiated, if there is good cause."

"This one *must* be."

Maybe, thought Proteus, *this man is somewhat deeper and trickier than I have thought.*

The captain was nodding. "As you say. But this truce of a day, before you are to be given into the charge of the temple priestess, will give us a little time to plan. My lady, you know your brother well. Can you think of any kind of stratagem . . . ?"

Medea stood looking at Jason for a time. She looked at Proteus. Eventually she said: "We have started down a road that will allow no turning back. Therefore we must go on. The decision to come with you was mine, to begin with—though I could have done nothing else. So now it must be up to me to find the remedy."

She raised the gaze of her blue eyes, until she was staring into the distance. "I will trick Apsyrtus into coming back to the island once more, to talk with me alone . . ." Now her gaze suddenly fastened on Jason. "Then, if you have the manhood to do it, kill him. That will throw their whole fleet into chaos."

Proteus felt a chill on hearing those words fall so calmly from such soft and pretty lips—but after observing the lady at close range for several days, he was not as utterly surprised as he would have been before the Fleece was taken.

But he thought that Jason was truly startled, and could almost read the captain's mind. The captain must have thought he was beginning to understand this woman, but saw now that she was still really almost a total stranger.

What a pair we have here, thought Proteus to himself, studying them; what a pair indeed. Either they will do great things together, or they will meet some truly spectacular end.

The Mouse was hovering at the side of her mistress. From time to time the maid cast a quick look at Proteus as if to see whether this plan met with his approval.

Ignoring everyone but Jason, who still had not responded, Medea repeated icily: "Kill him, I say. Do you fear I will blame you later for my brother's death? Never! As you have seen, he is ready to kill me."

Jason remained cautious. "He didn't say that. He said—"

"Bah, do you believe him? And as soon as the men aboard my father's ships learn that he is dead, we must make our break for freedom, fighting our way through if necessary. I know the officers, and they will be uncertain then. At that moment they will break and yield, if you attack them fiercely enough."

A moment later, as if in silent agreement, Jason and Medea both turned toward him.

"Proteus, what do you think?" Jason asked him abruptly, while Medea slowly nodded. Meanwhile in the background the little maid seemed also waiting anxiously for his response.

Proteus cleared his throat. "I think, my lady, that, in the first place, if you are indeed turned over to the priestess in the temple of Artemis, we will not see you again, but your father will. Otherwise your brother would not have liked the arrangement so well."

The reluctant adviser paused before adding: "As to the plan you've just put forward, it is a treacherous business, and I can't say that I like it much. But at the same time I can think of nothing better. This has now become a war, and in war treachery has its place. We're less than forty men, one ship against a fleet. We'll not survive an open battle."

And even as he spoke, Proteus was wondering in the back of his mind how the goddess Artemis, the archetype of chastity and honor, would react to such murder and betrayal as the princess was proposing to perpetrate on her sacred island. But gods and goddesses tended to be remote and unpredictable—Proteus trusted his own instinctive judgment that it was so—and any deity was much less of an immediate threat than a determined prince who enjoyed a great military advantage.

Jason put the same conclusion in different words. "My princess, I would rather face an angry goddess than see you go to what may well await you at home."

Medea's look softened with relief when she heard this, and her color heightened. "Colchis is my home no longer." She seemed reassured by Jason's attitude, though Proteus, who had known him longer, thought the captain remained uncertain.

In a calmer voice Medea said to Jason: "I know something of my brother, and I know my father's officers, those who must be leading the forces that he commands here."

Jason was still uncertain. "I have seen unhappy omens."

"We cannot live by omens."

"And what good will it do us to kill one man, whoever he is? We'll still be bottled up by the king's fleet."

"I do not think so," said Medea in the new voice that had been hers since the great anger came upon her.

Now Jason looked at her with a new appreciation. It was not hard to imagine his thoughts: what a great queen the young woman before him would make, beautiful, intelligent, and ruthless.

But still he was seeking some way out of the Colchian trap, short of murdering her brother. The great persuader tried another tack. "What if we did not kill Apsyrtus, but took him alive and held him hostage?"

And the princess, though much shorter than the man who faced her, seemed again to be looking down at him. She said implacably: "And when and where would you set him free? Would King Pelias, in your homeland, thank you for bringing home the kidnapped son of King Aeetes? I think not. Taking him alive will only guarantee a relentless pursuit."

Jason tried another abortive argument or two, but in the end he had to agree that Medea must be right. "What do you think, Proteus?" he asked again, and got the nod of assent that he did not really want to see, or Proteus to give.

"Then the only remaining question," Proteus said, "is where and how are we to do it?"

Once the main decision had been reached, the details seemed to arrange themselves. An ambush was to be set inside the Temple of Artemis, at a time when all attendants would be out of the way.

Medea willingly undertook the task of explaining her plan to a larger group of Argonauts. She was certain that, once her brother was dead, the Colchian forces would retire in disorder. "Not a man of them will dare to bring that news back to the king. So it is when men are ruled by terror alone."

And the Argonauts marveled at her silently, but none objected.

"Who shall we send to Apsyrtus with the proposal?" And again their two heads turned together to look at Proteus.

Proteus was reluctant, but when Jason and Medea both pressed it on him, he at last agreed.

At first, he more than half expected the clever son of King Aeetes to see through such treachery, and refuse to come to any further meeting—but then he reflected that Medea must know her brother pretty well.

And the Mouse found another chance for a brief private talk. Giving Proteus a penetrating stare, she demanded: "It's Jason you are really after, isn't it?"

He shook his head. "Remember, if I wanted Jason dead, I've already had a hundred chances to do the job, before we ever got to Colchis. For that I'd have no need of fancy plans."

She seemed caught in an agony of wonder and indecision. "Then have you really turned your back on Pelias?"

"Judge me by what you see me do. Trust your own eyes and sense, if you won't trust what I say."

The Mouse chewed on her lower lip. "I can't stop you. I wouldn't want to, for I fear being dragged back with my mistress. But it must never be known in Iolcus that I have turned on Pelias. Such fearful things would happen—"

But at that moment they were interrupted, and he had only time to give the Mouse a nod and wink that he hoped were reassuring.

Later, in a more open talk, the Mouse told him she was ready to work hard for the success of any plan that kept her and her mistress from being dragged back to Colchis. "There'll be no brass pins there for my lady's eyeballs, and she knows it, whatever she might say. She just doesn't want to go back.

"But my own poor little body is another matter, and it might have to bear the burden of the king's anger. I'll be held to blame for not keeping my mistress at home in the first place."

The image of Aeetes taking out his wrath on the Mouse was entirely convincing, and it bothered Proteus more than he would have expected. "I wouldn't want to see anything like that happen to you."

She brightened slightly, but only for a moment.

And later, when they were alone again: "Do you know what, Proteus?"

"No, but I'm sure you're going to tell me."

"I have a strong suspicion that it's too late now."

"Too late for what?"

She made swift uncertain gestures. "I mean that something's happened to make it impossible for us to do whatever it was King Pelias sent you to do. Is that it? And you're afraid you'll have to tell Pelias of our failure? So is he going to take his anger out on both of us?" The Mouse was still quiet, living up to her nickname, but it was obvious that the prospect left her deeply terrified.

"No, that's not it," Proteus said on impulse. Suddenly he felt an urgent need to relieve her terror. "That's not it at all. We'll never have to see King Pelias again if we don't want to."

For a moment the Mouse stared at him helplessly. But once again other people were coming near, and once again she mastered her fright.

The story Medea conveyed to her brother, using her faithful maid-servant as a messenger, was that Jason and his gang had kidnapped her, dragged her with them quite against her will. She was ready to return home with her brother, and even to help him steal the Fleece back from these marauders.

When the Mouse returned from delivering the message, she said she thought that Apsyrtus had no suspicion of what was being planned for him.

Proteus crouched waiting in the dark, amid trees and bushes near the temple entrance, watching the path which Apsyrtus would almost certainly travel when he came to the appointed meeting. Insects were loud in the nearby undergrowth, and now and then there sounded a whispered oath and slap. Half a dozen chosen Argonauts were waiting close beside Proteus. When Jason and Medea sprang their trap in the temple, these men outside would prevent interference by any escort that the prince might have brought with him. Meanwhile the rest of the Heroic crew were also alert and ready, keeping out of sight at a slightly greater distance.

The handful of men with Proteus had little to say, to him or to each other. He had the feeling that they were looking at him more than usual, in a way that made him feel uneasy.

At last he spoke up: "If any of you think this treachery dishonorable, well, I can only say that you must have little experience of war. Anyway, it is we ourselves, our whole crew, who are being unjustly held as hostages, surrounded as we are. We are free men, and I say we have a right to kill. To regain our freedom."

No one answered that. They were still looking at him grimly, their faces hardly changing; and he realized suddenly that he was probably arguing more with himself than with any of them.

Night fell, and the time set for the secret rendezvous drew near.

Medea's brother (who with an amused attitude had kept reassuring Jason that no treachery was planned) came just as arranged to meet with Medea. He had left his small escort outside the temple at a little distance, and he was personally unarmed as he entered the small room where she was waiting.

Now in Medea's eyes her brother looked different than he had when in council with their father, more as she remembered him from the good days of her childhood. He spoke to her warmly and kindly, recalling pleasant things that had happened when she was only a little girl.

His voice was mild. "You don't need to be terrified, little one, about going home. I promise that I will prevent our father's doing anything really horrible to you. You believe me when I say that, don't you? Don't you?"

The princess in turn looked at Apsyrtus wooden-faced, and told him that the simple fact of being forced to return home, of being separated forever from Jason, who now meant everything to her, would be quite horrible enough. As bad as having her eyes poked out with long bronze pins.

Apsyrtus seemed genuinely concerned. "Surely this ambitious stranger cannot mean that much to you."

"I tell you he means my life."

The prince was puzzled. "You first laid eyes on this Jason only a few days ago. And surely you can see he is too weak in some ways ever to be a worthy king—a man like him will come to no good end." Then the elder brother lowered his voice a little. "Tell me, Medea—are you still a virgin? Has he formally proposed marriage?"

"I love him in a way that you are never going to understand!" And she gave the arranged signal. And saw in her brother's face that he had suddenly realized what was about to happen to him.

Jason leaped out of the closet, where he had been waiting in ambush, and ran at the Colchian prince with his sword raised.

Seeing his danger mirrored in his sister's face, Apsyrtus turned at the last moment, and his right hand went to his waist in search of the sword-hilt that was not there. But in any case the move would have been much too late. Jason's first thrust was true and deadly; Apsyrtus died with eyes and mouth agape in vast surprise, all elegance dissolved in blood. He fell clutching at old dusty draperies, a kind of tapestry depicting Diana on the hunt, and pulling the fabric down with him to the floor.

After striking the man down, Jason fell to his hands and knees, and went through a hasty ritual of thrice licking up blood, from the stones of the temple floor, and spitting it out.

It seemed that this particular superstition was a new one to Medea, and she recoiled from it. "Have you gone mad?" she demanded. Her voice was a mere rasp of breath. "What are you doing?"

"Keeping a ghost at bay. I hope." And awkwardly he scrambled to his feet. "You who know so much of magic, have you never heard of that?"

Meanwhile, just outside the temple, the six men who had come as escort with the prince were alerted by a scream from within. They drew their weapons, but before they could move to interfere, Proteus and his chosen companions jumped out of concealment and blocked their way.

Proteus raised his voice in a commanding shout. "Your prince is dead, and there is nothing you can do about it."

And just as he finished speaking, Medea emerged from the temple bearing a lighted torch. Right behind her came Jason, carrying the head of Apsyrtus by its long, curly hair. He held up the gory weight so the Colchians could be sure that there was no mistake.

By now, the remaining Argonauts had come pouring out of their slightly more distant places of concealment, and the half dozen Colchians were fenced in on three sides by an overwhelming force of thirty men. Only the path leading back to their boat was open to them.

"Your boat is waiting," Haraldur told them harshly.

There was a stunned and angry silence. In accordance with

Jason's orders, no blow had yet been struck outside the temple. The more of these Colchian fighting men who remained alive during the next few minutes the better, the more voices there would be to spread the word to their fleet that the prince was dead.

In another moment, the supporters of the murdered prince had turned and were jogging in retreat back along the path. The boat that had brought them to the island was anchored a little way off shore, with only one man in it; and while he waited with oars poised, wondering what had happened, the prince's surviving escort stood on shore screaming the terrible news out across the water to all the waiting Colchian ships. Their voices were hoarse and unsteady but very loud.

When the yelling had gone on for almost a full minute, Haraldur turned to Proteus. "Enough?" he asked.

"Enough." Proteus gestured, and the thirty Argonauts who had been waiting rushed on the six and slaughtered four of them—the other two quickly discarded their weapons, and managed to swim away in darkness. Meanwhile the one man in the boat had also opted for strategic retreat.

Having trotted back to the temple to report success, Proteus looked in to see the headless body of Apsyrtus on the floor, and Jason on his hands and knees beside it, licking up spots of the plentifully spilled blood, while Medea stood by icily controlled.

"By all the devils, man, what are you doing?" But even as Proteus voiced his shock, some dim recess of his memory produced a kind of explanation: a superstition claiming that by this means the ghost of a murderer's victim could be prevented from haunting him.

With Medea and the Mouse running as fast as any of the men, the entire body of Argonauts hastened to get aboard the *Argo*. In a few moments some thirty sturdy oarsmen were putting their whole backs into the oars, forcing them rapidly downstream.

Proteus had never seen Jason so shaken. It was almost as if the captain had never killed a man before; and Proteus knew that was not the case.

"I do not like the taste of blood," he muttered, wiping his smeared mouth on his sleeve, and hastily gulped down first a draught of water, then one of wine. Then he shuddered and looked around him, like a man in fear of immediate pursuit.

A few hours later, Jason also made such sacrifices as he could to Artemis, with the limited resources available on the ship. He said that such omens as he was able to detect were all unfavorable.

"One would think," Medea pondered, "that Diana might be angry with us too. Can anyone think of some way to placate her?"

"It is quite possible," offered Proteus, "that she didn't even notice." But those who heard him only looked at him strangely, and went on making their own suggestions. Each man and woman aboard had a firm personal conviction of what gods and goddesses must be like, though none of them had ever seen one.

Then they were all in the ship, and shoving off. Jason with vehement gestures silently urged the men to speed, and to quiet at the same time. The helmsman had turned *Argo*'s prow downstream, and they were making the greatest possible speed in that direction, in an effort to break through the ring of their pursuers while confusion reigned aboard the Colchian ships, and reach the open sea.

Never had the ship's more than thirty oars sounded so loud to Proteus as they did now. Once there drifted over the water, from somewhere in the darkness to their right, a sound of confused and muffled shouting, as if the crew of one or more Colchian ships might be reacting to the news of their leader's death. At any moment it seemed that one of the ships that had been standing watch might loom out of the darkness and cut off the fugitives' escape, but so far the darkness just ahead remained empty of their enemies.

Jason, seemingly well recovered from his horror, directed the steersman to hold in his mind the image of any peaceful, welcoming shore or island that might be available. Ideally this haven would be neither uncomfortably near, so pursuers would not stumble on it, nor more than a few days away. In earlier phases of their flight from Colchis they had often yearned for such a goal, but the compass-pyx had consistently refused to show them anything of the kind.

"But now I see it!" There was sudden elation in the navigator's voice, even while the man's face remained glued to his instrument. "Captain, a vision of the very place we want!"

The words sent a murmur of relief up and down the rowers' benches, creaking with the shifting weight of large, hard-working men.

"I will hold that thought too," Jason muttered. "How far have we to go?"

All the indications were that such an island was only about three days away, though no one could remember such a place being in this region, or what its name must be.

Proteus asked permission to take a look through the compass-pyx. When his forehead rested on the ivory box, there grew behind his closed eyelids a vision of an island, a beautiful place that seemed to him hauntingly familiar, though he could not recall its name. The vision was so clear, the island looked so large, that he thought it could be no more than a few days away.

When daylight came, there was no sign of any pursuit. It seemed that Medea's assessment had been correct, regarding what must follow on her brother's death.

The latest entry in the log said nothing of Prince Apsyrtus, certainly nothing of the manner of his death. It said little more than that the *Argo* had taken advantage of thick fog to slip past her blockaders.

And in fact as soon as the ship reached the open sea, a thick fog did indeed close in. Everyone aboard was willing to accept it as a sign that their luck had turned. The image of the welcoming island, only a few days distant, held firm in the mind of anyone who bent over the compass-pyx.

∘ *S I X T E E N* ∘

Isle of Dawn

hinking back as he rowed in darkness and silence, and observing the moon, which was just past full, Proteus reckoned that four full months had now elapsed since he had linked his fate to that of Jason and the Argonauts. A very short time, compared to the length of most human lives, but it was all he had in the way of remembered life. Before that stretched the void, shrouded in almost impenetrable fog, thirty years or so that were almost as much a mystery to him as if they still lay in his future.

When it came his turn to rest, and he fell asleep, there came to him strange dreams, in which he was aware of holding some kind of immensely powerful weapon, without being able to see it clearly, or knowing what it was.

Dawn found the *Argo* long since free of the maze of waterways. For hours they had been clean out of sight of land, headed for somewhere near the middle of the Great Sea. Patches of thick mist drifted over the ocean's surface, a most welcome sight to people who feared pursuit.

Through most of the morning, the hard-pressed crew kept up a weary struggle to make headway in a choppy sea. They were urged on by the steersman's latest report that now their goal, that still-nameless happy island where they would be able to rest in safety, could be no more than a day's effort distant.

Jason stared at him. "It was only a few hours ago when you said it would take us three days to reach the place."

The navigator was apologetic. "I cannot always read the instrument with perfect accuracy, captain. Now I am sure it will be much less."

"Let us hope that you are right this time." Then Jason wanted to know: "What is the name of this place we're headed for, and why did it not appear on any of our charts?" He sounded skeptical. "I still don't understand."

The navigator shook his head. "There is much in my craft that I have never understood. But there is no need, if we can obtain results. Just thank the gods, and the powers of the compass-pyx."

Dawn on that morning was no more than a troubled transition from dark to pearly gray, that brought little increase in visibility. Shortly afterward a low curtain of sea-mist parted, revealing near at hand their destination, an island of indeterminate size, lush with tropical growth.

Jason sounded numb. "First you said three days. Then an hour ago, you said one day. And now . . ."

"I am sorry, captain. I was wrong again. This is the place. I am absolutely certain."

The waning moon, no smaller now than when they had fled the temple island, was fading swiftly in new daylight, as it sank wearily toward a western horizon that was free of any trace of land.

Proteus was staring at the beach and ranks of vegetation now before them. "I have been here before," he murmured to himself.

Beside him, the Mouse shivered. "I do not think I like this place," the maid said suddenly, and wrapped her bare arms around herself, as if the warm air drifting over the warm sea had suddenly turned cold.

Medea, sounding as if she were suddenly in shock, murmured something about having visited this island once in a vision.

Haraldur had no time for visions now. "There's an easy beach, and a small stream to refill our casks. It seems to have everything we need. But . . ."

Proteus was suddenly, inwardly, completely certain of one thing. He got to his feet. In a clear voice he announced: "This is Circe's Island of Dawn."

Men around him groaned. "Then we are lost," one rower muttered, fatalistically.

But not everyone was ready to give in to imagined dangers, and others growled at the despairing one. Still, the men's reaction, as they leaned on their oars, coming into calmer water, was generally subdued. Frightening legends abounded about this place, the worst of them telling of men turned into animals, at the cruel whim of the enchantress. And many of the stories hinted that even greater horrors could happen here.

". . . things too terrible to talk about," someone was muttering.

Proteus almost laughed at that. He knew he had been here before and had survived. "Really? That's not the way people like to tell ghost stories, in my experience. Usually the most gruesome details are spelled out with loving care."

But the island waited invitingly before them, green and soft and welcoming. There was nothing in the least gruesome or alarming about the prospect.

How far was the Island of Dawn from Iolcus? Almost everyone aboard had a different opinion on that—Triton thought it was just about as far as Circe wanted it to be.

Something about the place—he couldn't tell if it was the sound of the gentle surf, or the aroma of spices on the offshore breeze—kept jogging Proteus's memory. Something very important to him had once happened here—but what? Vital clues to his real identity seemed to be bobbing like bubbles in the foam of the gentle surf, just out of his reach. Now he was absolutely certain that he had been to this place before.

The whole place looked entirely innocent, a spot of garden rimmed by surf and coral.

There were certain moments when he almost believed that the waves nibbling at the sand were speaking words, in a long-drawn-out splashy voice—words in a language he had once known, but had not yet remembered.

And more strongly than ever he felt a persistent sense of some stupendous revelation, hovering near—or was it only that he had had his head stuck into the compass-pyx too long? They said you put yourself in serious danger if you ever fell asleep with your forehead resting on the ivory box.

When he mentioned this to the Mouse, he got the answer: "If that's the worst danger we've got to worry about right now, we're in better shape than I think we are."

Another man complained: "What I don't understand is how the compass-pyx could be so easily deceived."

"There may be no deception," Proteus told him. "This may be a good place for our refitting."

In truth he suddenly had little interest in what his shipmates might be doing. The Island of Dawn was before him now, its sands beneath his feet as real and solid as any part of the earth that he had ever trodden. And the more he looked at it, the more he experienced maddening hints of familiarity.

Jason was urging Zetes and Calais to put on their flying sandals, and go scouting to see what might lie in the island's interior. The two brothers eagerly agreed. They promised to come back soon, and briskly took to the air.

Jason, shading his eyes, kept watch on them for a full minute, while they climbed on and on. "They look like sea birds," he finally remarked in a distant voice.

Those Heroes who were generally considered to have the keenest eyes kept up the watch when Jason and others had to abandon it.

"I've lost them." The Argonaut to give up the search seemed puzzled, shading his eyes and squinting. "There's only a couple of albatross."

While waiting for his scouts to return, Jason chose a spot to beach the ship. There was no problem finding an inviting place. They faced a long, broad, concave rim of white sand, curving along one side of a peaceful, half-wooded spot of land rising out of a warm sea. This was a much bigger island than the one they would all have been happy to forget, the little lump of dirt enclosed by a rough circle of freshwater shoreline, where the acolytes of outraged Artemis must still be hard at work trying to scrub away the bloodstains from the floor of the profaned temple. At least most of the Argonauts were assuming that Diana must be outraged—as far as Proteus knew, none of them had actually heard from her as yet. But the course their voyage had taken since the death of Apsyrtus seemed to show that some great power had taken an interest in them, bringing them here at an unnatural speed.

Circe's power was known to be formidable, Proteus thought to himself, but was it truly as wonderful as this? Had she some special hold upon the ship?

The condition of the *Argo* seemed to have deteriorated badly, over just the past few hours, and it needed work, on the central hull and both outriggers. Also they were running low on water, though naturally they had refilled all the jugs and skins before leaving the river.

And he had nowhere else to go. When he tried the compass-pyx again, it would show nothing but stark gloomy clouds, drifting over the open sea.

Proteus was driven by a mounting urge to explore the island on foot.

"Any chance we could just fill up our water jugs and skins and be on our way again?" one Argonaut was pleading.

"She is a goddess, no?" It was Haraldur who asked the question. His home was distant, and many of the gods and legends of this warm sea were still unfamiliar to him. "The one who turned men into beasts, in the stories. And this bit of land was hers?"

"It still is. And some of the stories do say that she's a goddess, but she's really not. Some call her a witch; I'd say enchantress." There were technical differences between those two.

"She hasn't come to welcome us," another man observed.

Proteus said nothing.

"You know her, then?"

Disbelieving looks were turned on Proteus, by men who had been forced to respect him by what they had seen him do. Yet the same feats made them jealous, and he knew they would be ready to mock at any false pretensions he might have, secretly rejoice at any failure.

He responded calmly. "She's only a woman, right? Is there any reason I couldn't have met her?"

His questioner considered. "One reason is, you've not been changed into an animal. I hear that one of her favorite tricks is to transform men into pigs."

The other was shocked. "Only a woman! Whoo! Might as well say that King Aeetes is only a man!"

He turned away from them, to scan the island again. "I do say that. As for Circe, she is . . . what she is."

Jason had made up his mind and uttered a terse order. They bent to their oars again, driving the ship firmly to the beach. And Proteus's shipmates, who had grown to know and trust him, were silent, looking at him strangely. But anything else any of them might have said was forgotten by the others in the subtle weird-ness of the island as they drew nearer to it, and nearer still.

As soon as *Argo* ground her bottom on the beach, the men clambered out of the long ship, as usual groaning with relief to get their bottoms off the hard benches. Then, moving quickly in a practiced deployment, they ranged along both sides of their vessel to tug her up a little more securely on the land.

Even before the ship had been dragged entirely out of the sea, Medea was standing on the sand, her maid beside her. Both women were still wearing the same impractical garments, now torn and shabby, in which they had fled their homeland. Or some of them. Medea's soft mantle had long ago been lost, and the Mouse's felt slippers had disintegrated.

The beach where the *Argo* now rested made part of the island's southern rim, bathed in life-sustaining sunlight. Here the surface rocks and white sand were pleasantly warmed. The sea shells on the strand were pretty . . . though Proteus had to admit to himself that there was something wrong with the shapes of some of them.

To the right of the new arrivals as they faced inland, there gurgled a pretty little creek, pouring fresh water into the sea. Ordinary seabirds flew up squawking, but as far as Proteus could see, the place was deserted of intelligent life. Yet he had the sense that certain immaterial powers that served as guardians and keepers here were hovering close by.

Several members of the crew tasted the water of the small stream and one of them pronounced it clear and clean.

"But is it safe to drink?" another asked.

"If the lady of this island wants to poison you," Proteus assured them, "she can do it through the air you breathe, or the sunlight falling on your skin. So you may as well drink deep of her water, if you are thirsty."

A couple of men were already beginning to fill the casks and jugs, so they would be ready in case of a hasty departure.

Even before the *Argo* had been made secure—as secure as any ship could ever be made on this beach—Proteus, driven by a rapidly growing sense of familiarity with this island, turned his back on the others, and set his feet on a small path leading inland, through exotic vegetation. Before he had gone twenty yards, the growth around him was tall and dense enough to hide the sea behind him. It seemed to him that he almost knew—ought to know—where he was going. He felt a growing certainty that here he could find the answers he had been seeking for the past four months.

As he turned his back on the others, he could hear a querulous murmur of voices behind him, but no one asked him where he was headed. Just treading the white sand of this beach made people begin to behave strangely. For a start, it turned some of them uncertain in their thoughts and actions.

Not Proteus, though. He felt suddenly more certain of what he ought to be doing. Already he had become aware of whispering, giggling sprites and spirits, a small mob of half-material onlookers who remained somehow just out of sight. Or almost. He could get an occasional glimpse of one of them, from the corner of his left eye.

He had not gone far before he could hear the scuffling of several pairs of feet following him swiftly on the narrow path, and he knew without turning who was coming after him. If he listened he thought he could pick out the faintly squeaking sandals of Medea and Jason, and the patter of the maid's bare feet. Presently Jason and Medea were practically at his elbows, the servant girl keeping close behind them.

"More and more," said Proteus, as if continuing a conversation already begun, "the conviction grows on me that I have been here before."

"When?" the princess demanded. And then, before he had a chance to answer: "Have you met my aunt? This may indeed be her island, for all I know, but I have never seen her."

Proteus ignored her questions. "It seems to me there is a . . . house. Yes, a house built of cut stones, and it stands in toward the center of the island, where the land is thickly wooded." At least he remembered it that way. "There were palm trees . . ." And there had been other trees, as well as certain growths that Proteus would not have known how to attempt to describe.

Jason deftly caught a branch that Proteus had pushed aside, before it could swing back and slap him in the face. The branch had leaves, or buds, that when seen at close range bore a startling resemblance to human hands and feet. The captain put in: "So, you've definitely been here before? Can you be sure of that?"

"Almost sure. Could there be two islands like this in the whole ocean? But still . . . no, I can't remember."

When Proteus tried to pin down in his mind the circumstances of his previous visit, the only really clear image that came was that of a young woman, sitting in the stone house. He tried to describe it to his companions. "The woman was dark, and beautiful . . . and she sang as she worked at her loom."

"A weaver?" Medea asked. "Some artisan or servant?"

"No. But working as great ladies sometimes do, for their own enjoyment." He looked at Medea.

"They say my Aunt Circe is dark and beautiful. But I have never seen her. What was she weaving?" Medea sounded truly interested.

"A thin—web of some kind." The material, as Proteus remembered it, had looked incredibly soft and delicate. "Shot through with spectacular colors . . . you would think that no one but a goddess could have created such a fabric."

Jason was looking at him strangely. "How did you come to be here, Proteus? That other time?"

He was saved from trying to answer by the fact that the thin path opened abruptly into a sizable clearing. They had come in sight of the house, a low structure of irregular form; and it was truly strange enough to be worthy of its mistress. The stones of which it was constructed might have climbed up out of the earth of their own accord, and formed themselves into a shape that was certainly not natural, but not like that of any other building that any of the visitors had ever seen. No sound came from the house, no smoke rose from its odd chimneys. Several low, broad, shutterless windows and doorless doorways stood open—there was no apparent way any of them could be closed. But as soon as Proteus approached the nearest entrance meaning to look in, all of the seemingly unguarded apertures quivered, like so many reflections in water, and disappeared, leaving only the inhospitable stone wall to foil his curiosity.

Involuntarily Proteus retreated a couple of steps.

"The place looks deserted," Jason commented.

"Almost," amended Proteus. And the visitors were treated to a peal of tinkling laughter, nearby but proceeding from some invisible source that none of the hearers could identify.

Putting one hand in a pocket of his tunic, he felt the "Tooth" he had stuffed in there before Jason underwent the trial of the Bulls. Proteus had believed when he pocketed the Tooth that he had known someone who would be very glad to have a thing like this—someone, but *who?*

Probably not Circe.

Something moved, gathered itself into an odd visual patterning at one corner of the house. Proteus supposed that there might well be some real creature in that position, just beyond the corner, gripping the stone corner of the building with some of its overgenerous complement of ill-assorted limbs. Could human fingers sprout from a bear's paw, or a crab's claw at the end of a pale and girlish wrist?

. . . or all these appearances could be nothing but strange illusion . . . and might not the whole island be little more than that?

Proteus had turned, skirting the edge of the clearing, and was soon heading briskly away from it along another path. Now he knew, he remembered before he saw, which way this particular path was going to curve next. His companions were keeping up with him.

"Where are we going now?" Jason for the time being had become very much a follower. Medea and the maid diligently kept pace, as if they might be afraid of being left behind.

But Proteus was gaining confidence. Instead of disturbing him, each new marvel presented by the island somehow made him feel more secure. "I think I know where we can find her. All this . . . is somehow very familiar to me."

On leaving the clearing that held the house, Proteus had thought that he was still headed toward the very center of the island, but once he got in among the trees things became momentarily confusing. Then all the elements of his mental map seemed to straighten out, fall into place again in a new configuration. His feet kept carrying him along the path, and before he knew it, another part of the beach was right ahead of him. And over there in the distance, though not in the direction where it ought to be, he could see the *Argo* run aground like a toy ship on those distant sands, and a clustering of Argonauts around her, some of them no doubt trying to get started with their repairs. Jason should have stayed back there with them, he thought.

But he spared no more than a brief glance for ship and Argonauts. Some ten or twelve paces directly ahead of him, a nude young woman stood waist deep in the warm water, bending gracefully to bathe her long, dark hair in the soft foam of the gentle waves. Unalarmed, she straightened at his approach, tossing her head to throw back her wet hair, and fixed him with a look that slowed his steps on the firm sand.

And a moment later, a look of blank astonishment had come over her face.

In a regal voice the lady in the water suddenly demanded: "Who in all the Tombs of Tartarus are you? And what are you doing here?"

Circe

$\mathcal{S}$een at another time, and in another person, Circe's abrupt change from complete self-possession to amazement might have been comical. But Proteus felt no impulse to laugh. In Colchis, Bebrycos, and Samothraki, all lands entirely strange to him, he had been recognized—and here, where he had been certain he must be known, he was a complete stranger to the lady who knew so much.

He said to her: "My name is Proteus."

"Is it, indeed? Well, that means nothing to me." She tossed wet hair away from her face, and stared at him as if to see him better.

He said: "As to why I am here, I had hoped, my lady Circe, that you might be able to tell me that."

The enchantress was still puzzled. But not completely, not any longer. On some level understanding was beginning to creep in.

Now Circe was thinking hard, but had not yet quite found the explanation that she needed. "Proteus, is it? Am I supposed to know you, sailor? Your face is as unfamiliar as it is ugly. But you take a damned familiar attitude."

Proteus had no answer for that. While he waited for her to speak again, his gaze ran boldly over her unclad body—shapely, lovely almost beyond imagining. But some greater urgency hung in the air, formless but as effective as a threat of death, keeping his mind from dwelling on carnal matters.

Proteus did not turn to look behind him, but he knew his three companions must still be hovering there warily, in the shade at the edge of the forest. He had no doubt that Circe was fully aware of their presence, but she paid them no attention. For some reason she was still puzzling over her visitor, and at last she said to him:

"I had better call you Bringer of Bad Dreams. That is who you are, today."

"Why 'bad dreams,' lady?"

Ignoring the question, she stepped up onto the dry beach, past a thin wrack of drying seaweed, and picked up a single garment that lay there, swirling it about her in a burst of fragile color. A moment later she stood garbed in something like a rainbow . . . a cloud of fine fabric, woven of all colors and of none.

Then suddenly she rounded on him again. "Now I begin to suspect what has happened. I see a possibility, at least . . . but if that is true, what else have I misjudged?"

Proteus waited silently.

In another moment Circe was nodding to herself. "It must be so. And if your friends hiding back there in the trees are the people I have been assuming they must be—the situation grows very interesting. Though not at all amusing."

"They are the Princess Medea of Colchis, and Jason the adventurer. And—"

"Yes, as I expected. You need not explain *them*. But you had better explain yourself, if you can."

"My self is one subject about which I know very little. I may as well admit to you, lady, that I have suffered a great loss of memory. But," he persisted, "why did you call me Bringer of Bad Dreams?"

"Loss of memory, is it? Yes, that fits." And again the lady studied him. The silence between them went on until he began to feel seriously frightened. When she proceeded it was with an air of caution, and on what seemed another subject. "Only a few hours ago I was terrified by a nightmare. I think it must have been sent me by the Prince Asterion of Corycus—have you ever met him? No? You will, one day—and he was trying to prepare me for your arrival here today." The lady paused. "I do mean to have some revenge on the prince, for sending me such a nightmare. I think I will dispatch him in return something that will not amuse him, to join him in his Labyrinth."

And there came another flash of returning memory. It was a startling image, come and gone like a reflection in the shattered surface of a pool. At some time in the past he, Proteus, must have been in the presence of Prince Asterion, and not in any dream, either. Clearly he could recall looking at what legend called the Minotaur, a seven-foot figure with the head of a bull on the body of a powerful man, dwelling in the Corycan Labyrinth.

Circe was speaking to him again. "Do you wish to know about my nightmare, you who now call yourself Proteus?"

"That is my name. Who were you expecting, if not me?"

The lady ignored the question. "It seemed to me as I slept that I saw all the rooms and walls of my house streaming with blood, and flames consuming all my implements of magic . . ." Circe's voice of silvery beauty faded, and for a moment she seemed lost in inward contemplation.

"And how did you deal with this nightmare, lady?"

"Successfully, as I deal with most things. The red flames I quenched with the blood of a murdered man."

"Of which you just happened to have a fresh supply on hand?"

"You are a bold little sailor, are you not?—and so in time the hideous vision passed. When morning came I arose from my bed, and as you see, I have been washing my hair and my body in the sea."

"If you are trying to terrify me, my lady Circe—"

She raised an imperious eyebrow. "Why on earth should I waste my time doing that?"

"—then I would say you are having—no more than a moderate success."

That drew a laugh from the enchantress. Standing in a bold pose, her hands on hips, she said: "Nor do I seem to be doing all

that well in my actual endeavors. But enough of my difficulties."
She was looking steadily at Proteus. "I suppose it is useless to ask
what you have to report to me?"

"Report," he echoed stupidly. And suddenly, without warning,
he almost knew, almost reached the beginning of understanding. It
was like trying to recall an elusive dream, that kept slipping away
even as you sought to grasp it. There was a frantic turmoil inside
his head. Slowly he raised both hands, clasping his skull with the
feeling it might be about to burst. Memories were clamoring more
stridently than ever, trying to come through.

But the great explosion that must come sometime was not yet.
He said: "There are matters I know I should report to someone. I
feel certain that I have seen your face before, my lady Circe—"

"Oh, have you indeed? But the problem is that I have not seen
yours. You are not the man I was expecting."

"—but what I see in you may be only a certain resemblance to
the king of Colchis, who is said to be your brother. He of course
looks very much older than you. But . . ."

Circe ignored the king of Colchis. "And do you know how
and why this calamity befell you, this loss of memory? Were you
attacked by a Giant, by any chance?"

"I was—but by what magic do you know that?"

"No magic is necessary, only a little thought. Tell me whatever details you can remember."

That did not take long. As Proteus finished the relation, he
looked up, startled at the soft sound of approaching footsteps. For
a moment he had forgotten that he had not come here alone.

Evidently Jason and Medea had gradually taken courage from
the sight of what seemed a peaceful conversation, and had been
emboldened to come forward out of the jungle, with the maid
behind them timidly following her mistress.

But Proteus was not going to put up with an interruption, not
just now. He faced back to Circe. "Who am I?" The question
grated out in tones of desperation.

She squinted at him with what looked like sheer contempt, and the tone of her voice matched her expression. "You know full well who you are. Though it seems that for some reason you have been trying to deny it, even to yourself. Ah, what tricks the mind can play! Even a ruined one like yours."

As the three newcomers halted uncertainly a few steps away, Circe spoke decisively. "Come with me, all four of you. Come to my house." Then she threw a glance over her shoulder at the distant ship and the busy men around it. "Do you suppose your shipmates can manage to keep themselves out of trouble while we talk?—but never mind, I will send them something to keep them amused."

Then all four of Circe's visitors followed her as she walked briskly back to the center of the island. Once again the stone house displayed its full complement of windows and doors.

With a gesture she silently invited them to enter.

The interior was a cheerful place, with a small fire crackling brightly on a small hearth. A casual visitor might well have thought that some happy, industrious young woman, whose main concern in life was weaving, lived here alone. It took a closer inspection to discover the disturbing notes, like the peculiarities in the tiling of the floor.

But at the moment the sorceress looked anything but happy. Her great dark eyes were fixed upon Medea. When the enchantress spoke, there was true grief in her voice, and at one point it almost broke.

"You should realize that I had plans for my nephew Apsyrtus. He was to have done great things in the world, one day. But now you have murdered him—actually slaughtered your own brother— and I cannot forgive you for that. Now you are here, and I shall decide how you are to answer for your crime."

The girl gave a strangled little cry, covered her eyes, and collapsed in a heap upon the strangely patterned tiling of the floor, from which Proteus had to tear his gaze away before it hypnotized him. If Medea's action was a ploy to gain sympathy, her aunt was no more affected by it than were the floor tiles. Jason moved to Medea's side and knelt by her, touching her hair awkwardly. Then he stood up again and confronted the enchantress.

"That will do no good, my girl." Circe, with a graceful swirl of her fine clothing, seated herself in an elaborately carved chair. "But, I must not forget my own responsibilities. While you are here, you are all my guests. Be seated."

Suddenly stools were conveniently on hand, for all but the maid, who sat on the floor, tucking her feet beneath her. In the background Proteus was able to detect a half-seen scurrying of inhuman servants, almost imperceptible to human senses. Covered dishes holding delicious food appeared suddenly on tables, as if from nowhere.

For no reason that Proteus could see, the maid had put her hands over her eyes, and groped her way to a corner of the room, where she cowered down in silent fear. Proteus suddenly felt sorry for the Mouse, and moved to her side and touched her gently. She seized his hand in both of hers and held on tight, meanwhile keeping her eyes tightly shut. Her mouth was twisted into an unhappy line. Proteus understood that Circe must have given her something to look at that no one else could see—that no one would want to see.

Again Proteus could feel flashes of memory coming and going. Someone, long ago in what seemed another lifetime, had once said to him: "Circe is not always kind . . ." Had the speaker actually been Prince Asterion?

Memory suddenly produced ghastly pictures, of fiendish tortures, men turned into animals, as in the stories. And the anonymous voice went on: "But she is Apollo's friend . . . also other gods have been here, upon this island, coming and going over a long, long time."

Meanwhile the enchantress had given herself over to a long contemplation of her trembling niece who was now seated on a stool, and looked, if anything, unhappier than her maid. Jason had seated himself beside her, and she clutched his hand.

When Circe spoke again her voice was chill.

"And so you, my brother's daughter, have not only murdered your own brother, but have been voyaging, practically unattended, halfway across the world with a boatload of strange foreign men." Somehow it did not seem incongruous that she made the two offenses sound approximately equal.

Now Medea raised her head and sat up straight. Her fear was momentarily overcome by anger, and hotly she proclaimed that she was still a virgin. And anyway, she had not been traveling unattended.

Her aunt acknowledged those points with a nod. "Then perhaps your crimes are not as bad as they might be," she admitted grudgingly. "But let me hear from your own lips the story of what happened to your brother in Diana's temple."

Sitting at ease in her own strange chair, the enchantress listened to Medea's version of her brother's death, interspersed with the girl's anguished pleas for forgiveness. The story was not too different from the way that Proteus remembered the events.

These Circe abruptly interrupted. "And this one?" Her pointing finger indicated Proteus. "What part had he in this crime?"

"My part was one of loyalty," Proteus answered for himself. "To those I had engaged to serve."

The enchantress snorted her contempt.

He went on. "Call it a crime if you like, but it was no more criminal than any other stratagem of war. We were surrounded, unable to get away, defending ourselves against attack."

Circe looked at him as if she were disgusted beyond words. Proteus stared boldly back.

Jason spoke up at last. "What Proteus says is true. And had the princess gone back to her father the king, as he demanded, he would probably have killed her!"

"Would that not have been a just punishment for her crimes?" The enchantress shook her head. "But I really doubt that even Aeetes would have been so headstrong. Marriageable princesses are much too valuable in the games of empire."

"What else could we have done?" Jason argued weakly.

The enchantress stared at the captain of the Argonauts for a little, then looked away again, as if she considered him not worth even a comment. "I would see you all punished," she said at last. "But I begin to suspect that it is all out of my hands anyway. I see now that the great gods were foolish to depend on you to obtain the Golden Fleece for them."

Circe raised one slim hand toward Jason, and pointed two fingers at him, and his head nodded abruptly. In a moment he was fast asleep, though still sitting more or less upright on his stool. In the space of a few more heartbeats, Circe had done the same to Medea and the Mouse.

Now the enchantress and Proteus were effectively alone together. She arose from her chair and went to stand directly in front of him, while he let go of the Mouse's hand, and stood up straight, as if to be ready for anything. Circe looked directly into his eyes, for what seemed to him a long time. He was surprised at himself, at his own ability to stare back so boldly at this woman of whom most of the world would be utterly terrified. And indeed he was—no, not terrified, but wary, of what she might be planning to do next.

It was Circe who broke off the confrontation at last, took a few graceful steps around her room, and then turned to face her visitor again, this time from a slightly greater distance.

Her voice was regally amused. "I have said that *you* know who you are, and now I too have made sure of your identity. It was easy enough to discover, once I looked into your eyes. I saw more than a simple sailor looking back."

Now that the answer seemed almost in his grasp, he was

afraid to reach for it. "How did you bring us here?" he asked. "You have some connection to the *Argo*, don't you? Some means of control, built into the very ship herself."

Her dark eyes smiled at him. "And where do you think the money came from, to build and outfit your Hero-captain's gallant ship?"

"Ah," said Proteus.

Circe smiled. "There were intermediaries, of course, who did their job quite cleverly. Jason has not the least suspicion, that I am—or was—his real sponsor against King Pelias."

"I see."

"Now let me ask you again, you who now wear the body of the common sailor and blackguard Proteus—which Giant was it you encountered, just before you found your way aboard the *Argo*?"

And with a little help from Circe, the scene of that disastrous shipwreck and his succeeding struggle in the water, came back to Proteus.

The memory, when it finally came, was vivid and luminous as a drug-vision, and left him sweating and swaying slightly on his feet.

Circe's voice broke through, recalling Proteus to the here and now. "I never learned that Giant's name," he said.

She seemed faintly disappointed. "Never mind, then, it matters little. But now do you begin to understand? About yourself?"

"I am a god." The words came out in a low voice, deep and confident. Even in his own ears it did not sound much like the voice of Proteus.

"Indeed you are! And which god are you? Such little details do make quite a difference, you know. Does your recovered memory extend that far?"

"I am Triton, one of the gods of the sea."

"Of course you are."

"And I killed that Giant, the one who wrecked the ship, after he came near to killing me." Now he could remember the frothing waves, all black with the monster's blood.

"And I am glad we have begun to clear that up."

And Triton, who for the last few months had been as one with the human Proteus, raised his head and looked at the woman before him with new authority. In his changed voice he said: "I begin to remember other things. A few more. You and I had an agreement."

"Better and better!" Circe clapped her hands, and in response shrilling little voices cried out in all the corners of the room. "Of course we did. That was when you were in your previous avatar— the human body in which you walked around before acquiring this one—you do still understand how the business works? Ah, good. Terrible things the Giants' weapon can do to a god's memory! But in your case it might have been worse, for certainly there is still a good deal of Triton left. Probably more of your memory will come back in time." She sounded as if that were a mere detail.

She was still looking at him, but her voice changed. "And Proteus, worthy sailor, how do you do? I suppose I must accept you as a colleague now." The enchantress paused, studying him again. "Hah, but perhaps even as a mere human you were more than a worthy sailor! Or should I say you were less?"

Now she raised a slender hand, bejeweled with several rings, and slapped him stingingly on both cheeks, back and forth. Again she looked into his eyes. Jason and Medea still slumbered on their chairs, and the Mouse lay curled up on the floor.

"Proteus the sailor, whoever you are, or were—probably some poor fool of a wandering tramp—do you understand now that you have the glorious good fortune to wear the Face of Triton inside your head? To enjoy his powers, to blend his memories—such of them as that befuddled divinity has left—with your own?"

Proteus/Triton was nodding slowly, in agreement. Circe nodded with him as she went on, as if musing to herself: "I can see now how it must have happened. Your avatar with whom I had made alliance was killed at sea, when a Giant attacked the boat that was carrying Jason's would-be servants. And you, lucky Proteus, whether sailor or servant, you were quick enough to save your life by grabbing up the Face of Triton when it came popping out of the dead man's head. That, you may recall, is what Faces always do when their wearers' lives are quenched.

"The Giant must have seen that the god he meant to destroy was about to take up his abode in a different body. For he blasted you again, blasted the new body, with that strange infernal weapon Giants have, against which not even the greatest deity can stand. That wiped away still more of Triton's memory, and most of the human memory that had just become attached to it.

"But, lucky for both of you, dear Triton and dear Proteus, the residue of powers remaining were great enough to somehow enable you to escape with your life."

"I tell you, I killed that Giant," said Triton's voice, coming again from the throat of Proteus. The man knew that the god dwelt in the god-Face now resting inside his head, and that for the rest of his life Triton must share his identity. Human and god, on terms of greater intimacy than could ever exist between two merely human beings.

Triton/Proteus looked down at his empty hands, and his voice grew puzzled. "Somehow at that point I still had my Trident with me, and I struck him down. Though where it could be now . . ."

He let that worry drop, for there were even more demanding problems to be faced. Now that he knew who he was, the answers to certain puzzles became terribly clear.

There was one important thing about him that Circe did not know. Old Proteus had been no mere wandering sailor, but the secret agent of King Pelias. Probably a trained and skilled assassin, under orders to kill Jason, or at least to prevent his taking the throne of Iolcus.

But at the same time, whether Old Proteus had ever suspected it or not, Triton in his previous avatar had been working on the other side, secretly allied with Circe and probably with the great gods too, somehow bound and sworn to help Jason get the Fleece—but then to take the treasure from him, and deliver it to the great gods to fit some purpose of their own.

Complications within complications. It was enough to make a man's head ache, or even a god's head, and it did. He was no longer a secret agent. No, nothing as simple as that. In fact he was now two of them, working for opposite sides, each of whom seemed to have good reason to kill the other.

It was even possible that Old Proteus had somehow signaled or guided the Giant who wrecked the ship to the spot in the ocean where he might ambush and kill the god. But that was not to be.

Instead, Fate had seen to it that what was left of the human assassin Proteus had been coupled for life with what was left of his divine intended victim. Then the sole survivor, the product of their union, a hybrid as innocent—well, almost—as a baby, had come wading out of the sea, his only surviving purpose to join the Argonauts.

It was all a monstrous jest, so magnificently horrible that Triton/Proteus began to chuckle to himself. Proteus/Triton thought that there was no way anyone else on earth could fully understand his situation. Not even the powerful enchantress, who saw only half of it.

"What are you laughing at?" Circe demanded.

"Nothing. Everything. The world." And his roaring laugh burst out again. The man who was now also a god, the god who could never be anything if he possessed no human body, clutched at his throbbing head and groaned amid his laughter, so did the laughter shake him.

Now he could understand about the Boy. The god Cupid, somehow recognizing his divine colleague Triton and indifferent to what avatar Triton might currently be wearing, had passed on the orders of the great gods, who wanted some man called Proteus dead.

Looking at the Mouse, who still lay on the floor, Proteus could now begin to understand her attitude toward him. Being originally from Iolcus, she must have seen him there, and now she saw in him nothing but the evil tool he had once been. What exactly might Old Proteus have done, to make her hate and fear him so?

The enchantress refused to be amused. "If it is nothing, I would advise you to stop this hysteria. We have practical matters to deal with."

Slowly he got his feelings under control. Even the wishes of the great gods would have to wait for a little while. The practical matter first in Circe's thoughts at the moment was her own anger with her niece, and with Jason as well, for somehow getting the girl involved in all this.

Of course Triton had been involved too. But being openly angry with a deity was a little different, even for Circe. Even though she snapped at Proteus: "Do not think you will be spared, just because you are a god!"

That brought his fading laughter to a conclusion. "Are those the friendliest words that you can find to say to me?"

Circe appeared to reconsider. "Let us not quarrel, Triton. The god of the Trident and the waves is welcome to my home, as always."

"My gratitude for your hospitality."

"Any favor I may do my Lord Triton will be reciprocated, I am sure." Certainly there was as much mockery in her tone as in his.

"I shall do what I can for you, in turn," Triton said, more seriously, and paused. After a moment he added: "I have wondered sometimes why you never seek divinity for yourself. You must know, sometime, when Faces become available. I have heard from other gods that Circe has turned down more than one opportunity along that line."

"I am content with what I have." Circe's smile was serene and private. "As I am sure the Lord of the Sea must know, the fire of divinity is a consuming one, when it catches in a merely human mind and body."

"I doubt that that is always so." Triton was not much interested, it seemed, in pursuing the subject further—and Proteus was afraid to do so.

"Perhaps, my Lord Triton, I remember some of your earlier avatars much more clearly than you do." And Circe smiled in a way that was as old as sensuality. And Proteus, old memories suddenly prodded into life, experienced a brief odd vision of seeing what seemed to be himself in a handsome but totally unfamiliar body.

"One additional word of warning, my friend," the dark-haired woman said, after the silence between them had stretched on for a little while.

"Yes?"

"It is for the man called Proteus, and not the Lord Triton, and it is only this: that the human body when serving as the avatar of any god will eventually wear through and collapse; there is a limit to how long the power of any god can sustain it . . . the immortality of the gods is only a cruel hoax where human beings are concerned."

"And I have a question for you, friend Circe. What of these people?" And he made a sweeping gesture that included Jason, Medea, and the Mouse.

Circe's anger now seemed mostly spent. "When they have given me the Fleece, they can go on with their voyage, and I will leave it up to the great gods to decide on what punishment they may deserve . . . do you go with the *Argo*, Triton?"

"I do. I find that I am still an Argonaut."

Now his hostess rose gracefully from her chair, in what seemed to be an indication that she was ready for her visitor to take his leave. The Mouse rose from the floor, and, moving with the air of a relaxed sleepwalker, found herself a chair.

One of Circe's thin dark eyebrows rose. "One final bit of advice."

"Yes?"

"I strongly recommend that on departing from the Isle of Dawn the Lord Triton should cease to tie his fate to that of Jason the adventurer."

"And why is that?"

"Because Jason will never be king anywhere." With her eyes closed, Circe added: "It is irritating to find a god in a new avatar every time I look around. I prefer some measure of stability. Not to mention intelligence. In the old stories the gods are forever disguising themselves as humans, ordinary mortals, and prowling around the earth in search of adventure. But in a sense such a disguise is no disguise at all."

The walls of the stone house were thick, but Proteus/Triton had a god's keen hearing. Outside the gulls had fallen silent, but in the pines some wild birds that few human eyes had ever seen were screaming frantically at one another, caught up in some conflict that had nothing to do with either gods or humans.

Something had distracted him, but Circe was still speaking. "It is not out of kindness that the mighty god who shares your body refrains from seizing total control of the flesh and bone. Kindness has nothing to do with it. The real reason you retain your freedom is that Triton, who is granted life and being by your body, has no real life at all without a human partner. And as long as you are his avatar, he can do nothing that the man Proteus does not want to do."

"If you know so much about it, woman, answer me this: Where did the *powers that are captured in the Faces* come from, in the first place? Who created them?"

"I think it is a pointless question. As well ask where we humans came from, and who created us." Then Circe looked at Medea, and added: "Bad things will happen to that girl, whether she is allowed to make good her escape from her father or not. I might forgive her—though I do not—but that would not be the end of the matter. I have said that her case must now be left in the hands of the great gods."

Triton suddenly put in: "Circe, more of my memory's coming back."

"Oh?"

"Yes. I now recall something of what our agreement, yours and mine, must actually have been about."

"So now you are going to tell me what you think it was."

"Yes I am. You told me that our side, the side of the great gods who fight the Giants, must have the Fleece, that it would somehow be of enormous value to them in the war. 'Our allies in their secret workshops' is how you put it, now that I recall.

"You and I agreed that I should disguise my divinity and join the Argonauts. My avatar before this one was, like this one, a sailor—among other things. Our hope, yours and mine, was that the Giant who watched over the Fleece might not be on his guard if I approached him as only one of a group of common sailors. If he thought me no more than human, I could take him by surprise, get near enough to kill him before he realized the truth, then snatch away the prize."

"Very good, Master Triton." Now Circe's attitude seemed that of a schoolmistress grilling a difficult but promising student. "And what else do you remember?"

Slowly he shook his head. "Only that it seems to me I could have done as much without your help. What was I, Triton, sup- posed to get in return when I brought you back the Fleece?"

"That may come back to you someday. Let me know if it does." There seemed a hint of the demonic in her smile.

"There is one other point. If Zeus and Apollo want the Fleece, why should they not simply have gone to Colchis and taken it? Who could oppose them?" But even as he asked the question, the answer was there in his recovering memory.

"Oh. Giants, of course." Zeus and Apollo had feared to go to the grove in Colchis, because they knew it was guarded by a Giant who lay in ambush, ready to destroy their memories as soon as they came in sight.

Circe was saying: "Even the great gods have their weaknesses, and sometimes they even behave like idiots. But I am on their side in this; I have no wish to see the whole world ruled by Giants."

And she snapped her fingers sharply, once, and the walls of the stone house disappeared from around them, and the five people were all now sitting in chairs at the inner edge of a broad beach, with gentle surf a hundred feet away. In the distance Proteus could see the drawn-up *Argo*, and most of her crew busying themselves around her.

Once more Circe snapped her fingers, and the heads of three mortals rose from dreaming slumber, and their eyes came open. And Circe held out an imperious hand to Jason.

"Now bring me the Fleece!"

Waves

*J*ason stood up from the chair in which he had been sleeping, drawing his clenched fists close in front of his body, as if the Fleece were in them. But he was wearing only a loincloth and sandals at the moment, and obviously the treasure was somewhere else. If he was astonished by the disappearance of the house, his face did not betray the fact.

When he spoke, his voice held raw defiance.

"That treasure is mine, my lady Circe. I will not surrender it, even to you. The crown that was stolen from my family must be restored—"

The lady put on the manner of a nursemaid, dealing with a noisy child. "Cease your babbling and bring me the Golden Fleece at once. Unless you want to lose much more than a mere chance at a crown." And she flicked the fingers of one hand in a gesture of dismissal.

Even as the enchantress spoke, Medea stood up from her chair too. Now the princess looked as if she might even be able to defy her aunt. She had heard the threat and was afraid for Jason, and seemed determined to drag him away from Circe before he met some truly terrible fate.

Meanwhile the princess was pleading for the man she loved. "Forgive him, Aunt Circe! He doesn't know what he's talking about. If you really must have the Fleece, I'm sure that something can be worked out . . ."

Circe only glared at her niece imperiously. Then, as if struck by a sudden suspicion, Circe lunged forward and seized her by her dress, the upper part of which she pulled violently aside. Circe stared intently at the skin between the firm young breasts, then spun the girl around, as if she were weightless, and inspected the corresponding location on her back.

Then she turned to once more confront Proteus/Triton. "Suppose you tell me, little sailor, did you see anything of Eros in the course of your journey? Perhaps when you were at Aeetes's court?"

Proteus/Triton saw no reason to aid the enchantress in her discoveries. He tried to sound obtuse. "The god Eros?"

The voice of Circe crackled. "Do you know of any mortal human going by that name? I certainly do not."

"No. But I don't see what connection you think Cupid might have . . . wait, though. There was a Boy. Somewhat odd-looking."

"Tell me about him."

"He was carrying a bow and arrow—so small that they looked like mere toys. I thought them ritual objects."

Meanwhile, Jason had seemed about to protest Circe's rough handling of Medea. But then he only bowed lightly to Circe and walked away in the direction of his ship, both fists still clenched. Medea walked by his side, tugging at him as if to get him away from Circe as rapidly as possible, and the maid, who had wakened with the others, went with her mistress. Circe paid them no attention.

No, thought Proteus, he's not going to give it up that easily. He'll try something desperate first. Proteus/Triton was uncertain exactly where the treasure was now stowed aboard the ship—he knew that Jason tended to move it nervously from one place of concealment to another. He supposed that Medea had done what she could to give its current hiding place some magical protection, but it was hardly possible that the princess would be able to hide anything from her aunt.

The enchantress still concentrated on the visiting god. "And where did you happen to observe this peculiar lad?"

"In Colchis, not far outside the walls of the capital. He walked past me while I was standing guard. Jason and Medea were having their first private meeting. The Boy was wearing an odd kind of cloak, or robe, bunched up around his shoulders—"

"Hiding his wings." Circe nodded briskly.

"By all the gods!" Triton/Proteus feigned surprise. *Let the old witch go on thinking he was more befuddled than he really was.*

"By some of the gods, at least," Circe corrected, carefully studying the deity before her. "I am sure that in this case Eros had his orders from above."

"But why would he want to hide his wings?"

"In case some human did catch sight of him, despite his wish to remain invisible."

Triton shook the head of his human avatar, as if in a futile attempt to call up ancient memories. "I took the Boy for one of Medea's attendants. I thought they were planning some ceremony, or religious rite, and that he must have some role to play. In passing he gave me a wink—as if he thought we shared some secret."

"Fool!"

The voice of Triton changed. "A dangerous name to call any god to his face, old woman. Are you applying it to Eros, or to me?"

"Both of you were idiots, and probably still are! But Cupid at least followed orders. He was told to hit Medea with an Arrow, and he evidently did."

"Are you in the habit of giving orders to gods?"

"Not to important ones. But I happen to know that they were given to the Boy, by Athena herself, or maybe Aphrodite."

There was a pause. Both natures of the dual being before her were impressed by those names. "But I ought to have recognized him," Proteus said at last. He gestured awkwardly at his own head. "The god Triton should have sensed the presence of another deity."

"Perhaps not, if the god Triton had been stunned by a Giant, and was only half awake, as even now he seems to be."

"I told you, enchantress. I have forgotten almost everything."

"So I see."

Triton looked down at the human body that had become his latest habitation. He flexed the capable fingers, appraising the play of muscles in the strong forearms. Of course what a god could do did not essentially depend upon the natural strength of his avatar, but youth and health and strength in the human body were all to the good. Triton thought he might have done much worse than this fellow Proteus—of course in the long run it would probably make little difference. The presence of a god-Face usually worked a considerable transformation in any human form it came to inhabit.

Triton was angry at Circe now, feeling, knowing instinctively that she was somehow responsible for the awkward and dangerous situation in which he found himself. His divine nature had been put at risk of complete destruction. It was common knowledge that no power in the world could destroy a god-Face; but totally wiping out a god's memory would be effectively to murder him.

And it undoubtedly was the god, not the sailor, who now spoke. "Woman, I can't imagine how you talked me into this, playing games with Giants. That's one of the very many things I find myself unable to remember. But there must have been some dirty trickery involved!"

Circe's haughty demeanor did not change. "If you cannot remember, Triton dear, you do not know. And if you do not know what you are talking about, it would be wiser to keep your mouth shut."

"Tell me what kind of game you have been playing!"

"Would you believe me if I told you all the details? Why waste time?" And she turned to look at Medea's receding back, while the three ordinary humans continued their retreat. "Great Zeus, what complications! I never foresaw this. Now the girl is madly in love, of course, which I never expected to see in any niece of mine."

Triton/Proteus drew a deep breath. "But I think our effort to help Jason has been effective, so far. The great gods should be pleased with you and me."

"That may be."

"We helped him to survive the Bronze Bulls, and got the Fleece into his hands." Proteus paused, then added in the tones of argument: "If I am a god, I should be able to demonstrate some godlike powers."

"No doubt you can, at least when challenged by an emergency. Have you tried anything of the kind?"

"No, not really." But even as he spoke, Proteus recalled the improved progress of the ship when he was rowing, his tireless muscles, his easy swim through freezing water under icebergs, his consistent success at catching fish. There had been plenty of evidence, but something in him had refused to see it.

Circe ignored the comment. "When I have the Fleece in hand, I may be able to do something to help you regain your memory—but I would of course expect a consideration in return."

"I know who I am now, woman." He hesitated, but was reluctant to make any more bargains with this human trickster. "If I were to ask you for anything, it would be to let the Fleece go on with Jason. Our original idea was to help him, was it not?"

"The great ones' idea was to use him." Circe was brisk. "To get the Fleece away from the place where Giants guarded it. Now his usefulness is at an end. But Jason and his men can remain on my island for a time, if they choose, or they can leave. It will make little difference to me."

"What about Medea, and her maid? Perhaps you could free the princess from the spell of Cupid's Arrow."

"Oh?" The enchantress considered. "Does my Lord Triton also have a craving for her?"

"Medea is a beautiful woman." The god's tone implied that such were common enough. "But no. She and I are now bound together in quite a different way—by murder, and that is enough to have between us. Anyway, she is your relative, and I would think that you would want to show her mercy for that reason."

"My relative, as you call her, deserves no help from me. Rather would I see her punished for her crime. Besides, time and human nature usually provide sufficient antidote for Cupid's shafts."

"Human nature? I don't understand."

Circe evidently came to a decision that their talk had gone on long enough. "I have urgent business to take care of, and I will not stand here all day debating, not even with so eminent a deity as Triton." Her tone turned the compliment into a sarcastic taunt.

Now the woman, however great her powers, had gone too far. Triton said, in a quieter voice than before: "I think you had better stand where you are and answer my questions, until I tell you you may go."

Circe's fine, thin eyebrows rose in crooked arcs. "Bah! The little godling threatens, does he?" Her voice turned into a fishwife's shriek. "Remember who I am, little sailor! When you have put on the Face of Zeus, Athena, or Apollo, *then* you can come and give me warnings, and I will listen carefully, and bow my head and tremble. But the deity in charge of seaweed and seashells is not so terrible." The enchantress shook her head violently. "Not to me!"

Proteus stood taller, and met the gaze of the ancient, mortal woman with his own hard stare.

Circe was still not impressed. "If you think you can command the entire ocean, call its forces to your aid, you had better talk to Poseidon, and have your responsibilities and duties more clearly defined. I assure you that the Lord Neptune listens when I talk to him; he is master of all the water in the world, and he will be interested to discover that you are no longer his subordinate."

"Ah." The name of Poseidon, so confidently introduced, came as something of a shock. It tended to put things in perspective. Poseidon, better known to some as Neptune, was one of the triumvirate, with Zeus and Hades, who ages ago had divided up the universe among them—or so the tradition went. In that company, any powers Triton might be able to exert would dwindle to insignificance.

Circe put one hand out, in a reaching, grasping gesture that ended with the jab of an imperious finger. "Cease this stupid argument. Catch up with that fool Jason, and make sure that one of you brings me the Fleece!"

Now she had really gone too far. "Better think of who you are ordering about, woman. As for the Fleece, come and take it from us, if you can. Something tells me you may be lying when you say your only wish is to give it to the great gods." And having delivered himself of this speech, Proteus/Triton turned and walked away, heading at a deliberate pace down the long curve of beach toward the distant *Argo*.

Even as he walked, an awareness grew in him of ancient magic, tickling and probing at his mind. It was Circe, of course, doing her subtle best to confuse his sense of direction. But he could block that nonsense—Triton realized with satisfaction that he had not forgotten how to do everything. The woman was in for a surprise if she thought to treat him as an ordinary mortal.

Now he called upon the powers of the sea for help. And to his elation he saw the beginning of response come almost instantly, in the form of a rim of clouds beginning to grow along the horizon.

Striding on along the beach, Triton enjoyed the sensation of his returning powers rapidly replenishing themselves. A sense of unease began to grow in him, as he realized that he might have succeeded a bit too well. Help was certainly on the way, but possibly too much of it was coming, more help than he could readily control.

A few minutes later, with more elements of the god's memory still returning in a slow progression, he realized that he had actually summoned Scylla—the name meant She-Who-Rends—

something he would probably not have attempted, had he been entirely in his right mind. Probably all he would really have needed would have been a couple of simple water-elementals. They could have provided all the help the *Argo* needed to get free of the Isle of Dawn.

And memory, still returning in small increments, increased the god's unease. He had called for help, for fighting power, for anger and destruction on a truly massive scale. And now he was going to get it. But it was too late now to revoke the summons, and he would have to deal as best he could with whatever it had brought him.

Suddenly a new worry occurred—if Scylla was near, then . . .

Yes. Having called the way he did, he was going to get Charybdis too. The Sucker-Down, as the name translated from some ancient language of which the god was only hazily aware, lying as it did on the clouded horizon of Triton's divine recollection.

But other elements of memory were firmer. Scylla and Charybdis were much alike, being huge, half-sentient knots of water-currents, ceaseless flows of liquid and energy all interwoven and entangled. If Triton had ever known how such creatures came into existence, the details had been lost to him, along with so much else. But here they were, not half a mile offshore and bubbling closer—and had he been in full possession of all his wits, he would have tried to evoke such creatures only in a life-and-death emergency.

Well, perhaps that was really his situation now. With Circe it was always hard to be entirely sure. Anyway, the pair had now been summoned, and he would have to deal with them as best he could.

Was it only an accident that Charybdis and Scylla had been so conveniently nearby? He would come back to that question later, if and when he had the chance. Right now it was necessary to deal with the beings themselves.

Standing with arms folded, Triton watched the majestic

progress of their approach. Thunderclouds that had just material-
ized from a clear sky now stooped to mingle with the sea, in a
boiling turmoil that Proteus first caught sight of when it was still
halfway to the horizon, but which closed with something like the
speed of hurricane winds. Welling up a few hundred yards offshore, in forms that suggested to the water-god the waterspouts of
tropical typhoons, they pleaded, in great howling, gurgling voices,
to be released from their miserable existence. First one after the
other, then both together, they moaned about certain uncanny
adventures in the past, when they were called up by opposing
magicians, to fight against each other. Humans could never have
interpreted this bellowing as anything but the random raging of a
stormy sea, but the ears of gods were far more capable. Stoically
Proteus/Triton heard out the ghastly tale; he realized that unless
he did, it would be hard to get the creatures to do anything.

Their voices came at him in a barrage of strange, echoing
sounds, reverberating out of a dark green cave of curling wave
that did not crest or break, but only stood its ground while the sea
around it flowed up into it and through it, lending substance to its
strange twisted shape.

The shrieking of Charybdis concluded with a question. "What
do you say to that, Lord Triton?"

He tuned his voice to a volume higher than a mere human
could have managed, not sure how well the raving, roaring things
could hear over their own noise. "I quite agree, that you have both
suffered great injustices. But such matters are all in the past, and
not even Zeus himself can do anything about them. It is today that
I would command your strength."

The response was another shriek and a whistle of wet wind.
Now the monsters had concluded their ritual airing of complaints,
they were ready to go to work. "What will you have us do?"

His right hand rose in a simple gesture of authority. "You will
note a sturdy vessel on the beach, a little way ahead of me. The
ship and its crew are to be set free from the island, provided with

a lane of smooth water in which to ride, and given a swift current to carry them gently outward bound. Any powers on the island who might try to hinder this peaceful departure are to be pounded with your waves."

There was a slight pause. "Do you know who is on the island, Lord Triton? Who will be damaged and confounded by the work that you command?"

"I do know that, and that is my responsibility, not yours. Yours is only to obey."

"We hear and we obey!" The words of the answer dissolved in bellow and crash and howl.

And now, some truly tremendous water-walls began to stir and rise. Any mere human standing on the beach would have turned tail, if not suicidal, and run away. But the avatar stood firm, confident that the waves knew better than to strike at their lord directly.

At first, the powers Proteus/Triton had called into action were entirely obedient to the god's commands. Their hammering the coast with huge waves distracted Circe, and made her fear for certain works, some visible to human eyes and some not, she had established there.

Jason, marching stubbornly back to his ship with the two women, had looked up in amazement at the burgeoning storm and then had given the command for his men to gather close around the *Argo*, and shove her out to sea. Those Argonauts who were close enough to hear him, and able to move effectively, obeyed his orders with a rush. The Heroes were more than eager to leave the island, but at the same time understandably reluctant to put out into the teeth of a rising gale, what looked like the mother of all storms. But their terror of Circe, and Jason's orders, won out in the end. He was determined to save his treasure, or go down to the bottom of the sea still clutching it.

*   *   *

Suddenly a figure appeared ahead of him, running toward Proteus through the spume and sleeting rain. It was the Mouse, her single garment drenched and plastered wetly to her body.

"Jason sent me," she screamed at him when she drew near, her shouting barely audible over the mounting wind. "He wanted to be sure that you were coming. Didn't want to leave you on the island—" A brutal surge of wind and waves knocked her off her feet, left her floundering helplessly on the beach.

But even as her small figure was about to be engulfed by roaring tons of water, Proteus/Triton reached her side, and in a moment had scooped her into his arms. Briefly she tried to fight free of his grip, but the effort was completely useless. Two arms of divine strength held her in protective custody.

Instead of trying to dodge the next impending wave, he turned sideways to shield the burden he was carrying against his chest, and bore her right into the thunderous surf. When the Mouse, her eyes tight shut, drew in breath for a despairing scream, he clamped a broad hand over her nose and mouth, so that neither sound nor water might pass.

Then they were underwater, in Triton's natural domain. It came as no great surprise to Proteus to discover that he was able to breathe here (at least it felt almost like normal breathing) in perfect comfort. Of course he must have been breathing in the same way, without fully realizing it, when he rescued his shipmate in the ice-choked Bogazi, and on several other occasions after joining the Argonauts.

He looked down at the Mouse's face, still half covered by his hand. The girl was unconscious now, and of course she was going to have to breathe here too. But Triton could take care of that, and now he did.

Still looking at her, he thought: *It will be better if I can protect you here, in the sea, without showing you who I am.*

* * *

The Mouse, on first recovering consciousness, thought at first that she had been dreaming. And then she became absolutely convinced that she still was.

With eyes closed, she heard and felt the thunder of the surf pass by. Moments later, still gripped and supported in the man's arms, she felt a very strange though rather comfortable stillness envelop her, and opened her eyes to the greenish light of several fathoms under water.

The figure of a strong man loomed before her. It was a figure she felt she ought to recognize, but still thought very strange. The man was bending over her, while at the same time supporting her with one arm. The curls of his hair and beard seemed all the same color as the water that was making each individual hair stand out, forming a great bushy mass.

In drowsy confusion the girl said to him: "I thought that you were Proteus. I thought—I thought that you were going to drown me."

"Why in the Underworld should I do that?"

When she only looked at him in dreamy silence, he went on, in his strange and watery-sounding voice: "Is this not a marvelous dream that we are sharing? I think we have Triton to thank for it. He is one of the sea gods, you know."

She drowsily nodded her agreement. At least she tried to nod.

Now the man who held her said: "You will be safe here." Then, as if he were trying to make sure of something, his fingers brushed her nose and mouth, and rested gently on her breast. "As long as you are with me."

In a burst of bubbles she released her pent-up breath. Her aching chest gulped in—

Great relief. After the tingling touch of her protector's hand, her lungs did not burn with the inrush of water, but accepted it as gratefully as air. In a moment Mouse seemed to be breathing normally.

Any lingering suspicion that she might not be dreaming vanished. "And who are you?" she asked. Her voice sounded strange, but it was a voice, not mere bubbling air. "You look like—like Proteus." She felt revulsion and fascination at the same time. This could not be the same man she had seen some three years earlier in Iolcus, doing frightful things—and yet it was so very like him.

"Why, so I am," the looming figure assured her in its godlike voice. "And Proteus and you are dreaming—a certain god who likes you both has sent the two of you a happy dream to share. When you awaken, it will seem to you no more than that."

"A happy dream . . . ?"

"Yes. Of course. Gods can do even greater things than conjure dreams. Did no one ever teach you anything about gods?"

Mouse shook her head. "Only that they never pay any attention to our prayers."

"That is not true, not quite true, although I know what you mean."

Here was a good place to bring a guest, with a clean sandy bottom, not too cold and dark and deep for a mortal to feel comfortable. And here, in the side of an underwater cliff, the dolphins and other natural creatures might with a little effort create a pleasant grotto for a god like Triton, and for any human he might choose to entertain in that environment.

Triton's guest today said, drowsily: "People tell many stories about meeting gods, and most of them are untrue, I suppose. I have never met a god, until now."

"Few people ever do. The man named Proteus had never met one either—until he picked up the Face of Triton, and let divinity flow into his head." He paused, and when he went on, it was Triton speaking, though there was very little difference in the voice. "There are not all that many of us—of gods, I mean. And most of us tend to stay clear of humanity most of the time."

The Mouse was staring up into the wavering faint light that

filtered down from the surface of the sea. "Will the ship survive up there? The *Argo*?"

"I have given orders that it must." But having said that, he was not completely sure. Even if the local waves were gentle, the battered *Argo* might start to sink of her own accord. He would have to go up soon and look. But something caused him to delay.

In this environment it felt only natural to Triton/Proteus that he should grow a fishtail, and so he let the transformation happen. The Mouse stared, fascinated, as he demonstrated the extra speed of movement provided by the new appendage. His body reverted to full humanity as soon as he came to a stop again, right at her side.

"A moment ago you had a tail," said Mouse, with childlike directness. It was easy to talk that way when she knew that she was dreaming.

He nodded. "I did. A fishtail's a great help for serious swimming. Don't worry about it, it comes and goes as needed."

Her voice was suddenly so soft that he could hardly hear it. "I would rather not ever have one for myself, if you please."

That drew a chuckle from the god. "Don't worry, I have no plan of turning you into a mermaid. You shall remain as fully human below the waist as you are above. It would be truly a shame to change you in that way."

Triton knew that he himself would be able to see with great acuity, no matter to what depth he might descend. But any purely human guests that he escorted would need some form of light on going much deeper than they were now—in that event he could summon up some glowing creatures from the deep, who would accompany his party as guide and torch-bearer to the depths of the sea.

When Triton took thought, he remembered that there were certain ways in which he could entertain a human visitor to his domain with palatable food, not necessarily raw fish. Other varieties of entertainment could be provided too—he had done so often enough in the past, in other avatars. Now he could recall flashes, fragmentary hints, of a process for producing a good underwater wine . . .

Here in the depths the Mouse's sleepwalking eyes looked wider to Proteus even than they did in air. And the bottom of her shift, her only garment, kept rising up around her slender hips, making an image more seductive than ordinary swimmer's nudity. There were moments when Proteus thought she might be regaining consciousness, for her hands seemed to be trying to hold the hemline down.

"The next time you go bathing, you might take off your dress," he remarked, half in amusement, half in irritation.

"There wasn't time. Anyway, I wouldn't want to lose it. It is the only one I have." Her own voice sounded in her ears a little odd, but still she thought the words all came out clear and plain enough.

"Poor girl, you ought to have some better clothes . . . I'll see to that, when I have a chance." Then Triton suddenly lifted his head, listening. "In a little while we can talk. But first I must take care of some additional business. And you had better really go to sleep again; I will call a guardian to watch over you. Slumber deeply, and forget how we have talked. I tell you that you must forget."

What was Circe up to now?

Triton realized that she must know his abilities as well or better than he knew them himself. But it seemed the enchantress had convinced herself that she could defeat this minor sea-god, at least now while the god was dwelling in such an inexperienced avatar, and with his memory still lamed.

In this she was soon proven wrong. Circe's eyes went wide as she saw the chain of watery force, humpbacked as a whale but many times as large, rolling majestically up a slight ravine toward her house.

When Triton's head broke the surface of the churning sea, he saw with satisfaction that the two great monstrous beings had scrupulously obeyed his orders, inundating much of the island with enormous breakers. The waves did not behave in normal fashion, reaching a natural limit and then sliding back into the sea that owned them. Instead, each one seemed to gather itself for a second effort; a whole enormous mass of water, carrying a myriad of small common sea-creatures with it, went leaping, stretching, compacting and leaping again across the Isle of Dawn.

Meanwhile, according to his orders Charybdis and Scylla were leaving a narrow strip of relatively calm waters through which the ship could pass, with almost all its crew aboard. Proteus watching from a distance could see that Jason was pulling an oar as usual, presumably with the Golden Fleece stowed somewhere securely nearby or on his person. And he caught a reassuring glimpse of Medea's golden hair.

The waves and currents having been set in motion, they persisted for a time, simply in the way of nature. Now the bellowing, howling fountains that were Scylla and Charybdis came rolling up to Triton where he lay swimming in the deep, and reported to him that they had finished the job.

"Then you may go." Triton waved his free hand grandly. "You have my gratitude, for service well performed."

Yet still the howling vortexes lingered. One of the great elementals commented, in a voice of driving rain: "It is strange that Father Neptune has seen fit to punish Circe. They were on quite good terms not long ago."

Triton decided it would be best in the long run if he made certain matters clear. "What I have commanded you to do today is on my own authority, and Poseidon has nothing to do with it, one way or the other."

That news added volume to the watery uproar. "If Father Neptune calls us to account for this, we will of course say that it was done by your direct command."

"So be it."

The forces unleashed in the struggle had brought on something like a local hurricane, a natural turmoil that persisted after its instigators were departed. But the enchantress had managed to survive, though twice the wind had actually knocked her off her feet. From such sanctuary as she could find on shore, behind the rolling clouds of spume and spindrift, aided by such powers as she could hastily evoke, Circe shrieked curses at Triton and his latest human embodiment. She promised to call down on his head all the wrath of the great gods themselves. And in her fury she let slip, or gloated over, the fact that several of the Argonauts were still on shore and in her power. Some six or eight of them, who she was now holding penned up near her house, had started to turn into animals, displaying slender legs, with hooves on them, and fur.

When Triton through his divine powers saw at a distance what was happening to his shipmates, he was enraged in turn—Proteus could feel the divine fury as his own—and in some ancient-sounding tongue that Proteus had never heard before but now comprehended perfectly, began to work new spells upon the sea, threatening to drown the entire island, even submerging the enchantress's house, unless Circe let the whole company of Argonauts go, unharmed and fully restored to human shape.

Circe did not give up the unequal struggle against divinity until her island had been half-drowned in great waves, and herself with it. The stone stronghold at the center stood in danger of being buried in stinking mud, dredged up by her assailants from the bottom of the sea.

All that smothering mud was the last straw. When she saw that, she sued for peace.

The enchantress had no choice but to submit, and gave the necessary commands, freeing the men to run each on two human legs, through thick mud to the shore, where dolphins had been mobilized from somewhere to help them swim their terrified way out to the now-distant ship. Except that Jason's crew would now be two men short. The pair with winged sandals were gone for good, locked into the form of birds, beyond the range of her powers—or she said they were. It was beyond her powers now to change them back.

Circe expressed her surprise that Triton would be willing to stake so much on this contest, make an all-out effort on behalf of a handful of humans who were no close kin to him. But now the feelings of the wretched scoundrel Proteus were intimately involved. It was well known that when any deity passed into a new avatar, the quirks and emotions of the human became to a great extent those of the god or goddess.

Scylla and Charybdis in their departure from the vicinity passed so close to the ship that they endangered the vessel and crew again. But then Triton, working his way to full awareness of his rightful powers, contended with the vast whirlpool and saved *Argo* from being swallowed up and crushed in it.

Returning to the underwater grotto where he had left the sleeping Mouse, Triton dismissed her guardian, a killer whale, with a friendly pat on his blunt snout. Grampus gave Triton a glimpse of fifty enormous teeth, and with a swirl of rounded flippers turned away his thirty-foot black bulk, tagged with white on underparts, above each eye and on each flank.

"Come," the god said to the young woman. "Soon you will be awake again." Her eyelids quivered but did not open.

He had made certain pledges, and he meant to keep them. Triton was still a shadowy stranger, even to himself; and Proteus was still an Argonaut.

Today there was going to be no lengthy stay beneath the waves. He said to his guest: "We must return now to the ship." And he added in reiteration: "You must forget I am a god."

When the freakish storm and its aftereffects had completely died away, and it looked like there would be clear sailing for a time, the latest to play the scribe aboard the *Argo* took advantage of clear sunset light, and found time to make a long and very shaky entry in the log. It seemed to the writer that almost four months had passed since the ship's departure from Iolcus.

It was time for Jason to take roll call, and see just who was missing.

Zetes and Calais were still nowhere to be seen.

Wedding

he forces that had pried the *Argo* free of Circe's grasp had come near to destroying her in the process. The ship was no longer safe, even when the sea immediately around her had been calmed by the magic of a friendly god. After an hour or so of struggling at a distance to protect the *Argo*, Proteus, with the woman who had been called the Mouse still sheltering under his arm, caught up with the vessel and started looking for a way to get both of them back on board without being seen.

The need to return the Mouse was not his only reason for rejoining the *Argo* and her crew. He still felt himself drawn there, as naturally as a falling rock is drawn to earth; if he did not go back among his shipmates, where else would he go? A god he might be, but in all the world he had no other home, no family or friends away from Jason's vessel and those aboard her.

Deep down, there was something in him now that feared the distant ocean and Poseidon's wrath. He feared he had usurped some of the greater sea-god's powers—Circe had probably been right about that. And he had not forgotten that the great gods had wanted Proteus dead.

Now the unconscious Mouse was quivering in his arms. Water temperature was something that Triton's avatar could ignore at his pleasure, but he could tell that it was currently in the range of comfort for most humans. Still, the long exposure was having its effect on the slender woman and he could feel her insensible body shivering.

The ship was only drifting at the moment, as the rowers changed positions. Clamping the limp fingers of the Mouse firmly over one gunwale, Proteus/Triton placed one of his hands on her head, and a moment later she had regained full awareness.

"There was a huge wave," Mouse told him, as if she were seeking confirmation for something she remembered. And Proteus could see in her face that she remembered very little more.

"There was indeed." He nodded vigorously. "In fact there were several enormous waves. But we have come through all right."

Then he gave the Mouse a boost, a good start at climbing aboard.

"There you are," he heard the princess say, her voice issuing from somewhere just out of his line of vision. "I had wondered whether you were permanently lost." Triton's head was under water again before the Mouse replied, and he could not quite hear her words.

Darting under the ship, Proteus/Triton grabbed the edge of the outrigger on the other side, and in a moment had hauled himself aboard.

One man who saw him come out of the sea declared that it was a strange time to be taking a dip, and he muttered some excuse about having to check the hull, but no one seemed to realize that he had not been on the ship when it left the island. Every man must have been concentrating on his own survival.

Looking back toward the domain of Circe, he saw that the huge waves his creatures had raised against the island were now rapidly subsiding, leaving behind them a surface of gray slimy mud, from which the trunks of coated trees, their foliage all sluiced and scraped away, protruded like the poison spines of some enormous monster.

An oarsman nearby groaned to his benchmate between pulls: "Some god is helping us make our escape!"

"Helping us? You'd describe the beating we've just taken as getting help? Another minute or two of help like that and we'll be drowned!"

Then a third Argonaut chimed in: "It may be that two gods are fighting, and we're caught in the middle."

The one who had spoken first now looked up. "Proteus, you're here, thank the gods—we could ill spare you. I thought you were lost overboard."

"No, I was up forward."

And a little later, when the men up forward questioned him, he was to say:

"I was back in the stern."

Listening to the men and watching them, he reassured himself that despite the events of the past few hours, none of Triton's shipmates were suspicious, at least not openly, that for the past few months a god had been helping them row their ship.

His next move was to ask Jason for a look at the Fleece, to make sure it had not been lost in the struggle.

The captain obliged, and dug out his treasure from the small locker where it had been bundled away. Both men were taken aback when they saw it. The bundle was notably smaller than it had been when he put it away. The Fleece was indeed diminished in size, and its brilliance noticeably dimmed.

"This is Circe's work!" Medea exclaimed. But Triton/Proteus doubted that. If the enchantress had had access to the prize, she'd have taken the whole thing away.

But what had happened to the Fleece was shocking.

"Where's the rest of it? Have you cut pieces off of it, or what?" Proteus demanded of Jason. But even as he spoke, he found it impossible to believe that Jason would do anything of the kind.

When the Mouse, looking over Triton's shoulder, saw the object of their concern, she was as puzzled as everyone else. There was a substantial deterioration. The golden glow had dimmed, and the fabric was more the size of a towel than a bedsheet.

Jason, dreadfully worried by the discovery, turned to Proteus/Triton for advice. But at the moment the trusted counselor had none to give.

Their scrambling escape from the island had pushed the men

and their leader to the limits of their strength and endurance. And hope was fading that Zetes and Calais were ever going to reappear. Everyone had to acknowledge that the two winged Argonauts seemed to be gone for good. One man who boasted of his keen eyesight now claimed to have actually witnessed the transformation of flying men into birds, and described it at length for his shipmates.

Jason sounded as numbly fatalistic as Proteus had ever heard him. "I fear there is no hope. Add them to the casualty list next time you make an entry in the log."

Medea was looking at him in dull wonder. Finally she asked: "How did we manage to get away?"

"The Fates were with us. And your magic . . ."

The princess shook her head. "People always say that, about the Fates, and it means nothing. I would like to believe that my magic was strong enough to get us free—but I cannot. There must be more to it than that. It may be that some god was indeed helping us."

Jason could come up with no better explanation.

When at last it was possible to cease an all-out effort to make speed, Jason took roll call of the exhausted Argonauts, most of them leaning on their oars while two men bailed; the strained seams of the hull were now taking water in several places. Only Zetes and Calais were missing.

The Argonauts were talking while they rested at their oars. Listening to them, Proteus realized that the men considered Circe and Medea to have been the chief antagonists in the duel of magic just concluded. Since the getaway had succeeded, most of the men were now ready to offer the princess wide-eyed homage.

Jason seemed to agree with them. "It was the princess who somehow prevailed." There was wary calculation in the look he turned on Medea now. "It seems that you have saved us from your aunt."

The Mouse was still dazed, and only the princess herself

seemed to have real doubts. She nodded in silence, then shook her head. First Medea's lips were trembling, then her whole body. Finally she murmured: "A storm like that . . . I tell you, I was not even trying to raise a storm. I cannot take full credit. Powerful help came to us from somewhere. But from where is a complete mystery."

No sooner did Triton feel confident that Scylla and Charybdis had really departed, than he realized, with a feeling of doom, that bad weather of purely natural origin was setting in, and there was almost nothing that he could do about it. Neptune might clear an entire sea of storms if he so chose, but feats like that were far beyond the lesser god's abilities.

Bowing his head while he once more labored at his oar, Proteus/Triton offered up a kind of quiet prayer: "I have this to say to the great gods: If any of them should feel inclined to step in and help us out of this ugly situation, they are quite welcome to do so. On the other hand, if they do not . . ."

He let it die away. He was filled with a sullen anger at the world, but there was no point in mumbling ridiculous threats against Poseidon and Zeus. If they took note of him at all, which he doubted, they would only laugh. And what would they say if he brought them that tattered remnant of the Golden Fleece?

None of their majestic forms appeared before his eyes. He realized that in the past he had probably not dealt often with such eminences, and he had no recollection of ever having met them face to face. Yet somehow he felt he knew them too well to feel surprised at their failure to respond to his prayer. Zeus or Apollo or Athena might have heard his outcry, had they been listening for it, but the chance of that was so small as not to be worth considering.

Several times in the past few days it had crossed his mind that the great gods might reward him when they saw what a good Argonaut he had been, helping Jason obtain the Fleece, and seeing to it that the treasure was brought back to where the great gods might get at it without fear of Giants. He, Proteus, might be able to claim some reward from Zeus and his confederates. Maybe after Jason had presented what was left of the trophy to Pelias, and derived whatever benefit he might from that act . . . which would probably be none at all.

He could remember vividly something that Circe had said: *"I see that the great gods were foolish to depend on you to obtain the Golden Fleece for them."*

But Proteus could not believe that the Fleece in its present wretched condition would be worth much to anyone.

If Circe had been right in her estimate of the current situation, all the Olympians would now be extremely busy, preparing for a major battle against the Giants. And even Zeus could only be in one place at a time.

Anyway, Triton feared that if Poseidon came to take a hand in this business, it might well be with a different goal in mind than either Proteus or Triton. So far Poseidon, like the other divine masters of the world, was inclined to be elsewhere. All of the gods feared the Giants' terrible weapon, and with good reason.

Not one of the voyagers was willing to put unquestioning faith in the compass-pyx any longer, not after it had guided them to Circe's island. But they were once again in the open sea, with no other means of navigation save the sun and stars. And they had an urgent need to locate friendly land.

Still there were some who wanted to throw Tiphys's heirloom overboard. One man snarled: "The last time we trusted it, it brought us to Circe. It's only by the help of some benevolent god that we're not all pigs, rooting with our noses in the dirt!"

After all the damage that had been done to Circe's island in the violent course of their escape, there was no doubt that the enchantress hated them, that she would gladly destroy the *Argo* and its whole crew if she had the chance.

*   *   *

Triton found he could be of no direct help in guiding the ship; whether because of his damaged memory or natural limitation, he had no better idea than anyone else of their exact location in the Great Sea. Proteus, after thinking things over, advised that before anyone relied on the compass-pyx again, they should rip out the copper strip that connected it with the ship's oaken keel. He suspected that that was the means by which Circe had been able to exert a degree of special control over the *Argo*. Jason at once gave the necessary orders, and the thing was done.

Then he turned to Triton/Proteus. "Some of the men are saying you have some special influence with certain gods."

Guardedly Proteus searched the captain's face. "I don't know why they say that, Jason."

"Well. Nevertheless, if there is any truth in what they are saying, Proteus, I pray you help me in this matter. If you can persuade some deity to help me, I promise him or her rich sacrifices—"

"I tell you, there is little I can do."

But Proteus was worried too. "Bah, what do any of the so-called great gods care for promises and sacrifice?" he barked out. Heads turned in his direction. Some would take that remark for fearful blasphemy, but Triton was in a foul mood inside the sailor's head.

Now everyone on board was aware of the change; Jason had left his failing treasure spread out on the deck, thinking perhaps confinement in the dark was the cause of its shrinkage and dimming. But sunlight and rain proved to be of no benefit.

Medea had no more idea than anyone else of what to do about the deteriorating Fleece. She continued to be despondent because her Aunt Circe was angry at her and would now certainly be more determined than ever to foil Medea's plans for Jason. Looking worn, her sunburn peeling quite unprettily, the young princess was obviously exhausted from her recent physical ordeals.

From time to time Medea looked at Proteus, but it was doubtful that she ever gave him any real thought, except as to how he might be even more useful. And obviously it had never entered her tired and sunburnt head that he might be a god. If anyone else aboard had that suspicion, they were keeping it to themselves.

Proteus had no intention of revealing his divinity to any of them as yet. He was certain that he had succeeded in making the Mouse forget the revelation.

Thinking of Mouse made him think of King Pelias, her secret employer. Proteus still had no idea of what the old bastard looked like, or any memory of ever meeting him. But it seemed almost certain that Old Proteus and the usurper had met, for Pelias would want to personally confirm the qualifications of any agent he entrusted with the task of disposing of his rival.

The more New Proteus heard about Pelias, the less he liked him. Of course he had the same feeling about his earlier self, who had evidently been quite willing to work as a spy and assassin for such a human smudge.

But toward his earlier self he could feel no real enmity. He had realized some time ago that Old Proteus was dead.

Eventually the pictures in the compass-pyx came clearer. An attainable refuge was available, embodied in yet another island kingdom, this one named Drepane, only a few days' travel away.

Fortunately, the worst of the bad weather passed them by. But as the days dragged on the situation of the ship grew still more serious. Men were constantly bailing. Only one serviceable sail remained, and it had grown threadbare from constant exposure to wind and sun and salt, while the leaks grew worse day by day. He who ran out on his shipmates in this situation would be no Argonaut.

An ominous sight greeted the crew of the *Argo* as they rowed into the chief harbor of Drepane: a squadron of three large ships, marked with the insignia of Colchis. Weatherbeaten vessels, fresh from a hard journey, but still solid and capable. But at the moment there were no Colchians to be seen.

The first officials to greet the Argonauts on their landing were courteous but reserved. Thanks to Drepanian hospitality they were safely lodged on shore, well-fed, and their battered vessel temporarily secured against sinking. Some of the crew undertook such minor repairs as could be made without hauling *Argo* out of the water. Just now there was no drydock facility available, and there was no handy beach.

The ruler of this land, King Alcinous, had a widespread reputation for being just and fair. The Argonauts soon found, to their consternation, that the king was even now entertaining a strong delegation from King Aeetes, who was more determined than ever to get his daughter back at all costs.

Proteus heard with mixed feelings that the monarch of Drepane claimed to be a grandson of Poseidon; and for a time Triton thought of revealing his identity to this king. But that would not be a wise idea at all, if Neptune was truly against him.

Jason considered the idea of asking Alcinous for a meeting, at which he and Medea could confront their accusers; but none of his advisers thought that a good idea.

Ominously, only Medea was invited to see the king. But when she returned from the audience her news was not too bad. She described Alcinous as kind and thoughtful, eager to listen to her side of the story; but all he would tell her was that he was still considering her case.

Queen Arete had been present too, and the princess had appealed to her for help. Medea thought the queen was sympathetic to her cause.

Making a formal appearance before King Alcinous, the officers of the Colchian delegation accused Jason and Medea of murder, in the slaying of Apsyrtus. They strongly implied that the mighty King Aeetes of Colchis would consider as enemies anyone who sheltered the fugitives.

Alcinous did not react favorably to threats, even when they were so indirect. But for the time he kept his own countenance impassive.

That night, Queen Arete, to whom Medea had appealed for protection, kept her royal husband awake by complaining, in a general way, of the ill-treatment to which fathers too often subjected their daughters, whether the daughters were guilty of anything or not.

The queen said: "Everything we hear about this old Aeetes suggests that he is capable of treating this charming Medea with extreme barbarity, if you give him the chance."

The king grunted something unintelligible. He was trying to get to sleep.

And, now that they were able to go ashore and find a little privacy, Triton/Proteus found himself walking gloomily with the Mouse, yearning to tell her of his troubles, and of the joys and privileges he had discovered in being a god. Not that his divinity had yet afforded him much in the way of joy.

At his suggestion, they sat down together in the soft seaside sand.

He pondered whether he ought to intervene on Medea's behalf, if the decision of King Alcinous went against her. He felt confident that Triton's power could somehow save the princess from being sent home. But what would he do with her then? The *Argo* was now chronically in need of fixing; he wondered if Circe had somehow managed to burden the vessel with a lasting curse. If she had, it was beyond his power to do anything about it. Vaguely he supposed that he might somehow seize control of a sound boat or ship, turn it over to Jason and his surviving crew, and wish them well.

The Mouse interrupted his gloomy train of thought, by saying to him: "Proteus, we are both of us still a long way from home."

"I don't know, Mouse—is that your real name, by the way?— I don't know where my home is."

Mouse was silent for a time, as if thinking something over. She picked up a handful of sand and let it trickle through her fingers. Then she said: "You claim not to remember my real name?"

"I don't believe you've ever told it to me."

"Then I suppose it possible that you don't remember my husband, either."

"I didn't know you had a husband. Certainly I've never met him."

For some reason that caused her to turn her face away. "He's dead now," she said. Then after a lengthy silence, she turned back to him, eyes searching his face intently. "Do you have a family?"

Proteus made a helpless gesture. "I don't know that either. I don't know if my parents are living or dead, or whether I have brothers or sisters. Given what I have begun to learn about my previous occupation, I think a wife and children are unlikely."

She looked at him for a long time in silence. "But now you are a different man," she said at last—but hesitantly, as if a shred of doubt still lingered.

"If you knew me, or thought you knew me, before I joined the Argonauts—then you must understand that I am now a very different man indeed. Something happened to me, I suffered a blow to the head, and almost all of my old self was wiped away."

"Really? Did any of the Argonauts know you—before?"

"No." Then following a sudden impulse, he told her: "My new self, I think, is—very small. Or would be, if—" *If half of me was not a god.* He couldn't go on like this! He wanted urgently to tell Mouse, to tell someone, but the words stuck in his throat.

"And a blow on the head accomplished this transformation?" Her disbelief was plain.

"No." Suddenly he could hold it back no longer. He was a

god, wasn't he? To the Underworld with being cautious! He rushed on. "At the same time I saw the Face of Triton lying on a wooden deck before me; and I picked it up and put it into my head. It slid in smoothly, painlessly, just the way god-Faces do in all the stories. So now I am Triton, and I can do great wonders with the waves."

A silence began to stretch between them. She was staring at him in awe, in the way one might expect a mere human to stare at a god. At last she whispered: "With waves—and dolphins—and—"

"And breathing under water. Yes."

Mouse had a few more questions, and he did his best to answer them. At last she observed: "It sounds extremely complicated."

"Not really. It is easier to live with than to explain."

"Proteus—Lord Triton—hold me."

He held her. It was soon evident that certain elements of the sea-god's nature were emphatically human, with nothing of the fish about them. With a small part of the god's mind, he called up mist, and at a little distance sea-spray, to keep private, for a time, their little portion of the beach.

"Then I wasn't dreaming, that other time," she said after a while. "When we were coming away from Circe's island. Going under the waves with you."

"No, you weren't dreaming. I told you to forget, I wanted to keep my secret. But I was wrong. I need someone to talk to."

The Mouse was intensely curious about the details of his apotheosis, but actually he could tell her very little, though it was all he could remember, about the shipwreck, and his first fight with a Giant.

He concluded: "I suppose I had never seen a Face before, but I couldn't have had much doubt of what it was. I picked it up, and—here I am."

Mouse was silent for a time, her arms still around him. Then she said: "When I first saw you in Colchis, I hated you very much."

"But why?"

"Because I had seen you before, years ago, back in Iolcus, and there you were—a man who did horrible things. No, I don't want to say any more about it, please don't ask me to."

"I was a man who did horrible things, in the service of King Pelias."

"Yes."

"All right, I won't press you for details. I'm not that man any longer. And I'm glad that you don't hate me now." He stroked her tenderly.

"No, I don't. Now I will do whatever I am asked to do by the great Lord Triton, who has saved my life."

"When this voyage is over, Mouse, I will see what I can do, to arrange a better life for you. But don't expect too much. I have the powers of Triton, or some of them—I don't know how much I may have forgotten."

"How strange." She stroked his forehead tenderly.

"Yes, all new and strange to me. It may be that I can accomplish very little in the way of putting people on thrones, or knocking them off. I really don't care much about that. But I will at least keep you from being sent as a prisoner back to Colchis. I think I can promise you that much."

"I fear I can offer you no help in return, Lord Triton."

"You must remember not to call me that when others may be listening. I want to keep my secret for a while yet, if I can. And you have already given much help. The great Lord Triton, as you call him, finds himself in much need of such kind words and comfort."

Meanwhile there were two others, King Alcinous and his queen, Arete, who also lay wakeful in the night. The queen, considerably younger than her lord, was pleading with him: "My royal lord, save this unhappy girl from the Colchians."

"I have said that I will think about it." And Alcinous closed his eyes and tried, by regular breathing, to give the impression that he was already asleep.

The queen was not so easily deceived, but kept on talking in her normal voice. "Think all you want. Iolcus is not very many days of sailing from our island, and Jason may very well come to rule there. Whereas Aeetes lives far away and we hardly know anything about him but his name."

That stirred the king to a response. "We know he is a great and powerful monarch."

Ignoring what she did not want to hear, the queen took up another argument. "It broke my heart to hear all the troubles that poor girl has been through. She must have been out of her mind when she gave that man, Jason, the magic charm to help him deal with the Bulls." And she added: "He's the one who got her into this, you know. It's always the woman who pays."

The king grunted, in the way of listening husbands the world over, at moments when they would prefer to be asleep.

Queen Arete went on. "Then, as we sinners often do, she tried to cover one fault with another . . . why, only recently and not so far from us, the brutal Echetus drove brazen spikes into his daughter's eyes, and now the miserable girl is languishing in some dark dungeon."

Rolling over among a mass of pillows, Alcinous braced an elbow to raise his head. He asked: "Do you really believe that story about the spikes?"

Arete shuddered deliberately, making sure that the motion was strong enough to shake the bed a little, so that her husband would be sure to feel it. She said: "One hears the same version of the story from different people, which indicates there may well be some truth in it. And I know what terrible things I have seen men do."

The king shook his head: "I do have some sympathy for this little princess. As for the so-called murder she is said to have committed, doing away with her brother, it seems there was a kind of battle going on at the time. And in a battle, what do you expect but killing? But I should think twice before defying a just sentence from Zeus."

"We have no real evidence, my husband, that Zeus or any other god has any interest in the matter at all. That is only what the Colchian delegation tells us."

"True enough . . . nor would it be a good idea to hold King Aeetes and his power in contempt, even if he is far away. There is probably no greater king anywhere."

"So, what will you do?"

Alcinous sighed. "My duty, as best I can."

"And that is?"

"To give a decision that the whole world will acknowledge as the best."

The queen was nothing if not determined. "And what will that decision be?"

"If Medea is still a virgin, I shall direct them to take her back to her father. But if she is a married woman, I will not separate her from her husband. Nor, if she has conceived, will I hand over a child of hers to one who plans to punish her. Does that meet with your approval?" The question was a serious one.

"My noble lord is wise as well as brave."

"I am glad I have finally convinced you of that elementary fact. Now let me get some sleep." Alcinous punched his pillows and lay down.

But before the queen joined her royal consort in his slumber, she arose quietly, without waking her snoring husband, and sent a trusted servant to inform the Argonauts of her lord's decision.

Jason and Medea rejoiced—she at the prospect of being married (belonging to a husband she could manage, rather than a father she could not), and the captain was happy to have found a sure way out of his present difficulties.

*   *   *

Medea and Jason were married within the hour. Someone took pity on the Mouse, and gave her a new dress, so she might make a decent figure in attendance. The couple entrusted the ceremony to a well-known local priest of Apollo, with the idea that it would be good to have an independent official, trusted by the king, who could if necessary give credible testimony that they were really married.

They went to bed together in a cave-room the queen had generously and secretly made available. The walls sparkled with a thousand mineral crystals, and in that setting the Golden Fleece that Jason spread out on their bed seemed to have regained something of its size and luster.

When Proteus had witnessed the ceremony, and had seen the couple retire to their wedding night, he looked around for the Mouse. But now he could not find her, and so went to his bed alone.

In the morning the young maid was still missing, and when Proteus finally inquired of the palace authorities, they had no word of her. When he went out on his own and questioned the local people, he learned that a fast Iolcan ship that had been in the harbor for several days had left, suddenly and unexpectedly, during the night.

Of course he had no proof that the Mouse had been aboard that vessel, but he had no real doubt of the fact either. She was speeding back to Iolcus to make her secret agent's report to Jason's rival.

Bitterly he thought that Pelias ought to richly reward one who brought him such important news: that his enemy Jason had now been fortunate enough to enlist a god in his cause.

Medea, fresh from her wedding night, and reveling in new-found freedom from her father's tyranny, found time to complain about the unfaithfulness of her missing maid, who had suddenly run off. Meanwhile Jason did not seem to care one way or the other.

Proteus felt a growing sense of betrayal, which soon turned to private anger at the Mouse. This he did his best to conceal from his shipmates.

Quite possibly the dead husband had been a lie. Certainly there would be an Iolcan lover of some kind, or lovers, who would welcome her back.

When in the morning the king's decision went against the Colchians, they trembled with fear, and readily admitted that they dreaded the wrath of their own king, should they return to him with such news. In the next breath they begged for sanctuary, which Alcinous immediately granted them.

"I will see that your decision is conveyed to your sovereign through some neutral source." The monarch went on to say that if the Colchian king wanted his ships back, he could send crews at any time to sail them away. "And in the meantime I will charge him no dockage fees. If Aeetes keeps sending his best agents far afield, he will soon discover that he has none of them left."

And Jason led a cheer: "Let it be so with every tyrant!"

After joining loudly in the cheers for the wisdom of good King Alcinous, the Argonauts soon completed their necessary repairs, and sailed on, rejoicing, with Jason and his bride aboard.

The Argonauts were more than ready to believe that their luck had at last taken a permanent turn for the better.

Triton

*S*o far, no entry in the *Argo*'s log had mentioned the obvious deterioration of the Golden Fleece, and Anchaeus, still acting as logkeeper, did not propose to open that subject.

Several things of great importance had never been recorded. Evidently no one on the ship but Proteus had ever had the least suspicion that the Mouse had been a secret agent in their midst, working for Jason's archenemy. Proteus could not very well reveal the fact without disclosing the same thing about himself.

He was secretly relieved to find that the log book was still in its accustomed place—not that it would have done King Pelias much good if a thief had stolen it and brought it to him. Well, if the Mouse was on a fast ship bound directly for Iolcus, as no doubt she was, she would probably be carrying her exciting information to the king many days before the *Argo* came limping into home port—if it ever managed to do so. But the big news in her report would be something that had never been entered in the log.

Medea still grumbled now and then over what she perceived as the disloyalty of her missing attendant. But the attitude of the princess suddenly mellowed when it occurred to her that the Mouse might have met with foul play of some kind—it happened to young women sometimes, even in the most civilized of ports. Still, Medea spent little time fretting about her loss, for she was nagged by other worries. She told Jason and Proteus of a dream in which the ghost of her butchered brother had appeared, walking on water beside the ship, and seemed to beckon her to follow him.

But with grim determination Jason's bride managed to shake off the tentacles of guilt. Nothing would be allowed to distract her from her purpose. "I will not put up with such things. I will not. I have done what I have done, and that is that."

*　　*　　*

There came a time when Medea and Proteus were briefly alone, as much as any two people could be aboard the ship. He saw her looking at him, as if she had never quite focused on him before. And Medea said: "Sometimes I wonder who you are."

Feeling a faint chill of alarm, he offered a slight bow, really only a nodding of the head. "One who has served you and your husband faithfully, lady."

"Granted. Though that is not quite what I meant. Oh, Proteus, good Proteus! You are so devoted. If only life were that simple! But a woman must look out for herself. You are a good sailor, and an excellent fisherman, but I would not be much of a success as a sailor's or fisherman's wife." She gazed at him with the expression of a girl who had learned early in life that nearly every man who looked at her could be enslaved.

Feeling somewhat relieved, Proteus/Triton replied: "There I must agree with you, princess." Days ago he had begun to suspect that the effect of Cupid's Arrow was wearing off; he seemed to remember Circe saying that such was often the case, and the looks Medea gave her husband were more thoughtful than adoring.

If there was a slight edge in his comment, the lady did not seem to feel it. She only smiled, tolerating this very helpful man who was never going to be a king.

No matter who now tried to read the compass-pyx, the result was cloudy pictures and uncertainty—perhaps because no one on board still had real faith in the instrument.

Day by day, and hour by hour, the situation of the Argonauts and their hard-used vessel continued to deteriorate. Sails were useless, leaks had become chronic, and there was not much that Triton could do about it.

The driving wind and the smashing waves refused to bend to the control of Triton's will. Instead, those great limbs of nature steadily opposed him. His godhood had not been paralyzed, his powers were still his to command. But they were completely over-matched by antagonistic forces.

The only explanation he could come up with, apart from the sheer perversity of nature, was that Circe, or some other enemy, had successfully turned at least one of the greater gods against him. And of course some powerful deities might be against him anyway, bitter enemies of Zeus, taking the Giants' side in the ongoing war. Of course one excellent candidate would be Hades. The Lord of the Underworld was said once to have been a partner of Zeus, but for ages had been his chronic enemy; not equal to the Thunderer in strength, but still a deity of enormous power.

Doubtless more important, from Triton's point of view, there was Poseidon, who, it was said, with Zeus and Hades had once divided the whole universe among them. Triton had no idea of the great sea god's position in the current struggle.

And Proteus had to believe that if the great gods were supporting Jason, the Giants and any allies they might have must be his enemies. Jason's destruction might even be the enemy's current chief objective. If it came to another Giant attack, Proteus/Triton was the ship's only capable defender.

Of course there was nothing compelling him to stay on board. It would be perfectly easy for Triton to plunge into the sea, and have himself borne by by dolphins to some far corner of the world. No reason he could not withdraw to some quiet place, where gods and Giants seldom ventured, a part of the world where no one had ever heard of the Golden Fleece.

If the ship does sink, he thought suddenly, *I will not be able to save them all. But I will rescue Jason. Not that he is worthier than any of the others, but saving him will deny the enemy, King Pelias and the Giants, what they want most. I will save Jason, and as many of the others as I can.*

It was damned strange to be aware of your own divinity, and at the same time to feel trapped by circumstances, like some small, helpless animal. Every scrap of knowledge that had stayed with him, the essence of Triton's long, long lifetime, fed his certainty that he would be no more than a worm in the hand of Neptune. It seemed only a matter of time before the great gods would have time to spare to crush him, if that was what they wanted.

The wind that drove the vessel seemed perfectly natural, yet it was so strong that the only way to keep *Argo* from sinking or capsizing was to turn and run before it. There was no thought of trying to raise a sail, it would only be torn away. Scylla and Charybdis were somewhere far away, and out of touch with Triton, who felt very much alone.

Such overwhelming opposition as seemed to be arrayed against him could come, he supposed, only from the peerless Poseidon, who, like the other great gods Apollo and Zeus, and evidently Athena and Aphrodite too, wanted to see the Fleece go directly, and as soon as possible, into the workshop of Daedalus.

Triton had no doubt Hephaestus the Smith was a clever god—patchy memory gave some indication that it was so—and the human named Daedalus, also called the Artisan, might be something more than clever. Together those two could very well be able to wring some vital secrets from the unimpressive remnant of the golden wonder. Then gods might outlast Giants in their great struggle, and humanity would be better off.

They had reached the middle of another day of windy buffeting and helpless drift, when without warning a great calm seemed to come over their immediate surroundings. Then there was another upwelllng of the sea, much more slow and solemn than that which had attended the appearance of Scylla and Charybdis, She-Who-Rends and Sucker-Down.

"What in all the chambers of the Underworld is that?" the captain gasped.

Triton was afraid he knew exactly what it was. "Prepare for

some rough weather," he muttered, more to himself than to his shipmates.

An anonymous cry went up: "We're lost! Great gods, whatever that thing is, we're doomed!"

And some strange force, as far beyond Triton's ability to comprehend as it was beyond his skill to counteract, seemed to be holding the ship perfectly still in the water.

From the first moment of its appearance, he had no doubt of the identity of the mighty presence that had now taken control of the ship and everything around it. The Argonauts and their vessel were now in the presence of Poseidon, by some called Neptune. The great god was immediately recognizable on sight to many of Triton's shipmates, though almost certainly none had ever seen him before. Triton's own efforts to control the local water and wind were casually overruled, as was the natural gale that had begun to blow, so that for the moment the *Argo* was gently borne up in a sea of calm. Control of this portion of the Great Sea had been effortlessly assumed by its true master.

For a long moment, all of the other people on the ship were stricken dumb by their first sight of one of the triumvirate who had once claimed to rule the universe. In the eyes of mere humans, Neptune appeared a titanic figure, clad in gold, his golden chariot surrounded by leaping, bounding dolphins, and pulled by white horses which on closer inspection had something monstrously serpentine about some of their legs. He was not bothering today with a Trident—it would be foolish to think he really needed one.

The same Argonauts who had done their best to fight a Giant face to face were now cowering like children before this presence. One or two seemed to hope that they might be able to hide beneath their rowing benches. Even Jason's head was down, his face hidden in his hands. Medea was clinging to her husband's side, her own face buried in his chest.

Of all the people on the ship, only Triton/Proteus was on his feet, balancing himself with divine skill, keeping his body erect despite the swaying and dipping of the deck beneath his feet. Neptune was staring directly at him, with an unreadable expression, and Triton thought that in another moment or two, he would either be annihilated or his godhood would certainly be revealed to any of his shipmates who had not yet fainted.

Before Poseidon could say anything, there came a startling interruption. Half a mile from the ship, and with the ship between it and the god, there appeared a doubly fish-tailed Giant, bigger than a great whale, and breaching like a whale, dwarfing Neptune who like any other god must walk the world in human form, and be no more than man-sized after all.

The Giant's body broke the surface and fell back, with the roar and splash of some vast creature of the deep. In a flash, Triton understood that the Giant must have been tracking Poseidon and meant to destroy him with the special weapon.

In a moment, the monstrous panoply of waterspouts and clouds enshrouding Neptune had collapsed in a torrent of falling spray. The great god himself had disappeared. In his intense fear, Poseidon had quickly submerged to such a distance that the Giant, raising empty but powerful hands, could not take aim at him. Already even Triton, as he grabbed up a spear and dove over the ship's side, lost track of the greater god's exact location.

The mountainous disturbance resulting from Neptune's sudden plunge did not die away until it had engulfed the ship. Huge waves threatened to capsize the *Argo*, despite the stabilizing effect of the plank-bottomed outriggers on each side. Several men were swept overboard, and Proteus let himself go with the surge.

As soon as the waves had closed over Triton's head, he shifted into fishtail form, and launched a desperate counterattack, in defense of himself and his shipmates.

His previous encounter with a Giant in the water had taught

him something about the tactics the enemy employed. What little Triton could recall of that now helped him form a plan of battle.

On seeing him submerge, the Giant too sank below the surface.

The only weapon Proteus had on jumping overboard was an ordinary spear, and he knew he would have to get very close to his huge antagonist indeed to use it effectively. Especially under water, where the throwing range would be enormously reduced.

His huge opponent, well aware that Triton would have to close with him to do him harm, kept turning so as not to be taken by surprise from behind.

At moments during the whirl and fury of combat, Triton caught momentary impressions of Neptune, now more than a mile deep in the Great Sea, and still retreating. Closer at hand he had a momentary look at Medea on the ship, still at Jason's side, her hands raised in a gesture that showed she had not abandoned all hope of being able to do something effective with her magic.

The struggle in the sea went on. Triton, his body fish-tailed and darting with a shark's speed through the water, called up a school of fish to screen him somewhat from his enemy. He had to keep the Giant from locating him and focusing the invisible weapon on him—one more blast from that might well leave him with no more memory than a clam.

Proteus/Triton had to assume that by this time any Giant he encountered was likely to know what had happened to one of their colleagues in the Grove of Ares—and also how Triton had killed another, months ago, in the midst of the Great Sea.

The Giant roared out a few words, from behind the murky screen of fish.

"Triton, is it you after all? I thought one of my comrades killed you months ago. Whose head are you hiding in this time? Come out, little godling, come out and fight, you wretched coward!"

That was the second time in a few days that Triton had been called a little godling, and he was tired of it. By a subtle power he had not known that he possessed, he caused his underwater speech to issue from the mouth of a great fish swimming on the other side of his opponent. "Matter of fact, he did kill me. But don't you know what happens when you kill a god?"

Evidently the Giant was not deceived as to his location. A wave of radiance from the magic weapon, stirring the water like waves of heat, passed very close on Triton's right side. He thought that if that had hit him, his mind would now be entirely gone; forgetfulness spreading like a dark cloud, until it engulfed even the ability to think. The propagation of the wave was very fast. Yet under water it was not so fast that an agile god had no chance to dodge.

He made some effort to draw his huge antagonist away from the *Argo*, so that the ship and the people on it might survive even if their god-protector died.

The inconclusive duel with the Giant dragged on, and seemed no nearer its conclusion when a beast of the sea that Triton had not summoned came darting near him, with a long burden in its mouth.

At first he spun away frantically from the approaching bulk, fearing that some creature allied to the Giant was about to attack him. But then he heard the shrill speech of a dolphin, garbled by the necessity of carrying a burden in its mouth. Instantly Triton doubled back in his headlong flight, to hear what the creature had to say. It seemed to be telling him that it came from Neptune.

Again the streamlined shape swam near. Reaching out his hand to seize the object carried in its mouth, Proteus/Triton blinked at suddenly finding himself superbly armed. His fingers had closed upon a spearshaft with a triune branching; the three separate, parallel spearheads looked like splinters of black obsidian.

Who might have fabricated this weapon, and when, he could

not remember, but obviously something more than human skill and power had gone into it. This was his own Trident, his true Spear, of which all those he had been using over the last few months were only shoddy imitations. The whole unit had the look of a single piece of dark glass, rather than of metal, but the suggestion of fragility was utterly misleading, and he knew that all the parts of it were very strong. The triply-branching shaft was no more than about five feet long, and the three spearheads comparatively short, so any wounds they made must be less than a foot deep. Yet the triple impact of their keen points could strike with almost unimaginable force.

Neptune's messenger was a mere common dolphin, a being low enough on the ladder of importance to be impressed by the opportunity to talk with one as eminent as Triton.

Speaking in deferential tones and forms, the dolphin informed him that the Trident had been recovered from the bottom of the sea, about a month after the lesser god's last change of avatar.

The endlessly smiling dolphin mouth produced a form of speech that would have been opaque to merely human ears, but now that its mouth was free, Triton could readily understand. "The Lord Poseidon hopes that this gift will seal a reconciliation between himself and you."

Shifting easily into the rapid dolphin speech, Triton replied: "I have never considered myself our great lord's enemy."

The messenger looked at him closely with its very human eye. "Great Neptune now sees that the rumors of your enmity were false, and thanks you for your help against the Giant. He himself remains at a distance, because it may be that other Giants still infest this area. He advises you to seek your own safety."

"I thank Great Neptune for his concern. But tell the Lord of all the Oceans that I am much concerned with the survival of this ship, the *Argo*. If he wants to do me a good turn, he could help her on her way."

"I am to warn you, Lord Triton, that if you accompany the *Argo* farther in these waters, you must stay on the alert for more Giants. And for worse than Giants, too."

"*Worse?*"

"And I am to tell you, further, to expect no additional help from Lord Neptune just now. He urges you to put forth your best efforts to place the Fleece in the hands of the human Artisan, Daedalus. Lord Neptune cannot help you, because he must prepare for a great battle."

"Just what in all the watery hells of Ocean does he think we're having here?" the sea-god commented in a muttering gurgle.

"As to that I couldn't say, Lord Triton."

"All right. All right. Maybe Poseidon understands the situation better than I do. Bear him my thanks for this important gift."

The watery messenger signed assent, and a moment later had disappeared below the dark surface of the rolling sea.

Despite the Giant's continual wary turning in the water, Triton with his Trident in hand managed at last to get behind him, then dart in and strike before his enemy could bring the projected power of his hands to bear upon the god. In another moment the Giant was in floundering retreat, howling with the pain of deadly wounds.

Instead of beginning what might well have proved a long chase, trying to finish the Giant off, Triton/Proteus elected to stay with the ship. He had some hope that his restored weapon might be useful in a different way. But to his disappointment the Trident, shake and brandish it as he might, proved no help at all when he simply wished to counteract the prevailing winds and tides.

He even thought of trying to summon Scylla and Charybdis back, but he dimly sensed that they were far away; and earlier they had almost destroyed the ship, inadvertently, while under orders to protect it.

Once again he regretted, among other things, not being able to retain Circe as an ally. Well, maybe someday, a hundred years from now—with the enchantress doubtless looking not a day older—they would be on good terms again. Triton might very well have taken up residence in some new avatar by then, though that was not certain—a human frame infused with the powers of a god tended to last much longer than it would have done in the mere course of nature.

Certainly he must retain possession of the Trident, now that he had it back. But it might not be easy to do that, without alerting all his shipmates to his true identity. Casting about within himself for some power that might be of help, he came upon a means of magical concealment.

Currently Jason and his followers were having to contend with nothing worse than the natural aspects of the ocean, but those seemed quite sufficient to destroy them.

The most serious problem, and one beyond Triton's competence to do much about, was that the ship was damaged, her bottom leaking, and repairs were necessary. She was superbly constructed by any human standard—Triton thought that perhaps only the famed Daedalus could have done better—and any ordinary vessel would have broken entirely apart by now.

There was no choice but to find their way somehow to the nearest friendly beach, lying in the general direction they were being carried. They needed a place where a battered ship could come to land without having her bottom ripped out or being beaten to pieces on rocks. But for all any of them knew, including Proteus, the nearest beach of any kind in that direction might be hundreds of miles distant.

In his desperation, Jason continued to try to use the compass-pyx. Gladly he allowed Medea to take a turn, and anyone else who wished to try. Whoever was crouching over the instrument laid his or her forehead on the rest and held as clearly as possible the mental image of an anonymous, safe, and welcoming shoreline.

The ship's flying passage before the wind went on so long that those on board were in danger of running out of drinking water; but so far the driving rain fell thick enough, day and night, to keep them from total dehydration. The falling water was caught in pieces of a tattered sail, which were then wrung out.

The captain and his bride no longer seemed on the best of terms. Evidently, thought Proteus, Circe had been right about Cupid's Arrows. Their effects passed away in time, even as fire died out without new fuel. Love once planted could grow mightily, but then again it could be strangled. The couple still clung together, but there were hints of something wrong between them, deeper than a mere quarrel.

The driven ship was essentially lost. No way for it to reach any goal that the instrument might find. They were surrounded by a bleak seascape indeed:

Medea awakened abruptly from a deep sleep, announcing that she had just had a vision. "I saw a great gulf, or bay, from which no ship is ever able to escape, because of the fierce wind that drives all vessels on the shore. The water is shallow, and thick with tangled masses of seaweed. On the shore, there is nothing at all but sand, reaching out to the clouded horizon. No living creature stirs there, on the earth or above it."

And Proteus/Triton, when he fell asleep a little later, was drawn into the strangest dream that he could remember ever having.

It seemed to Proteus that he was wandering, afoot and alone, in some city where he had never been before, and with the secret knowledge that is given in dreams, he knew that everything around him was doomed to destruction. He stood on the portico of a great temple, surrounded by the statues of gods and goddesses, all of them sweating blood. A great inhuman bellowing sounded from somewhere inside the temple, so that even Triton grew terribly afraid.

Looking up into the noonday sky, he saw that the sun had somehow been eclipsed, and the stars shone out in the nighttime darkness that surrounded that terrible sight. Around the temple, men and women were wandering in the streets, dim ghostlike figures all wailing and crying out, some of them warning of war, others proclaiming that a plague was about to fall upon the land.

At last a figure approached Proteus directly, and it was physically monstrous, a great bull's head on a tall man's body, and he knew that he faced the Minotaur. But somehow the very strangeness of the shape was reassuring.

A quiet voice issued from the bull's mouth, saying: "I am Prince Asterion, of Corycus. It has been difficult to reach you, Lord Triton, god of the sea. I am glad to see that you have found the way into my house at last."

"I am only a godling," Triton heard himself reply.

"Welcome to my Labyrinth of dreams," the Minotaur said, and made a sweeping gesture with a very human hand. "It covers infinitely more space than my waking Maze on land."

Fear had receded from Proteus, and he asked: "Where does it lead, this Labyrinth of dreams?"

"Tonight it leads to sights that it would be well for you to see. Dreams can shadow forth reality. Have you met Hera yet? Or Aphrodite? They are divinities, of course, but like you they must dream, even as I do."

Out of the shadows beside the enormous temple loomed two shrouded female forms. Proteus knew, or thought he knew, that Hera, also known as Juno, was the wife of Zeus. And gray-eyed Athena, called by some Minerva, a traditional foe of Poseidon, but now here peacefully despite her helmet and her shield, seeming to demonstrate by her presence the unity of the great gods in this. From a few words that Proteus could hear them saying, he could tell that they were all here now as allies of Zeus, they all had a stake in helping Jason to succeed in his mission.

And somehow, with few words spoken, it was communicated to Proteus: The great gods were indeed on the side of Daedalus and Vulcan, and they had wanted Jason to get the Fleece away from its guarded place in Colchis. Their object was to take it away in turn from Jason, at the proper time, and hand it over to Daedalus, whose cunning wizardry would discover what secret strength it had to give its owner. For some reason, Zeus and his allies expected the Golden Fleece to be of great benefit in their ongoing war against the Giants.

"I know where the Golden Fleece is," Proteus heard himself saying in his dream. "It is in the hands of Jason."

"We all know that," Athena chided him in her deep voice, fixing him with ageless, depthless eyes.

"We all know that," said Hera, sweetly echoing. There was a peacock sitting in the graceful curve of her strong arm.

"What we must tell you," said the bull-man, "is that Daedalus may very well be here, on the island of Corycus, when the ship of the Argonauts arrives."

"You must seek out Daedalus," powerful Minerva commanded.

"You must give him the Fleece," Juno reiterated softly.

. . . and the goddesses and Minotaur all vanished, and Proteus dreamed that he was once more swimming with the Mouse. This time great metal fetters weighed her down, and he had to put forth all his strength to lift her from the very bottom of the sea.

Projecting upward from the muddy bottom was a strange object, like a huge tree-stump. Despite its being dead and underwater, it jabbered at Proteus/Triton in a strange language, saying words that he had never heard before, but yet conveyed a grotesque meaning:

"Full fathom five thy father lies;
Those are pearls that were his eyes;
Of his bones are coral made
Nothing of him that doth fade
But doth suffer a sea change
into something rich and strange.
Sea-nymphs hourly ring his bell . . ."

Triton's dream showed him a last blurry vision of sea-nymphs, appearing as fish-tailed maidens, chanting that song of nonsense with the tree-stump. And even as the dream began to shatter and disperse, Proteus heard the voice of the Minotaur, sane and practical, telling him: "One thing that no sane mortal wants to do is to get caught up in a conflict between gods."

"I'll heartily concur with that," said Proteus. And thought he was starting to wake up.

He told no part of the dream to any of his shipmates. He saw no way that it could be of any help.

Help of some kind was definitely needed. From hour to hour in the waking world, the survival of the *Argo* and her crew hung in the balance. Another day and night passed, and no one knew whether their next hour might be their last, but finally there came the welcome noise and feel of sand grating beneath her bottom.

It was in fact a flood tide that had caught the vessel and swept her up to the inner shore, leaving her high and dry when the flood receded.

For a time the stranded crew were surrounded by an impenetrable fog. When that cleared, it revealed a landscape that was a close match to that Medea had reported seeing in her vision. Away from the sea, a wasteland stretched into the distance, unbroken and immense.

The worn-out crew dragged themselves off the grounded ship and staggered ashore. For their survival they poured out prayers of thanks, expressing their gratitude to a hundred gods, none of whom were likely to be paying the least attention. In the relief of the moment, several brave adventurers improvised vows that they would never trust their lives on any ship again.

Then, in that ghastly, fading light they made an exhausting effort to drag the beaten *Argo* even farther up on the beach, beyond all traces of the highest waves. When they had secured the ship as well as possible, they all crawled a little farther inland still, where they tried to take shelter from the wind behind a series of sand dunes.

One of the crew groaned: "The curses of Circe follow us even here."

Triton thought that all too likely. He was now carrying his Trident slung on his back with a frayed piece of rope, and thought he had succeeded in making the weapon invisible to all eyes on the ship but his own. But he still felt powerless, despite what ought to have been the reassuring nearness of the sea.

Nearby he could hear Medea weeping in exhaustion as she clung to her husband. She had no maid to attend her now.

The future seemed clearer than the past, and both were bleak and terrible. What good was divinity, if you were still effectively powerless?

The whole crew spent a bleak and miserable night. In the morning, the sun rose on a featureless sea and desert. Even the god who moved unrecognized among them had only a vague idea of where they were. For once no one had any plan to propose.

At least the sky had cleared somewhat, and the wind abated.

As soon as the rain stopped, the need of fresh water threatened to become critical. But they could hope the clearing of the clouds meant that the wind might soon reverse itself.

Then Medea, dowsing for water with a twig of driftwood in her hand, located a place some little distance inland, where pools of rainwater had gathered among the rocks. No one was going to die of thirst.

The ship was in need of serious repairs. Another acute problem was that so many oars had been lost or broken in the recent struggles with rough weather that half the remaining crew would ride in enforced idleness when the ship was launched again. On top of that, the last remaining sail was almost useless—a large tear had started. All the spare canvas had been used up long ago.

One of the ship's lockers still held some sailmaker's tools and materials, and at Jason's orders an effort was begun to mend the sail.

Careened on a beach, tilted sharply to one side—that was the only way *Argo* could rest on solid ground, given her cross-section. It was in this same position that Proteus/Triton had seen her first, but then she had looked eager and young and new, and though she was only a little older now, she certainly looked tired. Instead of a few months, years might have passed; and it occurred to him that the same thing might have been said about Medea.

Working in turn on different sections of the ship's bottom, the workers tilted *Argo*'s bulk from one side to the other, as it balanced on the central hull. The massive weight came down each time with a crushing thump.

"Here's where we really could use Hercules," one lifter grunted.

Some of the Argonauts had started a driftwood fire shortly after coming ashore, and kept it going. Now the fire was useful for heating tar, as men began to go over the ship, poking and pounding the fibers of shredded rope into the leaky seams, and pouring on hot tar as soon as it had been softened to the right consistency. The general opinion was that she could probably be made seaworthy again—or almost. If they encountered no more storms, she would probably get them home.

The ongoing search for firewood turned up a few surprises. There were many wrecks, some old, some new, up and down this coastline. With here and there assortments of human bones, half buried in the sand, being unburied and reburied by the wind.

Haraldur was holding up a find. "Is this supposed to be a rib, or an arm bone? I'm not sure it's even human."

"What creature besides humans would haunt this empty land, without a plant or animal to eat?"

There were occasionally oars among the scattered wreckage, including a few of almost the right length.

"With work and perseverance we will win out," Jason assured his followers.

Still Triton had had no further word from Poseidon, and no more informative dreams. Triton supposed that the great sea-god, like Zeus himself and like Apollo, was simply too busy to pay much attention to this sideshow. The truly major deities must all be busy getting ready for the climactic battle with the Giants, and there was no reason to think that was going to take place anywhere around here.

At a time when no one was paying Triton/Proteus any particular attention, he walked along the beach until he was out of sight of all the others, then plunged in and swam out to sea, far enough to encounter several of its creatures, deep swimmers and a flying pelican, with whom he could converse. In a little while Triton had gained valuable information about the winds and currents up and down the coast.

On rejoining the others, he explained that a new vision had given him hope. In a few days, a seasonal change in the weather could be expected, and an offshore wind would set them free. They must be ready to take advantage of it when it came.

TWENTY-ONE

Corycus

*J*ason, who had now taken over the job of steersman for himself, lowered his head to gaze into the box of ivory and ebony. Presently he raised it again, and leaned upon the steering oar, turning the prow of *Argo* in what he now felt sure was the general direction of Iolcus. The Argonauts were setting out for home.

Something like five months had passed since the *Argo* had sailed bravely out of the harbor of Iolcus. "For all we know, Pelias may be dead by now," one member of the crew grunted as he pulled his oar.

Another shook his head. "I wouldn't bet on it. Old men like him will hang on to their power like grim death. You can tell by looking at him."

Proteus, who was listening nearby, nodded, not wanting to reveal that he had no idea what the old king looked like.

Another of his shipmates spoke up. "You saw the king in Iolcus? I never did. They say he keeps pretty much to himself in his high castle."

"Oh yes." His shipmate nodded. "He came down to the quay, to see us off he said, the morning before we left. I suppose to show that there were no hard feelings, between him and Jason."

"Not much there aren't."

"I didn't see old Pelias there."

"You only got aboard at the last moment, as I recall. He'd gone back into his fortress by then, a busy man with many things to do."

Someone turned his head to call out: "Captain, are we relying on the compass-pyx again?"

"What else?" Jason called back.

And indeed there seemed no other choice. But within a few hours, their journey began to be agonizingly protracted, as the precarious condition of their ship forced them to travel a zig-zag route, seeking out one mid-ocean island after another. Each time the weary crewmen came to land they had to labor on their leaky ship again.

At last the captain raised his head, his face indicating great relief. "I have a clear objective now," he informed his shipmates. "One you will be glad to hear. It is Corycus."

A cheer went up, and Medea clapped her hands. On Corycus, considered one of the most civilized of lands, a friendly welcome could be expected. Jason said that the island of the Minotaur lay almost in line with their course for home, and his own relief was evident when he announced that he was setting a course for the harbor of Kandak.

The man in the Labyrinth had been sending Proteus dream-messages whose full meaning was still far from clear to him—but they had strongly suggested that Daedalus was to be found on this island.

If that was true, then it should be possible to deliver the Fleece just as the great gods wanted it delivered. "Daedalus is on Corycus, is he not?" Proteus asked his shipmates.

But it seemed that none of them had any idea where the Artisan might be.

Meanwhile the princess, now that the pursuing forces of her father had been baffled, was looking forward to an interval ashore, hopefully in civilized conditions. She had her own idea of what would happen on Corycus.

"I will tell my troubles to Princess Phaedra, who has ruled the island since her father died, and the god Shiva was overthrown. Do you know Phaedra, Jason? I expect a woman will be more sympathetic to my case even than good King Alcinous. And Phaedra might even have some influence with my aunt. I hope she may at least allow me the luxury of a steaming bathtub in her palace. How fortunate she is to have her independence!"

Jason's mood had begun to darken again. He said he had never met Phaedra, daughter of the late Minos, nor her sister Ariadne, but had no reason to fear her enmity. "I can show her how it would be to her advantage to have me firmly established as king in Iolcus."

Proteus/Triton was as elated as anyone else aboard. He looked forward to this landing not only because Daedalus might be here, but because he had hopes of being able to visit in waking life with Prince Asterion.

Jason confided to Proteus his private worries that some of his men might be ready to jump ship when they came into this friendly port. So far only the maid seemed to have done that, but Corycus offered the most tempting refuge they had seen in a long time.

And in the discussion of recent amazing events on Corycus, the name of the Artisan came up. "I had heard that it was old King Minos who, before he died, brought Daedalus to this island."

Proteus simply nodded in agreement. If and when the moment came, he expected it would be easy enough for Triton to take the Fleece away from the captain. Of course Jason should also get some credit for the gift—Triton thought that would do the captain a lot more good than handing it over to Pelias.

Several days passed before they finally rowed and sailed their dangerously damaged vessel within sight of the harbor of Kandak. There were immediate indications that their stay might not be as peaceful as they had hoped.

The *Argo* was still more than a mile at sea when those aboard saw smoke rising from what appeared to be the center of the city, more smoke than could reasonably be expected from the cooking fires of even a large metropolis.

Whatever was burning on shore continued to burn, and the

smoke kept ominously rising, but they really had no choice but to put in anyway. One more serious squall would almost certainly finish off the chronically weakened *Argo*. Unless an opportunity for major repairs could soon be found, her days were numbered, even if the Fates should grant them good luck and good weather.

When Proteus asked to see the Fleece again, Jason hesitated but then brought it forth, carefully wrapped in layers of cloth and fur. Exposing it on deck had only seemed to accelerate its deterioration.

It was now so shrunken that Jason could carry it inconspicuously in a pouch or pocket.

Looking at the poor thing in the bright light of day, Jason said thoughtfully: "If it should ever turn out that I cannot be king in Iolcus . . ."

"Yes?"

"Then I must manage to be king somewhere else."

Medea and Proteus exchanged glances. Jason was still contemplating the wasted Fleece. "I have been thinking," he went on. "In the last six months I have come to understand the ways of royalty somewhat better than I did when we began this voyage."

"I suppose we all have," Proteus agreed.

The captain did not seem to be listening. "It is all too possible that when I get home, Pelias will refuse to honor our agreement."

Again his hearers exchanged a glance between them. Proteus said: "I would say that's more than a possibility. In that case, there would be no use handing over the Fleece to the damned old tyrant."

Medea asked her husband: "What will you do then?"

"Other means must be considered. The right to the throne rests with me."

Triton/Proteus wished his ambitious shipmates well. But basically he did not give a damn which human rump might rest on which elevated chair.

What did concern him was the fact that, whatever happened

when Jason brought his miserable treasure home, the Argosy would then be over. And Proteus/Triton would have to discover just what he was, what life might hold for him when he could no longer be an Argonaut.

The *Argo* was still separated by some hundreds of yards of blue water from the harbor's mouth, and the men aboard were still hoping that the smoke might have some innocent explanation, when Proteus suddenly had a sensation of familiarity. The port of Kandak was gradually coming into view before him, and there welled up in him vague memories of seeing this land and these buildings before, through mortal eyes. Suddenly he realized that for all he knew, his earlier, purely human self might even have lived here. That was an alarming thought, considering what he had begun to learn about Old Proteus—he could only hope that Princess Phaedra's men would not try to arrest the agent of King Pelias on sight.

It was soon evident that the authorities on Corycus had far more immediate things to worry about. The ship was now close enough to shore to convince its crew beyond all doubt that something was seriously wrong. At one edge of the city, not far inland, stood what had to be the royal Corycan palace, sometimes called the House of the Hammer. Right beside it stretched a vast, low-slung sprawl of walls within walls, walls upon walls, most of them roofless but mixed with low roofs and truncated towers. This could only be the fabled Labyrinth, the home of Prince Asterion and of a thousand legends. The great Maze was said to cover some four square miles, of which only a small part was visible from where the *Argo* lay offshore.

The smoke they had observed while still well out to sea could now be seen to rise from burning buildings, scattered about the city but all at some distance from either Maze or palace. It appeared to Proteus that some kind of war or insurrection must have broken out.

A weary groan went up and down the rowers' benches. "Not here, too!" a despairing voice cried out. "Is the whole world at war with itself?"

"Damn it all, but I was ready for a rest!"

"Not good." With a sigh Jason looked at the four men who were now bailing steadily. Yesterday two had been enough to keep the vessel afloat. "We have no choice but to put in. But let us not go into the harbor."

Jason and his crew had been out of touch with the world for several weeks. No ship outward bound from this port had encountered them at sea, to pass along the shouted news of any dreadful conflict.

The captain was pointing at a small boat that bobbed on the waves at no great distance. "Pull up to this fellow here, let's see what he can tell us."

Jason was looking at a single figure in a small fishing craft. The figure proved to be that of a gray-bearded man, tending a single fishing line. He was wearing nothing but a broad-brimmed hat, which offered some protection against the relentless sun. The fisherman looked up in fear at the *Argo*'s swift approach, and her practical appearance, but Jason soon put him at his ease. And if he was a man who kept up with the affairs of the world, it was even probable that he recognized Jason and his ship.

"What's happening ashore?" the captain called.

"Talus," was the laconic answer.

"Talus? But who's that? Or what? Some new kind of plague?"

The man seemed to be thinking it over. "Whether who or what is hard to say."

"Just what's that supposed to mean? Some invading king or pirate?"

"Worse than that."

"How could it be worse?" The Argonauts all turned blank looks on one another. Apparently the name meant nothing to any of them.

Surprisingly, the fisherman proved something of a linguist. "His name means 'sufferer'," he volunteered. "They call him that because of the awful noise he makes."

"But what is this Talus doing, apart from setting fires?" the captain asked.

"You'd not believe me if I told you, my lord Jason. But if you go into the harbor, you'll soon see for yourselves. You'd be better off to set your sail and head for some other island." Their informant shook his head sadly, and began to set his little oars into their locks. "I must go back into the port, but you don't need to."

Some Argonauts were ready to stop him, but the captain fatalistically shook his head. "Let him go."

"Then what are we to do, captain?"

"I think that under the circumstances it will be better not to enter the harbor. The surf's quite low. We'll pick out a spot on the outer shore, and run aground." Jason ran weary fingers through his hair. "And get out the repair materials again."

They had rowed only a little closer to the beach when one of the men pointed inland, and raised a cry of wonder. "A bronze man!"

Proteus turned his head, and saw the thing immediately. It was still almost three hundred yards away, but one look was enough to make him stare in wonderment. Nothing in his damaged memory was really any help with this—the nearest Triton's thought could come to it was a vague image of certain metallic entities that labored in the workshop of Hephaestus.

Some of the crew protested that the figure was not all that strange—it was only that the island had been invaded by some army wearing armor. But Proteus shook his head at that. There was only the single figure.

"It is a man in armor," said an Argonaut, squinting to see clearly.

His benchmate disputed this. "No, I don't think so. Whoever saw armor that covers a man's whole body?" Of course that sounded like a good idea, except that any mere human weighed down by so much thick metal would find it virtually impossible to move.

At first glance, the figure appeared unarmed and empty-handed, somewhere close to the size of an ordinary human. It seemed not nearly formidable enough to be responsible for a burning city. At the distance it was hard to be sure of details, but the person, or thing, looked nude and sexless. Very nearly its entire body was the color of bronze, with only a few spots of darker hue where there should have been a face.

"I know what it reminds me of," commented another Argonaut. "One of those misbegotten brass Bulls."

"Then maybe Jason can deal with it, as well as he did with them."

The face had two eyes, but they were as artificial-looking as the rest. There was almost no nose at all, and very little mouth, despite the loudness of the voice.

Jason sighed. "Well, we'd better find out who—or what—it is we have to deal with."

The Argonauts stared at Talus as they rowed, and Jason debated with himself, aloud, whether they ought to hail him. But before the captain could make up his mind, the figure startled him by calling out to him. In a loud penetrating voice, so harsh and metallic that it could come from no other source, Talus hailed the ship.

In his harsh, booming tones the Bronze Man announced that he had recognized the painted name upon the bow of *Argo*, and commanded those aboard to land immediately and surrender the Fleece to him. The tones of his voice made it indeed an awful noise, that turned the thoughts of Proteus to themes of suffering.

"Then someone does hold our find to be of value," Jason muttered. He filled his lungs and boldly roared back at the figure on the shore. "What master do you serve?"

"Hades!" The name came in a hideous shriek, so loud that Proteus felt the hair on the back of his neck trying to stand up.

And in the same instant, Talus bent to pick up something from the ground. Moments later a stone the size of a man's head came whizzing through the air, hurled by the bronze thing directly toward the ship, as if to prove that its demands should be taken seriously. The missile passed so closely above the deck that the men who were closest to its pathway dodged. It appeared the apparition did have fingers after all, at least enough of them to grasp a stone and hurl it with impressive accuracy and awesome strength.

At first some of the Argonauts, who had been looking elsewhere at the moment of the throw, insisted they were being bombarded with a catapult or trebuchet. But now all eyes were turned upon the uncanny thing as it stood on a seaside cliff. Again the bronze right arm flashed in the sun, quicker than a small bird's wing, and here came another flying rock, this one to send up a fountain of spray a few yards short of its target, then skip on to smash into an outrigger with wood-cracking force, so that the whole ship rocked.

"Armor or not," said a man on the right of Proteus, "that can be no man."

"No," responded another on his left. "But I don't believe it is a god."

"What else? What's left? It's not a Giant."

An Argonaut who had seen service in several navies exclaimed: "Truly it seems a kind of war machine, built in the shape of a man. But I have never seen the like of it before."

"Daedalus might make something of the kind."

"No mortal could!"

"We all saw those two other things, that had the shape of bulls. Who made them?"

Triton, knowing something of the habits of his fellow deities, suspected that Hades had found or created this creature somewhere in the Underworld, and then sent it up in the hopes of gaining the Fleece for his own mad purposes.

For a time the men had ceased to work their oars. The ship was slowly drifting a little nearer to the shore, and when the Bronze Man came into view again, he had his back to them and was running inland. He had been only a few hundred yards away by line of sight, but that distance was rapidly growing greater. A long inlet lay between him and the spot where the *Argo* meant to land. If Talus wanted to get at them without swimming, he was going to have to go the long way round, perhaps a mile.

Now his almost featureless face turned back toward the *Argo*, even as he ran on in the other direction, and again the strange voice, inhumanly loud, came booming at them across the water.

"Jason of Iolcus! Surrender the Fleece to me!"

But why, Proteus wondered, would Hades want the Fleece? Possibly only to keep Zeus and his allies from getting any benefit out of it.

"The damned thing is trying to drive us away." For the first time, Proteus heard something like a note of hysteria in the voice of an Argonaut.

His benchmate answered: "Aye, away to the Underworld! One more hit from a rock like that last one will send us to the bottom."

And another man put in: "Maybe he wants to force us into shallow water, and sink us there. Probably thinks we're loaded down with plunder. Once he sees the Fleece, he may change his mind on wanting that."

Jason was calm as usual when things got nasty. "Bring her around, steersman! We might as well pull in to shore, and close our eyes to flying rocks. Even if he doesn't hit us, we're going to go down. We're taking water faster than before."

"What'll we do, Captain? Form a line with spears and shields?"

"No. Most of you will concentrate on fixing the ship, while I fight off this latest monster." Jason turned to Medea. "No more magic ointments on hand?"

Wordlessly she shook her head.

"So be it, then," he grunted. "I managed two metal monsters in Colchis. Perhaps I can handle one more."

Proteus refrained from pointing out that the Bulls were not known to have destroyed a good part of a large city, nor were they capable of hurling head-sized rocks like pebbles.

Medea was looking at her husband proudly. "To win this battle would certainly increase your fame, and also your chances of becoming king. Of course I will help you with my magic. Proteus and the others will do all they can. Proteus! Do I not speak the truth?"

"I am sure we'll all do our best, my lady. But I advise avoiding battle if that is possible. If not, Jason, you must certainly not face this thing alone. I will stand with you."

By this time Talus, who was evidently no swimmer, had vanished, running, somewhere inland. It seemed very likely that he meant to run around the inlet and close with the *Argo* when she came ashore.

Urging his men on, Jason got them to drive the *Argo* straight at the scrap of beach. While they were still in relatively deep water, Proteus dove in; a few moments' swimming and he was in the shallows, then running up the beach at his chosen landing place. He supposed he risked revealing his godhood by swimming at such a speed; but this was an emergency, and he expected the crew were too busy to concentrate on him.

Within a matter of a few more heartbeats he was standing, dripping, at the top of the beach, from which a hundred yards or so of open field extended inland, with a grove of olive trees beyond that, shutting out the view of the harbor and its immediate surroundings. Looking back into the gentle surf, he saw with mixed feelings that Jason too had leapt out of the vessel before it grounded, and was about to join him on shore.

Facing inland again, he observed that Talus had not yet reappeared. Well, if the damned thing was a mechanical device, like the Bronze Bulls, then Triton the god felt capable of handling it. He was unafraid of any war machine made by mortals. Even if it were a creation of the redoubtable Daedalus, he told himself, though he had to stop and ponder before he could feel sure of that.

Now, if only the Bronze Man did not change his tactics and retreat . . . but no, here he came, approaching the long way round the deep inlet, evidently still determined to get at the *Argo*. Sun glinted on a figure no longer sprinting as no mere human would ever have the strength and speed to run, especially in full armor, but moving more slowly, stalking like a predator with game in sight, his steady advance punctuated with small lateral movements.

Another pair of running feet, these merely human, sounded behind Proteus. Before he had thought it was really possible, here was Jason, sword in hand, standing right beside him.

"It is some god, I tell you," Jason whispered, staring at their strange opponent, who still charged forward. "Or else Hercules come back to be revenged on us."

Haraldur had joined them, and here came Polydeuces, all of them fully armed. They all looked as if they would welcome the chance to fight, for a change, some other opponent than the endless sea.

The boxer snorted. "Revenge for being left behind when we set out? Instead he should thank the men who played him that trick. And this figure's nothing like Hercules, except in strength. What god would it be? It looks like none I've ever heard of."

Proteus/Triton considered trying to persuade the warriors who had joined him to go back to the ship and let him handle Talus; but he could think of no way of phrasing the suggestion that they would not find offensive. Well, their lives were their own to dispose of as they chose; he would try to keep them breathing.

Triton for his part preferred to meet this strange and formidable opponent with his own back to the ocean, and as close to it as possible. With this in mind, he retreated a few paces closer to the sea, and there took his stance, on the highest ground in the immediate vicinity.

Meanwhile, a handful of local citizens had begun to gather at a little distance from the Argonauts, standing on some higher rocks that doubtless gave them the illusion of relative safety. Half of these Corycan natives were begging for help, while the others urgently warned the newcomers to shove off in their ship again, and flee while they still had the chance.

One man pleaded with Jason to give the Sufferer anything he demanded, so then the monster might depart from their island and leave them in peace. "If it wants something from you, please hand it over!"

Jason raised one hand in a wave, including all of these advisers. And then he ignored them all.

But Proteus raised his voice and called to them: "What more can you tell us about this awful enemy?"

The citizens looked uncertainly at one another, and voiced disjointed theories, none of them of any help. There was not even general agreement as to where Talus had come from. However he might have reached the island, or exactly when, since his arrival the Bronze Man seemed to have spent most of his time lying low, though emerging for bursts of terrible activity. Over the last three days, he had wiped out several squads of soldiers sent against him. Naturally by now everyone was too terrified to approach him. Princess Phaedra had summoned all her advisers, but among them only Daedalus had offered any hope.

"Then Daedalus is here?" Proteus asked sharply.

"Oh, yes sir, if the monster has not killed him yet."

"Let us devoutly hope not," Jason muttered.

One of the local men offered the opinion that the Sufferer must be a demigod, at least. He had heard that Zeus had given him to Queen Phaedra, to stand sentry duty over the island of Corycus by running clear around its perimeter three times every day.

With the air of one privy to great secrets, the man concluded: "And they say that he is also going to visit each village on the island, taking a regular census of the inhabitants."

The natives began to argue among themselves. Most of what they were saying now made very little sense to Proteus, or to Triton either.

Talus

$\mathcal{O}$he Bronze Man had been advancing erratically, as if he might be focusing his attention on some prey closer to him than the Argonauts and their ship. And here, dodging between the trees of an olive grove that lay just inland, came confirmation of that idea, in the form of a lone human, running now at full speed toward the new arrivals.

Other people running had now and then come into view, in whatever part of the Corycan landscape Proteus happened to be looking at. But this man was the only one moving toward the Argonauts, and only he had Talus stalking after him.

The lone fugitive was lean and scantily clad, with gray showing in his hair. He was covering ground more speedily that most people of forty years or so could manage.

"It's Daedalus," Jason exclaimed suddenly. "I met the man in Iolcus, on the day of our departure."

Proteus stared when he heard that. Suddenly it seemed possible that the great gods had really begun to smile on him, after all.

As the Artisan drew closer, his appearance was somewhat disappointing. He was garbed in the clothing of a common workman, consisting of a mere loincloth and sandals, and a cheap vest whose small pockets jingled when he ran. Not with coin, Proteus saw now, but with delicate tools.

The name of Daedalus, if shouted in the marketplace, would not have created nearly as much excitement as that of Jason, but was perhaps just as widely known in the world. He was of no more than average height, with greenish eyes, a large nose, and brownish, gray-streaked hair tied behind him with utilitarian string. His fingers were ringless as a slave's, though there was no reason to believe his corded neck had ever worn a collar. Both hands were scarred, as if from the use of every kind of common tool.

He came pounding up to the Argonauts where they stood near the sea. He had lost one sandal somewhere, and his chest was heaving. "I am called Daedalus," he got out in a breathless voice. "And you are Jason."

The captain bowed. "Of course I recognize the famous Daedalus. You and one other, whose name and face have escaped my memory, were talking with Hercules, the day before we began our voyage."

When Daedalus turned to him, Proteus extended his right hand in greeting. It was enfolded by a callused paw that felt as hard as wood.

Then the Artisan, still breathing hard from what must have been a long run, turned back to the captain. "The machine means to kill me. Can you take me quickly out to sea?"

"Not as quickly as we would all like," Jason informed the fugitive. "Repairs are necessary." Then, seeing that the Bronze Man was not actually upon them yet, he turned away to help his crew in their rush to fix the ship.

Daedalus's face fell as soon as he was able to get a close look at the *Argo*, drawn up on the beach. Argonauts were laboring feverishly, with pieces of wood, canvas, and pitch, to patch two holes in her bottom planks. Medea was standing at a little distance, gesturing at the battered vessel, obviously trying to help in some way with her magic.

"I hope, by all the gods," panted Daedalus, "that Hercules is still with you. This island and its people have sore need of his strength today."

"He is not with us," Jason responded over his shoulder. He offered no explanation.

Puzzled, the Artisan looked to Proteus, who shook his head and said: "I have never met the man, he dropped out of our crew before I joined. What can you tell us about Talus? All we've been able to learn so far is that his name means 'sufferer.' "

Daedalus snorted. "Bah, the old word has nothing to do with suffering. It means an ash-tree. A smith told me that a race of bronze men once sprang from ash-trees. The charcoal from that wood burns with a tremendous heat, and so is good for smelting out the copper that must go into the alloy."

The Artisan sat down suddenly on the ground, as if his legs had grown too tired to hold him up. "Practical information about Talus is not easy to come by, but there is some evidence that he comes from the Underworld, and is in league with Hades."

Proteus said to him: "We have something we want to show you."

But Daedalus was wrapped up in some sudden new thought of his own. He called out to Jason: "You are on your way home, from your quest for the Golden Fleece?"

The captain turned his head again. "As you see."

"And was it a success?"

"It was," said Jason shortly, over his shoulder once again.

"Then may I see the Fleece at once? The matter is extremely urgent."

"That," said Proteus, "is exactly what I wanted you to see."

He looked hard at Jason, and after a moment's hesitation, the captain dug out the fragment from his belt pouch. It cost him another hesitant moment to actually hand it over to Daedalus.

The Artisan eagerly accepted the small wad, but then once again rising hope was dashed from his countenance. "Oh yes," he said in a lowered voice. "Marvelous stuff," he added glumly when he saw that some further reaction was expected. But his attitude belied the words.

A moment later he had handed the trophy back. "Marvelous," he repeated. "But useless to me. I already have a sample, very like this, in my workshop."

Proteus and the captain were both staring at him. "How can that be?" breathed Jason.

Daedalus threw a glance back over his shoulder, searching inland, but Talus still had not come into sight. He gave a slight shrug. "I managed to gain access to some of the materials left over when the Flying Ram was constructed, many years ago."

Proteus/Triton could feel himself growing irrationally angry. "Then you don't even want the damned thing after all?" he asked. "Are you sure? I heard—someone told me that the great gods were very eager to see this placed in your hands."

The Artisan did not seem at all surprised that the great gods took an interest in him. "One hears all kinds of things," he remarked, rubbing his forehead with a callused hand. He was still looking, wistfully, at the scrap of fabric as Jason stuffed it back into his pouch. "I was hoping that the Fleece would turn out to be something I had not seen before. Oh, this stuff is very interesting. At any other time I would be fascinated. But with Talus trying to kill me on the one hand, and the Giants to prepare against on the other, I have no time for merely interesting things. So keep your treasure, Jason, and derive from it whatever benefit you can. You have some kind of bet with Pelias, I understand?"

"But . . ." Proteus gestured his own disappointment.

Daedalus interpreted his puzzled look as a request for more information on the Fleece. "As a component of the Ram, it probably functioned to slow the vehicle down when a crash impended—then certainly it ought to have cushioned the final impact."

"Judging by the look of the Grove of Ares," said Proteus, "even twenty years after the final impact, as you call it, I would say it must have failed to do that. But are you sure that the great gods have no interest in this? I was certain they wanted it put into your hands."

Daedalus was getting his breath back, and now he regained his feet. He looked almost ready to run again—but only if he really had to. "Possibly they did, or do. But I fear Zeus and the others are somewhat out of touch with my work, having even more immediate threats to face." He turned to look inland again. "Where's Talus now? Do you see him anywhere?"

"No." Proteus was persistent. "I want to be able to tell the great gods that I have given you the Fleece!"

"I will tell them myself that you made the offer. I will also be happy to let them know that you have saved my life, if you have any way to manage that!"

Listening carefully, Triton could detect faint screams, coming from half a mile or so inland. The voices had a hoarse, male quality, that evoked an image of dying soldiers. "So, it's after you? You in particular, I mean?"

Daedalus nodded. "Unhappily, it is. Somehow it knows I am its only really dangerous opponent on the island. For days now I have been working, almost without sleep, to build a trap that will contain the Bronze Man if I can lure him into it."

Putting one hand in a pocket of his tunic, Proteus felt the "Tooth" he had stuffed in there before Jason underwent the trial of the Bulls. Proteus had known since he pocketed the Tooth that there existed someone who would be very glad to see a thing like this—and on an impulse he now held it out. "Here."

Daedalus took the gift, abstractedly, glanced at it and dropped it in a pocket of his vest. "Thank you."

What other comment he might have made was forestalled, by Medea who had now approached the men. She said to Daedalus: "There are still a number of ships and boats in the harbor. You might have got in one of those, days ago, and put out to sea."

Hasty introductions were performed, and the Artisan shook his head. "I might have. But I am pledged to defend the Princess Phaedra as best I can, and the princess refuses to leave her people in this crisis. But now it seems that I am cornered, and can run no more. Your ship may be my last chance to survive. I'll be no good to Princess Phaedra dead."

Jason was wrapping up the remnant of his treasure again. "What is this trap like, that you are building?"

"It is very complicated, sir. Not easy to explain." Daedalus swayed a little on his feet, as if his body dreaded having to run again. "Here comes Talus now. The gods be with us all."

Proteus turned to see that the bronze figure had reappeared, no more than a hundred yards away. The closer it came, the more human it appeared. It might indeed have been a man in armor, except that the waist and neck seemed too slender to have accommodated any normal human frame within them. If anything the figure now seemed a little smaller than Proteus had thought it when at a greater distance.

Jason was shouting at his men to heave on the *Argo*, get her back into the water at all costs, and they were scrambling to obey. Proteus glancing at the hull saw that some kind of patch, covering the worst leak, had been improvised with amazing speed.

When Proteus moved a few steps away from the Artisan, a little closer to the Bronze Man, the latter's attention stayed fixed on Daedalus.

"I cannot run much longer," the great man admitted in small voice. His breathing had returned more or less to normal, but his face had a look of exhaustion. "You must let me board your ship. I must have rest."

"Of course," said Jason, and he was gone to join his men in getting the craft re-launched.

"I'm not sure the ship will be any safer," said Proteus. "Instead of that, stand close behind me, and I can probably protect you there."

Where were the great gods when they were truly needed? Proteus thought. He supposed, and Triton's experience held nothing to contradict the thought, that one thunderbolt from Zeus, or an Arrow from Apollo's Bow, could easily enough have reduced this Talus to a small heap of glowing slag. But according to all that he had heard, Zeus was elsewhere just now, very busy lying low and trying to decide on the best way to fight the Giants.

Meanwhile, a ragged formation of what must be Queen Phaedra's loyal troops had appeared in the middle distance, watching Talus from behind, and advancing on him slowly. Triton supposed the Corycan Army had been doing their best to defend their princess and their city, and probably Daedalus too. He could see that they had grown very wary of their terrible opponent.

To the Corycan soldiers' credit, they had approached to within about fifty yards of Talus, and were having another try from there. But slung stones, spears, and arrows only bounced loudly and harmlessly from Talus's metal body. The Bronze Man did not even turn his head to look at his assailants; and Proteus thought that as much as the fabric of his body might look like bronze, it had to be something even harder and stronger.

Triton was impressed as well as Proteus. "By all the gods, I think even Hercules could do nothing against this!"

Talus continued to ignore the barrage. He had concentrated his attention almost fully on Daedalus, and Jason. And now, having apparently satisfied himself that no trap or trickery awaited him where they were standing, he began a steady advance.

As the bronze thing moved forward, its color was changing, growing brighter . . . with a sinking feeling, Proteus realized that Talus had the hideous power of heating himself red-hot, through some internal source of energy.

"The day before yesterday," muttered Daedalus from close behind him, "some intrepid soldiers tried to catch him in a net. But he turned on the heat, like this, and it fell away at once in burning strands.

"The idea had possibilities," the Artisan admitted. "But a different implementation would be required . . ."

Seen at closer and closer range, the face of Talus seemed to be grinning fiercely—which might be, Proteus thought, some effect of the radiant heat. Slowly the Bronze Man approached, as if he respected Daedalus and was wary of some trap or trick. Or was it possible that he had somehow detected the presence of a god among these new adversaries?

Jason had rapidly retreated, trying to save his ship, and Medea had gone with him. Triton meanwhile had been calling his own powers into action.

Meanwhile, some thirty men, their muscles energized by fear, had shoved the ship back into the water, where it seemed in no immediate danger of going down, unless its planks should be punctured by another rock. Some of the crew, benefiting by their experience of recent days, were becoming wizards at the use of pitch and oakum and odd bits of wood and canvas.

Jason was standing on the deck, roaring out orders, trying to get his vessel out farther from the shore, to at least make greater demands on their foe's strength and accuracy. And beside her husband stood Medea, her lovely face a mask of rage, as she tried to use her magic to bring down Talus.

The *Argo* rode a smooth path out to sea, while her crew bent to the oars. Meanwhile, as in their escape from Circe's island, the swiftly swelling surf came crashing in to right and left.

Unslinging the Trident from his back, the sea-god held the weapon ready in his right hand.

Daedalus had not retreated to the ship, and it was plain that he preferred to seek protection by staying with Proteus. It crossed Triton's mind to wonder whether the Artisan had been consorting so much with gods that he was able to recognize one on sight.

Proteus danced nimbly back before the glowing horror, with Daedalus somehow keeping just behind him, then suddenly clinging fiercely to his back, like a small child seeking protection. The god's strength easily bore the burden. The surf had swelled abruptly, until the waves were house-sized, and then larger. The rushing billows split behind the sea-god's back, not touching him or the helpless human he was carrying. Then the great waves joined again in front of Triton, went pounding on to deliver their rock-crushing blows on the harbor breakwater and the small figure of glowing bronze that danced along it, now trailing a massive cloud of steam.

Triton was sure he could outrun any mere human, but his divine powers were much better suited to underwater work than to this earthly dancing; and he was slowed to some degree by carrying Daedalus with him. He understood very well that the protective powers of his godhood were definitely limited, and resistance to great heat might not be among them. He strongly suspected that if Talus was able to seize him, the body of Proteus might very well be crushed and burned to death, despite the fact that he was carrying a god-Face in his head.

Still, with his magic Trident ready in his grip, he felt confident of being able to deal Talus a devastating blow, as soon as the metal man came within reach. And now, as swift as thought, the Bronze Man was upon them, hands outstretched like the taloned paws of a springing beast. And just as speedily the Trident shocked the attacker into staggering back, producing as it struck his metal a pyrotechnic show, like the eruption of a miniature volcano.

Evidently Talus was made of tougher stuff than Giant-flesh, for the killing machine was not destroyed. Instead it backed away, just far enough to be well out of Proteus's thrusting range, and there it began to dance about, industriously picking up more rocks and throwing them again. Now and then, moving with lightning speed, it feinted a new dash to close quarters.

Proteus used his Trident to parry the flying rocks, and waited for his foe to come to him again. He himself was wary of advancing inland even a step more than was necessary. As long as Proteus stayed within the grasp of roaring waves, Triton could keep not only the three points of his Trident interposed between himself and his adversary, but a protective shield of water too. Each time the glowing, grinning thing of bronze advanced on him, masses of water battered it. Great waves were torn asunder by its heat, shredded into hissing, roaring steam, so that the figure of Talus beyond was visible only as an orange glow through a cloud.

So far Triton's tactics were succeeding, but he realized that the man he was trying hardest to protect now stood in some danger of drowning. Deftly the god maneuvered to get his back turned briefly inland. Then, with the monster for once between him and the sea, he gently set down Daedalus, and from the corner of his eye saw the man go scrambling away.

Talus made no attempt at pursuing the Artisan, evidently realizing it would be a grave mistake to turn his back on his new enemy.

Proteus/Triton had to lure his metallic antagonist out on a spit of land almost surrounded by the sea. Once there, he called on a flow of ocean, creating titanic waves that swept ashore and enveloped Talus in a cloud of steam.

The Bronze Man tried to advance across slippery rocks, but the huge masses of stone were not much impressed by his furious burning. His metal foot slipped on slick rock, and he began to fall. Moments later another big wave caught him squarely, and hurled him back shoreward in a fresh explosion of steam.

A moment later he was advancing again, as rapidly as before. But Triton had all the water of the Great Sea to call upon. He tried to speed the timing of the waves, but that was hard to do, once a natural rhythm had been established.

At last a cross-current of green liquid force swirled his bronze antagonist away. Mountains of cold water brought up from the depths exploded into steam, hammered Talus between them, and seemed about to beat him to pieces on the rocks. Now it seemed that process had begun, for one of the Bronze Man's hands was dangling uselessly.

A cheer went up from the Argonauts, whose ship was still riding close enough to shore to let them see something of what was happening; but not even Triton could hear the cheer, for the thundering of the surf.

Even after being wave-damaged, Talus managed to climb a cliff and was preparing to hurl another rock. But something inside him had been damaged, or exhausted, and he could no longer summon up the strength. He stood there for a short time, high on the jutting cliff. And then, abruptly, his legs could no longer hold him up. His strength failed, and he pitched forward headlong into the place where the surf beat on the rocks.

Later, of course, the legend-makers were to have their way with that day's astounding happenings. One story had it that an Argonaut wounded Talus in the ankle with a poisoned arrow. Others somehow gave credit to a passing shepherd for encompassing the Bronze Man's destruction; most awarded the chief honor to Medea, and her reputation as a magician was enormously enhanced.

As soon as Jason saw Talus fall, he urged his crew to turn their craft around and row straight for the harbor, in search of a place where again they would be able to resume their work of repair. *Argo* at the moment was not fit to begin the last leg of her voyage home.

Everywhere, along the seawall and the docks, crowds were gathering, cheering lustily for those who had somehow caused Talus to be destroyed. From a distance, Medea on her ship's deck had been far more visible than Proteus, where he stood almost buried in the surf that he had raised. So it was only natural that she should be given credit for the victory.

Gasping, his muscles quivering in the aftermath of exertion, but ready to fight again if necessary, Triton/Proteus held his position standing on a spray-drenched rock, waiting for the bronze head to appear once more above the waves. Minutes passed, and then an hour, and there was still no further sign of Talus.

* * *

It now seemed that, after all, nothing could stop Jason from bringing the Fleece home with him. Medea was obviously still determined to help him succeed in his mission.

And Proteus thought: *I have stood by him so far, and I will stand by him till he confronts his uncle and claims his crown. However that turns out. Jason will then be on his own. But before I leave Iolcus, I think I will have a word or two to say to Pelias on my own account.*

Triton had begun, with spells and unobtrusive gestures, to calm the waters still beating on the Corycan headland. He had also issued a silent summons, for dolphins to come and help in the search for metal parts. But it might well take hours for the nearest such creatures to reach the scene. Meanwhile, Proteus/Triton preferred to spend his own personal energy making sure that *Argo* was still safe, rather than seeking the remains of Talus underwater.

Within minutes after the fight ended, and long before the summoned dolphins could arrive, agile Corycan youths and girls were clambering on the wet rocks, braving the subsiding surf, plunging their shining bodies into the deep pools between rocks, from which a hundred rivulets were now carrying back the surplus to the sea.

There passed a quarter of an hour, then a half. So far, no more than a few brassy fragments had been recovered, from between the sharp points of the hard black rock, evidently part of one arm and hand. That was all.

And Daedalus, afforded the chance to make a leisurely inspection of a few little fragments of his deadly adversary, observed that he was strongly reminded of the Golden Maidens in the workshop of Hephaestus.

In these small bits of bronze-colored metal he found true excitement. The largest piece was a single finger, more or less intact. Daedalus vowed to pay a substantial price for any additional part of the wreckage that had been Talus, bronze in this case

being deemed more valuable than gold. He asked that young people be ordered back into the surf to look for more parts, and he
himself, weary as he was, dared to enter the subsiding waves to
search.

Daedalus did succeed in carrying off whatever remnants of Talus
could be found in the pounding surf. Still some thumbnail-sized
pieces were being found, and not all of them were metal, a few
being of stuff much harder to identify.

Medea was being acclaimed across the island, given credit for
slaying the bronze terror with her magic. Daedalus, the only one
who might have let people know the true state of affairs, said
nothing, being utterly intent on his own ideas and work.

On the afternoon and evening following the defeat of Talus, Jason
and Medea and all their shipmates were royally entertained on
shore.

Triton/Proteus would take advantage of the delay of several
days, while *Argo* was being solidly repaired with the help of a
grateful Princess Phaedra, and would try to visit Prince Asterion in
his Labyrinth.

Jason and Medea were mildly surprised to learn that it was
their shipmate Proteus whom Prince Asterion wanted to see in
private.

Escorted partway into the Labyrinth, Proteus/Triton found it
vastly different in appearance from the site he had visited in
dreams. His immediate surroundings were of reasonable dimen-
sions. After only a short walk, through many turnings, he was
shown into a comfortable roofed chamber and asked to wait. He
was told that Prince Asterion would soon be with him.

While he waited, the man who had once come out of the sea to
join the Argonauts found himself confronted by (for the first time

in his life, as far as he could remember) a fine, clear mirror. And for just an instant it seemed to Proteus that he caught a momentary glimpse of the face of Mouse, as if she were right beside him, looking into the mirror too.

Surely he must have seen good mirrors at some point in his old life, and surely the god component of his compound being ought to be used to them. Still, this one was something of a shock, because of the image it presented. It was a fine sheet of glass or metal, beautifully silvered, and it gave him back an image that he thought must be very close to the reality. To what other humans saw when they looked at the man called Proteus.

It was not exactly what either Proteus or Triton thought he must look like, but he was ready to believe the glass could be right and his own ideas wrong.

Now it was not the Mouse, but the Bull-Man himself, the Minotaur in person, whose image joined his own.

Proteus turned and saw that this time the fantastic apparition was truly real, and Prince Asterion was standing just behind him.

"I have had it specially installed," the Minotaur told him, pointing at the glass with one huge but very human finger. "Because I want to know myself."

"I wish that I could know myself," said Proteus.

On that same evening, in the adjoining palace, Princess Phaedra offered Jason and his bride a new ship, in gratitude for the successful fight they and their people had made against the scourge that had almost destroyed her realm. He declined with thanks, preferring to complete his voyage in the same faithful vessel in which he had begun it.

When the princess expressed her curiosity about this decision, he told her that he had been granted a vision, to the effect that his fate and that of the *Argo* were inextricably linked.

Later Phaedra saw the visiting princess alone; what passed between the two of them was not immediately revealed.

*   *   *

The celebration of thanksgiving went on for several days. By that time Jason's ship had been made as seaworthy as the shipwrights of the port could make it, and he summoned all the Argonauts aboard. It was time that they pushed on for home.

Home

For some of the Argonauts, returning to Iolcus meant truly coming home. But Proteus had no feeling of familiarity when the rocky landscape of the large island first came into sight, or when he first beheld the Iolcan ruler's castle perched atop one of the rugged arms of land enclosing the ample harbor. Somewhere up there in that pile of stones, Pelias would be jealously guarding the throne that Jason wished to occupy.

During the last hour of the homing voyage, Triton noted, with his divinely augmented vision for all pelagic things, how the seaward side of the castle overhung a wilderness of jagged rock, whose only visible inhabitants were a few hardy bushes, and some nesting seabirds. A little farther inland, pine-clad promontories reared up, surrounding the harbor on all sides, save for its narrow opening to the sea.

But it was the seaward surface of the rocks just below the castle that Triton found most interesting. Certain faint but broad traces of oceanic slime, too faint for merely human eyes to see but reasonably fresh, marked the oceanside cliffs just below the castle's frowning outward face. The sight of that trail strongly suggested the possibility that a fish-tailed Giant might have come visiting old Pelias. The marks were such as might have been left by a two-handed but almost legless creature of more than human size, and they broke off before reaching as high as the castle itself, just at the level of a particularly well-defined crevice in the rocks. Triton/Proteus supposed the deep crevice might possibly hide an opening, maybe even the entrance to a tunnel big enough to accommodate a slithering Giant who had some good reason to drag himself that high above the water.

The castle's lowest windows peered out some forty or fifty

feet above the sea, clinging to the crest of a rocky peninsula. Looking up at the castle's inner face as the *Argo* pulled into the harbor's mouth, Proteus could see how in one place a merlon was missing from the battlement, like a broken tooth in a Giant's face.

Almost exactly one half year after her departure, the rundown *Argo*, her oars fanning the water jerkily like the limbs of a weary swimmer, bore her captain, his new wife, and his crew of tired Argonauts back into the seaport of Iolcus. The day of their return was chill and gray, the skies weeping gently at the beginning of what passed for winter in these parts.

Almost all of the tired men on board remembered that departure, and it seemed to them very little had changed in their absence; the harbor was still only moderately busy. The people on shore and on the piers who stood watching the long ship's arrival were wrapped in such clothing as they had available. Well, at least there were no mountainous walls of ice.

Princess Phaedra had given them a new sail, but there was simply not enough wind to make it useful, or Jason would have raised the mast and tried his best for a brave entrance. Anyway, it seemed somehow fitting that the last yards of the long voyage should recapitulate the difficulty of the rest. Everyone pulled smartly at the oars, and no one grumbled. They would make one last unstinting effort, and finish up the job in style.

Triton had been carrying his Trident ever since he struck down Talus. The three-pronged spear was slung quite openly on his back by a scrap of cordage, but it remained imperceptible to any ordinary humans. None of his shipmates could see the weapon, or hear the little sounds it made when it occasionally bumped or scraped on other objects. Nor could they even feel it, apparently, when one of them happened to brush past him. He had to be continually careful that no one was accidentally stabbed.

For the moment at least, there was nothing about either the port or the castle to jog his memory; they were as new and unfamiliar as any other place and any other royal dwelling he had seen on the long voyage.

His mind, compounded of human and divine abilities and memories, kept drifting back to Circe, trying to puzzle out what sort of agreement the previous avatar of Triton could have had with her. But the Triton of a year ago, a god with all his memories intact and dwelling in a different human body, was as remote and irreclaimable as Old Proteus. Whatever agreement that deity might have had with the enchantress had certainly been dissolved in those great waves pounding the Isle of Dawn, or buried in the mud that they had left behind.

Still, Triton toyed with the idea of someday paying another visit to Circe on her island, and trying to make peace with her. Well, after she had a good chance to cool down he might try it. There was no hurry. He felt reasonably sure that if he were to return to the Isle of Dawn in a hundred years, he would find her essentially unchanged. With a little effort on both sides, their relationship could be repaired. Vague memory assured him that the two of them had fallen out before, at various times over the centuries. Still their long-term interests coincided. Anyway, he seriously doubted the enchantress would be bothering him here in Iolcus.

In the meantime, the image of another woman kept intruding on Triton's thoughts. If the Mouse had come back here to report to Pelias, as it seemed certain she had done, then she was very probably still in the castle or the town. He told himself he wanted to see her just once more, just to make absolutely sure . . .

But absolutely sure of what?

Just as the *Argo* was poking her faded prow into the harbor, Jason suddenly brought up another gloomy detail: when preparing for this voyage, he had, as he thought, persuaded certain well-off foreign backers to invest in the construction and outfitting of his sturdy ship. Those backers would now surely be expecting some return on their investment—but any reward he might give them would have to wait until he sat on the throne. Meanwhile they must somehow have been putting up with the enmity of Pelias.

Proteus pondered whether he ought to tell the captain that his real sponsor had been Circe. Maybe someday, he decided. Now did not seem to be the proper time.

"Where we going to dock, Captain?" someone asked.

"We're not. We'd sink even while tied up at the dock. Unless people stayed on board to bail continuously, and I won't ask anyone to do that. I seem to remember that there's a little beach, over near the castle's foot. We'll run her aground there."

"Ship oars," was the last command ever given on the voyage.

After the bottom grated on gravelly sand, in a bleak and drizzling rain, there followed a long moment of silence, in which no one said anything, no one moved.

Finally the silence was broken when another Argonaut announced: "By all the gods, I'm glad I did it. But I wouldn't do it again, not for a dozen Fleeces and a crown." There was a murmur of agreement, stronger than Jason liked to hear, to judge by his expression.

Some of the folk on the docks had recognized the ship, and already a few onlookers had stopped and were staring from a little distance. One youth took a good look at the arrival, then turned and ran off with a purposeful stride. It would not be long before everyone in the city, and in the castle, knew who had come in.

One of the returning Heroes bent down and kissed the stones of the shingled beach, as soon as he had stepped ashore.

The two eyes painted on *Argo*'s prow, now staring into hopeless rain, were faded and worn almost to invisibility by sun and sea. Their blank stare encompassed the calm harbor, occupied by a fair number of craft of all descriptions. Here the *Argo* was not arriving in the midst of strife; but Triton/Proteus had a foreboding that she brought with her the potential for great violence.

Before anyone walked away from the ship, Jason insisted on

conducting a brief memorial service on the gravelly beach where they had run aground, a pouring into harbor water of the last mouthful of poor wine, as a libation. The captain's muttered plea to the gods recalled to all their minds the names and faces of their shipmates who had died in the course of the voyage.

Five or six of the crew turned their backs on the *Argo* and her captain immediately after the service and walked away, having nothing more to say to their captain or any of their remaining shipmates.

The eyes of the remaining crew watched without emotion as the last of the wine was given to wet rocks and sand—all the rest was already gone, and there had been no thought of saving the good stuff for last. Much better drink was soon going to be readily available, a short walk away.

Someone brought up the subject of what was to be done with the logbook—as soon as the last entry had been written into it. The writer juggled it in his hands, once, twice, and for a long moment Proteus had the impression that he was about to hurl it away, into the deepest water his throwing arm could reach. Jason may have thought the same thing, for he hastened to take possession of the log. He tucked it into a small pack he had dug out from somewhere and was carrying on his back.

He was carrying the Fleece in there too, and after a moment of indecision he took out the remaining scrap of fabric and handed it to Proteus. "Will you keep this for me, shipmate?"

Triton hesitated only momentarily. "I will, Captain. But for how long? And why?"

"Only a little while. Because I think it will be safer with you, for the time being, than with me. It's possible that the usurper's men will be waiting in the harbor, to arrest me on sight."

You are not alone in that, my captain. But Proteus did not say those words aloud; he thought he certainly could defend the treasure if anyone should try to take it.

Meanwhile Medea was standing by, wrapped against the chill

in a fine blanket given her by the sympathetic Princess Phaedra. She watched Jason hand over the Fleece as if it made very little difference to her what he might do with it.

When everyone walked away from the ship, for the first time in months leaving her unguarded, Jason and Medea followed slowly, lagging behind, deep in private talk or argument. For once they did not seem eager to have Proteus as a consultant, and this time he was well satisfied to let them settle their own affairs.

Others of the crew, now straggling forward in a loose gathering, had their own personal concerns. "I've not a coin left on me," someone was muttering behind Proteus. "Haven't had for months."

The line of Argonauts grew longer and more straggly, trudging around the edge of the water toward the buildings and the docks. One man raised an arm and pointed. "Look, lads. It's the very spot where Hercules threw us all in."

Haraldur chuckled. "I'll not forget that. Never felt so foolish in all my life."

"And the way the harbor water tasted."

"That's because you thought of all the sewage that runs into it."

"Never thought I could be glad to see the place again."

"Talk about not forgetting. There's many things been seen and done on this trip that we'll none of us forget."

For what felt like a long time, as their feet kept carrying them along the water's edge, it seemed possible that Circe had struck them with a curse of invisibility, so that now, when they had finally, actually, almost incredibly, regained their home port, very few people were going to take any notice of their arrival. But slowly there developed an additional movement of humanity along the docks, a slow gathering of onlookers.

Some of the voyagers, including Jason, Proteus, and Medea, had acquired new clothes on Corycus, but others had not bothered, and were still in rags, seeming to glory in their Heroic poverty.

"Use your imagination, man!" one of these was saying to another. "We won't need coins, not for a few days anyway. Anyone just back from a cruise with Jason, and bringing back the Fleece, will have the local barflies standing in line to buy him drinks and hear his stories."

"Wait'll they see the Fleece, they'll want their money back."

"But on the other hand," put in Proteus, "maybe some of us will be in no mood for telling stories." As the progress of the returning Heroes carried them closer to the quays and stores of the waterfront, he scanned the scattering of folk already there, trying to discover among them the men or women who might be already looking for him in the name of the king. The captain in all innocence thought that he, Jason, was the only one Pelias was going to be concerned about. Little did the captain know.

Proteus had no doubt there were anonymous agents of the king among the workmen and idlers who had witnessed the arrival of Jason and his ragged crew. It was very likely that he, Proteus, had already been recognized; and if he had not, he soon would be.

He had to fight down an irrational idea that the Mouse might somehow have learned that the *Argo* would be putting into port today, and that she would come down to the docks to greet her former shipmates. Perhaps to point him out to the king's officers.

One of his companions jarred him out of dark thoughts by bumping his elbow and demanding: "What's your plan, Proteus? Going to join us in the funhouse?"

"Not right away." He nodded more or less straight ahead. "I'll just wait yonder, in the big tavern, so I won't be hard to find. The king will want to see me."

Haraldur had fallen into step beside him. "So you wouldn't anticipate any trouble getting in to see the king?"

"Not in the least. I need only stand still, to be magically whisked into his presence. And if you're with me, Hal, you can expect the same kind of invitation."

Haraldur smiled at that, then, as the pair of them were entering the tavern door, frowned, as at some joke he had failed to understand.

"Sure, he'll ask you to drop in for a drink." Haraldur squinted at him, and his voice changed. "By the gods, I think you're serious." Then the northman seemed to experience a flash of understanding, followed by even greater mystification. "You mean you . . . have some connection with old Pelias?"

Proteus had finished the voyage without a coin of his own, but a day ago he had secretly arranged for a sea-creature to provide him with a few pearls, that he figured ought to serve at least as well as golden coins. He now handed one of these stones to a servitor, who looked at it with some suspicion and took it to the manager.

In moments the two shipmates were settling into tavern chairs, that felt so gratefully different from a rower's bench. Haraldur sipped from his mug—the server had swiftly returned—looked round him at the smoky room, which was sparsely populated at this time of day, and sighed with satisfaction.

"Used to have." Proteus turned his gaze toward the window, and the high castle beyond, looming over everything. "But it may be that he thinks I'm still working for him. If so, then as soon as he learns I'm back, and Jason's back in good health, he's going to want to ask me why a certain job never got done."

"What job?" The northman wiped mead from his mustache.

"He wanted Jason dead, and I was supposed to handle it." Proteus poured more golden liquid from the big jug left on their table by the server.

There was a pause, while the northman digested this revelation. At last he said again: "You're serious."

Triton/Proteus nodded.

"But you didn't."

"You wouldn't think a man could forget an assignment like that, would you?"

Haraldur leaned forward and lowered his voice. "Proteus,

have y'gone raving mad? To betray the king and still come back here?"

"Raving maybe, but not crazy. Though my brains were scrambled; that's the point, you see. That's what caused most of the confusion. Remember the day I joined the company?"

The other leaned back. "Not likely to forget it. The way you buried that spearhead in the log. Then, I thought I was making a joke, when I said you had to fight three of us. But now I think you might have."

Proteus nodded. "Almost all my memory was gone. I didn't know who I was—anything beyond my name. When Jason asked me, I managed to come up with that. I didn't know who I had been the day before, whether I had family or not, or if I was coming or going. No idea what I had been trying to do before the Giant sank the other ship. I thought it was the knock on my head that had wiped me out, but I was wrong."

"What was it, then?"

"I know now I killed that Giant." Proteus drank.

"By all the gods!"

"But before I did, he swept me with his special weapon. Scrambled my brain for sure."

The northman was following him closely. "But their special weapon has no effect on us poor mortal humans. It works only against . . ."

Haraldur's speech trailed off gradually. He sat there while his face changed slowly, until he was staring at the man across the table from him in a way that Proteus had never seen him look at anyone or anything before.

Proteus nodded slowly. "That's almost right, shipmate. But it does work against human minds, sometimes. It works inside any human head where a god-Face has come to dwell."

"So you . . . are . . . oh, by all the gods, I should have seen it! What's your name?"

"I picked up the Face of Triton a couple of hours before I

joined the Argosy. Right after the Giant killed the previous avatar."

"Oh, by all the gods!" The discovery called for a deep drink, from which Haraldur emerged once more wiping his mustache. "Triton! The fish, and everything. I should have seen it—I've met a god or two before. And the waves. It was you who pried us free from Circe's island." He made it sound like an accusation. "Or washed us free, was more like it. And then on Corycus. It was you finished the Bronze Man, it wasn't the princess and her jabbering."

Proteus nodded again. "I expect that Pelias already knows what's happened to his secret agent."

"How could he know?"

Proteus didn't answer that directly. "But just possibly he doesn't. In that case he'll be very interested in finding out why the man he sent to kill Jason has been so busy saving his life instead."

Haraldur wiped his forehead. "Not only saving Jason's life but getting him the Fleece—and what about that Giant in the Grove of Ares, I suppose you settled him too? Hah! And now you're just hanging around here so you can explain your conduct to King Pelias? You've got—" He stopped suddenly and lowered his voice, though no one else in the tavern seemed to be paying them any attention. "Were you a mere man, I'd say that you've got balls, standing up to a king!"

Triton nodded. "I do want to see old Pelias, face to face. There are some other things that have to be cleared up between us."

"Like what?"

"I don't know if I can explain it, even to myself. But I won't be sure of who I am now, until I know who I was before I became an Argonaut. Does that make sense?"

Haraldur snorted. "Shipmate, you're asking the wrong man about what in the world makes sense, what doesn't. Anyway, I'd give much to be there, when you confront the king and he tries to figure out if you're really a god or it's all some crazy story. Triton, by all the hells!"

"I was hoping you'd say that, Hal." Proteus sat up straight in his chair. "I have many of Triton's powers, but perhaps not all have come back to me. There are times when even a god can use another pair of hands, another pair of eyes to watch his back. I'd much like to have a reliable shipmate at my side when I go to talk to Pelias."

When Proteus had looked out the tavern window at the castle for a while, some ghosts of memory did indeed begin to stir. He remembered, or imagined he did, something of the vast structure's interior layout, as if he had indeed spent time inside it. Up there would be the private apartments of the monarch, and over there, somewhat lower, the long windows of the great hall. And lower still, of course, and almost windowless, would be the dungeons, which were still considerably above the level of the sea.

Half a dozen other Argonauts had come into the tavern, and settled at another table, where they began to drink and grumble. These were not men that Proteus would particularly have chosen as companions. Drifting over from their table came unhappy words concerning money. Well, considered as a pirate enterprise, the Argosy would have to be rated a financial disaster for those taking part, and for any backers they might have had; a lot of efforts at piracy ended that way, as did a lot of honest trading voyages.

Still, the casualties on such an expedition might easily have been much worse. And considered in terms of its real mission, the voyage could hardly be described as a failure. Jason had brought back the Fleece, exactly what he promised to do when he set out. Almost everyone else aboard had promised the captain they were seeking only adventure, and they could hardly allege they had been cheated out of that.

Those few among the Argonauts who had families or friends waiting in the city or nearby would no doubt be given a joyous welcome, as soon as their loved ones learned they had come home; but only a few of the adventurers were so lucky. In these men's young lives, there had yet been time for nothing but restless adventure. For them the voyage was not really over—for some among them, the Argosy had been only one leg of the long wandering voyage of their lives. Some of those men still had countless miles and many years to go. Others, Proteus thought a majority, were ready to return to their own homes and settle down—at least until the itch for change and danger grew in them again.

Wherever they meant to go, home, or to the nearest brothel, the great majority of the surviving crew had dispersed very quickly. It was as if they were tired of looking at one another, and listening to each other's voices.

The men at the other table all seemed to have come ashore with money. Still, they were voicing their general dissatisfaction with the world.

Now one optimist among them raised his voice. "Look at it this way—you can soon be getting laid."

"That might be easier if we would soon be getting paid. How's that for a rhyme?"

"You've missed your calling—should have been a minstrel."

Of course there was no prospect of anyone being paid off—not one of the crew had been a hireling.

Proteus produced another pearl, which he used to buy a round of drinks for the other table. The men there waved their thanks, and gave him a rousing cheer.

Proteus got the idea that not one member of the crew wanted to hang around with Jason any longer. Well, he could understand that.

"It was a wonderful voyage," said one of the men at the far table softly.

"More wonderful than you ever knew," Proteus called back.

They waved their respectful thanks to him for the drinks, and one called over asking him what he was going to do next. In response he only shook his head. As far as he could tell, not one of the crew, now excepting Haraldur, was yet aware that a god had been rowing and sweating among them as their shipmate.

Proteus thought whatever he did would have little to do with human politics. Kingmaking was not something that could be accomplished simply by stirring up a few big waves. And Triton certainly had no intention of trying to use his seagod's power to establish Jason on a throne—though maybe the man would be a good king. *There are no good kings,* said a proverb that might have been as old as the gods themselves, *but there are certainly bad ones.*

It was, or should be, up to those who were purely human to settle the matter of kingmaking among themselves. Gods really lived in another world; he knew that, though he could remember almost nothing of what that other world, the society of deities, was like.

It ought to be fun, trying to find out.

Meanwhile Haraldur had been pondering something, and at last he came out with it. "Will Pelias still be on his throne when you walk out of his castle?"

"I don't know. I suppose he can keep it, for all I care." Pelias was doubtless bad enough, but Proteus thought that he had encountered worse—Amycus, for example. Looking out the tavern window, he thought that most of the people in the harbor here seemed to be getting along fairly well. No doubt there were some in the castle dungeon who would disagree with that assessment, but the same thing would be true if and when Jason came to rule.

Hal was almost whispering. "Take a look behind you when you get the chance. What *have* we here?"

Proteus turned casually in his chair. Four tough-looking men, not uniformed but with a certain air of officialdom about them, had entered the tavern and taken a table. They looked toward Proteus and Haraldur from time to time. Proteus guessed they were prudently waiting until most of the Argonauts had dispersed before moving in on their prey. Hard-looking men, but probably not wanting to chance a fight with half a dozen of Jason's picked companions. Not when they had no need to hurry.

And now, here came Jason and Medea into the tavern—apparently some business outside had delayed them. Jason immediately went to talk with the other Argonauts at their table, where he was received respectfully but with no eagerness. Meanwhile the princess surprised Proteus by coming to where he and Haraldur were sitting. When they rose politely, creating room, she surprised him again by sitting down with them, though brushing aside the offer of a drink. When Haraldur made tentative motions as if to take himself away, Medea put a hand on his arm and asked him to stay.

Proteus asked: "Have you had any new word, Princess, about your missing maid?"

She gave him a puzzled look. "No. Why?"

Proteus said: "I suppose she may be here."

Medea blinked at him. "Here in Iolcus? Why? How?"

"It is only a feeling I have, my lady." He made a dismissive motion with his hand.

The princess gave him another strange look, then decided to get down to business. "The voyage is over, Proteus. What are you going to do?"

Everyone seemed to be asking him that. "I am not at all sure," he said, and it was sharply borne in on him that he really did not.

In a way he wished that the *Argo* had not yet reached this port, that the long struggle could still go on, giving some meaning to his life. The goal of the Argonauts, like the Fleece itself, had begun to vanish as soon as they achieved it—he was reminded sharply of something Asterion had said, about how goals were not meant to be achieved.

Thoughts of the Minotaur in his Maze suggested to Proteus that he might possibly return to Corycus—neither the god nor the man within him had any special attachment to that place, none he could remember anyway, but it would be good to talk to Asterion again. Princess Phaedra had been grateful to the woman she thought had disposed of Talus, and Phaedra would doubtless be just as grateful to the god when he told her the whole truth. It seemed strange to Triton/Proteus that a god might feel a need for human gratitude—maybe it was just human companionship he really craved.

There were other things he craved as well.

And now that the voyage was over, he noticed in himself also a yearning for the deep sea, the endless realms of ocean that existed far out of sight of land—and the pleasant knowledge, sure and secret, that the next time he went there, he would need no boat or oars.

Whether he went to Corycus, or sought the depths of the ocean, something would be missing. Suddenly he had a sharp, clear memory, carrying a pang of regret, of the curve and warmth of the Mouse's firm young body when his arm had cradled her, first beneath the sea and then above it. He had a good memory, too, of the satisfaction he had felt when his god-power forced deep water to treat her tenderly, induced the Great Sea to nourish her with dissolved air instead of drenching out her life.

. . . the warmth of the Mouse's body. The life and courage in her voice, even when she was afraid. Even the way the hem of her shift, underwater, had teasingly played around her hips . . .

But this was foolishness, because the woman he remembered fondly had gone to betray him to Pelias—he was almost completely certain she had done that. Well, there was certainly no shortage of other women. He half-remembered some old proverb, about there being as many as fish in the sea. As a god he knew he could enjoy almost any of them whenever he wanted.

Which made it all the more remarkable that there were moments—he expected there would be more in the future—when Proteus, and maybe even Triton, no longer wanted to be a god. Not that the avatar had any choice about it. Not as long as he wanted to go on breathing. Not even Daedalus, not even Hephaestus or divine Asclepius, could extract a god-Face from inside a human head without killing the avatar.

Meanwhile, the four hard-looking men were keeping a casually determined watch on Jason, and on Proteus. But the four were content to bide their time, remaining on their own side of the big room. If Jason was aware of their scrutiny, he gave no sign. He was still talking to the Argonauts at the other table, where he had taken a chair and was sipping at a mug.

Medea was sitting with her back to her husband, paying him no attention.

She was purposeful and energetic. "You must remember, good Proteus, that I once made you a little speech about how unsuited I am for the life of a fisherman's wife."

"I do indeed remember it, my lady."

"I must have greater things. In fact I am determined to be a ruler somewhere, someday."

"I see."

She nodded. "That seems to be the only way I can be free. I thought my magic was powerful enough to bring me freedom, but it seems not."

Proteus wondered what spells she had most recently been trying out. Whatever they had been, evidently they had not worked. "I understand what you mean, Princess. So what is your plan?"

"Soon I will be leaving Iolcus, without Jason. He has his own plans."

"I see," said Proteus again, and Haraldur muttered something.

The young woman facing them went on: "Where I will go I am not entirely sure as yet, but it will be in the pursuit of power."

Triton/Proteus was curious. "I had thought, Princess, that there was a great love between the two of you."

"I had thought so too. No, it was more than thinking, there really was." She shook her head. "But that is all finished. What I am asking you, Proteus, is this: Will you come with me as my counselor?"

"As your servant, lady?"

She shook her head briskly. "Certainly not as a menial. The servant of a princess may enjoy high caste, even a status of nobility. Before you answer, I will tell you—and you, Haraldur—something even my husband does not know as yet: I now have wealth, in the form of jewels. Real wealth, enough to hire ships, and men, when I know whom to hire. Princess Phaedra was grateful for my help, and more sympathetic to my position than I dared to hope."

Proteus said: "I am glad of your good fortune, my lady. But no, I will not come with you."

Medea did not seem much surprised at this response, only a little disappointed that it came so quickly and was so curt.

With steely imperturbability she raised the offer. "Then will you come with me and be my friend? I do not mean my lover. But someday the commander of my navy, or even chief officer of state?"

"No, my lady, I will not do that either." And Proteus offered no explanation.

For a moment he thought that the princess was going to insist on one. But instead she only turned her gaze to Haraldur. "Then will you be my counselor, on the terms I have just stated?"

The northman needed no time to consider. "I will, Princess. Gladly. That is, provided you can first spare me a few hours, to keep a promise I have made to Proteus, here."

The princess looked at them both. "I see no difficulty in that." She rose to her feet. "Tonight we will talk again. I have been told I am expected at the castle." In another moment she was gone, walking gracefully.

Triton, looking up once more from the tavern window at the high castle, knew he would soon be going there. The god invisibly continued to push forward certain magical arrangements he had begun while the *Argo* was still miles at sea.

When Medea had gone outside, Jason, as if he had been waiting for his wife to leave, came over.

The captain approached without haste or excitement, and stood before their table. "I trust you have the Fleece still with you, Proteus? Let me see it."

Jason seemed not to care if the other people in the tavern got a look at his shabby treasure, so Proteus simply drew it from his pack and held it out. Jason only looked at it and nodded and asked Proteus if he would keep it for him a little longer.

Then Jason said: "I have one more thing to ask of you, Proteus, and you, Haraldur. You certainly have no duty to comply, for I am no longer your captain. Our voyage is over, and both of you have done very much for me already."

"Ask," said Proteus, and heard Haraldur utter the same word at the same time.

"Will both of you come to the castle with me, while I confront the man who now sits upon the throne? It may be dangerous," he added in frank warning.

Proteus pushed his tankard aside and got to his feet. "I was planning to see your uncle anyway." Haraldur stood up also, saying: "I wouldn't miss this for the world."

Jason blinked at him in surprise. He seemed grateful for what he took to be fervent loyalty.

"Jason, let me first have a private word with our shipmate here. Then we will join you outside," said Proteus/Triton.

When he was effectively alone with the northman again, Proteus said to him: "Since you are coming with me, there is something I want to do for you first."

The magical business took Triton only a few moments, touching Haraldur's axe and dagger with his hands, and muttering an old formula that came when it was needed. When it was done, he said: "I am not as clever at these things as Circe—maybe I never was. But there, that should do the job." And now he was satisfied that Haraldur's weapons would be concealed as well as his own.

The northman looked doubtful, inspecting the business end of the battle-hatchet that rode head-uppermost at his belt. "I see no difference."

"You and I will still be able to see the tools of our trade, both yours and mine. But I hope and expect that no other human eyes will be able to detect them."

Haraldur still looked doubtful. Then his eyes suddenly focused on Triton's Trident, riding over its owner's shoulder on a sling. "Where in all the hells did *that* come from?"

Proteus/Triton smiled. "A dolphin brought it to me from the bottom of the sea. Now do you believe me?"

They went out of the tavern and joined Jason. As Proteus passed through the door, he saw the four thugs getting to their feet, with a great show of casualness, and following.

○ *TWENTY-FOUR* ○

Reckoning

*O*n emerging from the tavern under a gray sky, from which the drizzle had now ceased to fall, Proteus contemplated the slate-colored water at the harbor's mouth, and realized that he would probably never again travel any great distance from the sea. He might never again be entirely out of sight of deep water, or beyond reach of the smell of the sea-breeze, though he was sure Triton could survive a few such jaunts. Not even if his life extended vastly farther into the future than Old Proteus had ever dreamed of living. The god-component in his head was virtually immortal, and long after the body of the man Proteus had been destroyed, and his shade had descended to the Underworld, some trace of him would remain attached to Triton until the end of time. *Once a god, always a god.*

Assuming that Triton could keep from having his memory expunged entirely by another Giant. Remembering the faint trail of green slime on the outer cliff, he thought it quite possible that Pelias had arranged a special welcome for him in the castle.

Eyeing the strong-arm lads so patiently waiting to collect him for the king, Proteus wondered if any of them could recognize him from the old days. There had been a moment when one of them nodded in his direction, what could have been a kind of personal greeting. Another of their number kept looking back over his shoulder, as if he expected more Argonauts to come in at any moment—which was a real enough possibility to keep the king's men on their good behavior.

"Proteus." The leader of the king's irregulars nodded to him in a friendly way. "Ready for a little walk up the hill?"

"I've been looking forward to it."

"Really. That's good. The king says he wants to invite all the Argonauts to pay him a visit. Of course, it wouldn't be polite for you to carry any weapons in. If you've got any iron on you, might as well hand it over now." The fellow, despite his tattoos and suggestive scars, had a knack for sounding as innocent as a schoolgirl.

Proteus lifted his arms away from his sides. "Search, if you like." And he stood there smiling faintly, while another of the escorts briskly patted him down. The searcher was totally oblivious to the murderous Trident, although his probing fingers actually touched it more than once. Haraldur allowed himself to be searched also, and his eyes went wide and marveling when the procedure somehow failed to discover either battle-axe or dagger.

Jason had already disarmed himself, voluntarily, and so Proteus offered him no magical assistance.

Meanwhile, Pelias's respect for protocol had caused him to treat a genuine princess very differently. He had sent a carriage and a courtly official down to her with an invitation, which she accepted with the aplomb of one brought up as royalty. The carriage behind its two strong-pacing cameloids soon passed up the walking men, and was swallowed by the main gate of the castle.

The three Argonauts and their four-man escort were steadily retracing the path taken by Jason and his men on leaving the *Argo*, trudging around the harbor toward the castle and the long ship beached at its foot. The closer they came to the great structure on the ridge, the older it looked to Proteus. Much older than the palace in which King Aeetes held forth, and its grandeur was of a different and more rugged kind. Torches and lamps were being lighted in its windows, against the cloudy dusk.

After their escort had conveyed them in through the first gate, there were many stairs to climb, first out-of-doors and then inside. Most of the climbing was done in silence.

Looking through a distant doorway from one of the last corridors they traversed, Proteus caught sight of the Princess Medea seated amid luxury, in what appeared to be a small anteroom. She was being entertained by the same courtly official who had come down to the town to fetch her.

Pelias was evidently as eager for the confrontation as Proteus. The Argonauts were kept waiting only briefly, just outside the brightly lighted chamber in which the usurper was sitting on a kind of low throne, attended by three men. Two of these were graybeard counselors, but one was young, and royally dressed.

Looking in from just outside, Haraldur nudged Proteus with an elbow, and whispered: "Looks like the king's son is here. Acastus. Must be wondering when he'll get to take over."

On entering the room, getting their first good look at the man on the small throne, the three Argonauts were all startled to see how ill and old he looked. Proteus had all along been picturing a more vigorous opponent. Directly behind the throne was a stonework screen, an intricate design of curving blocks and spaces. Some six or eight feet behind the screen were the massive stones of the castle's outer wall, here pierced by a couple of large windows, one on either side of the low throne. These apertures were generously wide and open, looking out as they did upon the seaward side, where it must have seemed to the builders that no attackers could ever climb. The space between the windowed wall and the interior screen was heavily in shadow.

Ignoring his other visitors for the moment, King Pelias glared at Jason for a time in silence, and then bluntly demanded of him: "What have you brought me?"

"What I promised I would bring, Uncle." And Jason held out his hand to Proteus, who in turn produced the ball of dull stuff, which Jason in turn held out to the old man. "It is the Golden Fleece."

The king stared at the shabby remnant for a long moment, then grabbed it roughly, so he could hold it closer to his old eyes. At last he growled: "Is this some joke? To me it looks more like a handful of ass-wipe. What could this do for me? Nothing but make me a laughingstock."

Proteus spoke up boldly. "Daedalus, on the island of Corycus, said he found it interesting."

The king and his attendants only looked at him. He half-expected to be ordered to keep silent, but no one bothered to do that.

Anyone who looked at Pelias with open eyes would have to judge him not to be many days away from death by natural causes. Acastus ought not to have long to wait. It seemed plain to Proteus that the old man was managing to deny within himself, clinging fanatically to power as a means of staving off fear of death and of the Underworld. *And why would a mortal man take the desperate step of attempting to ambush a god?* There was one likely reason. *Because whenever the avatar of a god died, a Face always became available. And to assimilate a Face into one's own body was the best way ever invented to stave off death.*

Jason now spoke up to say: "Had I not seen it gradually change, over the months, I would certainly have doubts too. But I remember how glorious was the Golden Fleece, what a miracle it seemed, when first we took it into our hands."

The king only made a strange sound, that seemed to be intended as a laugh.

Jason remained calm. "Whatever else it may be, Uncle, it is no joke. Men have died to bring it to Iolcus."

"Then it looks like they died for nothing." And Pelias barked out another laugh, that turned into a fit of coughing.

"Uncle, you and I had an agreement," Jason insisted. His voice was bitter, but not surprised.

"Did we?" The old gray eyebrows went up, an exaggerated miming of surprise. "You mean that nonsense about how I must abdicate in your favor, if you brought home this rag? There was some foolish rumor to that effect, or so they tell me, but why in the Underworld should I do that?"

Acastus, standing at the king's elbow, now spoke up, dryly, saying he wished to impart some information. A month before Jason returned home, his bargain with Pelias had been declared irrelevant, or moot, by the Iolcan Council, who referred to it only in a hypothetical way when they met to name Prince Acastus as his father's legitimate successor. Then just for good measure the council had passed a sentence of banishment on Jason. But the terms of the ban were mild, graciously allowing him to remain long enough to repair his ship.

Jason had no immediate response to make, and silence held in the great room for the space of several breaths. Then the old man on the throne said to his nephew: "Yours is a fantastic story, and no one will believe that I ever made any such agreement. Unless of course you have some proof to offer? Witnesses, perhaps? I thought not. My dear young fool, no one's going to believe you." There was a pause before he added softly: "I may as well let you go."

And the king scornfully crumpled what was left of the Fleece into a ball, and threw it back in the direction of Jason's face. "Get out of my sight. If you are wise, you will get your ship out of my harbor too. Unless you want to see it broken up for firewood, which is probably the best it's good for."

The soft little missile traveled more slowly than the king had intended—which might have roused his vanishing interest, had he been paying attention. Jason easily caught the balled Fleece in his hands at the level of his waist. "I will be moving my ship, Uncle, as soon as I can make it ready to sail again."

"See that you do." The king waved his hand dismissively, then shifted his gaze to Proteus and Haraldur. "You two men, remain here with me for a time. I would have some words with you."

Jason looked at his shipmates, evidently decided that this was not the time or place to tell them anything, turned his back on his uncle and went out.

*　　*　　*

The Princess Medea was still waiting, in the same neat, well-lighted anteroom, for her meeting with the king. And she was still burdened with the company of the same minor official who had been with her from the start, and she was beginning to be irritated with the length of the delay. To her surprise, another official, this one of higher rank, came to tell her that, regrettably, the king had been called away on vitally important affairs of state. His majesty sent his profound apologies, and he would see her on another day. Would tomorrow be quite suitable?

So, Medea thought, *he is going to talk to Jason*. She got gracefully to her feet. "I will consider tomorrow. Has His Majesty been taken ill?"

"I have heard no such rumor, Princess."

In a corridor immediately outside her anteroom she encountered Jason, looking no worse for his visit with his uncle. Medea was surprised and somewhat relieved to see that her husband was free to go; that his uncle had not handed over the kingdom to him came as no surprise at all. Beginning a quiet argument, much like other debates they had had in recent days, they started to look for the best way downstairs, while her previous escort diplomatically bowed himself away.

"Shall we take the private stair?" Medea suggested. That was how she had ascended, along the inner cliff and through the castle; the stair went all the way down through an enclosed tunnel, whose lower end debouched directly on the beach, near the place where the Argonauts had left their ship.

"No, the regular stairs are good enough for me." Jason started that way.

Medea sighed and followed him. There were a few more details she wanted to get straight with her husband, though it was already settled between them that they would separate.

As they began their descent, Jason told her of his short meeting with the man he called the usurper.

"There is no way I can force my uncle to my will."

"Obviously."

"I know that this is not what we had planned—"

"I know it too. Will it surprise you to hear that I am not surprised?"

"Medea, believe me, I—"

"Why bother asking for my belief? Jason, I am bitterly weary of this."

"Of what, my love?"

"I am your love no longer."

"I have been faithful to you."

"You mean that you have lain with no one else. If that is true, it is only because you care very little about women—or about men either, for that matter. All you really love is the idea, the image, of that golden circlet, that must someday rest in your black hair. But I think your hair will be quite gray before that happens. You are a cautious sort of Hero, after all. You may live for a long time."

It was as if he could not hear her words. "I think I have kept the essence of every promise I ever made to you. Here you are, in safety, a free woman, beyond your father's reach."

"You were ready to send me back to him. But you did marry me. That was one promise you kept—as soon as it became advantageous."

"And I have given you all I have to give."

"And in turn taken from me everything I had—which was much. Very much indeed. I gave you my innocence. I sweated and starved and almost died of thirst. And then for you I committed murder. I have lost my entire family, and made an enemy of my Aunt Circe, for you and your ugly Fleece. I suppose you still have it?"

Jason tapped the small pouch at his belt. "It was on our wedding bed. Remember?"

"How could I forget? It was a glorious sight then."

"Now much reduced."

"Still it is more than big enough," Medea said, "for all the love-making we are likely to do with each other from now on."

Proteus/Triton was morally certain that the king knew of his changed identity, and that he had been invited into the castle only so he could be ambushed by a fishtailed Giant. That dark space behind the throne, between the stone screen and the outer wall, was where he must watch. At the invitation of King Pelias the monster would soon be climbing up the cliff on the seaward side of the palace, adding another layer of thin slime to the faint trail that Triton had earlier spotted on those steep rocks. It would have to be one of the smaller members of the Giant species. He doubted that any over fifteen or twenty feet in length would be able to actually enter the castle and move about effectively inside.

Pelias could not have known beforehand exactly when the *Argo* would come into port. Therefore there was probably no Giant hiding in the castle yet; but a summons would have been sent, somehow. And now that darkness had fallen, to conceal from the eyes of honest citizens the thing's climb out of the sea and across the lower cliff, Triton had to assume that a monster bent on killing him might make its appearance at any moment.

The king was letting his full anger show. Ignoring Haraldur, he said to Proteus: "Well, sirrah? Anything to say, before I order you skinned alive?"

"Only one question, Majesty: Did anyone warn you that a god was about to pay you a visit?" Even as Proteus spoke, he saw from the corner of his eye how Hal stood up straighter, and moved his right hand to what the guards must see as his empty belt.

The old man's eye stayed bright and steady, fixed warily on Proteus. He did what was apparently a kind of unconscious ritual, moving his eyebrows. "Oh, is that so? What can you tell me about this god?"

"One very important thing: He is already here."

And Triton/Proteus saw, with a pang of inner sickness, that Pelias was only smiling faintly at the revelation that should have stunned him. "Yes," the old king said, slowly nodding. "In fact they did warn me about that."

Triton saw that he had been right about the Giant, wrong about the timing. Now, minutes sooner than he had expected it, there came a slight stirring in the darkness behind the stony screen. Through its gaps there now protruded what could only be a Giant's enormous thumbs and fingers. One of the smaller specimens, indeed, though still enormous by any standard of humanity. From those digits the invisible, soundless beam that wiped out memory would, in the next moment, come lashing at the speed of thought.

But Triton was already rolling aside, getting himself out of the way of the weapon that would do Haraldur no harm at all.

The Usurper screamed out something, a warning or command, and Acastus shouted also. The guards were not slow in getting their weapons into action, but they were still overmatched.

Two of the Usurper's men had fallen to Haraldur's invisible battle-axe before the others realized that the northman was indeed armed.

The old king had tottered from his throne and was crouched down beside it, taking such shelter as he could.

In those first savage moments of the fight, several guards had lunged at Triton/Proteus, only to be scattered, flung away like mud from a spinning wheel, by the arc of the whirling Trident. Then the god hurled himself on the floor, rolling forward beneath the Giant's blast. One stroke of the Trident against the screen of stonework blasted a sizable hole.

In the next instant Triton had lunged forward, reaching through the gap, and stabbed the Giant on the side of his massive head. The triple impact of the Trident made an explosive noise in the confined space, and sent his huge opponent bellowing and tumbling down the secret chute leading to the open cliffside, and its sheer slope to the sea.

From the position in which he had finished his lunge, with his head and the upper part of his body inside the shattered stonework screen, Proteus could see the upper end of the tunnel whose existence he had already deduced.

The Giant had fallen that way, but was the Giant dead? Not wanting to take any chances, he plunged down after his defeated foe.

Meanwhile Hal had been using his axe to good effect, finishing off the guards. But now he looked around and discovered his partner gone.

"Damn it all, Proteus!" he complained to the empty air. He could easily enough kill the cowering king, or the paralyzed prince, or both of them, but that might create more problems for him than it solved. Triton had not been interested in killing them, and he, Haraldur, was here today as Triton's man.

He knew that reinforcements for the royal guard must be on the way, and he decided that a strategic retreat was definitely in order, a withdrawal at least until the god he served came back to look for him.

One glance down into the dark tunnel, with no handholds or footholds in sight, convinced him he was not going to take that route.

Choosing another way, Haraldur stepped through first one ornate door and then another, closing them quietly behind him, penetrating into luxurious lodgings, at the moment unoccupied. Here the quarters were a little close for convenient axe-work, and he drew his dagger and held it ready in his left hand. Feeling imprisoned by walls and doors and ceilings, he could feel himself growing confused and jumpy. There ought to be a stairway here somewhere, but perversely—might it have been done by magic?—the stairs seemed to have moved elsewhere.

Suddenly he froze, axe ready, listening to a single set of

rapidly approaching footsteps now a room or two away. He could only hope they might be Triton's.

For a long moment after all the Argonauts had gone, there was near silence in the torchlit audience room. The only sounds were the ragged breathing of the two men who were still alive, and the muted roar of distant surf, drifting in through the big windows. Then slowly, shudderingly, the king got his old legs under him, and stood up from where he had been huddled beside the throne. Looking around, he saw that the only living presence in the room with him was that of his son, who, unarmed, had flattened himself against a wall where he clung, quivering. The bodies of several of the castle guards, all dead, lay scattered about the chamber, jumbled with their useless weapons.

Looking at the huge hole broken through the stone screen, Pelias assumed that the god had exited by that means, either in flight, or pursuing the wounded Giant into the sea. "Of course he may come back," Pelias muttered to himself. "That is quite possible."

He noted with satisfaction, by the look on his son's face, that the young man was utterly bewildered. Acastus still had no idea that his father had been trying to ambush a god, or why.

Now the prince had peeled himself away from the wall, and was standing near the center of the room, wringing his hands. "What in all the hell is going on, Father?" he demanded in a cracking voice. "What are you talking about?" And Acastus clutched at his father.

Pelias brushed him aside with a savage jerk of his arm. "I'll explain it to you later!" What if the god did not come back? Then all his planning and scheming would have gone for nothing. His chance for virtual immortality was slipping through his fingers.

Barking orders at his son, telling him in afterthought to summon the captain of the guard and search the whole castle for the man in the horned helmet, Pelias stalked angrily into the nearby room where, according to his orders, the Mouse had been brought for a confrontation. This room contained the upper end of a private stairway, and its outer wall was pierced by two windows similar to those in the audience chamber. Here there was no stone decorative screen.

Planting himself directly before the Mouse, Pelias told her: "I want to have another little talk."

Her response was to immediately collapse on the floor, either in sheer terror, or through weakness brought on by her days in a dungeon cell. Pelias noticed that the two guards who flanked the woman looked half stunned, like gods struck dumb by some Giant's weapon—of course they had heard the uproar in the adjoining room, and of course they did not dare ask the king just what had happened. They had continued to do their duty, guarding this important prisoner. Now they had simply let her fall.

Mouse's wrists were chained together in front of her, and from them more links ran down to a similar joining of her ankles. She was still wearing the same clothes that someone had given her, out of charity, at the court of King Alcinous.

Now Pelias ordered one of the guards to go and fetch the woman's two small children. Ever since sending her as an agent to Colchis, he had been careful to make sure that her offspring were still around, being cared for, more or less, by people on his household staff.

Taking a step forward, the king kicked the fallen woman where she lay—he could no longer kick with much force, but he tried— and said to the remaining guard: "Give this sow a taste of water, I must have some coherent speech from her." Then he shouted after the other man: "And hurry up with her two brats, I want them here!"

Someone splashed water over her, and rough hands hauled her to her feet. After the darkness of the dungeon in which she had spent the last few days, her eyes found even this torchlight almost painful in its brightness. A chair was pushed forward for her to sit in, and from it she stared in fear and amazement at the new presence that now stalked into the room. It was a smallish figure that seemed to be made entirely of metal, but shaped like a man, except that one hand was missing. It was utterly strange, almost incredible. The young woman listened with horror when an almost human voice came from the thing, a kind of screeching whisper. She heard with fear the words the incredible figure exchanged with Pelias, regarding the hunt that had now been launched for Triton, and for the god's companion, a burly man in a horned helmet.

The king addressed him, or it, as "Talus." The eyes of the Mouse's two guards bulged at the sight of Talus, but once more they continued to do their duty.

The Mouse's mind worried at the problem of the Bronze Man's nature, which offered at least a momentary escape from her own terrible situation. It might have been a man in a suit of metal armor, but the encasement fit too smoothly, tightly, and completely, and it was very hard to imagine that there could be a human being inside it. Besides, the right forearm ended in a jagged stump, as if wrist and hand had been torn violently away.

The king was allowing Talus to feel a taste of his royal anger. "Could Hades not have sent you to me more swiftly? You have given me very little time to prepare for Triton."

The screeching thing came boldly back, as if it were a god, and royal anger could safely be ignored. "Understand, Pelias, that I could not travel swiftly after the god did this to me." And the Bronze Man held up the stump of his forearm. The king seemed ill at ease in the thing's presence, and regarded it nervously. After a moment he turned his back on it, and once again gave the Mouse his full attention.

"Well, bitch? What have you to tell me now?"

He was not distracted by the quiet entry of Acastus into the room; presumably his son had followed orders, and reinforcements were on their way.

Mouse murmured something indistinguishable, about her children.

Pelias told her: "Your brats have not gone to join your husband yet, but I can assure you that they soon will. First, of course, they will get to watch what happens to their mother. What you knew would happen if you failed in your mission."

The woman whimpered. And the king allowed her a quick look at her twins, four years old, to show her they were still alive, and so far not much hurt. They had grown, had changed enormously in the more than two years since she had seen them, yet she had no doubt of who they were.

A chill of horror went through her when she saw that her babies were now wearing slaves' collars, their tender necks encircled by bands of some cheap silvery metal. The surpassing joy of seeing them alive was poisoned by the knowledge of what was going to happen to them soon.

"You have one more chance. Speak truly and I will let them live." The king leaned forward, cupping an ear with an old hand. "Speak clearly, so I can understand you."

She made an effort, gestured at her guards, and said: "I have been telling these men the truth ever since they kidnapped me. And the truth is that the man Proteus never gave me any orders."

"Then both of you were getting your instructions directly from certain of my enemies."

The woman let out a despairing cry. "Great king, take pity on me and mine! I have never been in anyone's pay but yours. As to who might be paying Proteus, I do not know."

"Is there perhaps something about him that you forgot to tell me? Some little detail, maybe—of how Proteus *became a god*?"

The Mouse started to shake her head, then slumped. It seemed that her determination to keep silent about Triton, to help him if she could, had gone for nothing.

"Let us see if I can induce you to remember it." The king drew a small knife, and gestured. The two men heaved the chained woman to her feet, and dragged her forward.

Pelias seized one of her manacled hands, and wheezing, began to dig the keen point of his knife under one of her fingernails.

The Mouse screamed, loud and hopelessly.

A wooden door that had been locked burst open, splinters flying. The Mouse looked up to see Triton/Proteus rush into the room, Hal brandishing his axe beside him.

End

$\mathcal{A}$castus turned and ran from the room, with his aged father panting two steps behind him, falling a little farther back with every stride. The young man whimpered and ran faster as he felt a splash of warm blood on the back of his neck—the guards who had stayed to fight, whether out of bravery or necessity, were being cut down.

Triton for the moment was willing to let the Usurper and his princeling go.

He was amazed to find himself once more confronted by the Bronze Man, but he unlimbered his Trident, and used it again to good effect on Talus. The triple blast of the thrusting spear hurled the metal figure violently back, across the room.

Facing an opponent who had beaten him once before, Talus was evidently unburdened by any concern for honor, feeling no duty to die in his tracks. He turned his back on the angry god and sprang clear out the window. It was entirely possible that the long, skidding, and tumbling plunge toward the rocks and the sea that waited far below would do him less damage than the close-range anger of an armed god.

Gripping the Trident, Triton darted to the window and looked down, in time to see the metal body of his opponent vanish with a splash.

"See to the Mouse," he commanded sharply, and Hal bent over her. The children were clinging to their mother, who was unconscious. The northman tugged at the woman's fetters, then reached to take a key from the belt of one of the dead guards. In a moment the shackles and chains had been undone, and Hal tossed them rattling down the stair.

*   *   *

For the second time in as many fights, Triton/Proteus had seen the waves close over the head of Talus. This time he meant to finish off the Bronze Man, as he had just done for the Giant, but there were other matters to be taken care of first.

The deep water down there was reacting to his presence, to his staring eyes that conveyed his divine fear and rage. A whole arm of the Great Sea was stirring with an elemental kind of life.

"Mouse's fainted, but she'll come round," said Hal, panting and gloating at his side. "What next?"

"Now I think it is time for a thorough house-cleaning."

Reaching forth with all the power of magic that he still possessed, Triton evoked a great, gray-green foaming column, thick as a house and straining more than a hundred feet above the sea, brought it curling and foaming to such a height that its crowning spray blew in at the castle's upper windows. Triton could not maintain it at that altitude indefinitely, but he thought he could prolong the feat for long enough.

For the past two days, beginning while the *Argo* had been still many miles at sea, he had been silently calling for Scylla and Charybdis to approach the harbor of Iolcus, and to wait a few miles offshore for new tasks he would assign them. They had been far distant in the Great Sea when Triton's summons reached them, and only now had their amorphous shapes appeared on the horizon, moving under a strange sky, a sunset glowing through what looked like the natural cloud and lightning of an early winter storm.

Minutes ago he had urged them to come on at their greatest speed. And now they were on hand.

"Lord Neptune has urged us to follow you, and fight for you with all our strength!" came a great gurgling howl.

The god's voice roared in command. "Charybdis, Scylla, combine yourselves into one creature. Come to me now!"

"We hear, and obey!"

And by an act of concentrated will, Triton and his willing helpers set the roaring, rising column into full motion, even as the jet of a geyser explodes upward from the tormented earth, in some ill-fated land where the Underworld lies near the surface. The result was a great reaching fist of a wave, ready to strike with crushing force. More than a wave, but a great columnar upwelling that took within itself the power of many waves.

Looking out from one opening in the castle's wall, admiring his magical handiwork, Triton did not see the huge fingers of the second crawling, climbing Giant, as they reached inside the chamber through the room's other window.

One moment Triton was savoring the triumph of the powers he had set in motion; and in the next his conscious memory had been wiped away.

And in the moment after that, the head of the towering column of water he had raised came smashing into the high rooms of the castle and right through them, pulling the rest of the watery avalanche after it, like the body of some huge climbing serpent.

Haraldur saw the gigantic thumbs and fingers at the window, but his yell of warning came just too late. The hands were not quite as huge as he had once imagined those of all Giants had to be—only comparatively small members of their race could make the climb up through the hidden tunnel.

The Giant turned his massive head to see a single human rushing at him, apparently unarmed, empty hands raised as if they held a weapon. It was not a sight to make a fighting Giant try to dodge, or get away.

Hal took one sideways step, charged at the window from its flank, and swung the blade of his battle-axe between his vast opponent's eyes, right through the thickness of his skull, driving death into his slow-working brain.

And in the next moment, the towering flood that Triton had

evoked came thundering and splashing through both windows, a tremendous cataract of seawater in reverse.

Through the window of another room, Pelias had caught a glimpse of the second Giant climbing into position to attack. Reversing the direction of his panting, limping flight, the king had just started back to renew his confrontation with the god. Of course it would be deadly dangerous, but Pelias was quite ready to risk what little life he had left, for a chance of added centuries.

Everyone knew that it was impossible to destroy a Face, and Pelias had no idea of trying—he meant to put the Face of Triton on himself. The mind of the god dwelling within it would be severely damaged, and his powers no doubt diminished. But Pelias could still hope that it would bring him virtual immortality.

Several times he had imagined himself ordering his officers, when this moment came: "Butcher him when he falls helpless, and then get me his Face!" But finally he knew he would not dare to say those words. One of his aides, young and agile, might easily be daring enough to seize the Face for himself as soon as it became available. With a god's powers, if not his memory, infused into a young and healthy body, the defector would have little reason to fear a merely human king.

When Triton fell victim to the Giant's invisible weapon, the Trident tumbled from his hand, and Hal watched it go clattering on the floor.

In the next instant, just before the cataract of water struck, the northman grabbed up the spear. The glassy surface of the dark shaft burned his mortal hand like frozen metal, but still he held it tight, knowing that without the help of Triton, he would need every weapon he could get to fight his way out of this place alive.

And then the crash of water came through both windows, like a blow from the Great Sea itself.

*   *   *

Prince Asterion was watching from a distance, watching as he dreamed, and as he dreamed he felt the shock, and knew in his bones how severe it was. But there was nothing the bull-headed man could do. He was left uncertain how much of Triton had been destroyed this time.

Haraldur, struggling not to drown, clung desperately to the Trident, which had somehow become wedged in an upper corner of the descending stair. There it held fast, keeping him from being washed down with Pelias and Acastus. Father and son had both been swept in that direction, their screams turned to gurgles in the flood, their bodies beaten and broken against the stonework on the next landing down, then flushed away and out of sight in the continuing torrent.

The woman, with her children scrambling to stay with her, had dragged herself across the floor to Triton the moment that he fell. Even as Haraldur came near to drowning, he saw how the rushing, roaring, cascading waters in their furious passage divided neatly around those four clustered living bodies, leaving them undisturbed. Scylla and Charybdis were refusing to do Triton any harm.

He had been thrashing and splashing in salt water—
—and now the flood had stopped, leaving him utterly drenched, shivering with more than cold, lying on stone tiling in a strange, torch-lit room, utter darkness outside its windows. And he could not remember who he was, or where or how or why.

A strange-looking man in a horned helmet, heavily armed and also dripping wet, was standing over him, and had been shouting words at him, words that might have been names, but none of them made any sense.

The man on the floor dragged himself up to his elbows, and then to his knees. Now he noticed a woman in a tattered garment who knelt nearby, wet as everyone else, cradling a pair of small children who were dripping too, and naked but for their bright slave collars.

He said to the woman: "I remember you—I think I do. But not your name."

She did not answer him at once. The whole room and everything in it was littered with bits of seaweed and small crustaceans, and the smell of the sea was very strong.

And now, somehow, the woman struggled to her feet, managing to lift both babies with her, cradling one in each arm. For one of her size and emaciated condition it seemed quite a feat of strength. To the man on the floor she said: "Can you walk? Yes, you can, you must. Downstairs, hurry, we must get out of here."

Getting to his feet was surprisingly easy. He looked down at himself, saw an ordinary loincloth and sandals that told him nothing. He seemed fundamentally uninjured, no blood, no broken bones. His only problem was that he did not know who he was, or where he might belong.

The man in the horned helmet, who was clearly a friend, went ahead of them down the wet and slippery stair. He was armed in one hand with an axe, and in the other with a strange, three-pointed spear. The woman kept on urging the nameless man along. When they had gone down a few steps, he said to her: "I think there was a time when the two of us went swimming together in the sea."

"Yes, there was, I'm glad that you remember that. Now hurry!" And on she went, towing a child with each hand, eager to get out of the half-drowned castle.

Jason, pondering to himself what he ought to do with his remnant of the Fleece, the priceless trophy that nobody now wanted, decided that he would probably go and hang it in the temple of Zeus. Yes, maybe right in front of the gigantic statue of the great god.

In his imagination, he did so. Then he sat there in the temple, waiting for someone to notice his donation. No one did, though many people passed and some glanced at the gift.

On parting from Medea he had said to her: "We found the treasure that everyone had dreamed of, and it turned to dust and ashes in our hands."

Her voice was cool and practical. "I think you might have to recruit an entirely new crew for your next adventure."

"Yes, I have come to understand that. But—I think it will probably not be too hard." Once the word of his successful quest had time to spread, his reputation would be greater than ever. Whether the Fleece was now worth anything or not, he certainly had brought it back just as he said he would. Actually he still had hopes of finding a number of the original Argonauts ready to rejoin him, once they had had their spree in port, and a little time to think about it.

On leaving the castle, Jason walked out alone into the darkness of the surrounding night. As was customary when visitors of no particular importance were departing after dark, one of the servants had given him a cheap oil lamp, no more than a shaped and hardened lump of clay, by which to find his way along the path that led around the harbor, to whatever destination he might choose.

The only destination that interested him right now was much closer at hand. Jason carried the lamp with him as he crawled in under the worn-out hull of *Argo*. He was trying to assess the full extent of the damage, how much of the wood might still be sound, so he could waste no time in getting the ship ready for another voyage.

If he heard in the distance screams of terror, and a certain muffled roaring, the pouring of an enraged and sentient portion of the Great Sea through hollow corridors of stone, he paid such noises little attention. So he was still directly beneath the hull when a great surge of sea-water, the outpouring of Triton's flood, came rushing out of the mouth of the private tunnel-stairway. It bore with it various fragments, some of them human, of the castle's inner life, and these were stopped by the iron grating of the gate covering the mouth. The flood itself was not slowed down at all. The impact of this wall of water tipped the ship sharply from one side to the other, so the man underneath it was caught there and severely crushed.

Given the nature of the other events transpiring at the same time, many minutes passed before anyone noted Jason's protruding feet and tried to come to his assistance. Those who lifted the overwhelming weight at last and dragged him out heard his last words upon the earth: "I will call another Tiphys, and launch another Argosy, manned by chosen Heroes . . ."

And he thought he heard a high voice, answering. *Call all you will, unhappy man. But who will answer?*

None of those who came to help the dying man that night reported finding any trace of the Golden Fleece.

The man in the horned helmet, and the woman with the two children kept urging him along. He supposed he ought to go with them—but something was very wrong. The days of imprisonment and abuse had left her weakened, and when she handed him one of the children to carry, he accepted the small slippery body automatically.

"But why should they be wearing collars?" he wondered aloud.

"They shouldn't!" the woman told him forcefully, over her shoulder.

That settled that. He took the ring on the girl's small neck between his fingers, and, being careful not to hurt the tender flesh, pinched the metal firmly until it broke. Then he twisted the circlet off and tossed it away.

He descended a few more steps. Then: "Who am I?" he asked again.

"Proteus is your name," the woman said, still going down, not looking back. "I am Rosalind, and you are Proteus. Come along, keep moving."

"Rosalind. You are my woman, then?" Absently he reached out with one hand and started working on the boy's collar. Soon it too parted and was cast away.

She looked back and nodded wordlessly.

Meanwhile, the friendly man in the horned helmet was keeping up with them in their descent, sometimes scouting ahead a bit, sometimes falling behind, now and then nodding encouragement. Proteus had to assume that, for the moment at least, everything was somehow working out for the best.

Proteus was making his way out of the half-drowned castle, coming on shaky legs down one long curving stair after another, with the woman and her two children, and their armed attendant.

Proteus was dizzy, and part of the time he had to lean on other people for support. His body ached as if he had been fighting. There were more stairs to go down, and then yet more. Innumerable stairs, it seemed to him. He thought they must be out of the castle now, and nearly down to the level of the sea; he could hear surf in the background and somehow the sound was welcoming. Where was he, anyway? Was this where he belonged? For all he knew, it might well be, but it was hard to imagine how, and why.

Down and down and down they went, and at every level more people joined them in their flight, until they were inconspicuous and unnoticed among the flow of other refugees, some servants in rags or very nearly, some nobility in finery. It seemed that much of the interior of the castle had known a devastating flood.

Finding himself still leaning on the shoulder of the man in the horned helmet, Proteus asked him, simply: "Who am I?" He wasn't at all sure that he had the right answer yet.

The other hesitated before replying. Then he said: "You are whoever you want to be, my friend."

And now at last they were outdoors. And here the man in the

horned helmet left them, to join a small, blond, well-dressed woman who appeared to have been waiting for him. She stared at Proteus and Rosalind, but made no move to approach.

Before going away with the blond woman, the armed man handed Proteus the strange spear, saying: "Keep it. No doubt it'll come in handy, fishing. And if you ever remember, later . . ."

Unable to find the right words, he sheathed his axe, and made a two-handed gesture of casting the whole business from him. "Never mind, just keep it. I wouldn't know what to do with it. And the gods be with you, both of you." He waved a hand and moved away.

Rosalind was staring at the strange spear, as if it mystified her, but she was too exhausted to ask unnecessary questions. And Proteus heard a strange inner voice, that said to him: *The magic of a dying god begins to fail.*

Proteus had no idea what that meant, but it was indeed an impressive spear. His thoughts on the subject were interrupted by an anonymous voice, calling out: "He's dead!"

Turning his head, he saw by the light of torches how a number of people were pulling a man's body from under a large beached boat, or ship, that had two great eyes marked on the prow in faded paint.

"Who is it?" some anonymous bystander asked another.

"Jason," came the answer.

There was a general murmur. "Who is Jason?" Proteus asked his companion.

"Hush." The woman squeezed his arm with her free hand. "Never mind, I'll tell you all about it later."

He couldn't help struggling to gain more information. "What's happened?" Proteus gestured helplessly at the castle behind them. From many windows there came torchlight, and the sounds of lamenting and confusion. "Where are we?" He felt somehow that he should be angry, but had no idea of who or what deserved his anger.

They moved on, heading away from the glow of gathering torches, and into darkness. "I'll tell you all about it later," Rosalind promised him again. It cost her something of an effort, but her tears came to a stop. "Trust me. I think we have a chance now, at least we have a chance."

"That's good," said Proteus. He looked at her—this time he thought he *almost* remembered her. He looked at the clinging children, one girl and one boy. He nodded. The thought crossed his dazed mind that soon he would have to find out his son's name, and his daughter's. Something truly terrible must have happened to him, to all of them, just now, up there in the castle, to wipe his life away. And if he and his family were just fisherfolk, how had they come to be up there anyway? There was something ominous about that.

But it was going to be all right now. He was alive, unhurt, and had his woman and children with him. He asked: "Where are we going?"

"That way." Rosalind pointed away from the uproar, into darkness, and he thought he could hear waves beating on a rugged coast, outside the harbor. His instinct had been right, they were now almost at the level of the sea.

"Home," she said. "Back to the village where my—where our house is. No one will bother us there. No one here in the city will care about us anymore."

"Home," repeated Proteus.

It sounded good to him.